CW01662590

THICKER THAN WATER

A DI Crow Novel

HJ REED

Malago Press

Published by: Malago Press

www.malagopress.co.uk

ISBN (e-book): 978-1-0683091-7-5

ISBN (paperback): 978-1-0683091-6-8

1

New Year's Eve is the one night of the year when a large number of normally sensible citizens leave their brains at home and descend on the streets, clubs and pubs like lambs to the proverbial slaughter. For the city's dealers, muggers, sex offenders and house-breakers, it's the opportunity of a lifetime. For the emergency services, it's an annual test run for Armageddon. Most police officers lucky enough to be on leave are more than happy to lock their front doors, break out the earplugs and hope the phone doesn't ring. Thanks to Grace Helston, my DSI, I'm not expected back in my office until the second of January, so I arrive home from a day with the family well before the revellers hit the streets, eagerly anticipating an hour or so of blessed solitude in the absence of drunken renditions of *Auld Lang Syne*, fist fights, stabbings, drug overdoses, break-ins and general vandalism.

I spend the hour up to midnight staring wistfully at an unopened bottle of single malt, courtesy of the chief constable, for 'services rendered' – in other words, nearly getting killed in the line of duty – and make do with an unsatisfying mug of decaffeinated coffee, a concession to my consultant's latest attempt to reduce the nightmares that still regularly plague me in the small hours, ever since a drug dealer's bullet lodged itself in my frontal lobe, shattering my sergeant's skull right in front of me on the way. More than six years later, my dreams still can't shake the image. I make my way upstairs, hoping that for once I can indulge myself in the rare pleasure of uninterrupted sleep. Hope, however, doesn't quite cut it.

The phone rings at just past 2.30 a.m., first my mobile, then, louder and more insistent, my house phone, which I've been stupid enough to leave on my bedside table. I brace myself for a waft of dog breath and the warm, wet sensation of a canine tongue in my ear, and then remember that my Doberman, Bluebell, is staying over with Rosie and John Larson, my daughter and son-in-law, keeping my grandson, Ben, occupied for the last day of the school holidays. I groan, reach out an arm, scrabble for the phone and grunt into it.

'Al? Sorry about this. Are you awake?'

It's the DSI. 'No,' I reply. 'At least I wasn't until a minute ago. What's going on, Grace?'

'That's what I'm hoping you'll be able to tell me,' is the terse reply. 'Two calls within minutes of each other around half an hour ago, one from Downside Care Home in West Hill, and another from a house just off Pembroke Road in Clifton. We've got two dead bodies, and one survivor just arrived at the infirmary. I've called Polly Sillitoe in and she's on her way to Downside. DC Robbins has gone to the hospital. I can't get hold of Daz Jackson yet, but I'll keep trying. We've been with a skeleton staff the last couple of days, and so has Clifton – apparently, they can't rouse anyone from senior ranks. I know you're not officially back for another day, but …'

'Jesus Christ, Grace!' I'm fully awake now, on my feet and hunting for a clean shirt. 'You do realise,' I tell her, 'you almost managed to make it to the end of my leave without finding some excuse to get me back to work. Lucky for you I decided not to break open that Scotch tonight.'

I hear her sigh. 'I'll make it up to you, Al – I promise. Can you get straight over to the Clifton house? DC Draper has gone up there with some uniforms, but from what I've heard so far, it may well be beyond his ability to deal with. He'll need you to hold his hand if I'm any judge.'

If I had any reservations about being dragged out of bed in the middle of the night, the thought of Colin Draper, our newly promoted, over-enthusiastic and under-experienced DC, in charge of a major murder investigation, makes my mind up.

'I'll be there in half an hour, ma'am,' I say, and head for the bathroom.

Forty minutes later I'm standing outside a large, Georgian detached property that probably has its own indoor swimming pool and gym in the basement, and that any up-market estate agent would consider a snip at four or five million. The four-foot-high stone wall separating the front garden from the road is festooned with police tape, snapping in the stiff, icy breeze and already rimed with frost, even though it can't have been in place more than an hour or so. Two arc lamps have been placed on the front lawn, trained on the steps leading up to the front door, steaming like boiling kettles and creating more fog than illumination. Despite a thick sweater, overcoat, scarf and ski socks, my feet have gone numb within seconds of getting out of my car. At least, thanks to my ever-thoughtful ex-mother-in-law and her Christmas gift of a new *Thermos* flask, I have a supply of hot coffee tucked in a large pocket under my coat.

I show my credentials at the front gate and am ushered through to where DC Colin Draper is hovering under one of the arc lights, stamping his feet and batting his arms round his torso, woolly bobble hat jammed down over his ears.

'Jesus, sir,' he says as I come up to him, 'it's bloody freezing. I've been out here an hour – Professor Ainsworth's inside with the SOCOs, and they won't let anyone in until they've finished. God knows how long that's going to be. There aren't any all-night cafés or petrol stations around here either – I could murder a hot chocolate.'

'For goodness' sake, Colin,' I reply. 'You've been with us, what – six months now? Long enough to have learned that the detective's motto is the same as a boy scout's – be prepared.'

'Yes, sir,' he mumbles. 'Sorry. It's just the DSI said it was urgent, so I thought I should come straight over, but all I've done since I got here is wait around. To be honest, though, I think I'd rather be out here than in there. It's – well – it's not a pleasant sight, sir.'

'You went and had a look, then? What's the story?'

He shakes his head and swallows, and I realise his pale complexion isn't entirely down to the freezing weather. I take pity on him and pull out my flask, a state-of-the-art number with two cups screwed into the top. I detach them and hand them to him. 'Here, hold these, and for God's sake don't drop one, or I'll have you on surveillance at Vista House for a week.' I pour out the coffee,

'How can you tell that?' I ask, knowing that ninety-nine per cent of the time, Maggie's bets are pretty accurate.'

She shrugs. 'The amount of blood. See here?' She reaches out with a gloved finger and carefully pushes aside the top of the pyjama jacket so as not to disturb the knife, revealing a neat entry wound just below the ribcage. 'If he'd been alive,' she goes on, 'there would have been a hell of a lot more of it. The blow was up through the ribcage and into the heart, and would have created quite a mess if the heart had still been beating.'

'So, what did kill him, then?' I ask.

'No idea, yet,' Maggie replies. 'All I can say at this stage is that it very likely wasn't being stabbed.'

'Bloody hell,' is all I can comment. 'So, what about the wife? Maybe she disturbed whoever it was, and was simply collateral damage?'

'Possibly,' Maggie agrees, 'but if this was done by a professional, and she'd seen them, she wouldn't still be alive. You know as well as I do that this kind of attack doesn't fit with the local gangs, or even professional burglars. It's as if it was carefully staged, sending some sort of message to whoever found the body. Something else for you to think about – if the wife hadn't managed to alert the ambulance service, the body, or bodies, might not have been found for quite a while. It's just luck we've managed to get here so quickly.'

'So, you reckon it's a revenge killing?' I ask. 'But revenge for what?'

'That, Chief Inspector, is for you to find out.' Her phone trills, and she digs underneath her paper suit and yanks it out.

She listens for a minute, eyebrows coming together in a confused frown, then gestures an apology and turns away, phone still glued to her ear. I take the hint and make my way out to where DC Draper should be. There's no sign of him.

A PC flags me down. 'You looking for your lad, sir?' he asks. 'He just nipped next door – got caught short, he said.' He points towards the pathway to a neighbouring house. 'There he is now,' he adds, and squinting into the darkness I can just see a shadowy figure trotting towards us carrying what looks like a tray covered with a tea towel. Draper comes up alongside me and gives me a nervous grin.

'Sorry, sir,' he says. 'I was desperate for a pee, and Mrs Fontwell – that's the next-door neighbour – wouldn't let me leave without this.' He sets the tray down on top of an empty planter and whisks off the tea towel to reveal two large, steaming mugs and a plate of crusty bread. 'It's homemade vegetable soup, sir. She said to take one for you as well. I hope that's okay.'

'You mean you've been taking bribes from potential witnesses?' I ask. 'That, Detective Constable, is what I would call inappropriate behaviour, wouldn't you?'

He looks utterly crestfallen. 'Sorry, sir, I didn't mean ...'

'So,' I continue, 'I think the best thing to do under the circumstances is get rid of the evidence as quickly as possible. Hand me one of those mugs, will you? It's not getting any warmer stuck down there.'

For the next couple of minutes, we stand in silence, giving the soup – which is delicious – our full attention. It seems the next-door neighbour has prepared a vat of the stuff, as a steady stream of SOCOs and uniforms are making their way to her front door, and milling in the front garden clutching mugs. Maggie joins us, minus a mug and looking unusually subdued.

'What's up, Maggie?' I ask. 'It's not like you to pass up decent food.'

'If you'd heard what I just heard, you wouldn't have much appetite either,' she replies. For once, she doesn't beat about the bush. 'That was my assistant, Maisie Phillips, on the phone. Given there have been two suspicious deaths reported within minutes of each other, I sent her over to West Hill to act as my number two. She's just got back to me with the details – a ninety-year-old woman, Alice Walker, resident of Downside care home for the last five years. She was found in her room, tied to a chair with a knife sticking out of her chest. Maisie reckons the stab wound was post mortem.'

I freeze, mug halfway to my lips. 'You've got to be joking, Maggie.'

'I wish I were. If you've seen enough here, we'll get the body moved over to the mortuary and take it from there. Maisie says she's about to transfer the other one as well, so between us, we may be able to get started later today. If I were you, I'd get myself into the warm, and start looking for a very nasty killer with a predilection for old people and the ability to be in two places at once.'

2

There's nothing more to be done at the scene for the moment, so I retrieve my flask, send DC Draper home to get a few hours' sleep and set off for West Hill station. When I get there, I find Polly Sillitoe, my DI, and DSI Helston huddled round the filter coffee jug in the main squad room, deep in conversation. They both greet me with weary smiles, and Sillitoe pours me a coffee.

'Morning, boss,' she says, and adds, 'I hope you don't feel quite as bad as you look.'

'You took the words right out of my mouth, Inspector,' I reply, taking the proffered mug. 'I take it you've been brought up to speed on the situation in Clifton?'

She nods. 'The DSI's just filled me in. What the hell is going on, do you think?'

Grace chips in before I can comment. 'I suggest we go up to my office,' she says. 'It's bloody freezing down here, and I grabbed some croissants from the all-night petrol station on the way in. I've got a decent space heater up there as well.'

We don't need a second invitation, and make our way up to Grace's much less draughty third-floor office, where the chairs have cushions, and the desk, as well as housing the usual glut of box files and electronic equipment, provides a seemingly endless supply of my boss's go-to stress reliever, chocolate croissants.

We've just settled ourselves when Sillitoe's mobile trills. She digs it out, answers, and listens.

'Hang on,' she says after a few seconds, 'I'm with the boss and the DSI. I'll put you on speaker.' She jabs the button. 'Okay, Robbie, go ahead.'

'Morning, boss – ma'am,' she says, stifling a yawn. 'Oh, and Happy New Year!'

'We can live in hope, Robbie,' I reply. 'What's the story?'

'Mrs Malden's awake, boss,' she says, 'and she's going to be fine. That's the good news. The bad news is, she didn't see anything. She says a noise woke her up sometime after midnight, but at first, she didn't think anything of it – thought her husband had got up to make a drink or something. It went quiet, she waited for him to come back to bed, then smelled burning and thought he'd lit a fire, so she got up to see what he was doing. That's when she found him, dead in the chair, and collapsed with the shock.'

'Damn it!' I comment. 'She said she smelt burning?'

'Yes – apparently, something was smouldering in the grate in the room where he was found, but she doesn't know what. She saw his body, and her heart gave out. She's got a history of cardiac problems, hence the alarm she carries around. Sorry, boss – that's all I could get out of her. Whoever did it was long gone by the time she got downstairs, so no chance of a description, or even an idea of how many. Looks like we'll have to wait and see if forensics picks up anything. Her son, Jacob, is with her now, and kicking up a bit of a fuss about us lot disturbing his mother.'

'Okay, Robbie. I suppose there's nothing more you can do for the moment. Hang on.' I turn to Grace. 'Have we got a uniform down there, just in case the wife is still a target?'

She nods. 'One of the night shift's outside the room, and I've arranged a relief for when they come off duty.'

'Did you hear that, Robbie?' I ask, and when she replies in the affirmative, tell her to leave things for now and go and get her head down.

'I think that goes for all of us,' Grace decides. 'I've arranged with uniform to take statements from any neighbours who are awake and start door-to-door at 8 a.m. The pathologists have got their hands full for the moment and Maggie's called her team in – at least, the ones who aren't away on holiday. The scenes are secure, so I suggest we all get a few hours' sleep, have a decent lunch, and reconvene this afternoon, say, 2 p.m.? By the way, I finally tracked down Sergeant Jackson. He's in Edinburgh with the latest girlfriend, and says he'll be back by the end of the day. God knows how he can afford a hotel in Edinburgh at Hogmanay on his salary – whoever this new woman is, it sounds like it's serious. Maybe we ought to keep it under our hats for the moment?' She raises a judgemental eyebrow.

'The squad won't hear anything from me,' Sillitoe says, grinning. I just hold up my hands, and stop myself from commenting that he probably doesn't know what he's getting himself into – or, more accurately, his new girlfriend doesn't.

Sillitoe gets up and stretches the kinks out of her back. 'I'd better go and pick up Robbie. She went to the infirmary in the ambulance, and I doubt there's a patrol car handy at this time in the morning to give her a lift back here.'

'So, what are your thoughts?' Grace asks, when Sillitoe has gone.

I give her a shrug. 'You mean, apart from the ones about getting back to my bed? Assuming we're not dealing with a supernatural occurrence, we must be looking for more than one killer, working together, and targeting these individuals in particular. Apart from a similarity in age, though, I can't see any immediate link between the victims. Malden was pretty well-heeled by the look of it – Clifton old money – and the other one, Alice Walker, was in a state-run care home in West Hill – not very well run either, if someone could sneak in, murder a resident and disappear without any of the staff noticing. These places are supposed to have some kind of security, for God's sake, if only to stop the dementia patients wandering off in their nightclothes.'

'According to Polly,' Grace says, 'there was a shift change at midnight, and the old lady was killed sometime between then and 1.30 a.m. when a room check took place. It's possible someone could sneak in at the changeover, but we won't know anything more until we've interviewed all the staff from both shifts. That's upwards of thirty people if we include the casuals and agency carers, cleaners, cooks and nursing staff. They are all supposed to sign in and out, but it's a bit of a pig's ear. The permanent staff use electronic swipe cards, but all the others have to do it the old-fashioned way in a book at reception and aren't necessarily familiar by sight. That means anyone could have chucked on a blue overall and signed in with a false name. Polly has the books, and we've also got the files from the CCTV on reception. Luckily, they keep it running permanently, so we might get some luck there.'

'Where?' Joyce asks, looking suitably concerned. 'And who? Do you know?'

'One of them not too far from here,' I say. 'Near Pembroke Road – Charles Malden, a retired city councillor …'

I stop short. Joyce has gone white, and for a moment I think she's going to faint. Chrissie is staring at me in absolute horror. I'm about to dash out to get some water when Joyce takes a deep, shuddering breath, and comes back to life.

'I'm okay, Al,' she says. 'Just pass me my coffee, will you?'

I hand her the cup. 'I'm sorry,' I say, with a glance at Chrissie, who thankfully also seems to have recovered a little. 'I take it you both knew him?'

Joyce nods. 'The Maldens have been family friends for decades. Charlie is …' She hesitates. 'He *was* my brother Jack's closest friend at school, and best man at his wedding. I must admit, when I was a girl, I fancied Charlie like mad!' She smiles sadly. 'He was a good ten years or more older than me, though. I probably annoyed him no end. Jack died twenty years ago, but our families stayed close, and I still see a lot of Iris …' She pales again, and slaps a hand to her mouth. 'Oh, God! Iris – is she all right? Please don't tell me …'

'Iris is going to be fine,' I say quickly, reaching out to squeeze Joyce's hand. 'She was upstairs in bed when it happened. She's in hospital – it was a big shock, but she's being looked after, and the doctors say she'll recover completely.'

Joyce puts down the cup and gets unsteadily to her feet. Chrissie leaps up to support her, but she shrugs her daughter off with a scowl. 'Don't fuss! I'm perfectly all right. I'm going to the hospital – I have to be with her.'

'Mum …' Chrissie begins, but is immediately cut off.

'I'm not going to argue,' Joyce snaps. 'If you want to be useful, you can give me a lift. I'm going to get some things to take. I doubt the poor woman was able to take anything with her. I'll be ready in twenty minutes.'

With that, Joyce sweeps out, leaving me and Chrissie side by side in an eerie silence, broken by the occasional muffled sound of arguing drifting through from the kitchen at the other end of the hall.

I turn to Chrissie and tentatively take her hand. She doesn't resist. 'Are you okay?' I ask.

She nods unconvincingly. 'I suppose so. I wasn't as close to Charlie and Iris as Mum, but …' She looks up at me. 'Why would anybody want to do something like this, Al? He was an old man, no threat to anyone. I suppose it was a burglary gone wrong – was that it?'

'It's possible,' I tell her, 'but we don't know yet. That's why I've been called in – so we can try to work out what happened as soon as possible, and hopefully catch whoever did it before the trail goes cold.'

She opens her mouth, but I cut her off. 'Don't ask me for any details, Chris. You know I can't say anything while the investigation is ongoing.'

Although technically that's true, the fact is, I simply don't want to tell her he was found tied to a chair with a knife stuck in his chest. I figure she and Joyce have enough to cope with.

We lived together long enough for her to understand at once, and her mouth twists into a knowing grimace. 'Has someone told Jake?' she asks, changing tack.

'Jake? Ah – you mean the son, Jacob Malden? Yes, last I heard he was at the hospital, with his mother.'

'Oh.' She nods slowly, but doesn't elaborate. 'You said there had been two murders,' she goes on, veering off before I can ask how well acquainted she is with the family, 'and that they might be connected? It's not someone else we know, is it?'

'I doubt it,' I reply. 'The second was an elderly woman in a nursing home in West Hill. And I can't talk about that either,' I add, trying to pre-empt any further questions.

Chrissie takes the hint, gives my hand a squeeze and gets up. 'I'd better go and see if Mum needs any help.'

'I'll let Rosie know what's happening,' I say, 'and I'll see if I can sort Ben out before I run off with her husband. It looks like she's going to be left to hold the fort after all.'

At the door, she pauses and turns back to me. 'I'm sorry, Al,' she says. 'I shouldn't have said – you know, about what you're doing not being important. When it's someone you know – well …' She shrugs. 'Just bloody well catch them, okay?'

'Don't worry, Chris,' I reply. 'I intend to.'

show off.' He thinks again, and adds, 'And Mel's got one – she's had hers since she was seven.'

'Okay, that's two, out of how many? Thirty in your class, more or less? So how many haven't got a phone at all?'

'Millie's got a rubbish one, like mine, and Ollie and Joe have, too.'

'In that case,' I argue, 'you've clearly given a false statement when you say that everyone in your class has a smartphone. The fact is, hardly anyone has a phone at all – right?'

He shuffles his feet and snorts out a frustrated breath. 'Yeah, but …'

'No buts,' I interrupt. 'Those are the facts. As for being able to access your Kidcard account, haven't you got a state-of-the-art computer in your room that your dad built for you? If I remember right, Marcus comes round to your house to play games because he's not allowed one. Plus, you got the latest games console and a tablet for Christmas as well as the phone. I'd say you were doing pretty well, and what's more, your mum and dad trust you to know what you're doing online and not get into any trouble, or they wouldn't let you have your own setup in your bedroom.'

'So why won't they let me have a proper phone?' he protests. 'I'm not stupid – I'm old enough to have one and use it properly – I'm not a baby!'

'No, you're not,' I agree. 'But you're not grown up either. They are worried about you, Ben, that's all. They want you to have a phone so you can contact them in an emergency, but at the same time, they want you to be safe. How do you think they'd feel if you were attacked, maybe stabbed or beaten up because some toe rag from West Hill fancied your expensive phone? And how would you feel if it was stolen and you couldn't afford to replace it? I'm sure they'll let you have one when the time is right, maybe when you start at the big school. In the meantime, why not give them a break, and try to understand their point of view? The thing is, if you keep behaving like this, all you're doing is proving that you're not responsible enough.'

He considers for a while, and then says, a note of challenge in his voice, 'So how am I supposed to prove it if nobody gives me the chance? You all just make your minds up anyway. It's not fair!'

I heave an inward sigh of relief that my strategy, so far, is working. 'I can think of one way you can really prove you're grown up,' I tell him. 'And you can start right now. Your great-grandma has just had some really bad news. An old friend of hers has died very suddenly, and she's got to go and look after his wife at the hospital. Grannie is going with her to help. My boss has asked your dad and me to try to find out how it happened.'

His eyes widen. 'You mean he was murdered? And you and Dad are going to find out who did it?'

'We don't know how he died yet,' I lie. Ben might be ahead of his years in some ways, but when it comes to certain truths, he's still way too young. 'The important thing is that your mum has to stay here, and she's going to need your help looking after your sister and Blue. There's a pile of food in the kitchen as well that needs to be sorted out so it's ready when we get back. What do you say? Do you reckon you can put your gripes to one side for a little while and help us all out?'

His brow furrows briefly, and then he bounces off the bed, lips set in a thin, determined line, as I was almost certain he would.

'Sure, Grandad. I'm on it!'

Before I can say another word, he's thundering back down the stairs. Bluebell raises an eyebrow at me, barks her approval, and chases after him.

An hour later, after seeing Chrissie and Joyce off to the hospital and grabbing a hasty lunch of beef rolls and slices of apple pie, I pull into the car park at West Hill, with Larson in the passenger seat, clutching a huge, military-style backpack.

'Do you really need all that?' I ask, as he tips himself out of the car and shoulders the pack with a grunt. My imagination adds a couple of tin mugs dangling from it, and I just manage to stop myself from whistling a chorus of *Waltzing Matilda.*

He shrugs. 'Maybe not, but if previous experience has taught me anything, it's that having a grab bag is a good idea. I always work best if I'm using my own equipment. Plus, it saves an awful lot of paperwork.' He grins. 'You'll appreciate that, I'm sure.'

'Oh, I do, son,' I reply, thinking it's another thing I can put on the short, but growing list of things my son-in-law and I have in common.

Up in the squad room, we find Colin Draper on his knees wrestling with a cardboard package at least five feet long and secured with more heavy-duty sticky tape than wrappings on the average Egyptian mummy. He's so engrossed in the task he doesn't hear us come in.

'What the bloody hell is that?' I ask loudly, and he jumps to his feet as if I've caught him raiding the petty cash tin, flushed with either excitement or exertion – with DC Draper it's often difficult to tell.

'Oh! Sorry, sir. I was just – well – just trying to get it open, sir, but it's done up tighter than a …' He stops, coughs, and turns a shade redder, if that's possible. 'Sorry,' he says again.

'I can see what you're doing,' I say, trying not to roll my eyes. 'I asked you, what is it? And what's it doing in the middle of our floor?'

He looks at me as if I've just stepped off another planet. 'It's the new electronic whiteboard, sir' he replies, as if it's obvious. 'It came on Christmas Eve, but nobody fancied messing with it, because most of the squad were going off on leave.' A spark of realisation hits his eyes. 'Ah, of course. You were on leave already, so you probably didn't hear about it. All the major crime units are getting one, for briefings and so on. I thought it might be worth getting it set up, seeing as we've got two murders to deal with.'

I glance at Larson, who is looking equally excited. 'Looks like you thought right,' I say to Draper. 'And lucky for you, our resident geek is here to give you a hand. Mind you, before you start on the complicated technical stuff, maybe a Swiss army knife would be useful?'

I leave them to it and head for my office just as Sillitoe and DC Robbins bowl in through the squad room door, looking almost as excited as Draper. I beckon them over, and they join me at my desk.

'What the hell are they doing?' Sillitoe asks, staring out of my window at the mess of cardboard building up on the carpet.

'The new electronic whiteboard,' Robbins answers, almost jumping up and down with glee. 'Exciting, isn't it?'

'Oh, for God's sake,' I comment, sinking into my chair behind the desk, 'not you as well? Anyone would think we didn't have two murders to sort out. From the look on your face when you came in, Robbie, you've got some news?'

'Yes, sir, I have. Polly – I mean, DI Sillitoe and I stopped over in Clifton on the way, to see if anything's come up in the door-to-door. They've been at it around six hours now, and it looks like we might have something. There's a guy lives just across the road from the Maldens whose hobby is classic cars – the really expensive sort. He's got a Rolls, a couple of Bentleys, an Alvis – worth a fortune apparently, and a workshop along the side of the house. Anyway, he has surveillance cameras running 24/7 in case of theft, one of which is trained on the road outside. Uniform got the hard drive off him, so we picked it up and brought it with us.'

'Apparently,' Sillitoe puts in, 'we've been assigned both cases. The chief constable didn't want two teams tripping over each other's toes. Clifton isn't too happy, but they didn't get much of a say. Their DCI is away for another week, and their DS is off sick – got measles, would you believe? At least we'll be more or less up to strength when Daz gets back in the morning, although we could do with a couple more DCs if we're split between two crime scenes.'

'Measles? You've got to be bloody joking!' I shake my head. 'As if we're not short-handed enough. Still, you're right about needing more bodies, at least for the next few days. I'll talk to Grace, see if she can't bend the chief constable's ear. Meanwhile, Polly, can you stick with the care home, see if any of the permanent evening staff are back in this afternoon and make sure they've all been interviewed? Robbie, go back to the infirmary. Mrs Malden might have remembered something else. There's the son to consider as well. Maybe he can shed some light on possible motives for the attack. While you're at it, ask both of them if they've heard of Alice Walker – there must be some sort of connection between the two victims somewhere along the line.'

I pause, not quite knowing how to tackle what might, if I'm not careful, become a problem. I consider Robbie for a moment, and make my mind up. 'There's something you both should know,' I go on. 'My ex-wife's mother was a close friend of Charles and Iris Malden. She and Chrissie have gone down to the hospital to see Iris.

They may be able to add to the general picture. Robbie, I need you to interview them as well, see if you can get some information on Malden's general history – what jobs he had, what exactly he did for the council, any political scandals he might have been involved in and so on. It's possible he rubbed somebody up the wrong way in the course of his career, and if so, we need to know about it. Do you think you'd be comfortable with that?'

She looks a little doubtful, but nods. 'Yes, sir. I'll do my best.'

'I know you will, Robbie. Don't worry about sparing my feelings. Chrissie and Joyce know the score, and I'm sure they'll both do their best to help.'

As I'm speaking, the squad room door opens and DC Karen Wyatt, the station's family liaison officer, appears.

'The DSI called me, sir,' she says. 'She said you might need me. What can I do?'

'You bet I need you,' I reply. 'Did she fill you in on the Clifton murder?'

'Yes, sir,' she says. 'Do you want me to stick with Mrs Malden?'

I mull things over for a minute, then shake my head. 'No. I don't know when she'll be discharged, but for the moment she has people with her, and Robbie is on her way down there. I'd rather you kept an eye on the son, Jacob. With a bit of luck, he'll want to be with her, wherever she decides to go, and you can look after both of them. She won't be able to go back to her own house just yet, and the chances are she will be staying with family. Find out what their plans are, and see what you can get out of him while you're at it. If he goes anywhere, go with him. Tell him it's necessary for his protection, or whatever. You know the drill.'

She smiles. 'No problem.'

'Where will you be, boss?' Sillitoe asks.

'First stop, the pathology lab,' I tell her. 'I want to see how Maggie's getting on. If I know her, she'll have been at it all night.'

I push back my chair, but before I can get up, the squad room door bursts open again, and the unexpected figure of George Saint, our desk sergeant, lumbers across to my office. At once, the hairs on the back of my neck start to prickle. I've known George for more than twenty years, and in all that time, I can only ever remember him venturing up to the CID offices once. His usual excursions take him no further than the basement canteen to replenish his supplies of bacon sandwiches and sausage rolls. There are only two possibilities – either he's somehow gotten wind of the stack of beef rolls Rosie insisted I bring in to share with the troops, or he's got urgent, and not good news. My money's on the latter.

'A bit out of your comfort zone, George,' I comment as he reaches my office door.

He grunts, then sniffs. 'Afternoon, Al. Something smells good.'

I slide the large plastic container across the desk. 'Help yourself. You need to keep your strength up if you're going to start climbing stairs. Either you've taken up a new fitness regime, or you've got something to tell us, and somehow, I can't see you in joggers and a hoodie.'

He manages a fleeting smile and plucks a beef roll from the stack. 'I would have phoned, but there's an engineer messing with the internal switchboard, and it was quicker just to come up,' he says, between bites. 'We got a shout from the ambulance service around fifteen minutes ago. A woman called them out to her father, but when they got there, they found a body, dead for some time, they think. We sent uniforms straight out, and it's pretty clear it's one for your lot. We've sealed the house off and called the SOCOs in. The DSI isn't back in yet and she's not answering her mobile, but I've left a message.'

'Shit!' I mutter, the sentiment mirrored in the expressions of the others huddled round my desk. 'Details, George? Where, who and how?'

He ponders for a minute, jaw working slowly around his second breakfast, giving him the appearance of a ruminating cow. I know from long experience there's no point trying to rush him. If the station were on fire, Sergeant Saint wouldn't dream of heading for the exit until he'd finished his tea and sausage roll.

He finally swallows, clears his throat and gets on with it. 'I don't think you're going to like it, Al.'

'I already don't like it,' I tell him, 'and unless you get a move on, I'll never find out what it is I don't like. Just give me a break, George, and bloody well spit it out. We're all far too tired to mess about.'

He nods. 'An old chap, name of William Harcourt, address, 10, Bridge Close, on the border between West Hill and Ashfield.'

'I know it,' I comment. 'There are some pretty big houses up there if I remember right. It's not an area we're called to that often.'

'That's the place,' George agrees. 'The folks round there think they're a cut above. Anyway, the daughter went round to check on him and found him sitting in a chair with a knife through his chest. The paramedics reckon he'd probably been dead a few hours, but I suppose we'll have to wait for Maggie Ainsworth's lot to confirm that.'

'Jesus bloody Christ!' A glance around the room tells me I've pretty much voiced everyone's thought. 'Right,' I say. 'I suppose that saves me a trip to the pathology lab. Everyone else, stick with what we've discussed. I'll be at Bridge Close. George, you'd better get back to the front desk. Can you keep trying Grace, and let her know what's happening? Larson will be staying here, so he can collate any incoming information and pass it on if necessary.'

I head back into the squad room, where Draper and Larson are both on their knees sorting out piles of metal parts and screws. I quickly fill them in, and tell my son-in-law to mind the shop. 'Grab your coat, Colin,' I say to Draper, who is reluctantly getting to his feet. 'Playtime's over. We've got another dead body to go and look at.'

4

The light is already beginning to fade as, clad in paper suits, we duck under the police tape at the gates to the late William Harcourt's driveway. The large, mid-century detached bungalow, set in the middle of a substantial plot overlooking south Bristol's heathland, isn't as imposing as the Maldens' Georgian pile. Nevertheless, despite its dubious postcode, whoever owns – or owned – the place would need to have been earning a pretty healthy salary. A pity, I think, that their taste didn't match their income. Two brick pillars at the entrance are flanked by poorly moulded replica stone Alsatians, one of which has a notice round its neck announcing *We live here*, while the other warns *No trespassers or hawkers*. The bungalow itself is guarded by a battalion of gaudy garden gnomes, arranged around a mix of evergreen shrubs and clumps of pampas grass. The whole place has an air of homage to the 1960s.

'Bloody hell, sir,' Draper mutters, as he almost kicks a bare-arsed winking gnome into the front step. 'I didn't think anyone bought this kind of thing anymore. It's all a bit ...'

'Tasteless?' I finish for him. 'Believe it or not, son, this was the height of fashion back in the day. I'm not so sure about this, though.' I point at a shabby wooden name plate by the door that reads, *Fourcars*. 'Now, there's a man who wants the world to know how well off he is.'

'That, or how much of a dick he is,' Draper comments. 'I mean, who on earth would name their house after how many cars they'd got?'

'I'd guess someone who had to work bloody hard to get them,' I answer, thinking that given he chose to live in West Hill, a lot of that hard work might well have been on the wrong side of legal. 'In any event,' I add, 'whoever he was, he's now a murder victim, and somehow, I don't think he was killed for his lack of finesse in the fine art department. Are you ready?'

'I suppose so, sir,' he says, without enthusiasm, avoiding my eye and crouching to fumble with his plastic overshoes.

I want to tell him to bloody well pull himself together if he wants to stay on the team. After all, a detective on a serious crime squad who can't cope with the odd dead body is more of a hindrance than an asset. In the end, I just say, 'Come on, son. None of us like this part of the job – except maybe the pathologists. I had to get used to it, and so do you, understood?' He straightens up, swallows hard and nods. I give him an encouraging pat on the shoulder. 'Okay, then – let's get on with it, shall we? And if you feel ill, whatever you do, don't puke on the carpet. The SOCOs have got enough on their plates as it is.'

I tap sharply on the front door, and a hooded, masked head pops round an inner doorway to what I assume is the bungalow's lounge.

'Afternoon, sir,' a muffled voice behind the mask says. 'Professor Ainsworth says you can come in now, but make sure you stay away from any walls. We haven't quite finished taking samples yet.'

'Thanks,' I reply, and we make our cautious way into the lounge, where two officers are busy dusting windows and doors, while a third, under Maggie's direction, is taking photographs of the dead body of an elderly man, securely taped to a dining chair in the middle of the room, an ornate knife sticking out of his chest. Maggie turns as we enter, and greets us with a grim smile.

'Come on in, Al. I think we can safely say that any similarities between this one and your first two victims are far from coincidental. The knife is the same style as the other two, and it's my guess he died either late last night or early this morning. I can't confirm that just yet, of course, but if the window for time of death is correct, it means you have at least three killers in three locations, coordinating their efforts. I don't think I've ever seen anything like it before.'

'Me neither, Maggie,' I say, stepping up to examine the corpse more closely. Draper, I notice, is still hovering by the door. It's not a good sign. Now is not the time to make an issue of it, though.

'Those knives are pretty distinctive,' I go on. 'I'd like photos of all three as soon as you can manage. It probably won't get us anywhere, but we might as well try to find out where they came from.'

She nods. 'It might be worth getting an expert in to take a look. If they're replicas bought online, you'll be on a hiding to nothing, but on the other hand, if they're genuine …' She shrugs. 'It's worth a shot. What I can't understand is, why stab someone if they're already dead? Still, that's for you to find out. I'll get this one down to the lab, but with three to sort out, I can't say how long it will take. I'll let you know as soon as I have anything useful.'

'Thanks, Maggie. Do you know where the daughter is?'

'In the kitchen with a PC last time I looked,' she replies. 'I'm not sure how much sense you'll get out of her though. She looked pretty shaken up. I'd go carefully if I were you.'

'Don't I always?' I say, and she responds with a doubtful grunt. I turn to Draper. 'You stay here,' I tell him. 'And note down all the details Maggie can give you. Then, go and find the first attending officers if you can, and see what they have to say. I'll find you when I've finished.' I don't give him time to reply, but make my way out into the hall. I glance backwards and see Maggie enthusiastically beckoning my green-faced but determined DC closer to the corpse. To his credit, he's doing his best, but the way this case is going, I won't have the time to act as his nursemaid, and neither will anyone else in the team.

In the kitchen I find a woman, at a guess in her mid to late forties, sitting at a small table, hunched over a mug. A young female PC is sitting next to her offering tea and sympathy. The PC scrambles to attention as I put my head round the door, and I gesture for her to join me in the hall.

'Anything I should know before I talk to her?' I ask.

'Her name is Cathy Turner,' the PC replies, 'married, no children, lives over in Portishead. She came over to check on her father and bring him a meal and some shopping. She turned up just before 3 p.m., found his body, rang 999 and asked for the police.'

'The police? Not an ambulance?'

'No, sir. I think she realised there was no point – her father was obviously dead. We arrived within ten minutes of the call and found her sitting in the kitchen, just where she is now. She hasn't moved at all – in a state of shock. We called the ambulance on our way here and asked the paramedics to check her over when they'd taken a look at the body. They confirmed there's nothing physically wrong, but said to keep an eye on her and make sure she didn't leave until someone could be with her. We've notified the husband, and he said he'd be here as soon as possible, but he's a long-distance lorry driver and has to come from Birmingham. It could be worse, I suppose – he might have been in John O'Groats.'

'Okay,' I say, and check my watch. 'If he set off as soon as he got the call, he should be here in an hour or so. Are there any other relatives?'

'Just one, sir, as far as we know. The deceased has a brother, James Harcourt, lives down the coast in Weston. We've tried to contact him by phone, but no luck so far. A couple of officers from Weston have been sent to his home address.'

'Good. Thank you, Constable. I don't think we've met before, have we?'

'No, sir.' She smiles. 'I've only been at West Hill a couple of months, transferred from North Bristol. I've applied to join CID, but no vacancies have turned up so far. My name's Molly – Molly Shaw.'

'Well, PC Shaw,' I say, 'I don't know how long you have left on your shift, but I'd appreciate it if you could stay on with Mrs Turner until her husband arrives. I don't want her left alone. I'll have a word with Inspector Fosbury, make sure it's okay with him.'

Her smile widens. 'No problem, sir. My shift ended an hour ago, but I'm happy to stay as long as you need me.'

'Right, then. Let's go and see if the lady can tell us anything.'

Within minutes, it's clear Cathy Turner can't give us any useful information, at least, not yet. What is obvious is that she has no idea why her father has been targeted – he's a good man, no enemies, no reason why anyone would want to do him any harm – just like Charles Malden and Alice Walker, names Turner doesn't recognise. If she is lying, she's the best actress I've ever seen. After ten minutes I give up, get her address and contact details, and leave her with PC Shaw until the husband arrives.

I find Colin Draper in the front garden, chatting to the constable on duty at the gate.

'Anything useful from Maggie?' I ask him.

'Not really, sir,' he replies. 'She only said that she wouldn't be able to tell what killed him until the post-mortem, and not to ask.' He frowns, and then goes on, 'There is one thing, though.'

After a pause that would do George Saint justice, during which his eyebrows come even closer together, gaze fixed on some vague point in the distance, my patience starts to wear thin. 'What? For God's sake, Colin, spit it out!'

He jumps. 'Sorry, sir – it's just – well, it might be nothing, but those notices …' He points at the two stone dogs on either side of the gate. 'I'd have thought he had some real dogs if he's going to have signs up like that. But we haven't seen any, so if he has got some, where are they?'

He's got a point, and I kick myself for not asking the same question. I didn't even look to see if there were any bowls on the floor in the kitchen. 'Damn it!' I mutter, half to myself, then 'Wait here.' I go back up the drive and almost through the front door, but remember, just in time, that I've taken off the plastic overshoes. I shout instead, and one of Maggie's assistants appears in the hallway. I ask her to give the message to PC Shaw, and wait. A minute later, Shaw comes to meet me on the step.

'According to his daughter,' she tells me, 'Mr Harcourt had two German shepherds, Bonnie and Clyde. They weren't here when we arrived, though, and nobody's seen them. That's a bit worrying, isn't it?'

'More than a bit,' I agree. 'Thanks, Molly.'

I make my way back to where Draper is waiting, turning things over in my mind, wondering how Bluebell would react to someone breaking into my house and trying to murder me in the middle of the night.

'What do you make of it, Colin?' I ask him as we get in the car and set off back to West Hill.

'It's a bit weird, sir,' he says. 'I mean, if the dogs were there, they would probably have made a hell of a racket. My Mum's got a little Yorkie, and she barks like mad every time someone comes to the door, even if it's someone she knows. Two Alsatians would be a lot louder. Maybe we should ask the neighbours if they heard them, and if so, what time.'

'A good thought,' I agree. 'But where are they now? And if they were there last night, how did the killer get past them? Two dogs that size would be quite an obstacle to deal with.'

'Unless they knew the killer?' Draper suggests.

'That,' I reply, 'or the killer disposed of the dogs somehow.' I leave him to mull over the possibilities as we make our way back to West Hill.

On the way up to the squad room I drop in on Dick Fosbury, the station's uniformed inspector. Our paths rarely cross these days, but we both started as West Hill rookie constables some quarter of a century ago, and somehow managed to avoid all the sensible options of moving on to the kinds of districts that at one time didn't require the regular deployment of bullet and stab-proof vests. These days, of course, those options no longer exist, and police officers are as likely to come under attack in the leafy streets of Clifton as in the gangland drug dens of West Hill. I find him hunched at his desk, frowning at a computer screen that's probably displaying some spreadsheet or other on budgeting or duty rosters. He looks up when I tap on the door, and pushes his chair back with a long sigh.

'It's bloody ridiculous,' he complains, as I draw up a chair on the other side of his desk. 'I joined the force to be a policeman, not a sodding desk jockey. I don't know how you cope, Al. You're worse at form-filling than I am!'

'I don't,' I reply. 'I've got Polly Sillitoe, and she's got a first-class degree in economics. She can do in five minutes what would take me all week.'

He gives me a resentful look. 'Why am I not surprised? You've always been a slippery bugger – and scaling the dizzy heights these days. You'll be joining the golf club next.'

'Not if I can help it. Can you imagine having to spend every Sunday afternoon with CC Gosford?'

Fosbury laughs. 'In your case, it would be a one-way ticket to demotion. I can't see you ever letting him win. But I'm guessing this isn't just a social call. What exactly is it you want?'

'A couple of things,' I reply. 'I know you're as stretched as we are, and I'm sure you've had officers searching the grounds both at

Downside Care Home and Bridge Close, but I'd like another sweep at Harcourt's house, maybe taking in the fields at the back of the house as well.'

His eyes narrow. 'Looking for what, precisely?'

'Any evidence that someone might have got rid of a pair of large dogs. They could have been poisoned, abducted, killed and possibly buried – there's no way of knowing, but the victim had two Alsatians last night, and they're not there now.'

He nods. 'And the second thing?'

'Molly Shaw – what's your opinion of her?'

He stiffens. 'Why do you want to know? Don't tell me – you want to poach her, right? Crafty bastard! I'll bet you've bent the chief constable's ear already. Jesus, Al, you've got to leave me with *some* decent uniforms – otherwise, who's going to do all the boring stuff for you?'

'In other words,' I translate for him, 'she's brilliant, and you've been fobbing her off by telling her that despite having an active application, she's not been here long enough to get kicked up to CID – or something along those lines. And you're calling me a crafty bastard! You can at least agree to let me have her for a week until DC White gets back off his holidays. God knows we could use the help, and it will allow us to see whether she's cut out for it. Besides,' I add, 'I know you, Dick, and you're not so mean as to stand in the way of a promising career. If my gut feeling is right, she's far too good to be knocking on doors and seeing old ladies across the road.'

He slumps back in his chair, defeated. 'The last one of my constables who tried to see an old lady across the road down by Vista House ended up in A&E having four stitches in his head. All right, Al. If you can clear it upstairs, you can have her – but on a temporary basis, at least for now. Understood?'

I get up. 'I owe you one, Dick. If you pick up anything on those dogs, let me know. Meanwhile, if one of your lot finds any more dead bodies, tell them they'll have to ring in and make an appointment, preferably for one day next month.'

5

I get up to the squad room to find it in semi-darkness, and for a moment think I might have taken a wrong turn and walked into the local fleapit round the corner. Grace and DCs Draper and Robbins are huddled in front of a large screen on the end wall, intent on a patchwork of images and documents linked by a web of lines and arrows. Larson, hunched over his computer at a nearby desk, is playing the role of projectionist. I'm about to ask whether I should have bought a few cartons of popcorn on the way in when Grace turns and beckons me over.

'You're just in time, Al. Grab a coffee and come and look at this.'

I do as I'm told and join them in front of the giant screen. On one side, there are two sets of photographs, presumably sent through from the lab, of the knives used in the attacks on Charles Malden and Alice Walker. On the other, various documents show patchy histories of the first two victims, information that Larson has managed to gather during the few hours I've been at Bridge Close. So far, there isn't a lot, but if there is even the smallest connection between them, my son-in-law will find it, and probably not rest until he does.

'I came straight in as soon as I got the message,' Grace says, 'and helped John get this set up. It's impressive, don't you think? A hell of a lot better than marker pens and sticky-notes. The whole team can see all the important stuff instantly, and update it when new information comes in.'

As if on cue, Larson's computer pings, he taps away for a few seconds, and another photograph appears on the screen – Maggie must have extracted the knife from Harcourt's body and sent the images straight through to us.

'Bloody hell!' Draper comments. 'They're identical.'

'Almost,' Larson puts in, leaving his desk and coming up to the screen. 'The blades are the same, but there are some differences in the hilts if you look closely. They are Scottish dirks, definitely from the same period, possibly nineteenth century, and I'd guess they are genuine, not reproduction. Only a dealer would be able to say for sure, though.'

'So how come you are such an expert on ancient weaponry all of a sudden?' I ask.

He gives me an almost pitying look. 'I'm not – just an expert on Internet searches. I've been comparing these knives to a selection up for sale on antique dealers' websites. I could be wrong, but I'd be willing to bet they all come from the same collection, and whoever bought them isn't short of money. The going rate for one of these, if they are the real thing, of course, is upwards of two thousand pounds – some go for a lot more, depending on the provenance.'

'Christ almighty!' I step forward and take a closer look. 'Okay,' I say, after a moment's thought. 'If these things really are genuine, we should be able to trace the owner – or owners. If they've been stolen, and they were purchased legitimately, the thefts would have been reported, if only for insurance purposes. That means there will be a record on the national database. Maybe you can take a look through in the morning?'

He smiles. 'I'm already on it.'

Of course he is. 'The big questions,' I go on, 'are firstly, why the killers would use something so distinctive, and secondly, why stab somebody *after* they were dead, and leave upwards of two grand's worth of weapon in the bodies? At least, whoever did this, we can rule out money as the motive.'

Draper suddenly pipes up. 'What about the swords, sir?'

I blink at him. 'What swords? Come on, Colin – what are you talking about?'

'The ones in the hallway, sir, at the Malden's house. You must have noticed them – on the wall above the staircase. They were really old, like they were from the Civil War or something. I thought they must be fake, but if they were real …' His eyebrows crunch together with the effort of thinking. He finally looks at me. 'It could be a connection of some sort, couldn't it?'

I swear under my breath. The fact is, I'd been too taken up with the body in the living room to pay attention to the interior decor. I'm also irritated with Draper for not mentioning it earlier, which, given that I'd missed it altogether, is totally unfair.

I mentally count to ten, and manage, 'Good work, Colin. Get down there in the morning, go through the whole house and check them out, plus any other similar items you find. It might be worth checking with Maggie and the SOCOs, too, and see if they've got photographs they can send through.'

He puffs out his chest and, not for the first time, reminds me of Blue after a perfectly executed training session. I almost reach into my pocket for a treat. Instead, I turn to Robbie. 'Did you manage to get any more out of Mrs Malden?'

She shakes her head. 'Not really, sir. She's still pretty shaken up, although the consultant says she'll be fit enough to be discharged tomorrow morning. She'll be staying with her son for the time being.'

'Good. That means Karen will be able to keep an eye on both of them. What about Joyce and Chrissie?'

'Your ex-wife wasn't able to say much. She didn't know the family all that well, but Joyce – Mrs Barrett, I mean – knew quite a lot about the Maldens. He started in management, worked as an administrator for the NHS, and then for local government in charge of social services. When he was elected as a councillor he got onto the boards of a couple of private medical facilities – that was in the early 1990s. He's still got financial interests in them, shares and so on, but stepped down when he retired in the mid-2000s and didn't stand for re-election to the council. I've given all the information to Mr Larson so that he can chase up the details.'

'Thanks, Robbie. It's getting late, so you and Colin get off home, and we can take it up again in the morning. Polly's going to be stuck at Downside for a while yet. Have you got a ride home?'

'I can drop her off, sir,' Draper chimes in. 'It's more or less on my way.'

'Thanks, Colin. We'll have a briefing at 8 a.m. In the meantime, make sure you both get some rest.'

I watch them go, leave Larson communing with his keyboard, and signal to Grace that I want a private word.

'You've got that look in your eye,' she says, as I close my office door.

'Oh? Which one?' I do my best to look innocent.

'The one you always use when you're about to land me in it with the chief constable.'

'I've no idea what you're talking about, Grace.'

She sits back with a derisive snort and folds her arms. 'You might be an excellent interviewer, Al, but you'd have bugger all chance on the other side of the table.'

I shrug. 'It's nothing really. I just happened to bump into Dick Fosbury, and asked if I could borrow Molly Shaw to stand in for DC White until he gets back from Benidorm.'

'And I'll bet you told him you'd cleared it with me, and I'd cleared it with CC Gosford, right? For fuck's sake, Al!'

'Something like that. She *is* CID trained, Grace, just waiting for an opening. If we don't snap her up, somebody else will, and I've got a feeling she'll make a damned good detective. Plus,' I add, a bit lamely, 'we're short-handed.'

'So is Uniform,' she retorts, and lets out a sigh. 'And what am I supposed to tell him? You know he's got a bee in his bonnet about the police being a "visible presence", especially in places like West Hill.'

'That's simple,' I say. 'Just tell him one of the three murder victims is a retired city councillor with powerful friends at the golf course. It's my guess he's already had his ear bent by some of Malden's influential friends. He must know that the more manpower we've got, the better the chance of a quick result.'

She ponders for a long moment, and then treats me to a mischievous grin. 'Don't worry, Chief Inspector – I spoke to Gosford at lunchtime. He's agreed to let us have one officer for the duration of the case. I agree, Shaw is the best candidate. I'll leave it with you to liaise with Dick, okay?'

'Bloody hell, Grace!' I take a deep breath, and can't help but laugh. My DSI didn't get where she is for nothing.

We're interrupted by a tap at the door, and Larson sticks his head round. 'I've just had Rosie on the phone,' he says. 'Chrissie and Joyce are back from the infirmary, and they're asking if we'll be back for a meal anytime soon.'

I glance at Grace, who nods. 'There's nothing more we can do tonight, Al. With luck, we'll get more through from forensics tomorrow. Plus, Polly won't be finished until after the night shift gets in over at Downside. Let's call it a night and grab some downtime while we can. I get the feeling tomorrow is going to be a busy day.'

I'm not about to argue. 'Tell Rosie we'll be around half an hour,' I say to Larson, and add, 'You can leave your stuff here overnight. Rosie's going to need you, and you won't be much use if you're staring at a screen all night.'

He gives me his long-suffering look, and goes to get his coat.

By the time we sit down to what should have been lunch, it's well past eight p.m. Ben and Alex are both in bed, and we are all utterly exhausted. We eat mainly in silence, and, despite her protests, shoo Joyce into the lounge while we set about the clearing up. When I get to the kitchen, Chrissie thrusts two cups of coffee into my hands and waves me away.

'Will you go and talk to Mum, Al? She's pretty shaken up, and I think she wants to talk to you.'

'About what? You know I can't give her any information about the investigation, particularly as she knew the victim.'

Chrissie shakes her head and gives me an almost apologetic smile. 'I've got a feeling it's the other way round – she wants to tell you something, but I don't know what.' She frowns. 'Apparently, it's on a "need to know" basis, and whatever it is, I don't need to know.'

I find my ex-mother-in-law slumped in an armchair, absently stroking Blue's head. One thing about Bluebell – she has a better talent than any human I know for zoning in on people's moods. She pads across to me and lets out a quiet, questioning 'woof', a clear challenge for me to do something about it. I dump the cups on the coffee table, give Blue's ear a scratch and sit opposite Joyce on the sofa.

'Are you all right?' I ask.

Joyce sighs, and manages a weak smile. 'Not really, Al. It's all so – 'She struggles to find a word, and finally concludes, '– terrible. Iris told me what she saw …' She shakes her head. 'She's not had an easy life, and now this? It's so unfair.' There's a pause, and then she looks me in the eye. 'I suppose you're used to it. You see this sort of thing all the time.'

'Not all the time,' I say, 'and I don't think anybody ever gets used to it. But Iris is going to be okay. That's something, isn't it?'

'I suppose so,' she agrees, and falls frustratingly silent.

'You said she hasn't had an easy life,' I prompt.

She nods. 'Not at all,' and then adds quickly, 'Nothing to do with Charlie – you mustn't think that. They loved each other very much. I don't know what she'll do without him. She grew up in West Hill – did you know that?'

'No,' I say, 'I didn't.'

'The father was a bad lot – it was more thieving and black market dealing than drugs in those days, just after the war. There were so many guns about, you see, with servicemen keeping them as souvenirs. He got himself shot trying to rob a local newsagent. He died, and another member of the gang was hanged for it. The mother was left with Iris and two boys. One of them took after his father, more in prison than out – a bit before your time. He died in Wandsworth around fifteen years ago. The other joined the navy at sixteen, and according to Iris, made a good career for himself. Iris went to secretarial college – there weren't that many options for women back then – got an admin job at the hospital and met Charlie.'

'It does sound like she had a tough time,' I comment. 'It would have been hard for a single mother in the forties and fifties. It sounds like Iris fell on her feet, though.'

'She definitely did,' Joyce agrees. 'But later on, when they wanted to start a family, they had problems. They both went for all the tests, but things weren't as advanced as they are now and they didn't have any luck. Anyway, one day, she turned up on my doorstep, smiling all over her face, saying, guess what, she was pregnant. I was delighted for her, of course. I was expecting Christine, and for a few months, everything was wonderful. Then, she said the doctors were worried on account of her age – around forty by then – and Charlie had booked her into a private nursing home in the Yorkshire Dales for the rest of her term, and she'd be back when the baby was born. There was no visiting, but she'd write regularly – which she did. I do remember Charlie going up there quite a lot, though. I had Christine, and a few weeks later, Iris came back home with baby Jacob. It was lovely – we used to push our prams round the park almost every day, and she was so happy.'

'It sounds like things worked out well for them in the end,' I comment, not quite sure where this is leading. Maybe, I think, she just wants to talk, perhaps about things she wouldn't feel comfortable discussing with Chrissie.

She shrugs. 'Yes, to a point. But it's always worried me, Al …' Again, she pauses, working up to whatever has been on her mind. I'm about to say something encouraging when she takes a breath and goes on. 'He wasn't an easy child – Jacob, I mean. He never seemed to get on with his father, although I could tell he was close to Iris. The thing is, though, Iris never talked about her time in Yorkshire. I asked her about it, of course, but all she would say was that it was pretty boring, and in the end, everything had gone smoothly.'

'So, what are you saying, Joyce? You think there was another reason Iris went up to Yorkshire? Perhaps she had an affair, and Jacob wasn't Charlie's son so he sent her away, but then changed his mind – something like that?'

She looks horrified. 'No! Of course not! I said Jacob and Charlie didn't get on, but … No, Iris couldn't have done anything like that. She adored Charlie. I just thought – well, maybe I didn't think. But your young detective, the one who spoke to us at the hospital, said that anything I could remember about Charlie and Iris might be useful, and I told her everything else. I didn't like to mention that, though, because other people might come to the same conclusion you just did, and poor Iris has enough to deal with. At least she has Jacob now, so I suppose that's some consolation.'

'I'm sure it is.' I reply, not really knowing what else to say, and still wondering why I'm the one she's decided to confide in, rather than Rosie, who is, after all, a trained psychologist. 'Don't worry, Joyce,' I say. 'Whatever is going on, I'll get to the bottom of it, I promise you.'

'I know you will, Al.' She sits back and closes her eyes as if relieved at having got something off her chest.

I leave her to rest, and find Larson and Rosie in the now pristine kitchen, sitting at the table sipping their coffee.

'How's Gran?' Rosie asks at once.

'Okay, I think,' I reply, 'just tired, and worried about Iris Malden.'

Rosie nods. 'Mum's the same – she's gone to bed. They both must be exhausted.'

'We've been talking,' Larson puts in. 'The kids are both back at school tomorrow, and Rosie wants to stay here tonight.' He shrugs. 'It seems you and I are surplus to requirements. If you can give me a ride home, I can get a couple of hours in on the searches before the briefing tomorrow.'

I'm about to start on my usual lecture about my son-in-law needing to take proper care of my daughter when Rosie pitches in.

'Before you say anything, Dad, we don't want either of you here. It's a woman thing, okay? You've both got a job to do and so have I. Yours is to get the bastard who killed those people, and mine is to take care of Mum and Gran. I'm not due back at work for another week, so I have the time. You two don't. I'd call that a no-brainer, wouldn't you?'

I've never been able to argue with Chrissie, and find myself facing the same steely determination in my daughter's eyes. Even Blue is giving me her 'don't even think about it' look. I can't help but smile, go across and kiss her cheek.

'Okay, sweetheart. But if you need anything …'

'I'll call you,' she finishes for me.

Twenty minutes later, having dropped Larson off in his driveway, I'm heading for home and some much-needed sleep, with Blue's tail thumping its approval into my back seat upholstery.

6

I get to the station just before 8 a.m., Blue trotting happily at my heels, to find a comforting 'business as usual' buzz around the front desk. George is in his regular spot, elbow propped on the counter behind the transparent safety screen, dividing his time between his bacon sandwich and two PCs about to go on shift. They greet me with a nod and make their way out as I walk over to join him.

'Anything I need to know?' I ask him.

'Not so far,' he replies, taking the last bite of his breakfast, much to Blue's disappointment, and wiping his hands with his handkerchief. 'I've been reminding the patrols to keep an eye open around Bridge Close and Downside, though. I saw young Draper dashing out half an hour ago – he said you'd given him a job up in Clifton. Are you sure you want that lad chasing about by himself? His brain's too little to be out on its own.'

'You're not wrong, George,' I agree. 'Sometimes I think when he joined CID, he was looking for the stationery cupboard and walked through the wrong door. God knows how he managed to get through training. I mean, which bit of "briefing" did he not understand? He won't be on his own for long, though. I'll be going up there myself as soon as I've sorted out the rest of the team. I need to look around the place in daylight, now that Maggie's lot have everything they need. Keep a sharp eye out today – you never know, somebody might walk in and confess to triple murder.'

'If they do,' he says, moving his lips in what passes, in his terms, for a grin, 'I'll give them a nice cup of tea and direct them straight up to the third floor.'

Up in the squad room, yesterday's atmosphere of abandonment has almost disappeared. Larson has taken charge of Ollie White's desk and is already absorbed in whatever is on the array of screens in front of him. Sillitoe and Robbie Robbins are deep in conversation by the coffee machine. As I move to join them, the door flies open and Daz Jackson appears, looking much fresher than he should, considering he was busy partying in Edinburgh until teatime yesterday.

'It's good to have you back, Sergeant,' I tell him. 'I hope you managed to get some sleep – it's going to be a long day.'

'So I heard, boss,' he replies, heading for the coffee. 'Don't worry, I'm fine – managed to get a flight and was back here by midnight. What do you want me to do?'

'I'm not sure, yet. Let's see what the briefing throws up.'

I grab a coffee and am about to call everyone to order when there's a tap at the door and it opens again. A slight, nervous-looking figure takes a step inside. It takes me a couple of seconds to recognise PC Molly Shaw, out of uniform and decked in jeans, trainers and an oversized Denim jacket.

'Sorry if I'm late, sir,' she says. 'DI Fosbury told me to come up here as soon as I got in this morning. I wasn't sure what to wear – I hope this is okay?'

'It's absolutely fine,' I tell her. 'Come on in, Molly. Everyone, this is acting DC Shaw. She's going to be helping us out for the next week or two.'

On cue, Daz takes over, pours her a coffee and ushers her to a seat. Given the way he's sizing up the new recruit, I decide that whoever he took to Edinburgh, they *definitely* have no idea what they're in for.

'Okay,' I say, when everyone is settled. 'Has anybody seen the DSI this morning?'

'Gone to headquarters, boss,' Sillitoe replies, 'to try to get us more manpower. She said she'd be back as soon as she's had it out with the chief constable.'

'Sounds like CC Gosford won't get much of a word in,' I comment, wishing I could be a fly on the wall for that one. 'What's the latest from Downside, Polly?'

'We've taken statements from all the permanent staff on the evening and night shifts,' she says, 'including the nurse who found the body – she's been at the home for over ten years, full time, so she was able to identify a lot of the long-term agency staff as well. I've brought all the records of the last two weeks. With a bit of luck, we'll be able to account for the ones that have fallen through the net. So far, nobody saw or heard anything, and nobody noticed anyone doing anything unusual, or being where they weren't supposed to be. They probably wouldn't, though, with the number of one-off agency workers they get in most days.'

'I'm working on that now,' Larson puts in, 'plus the CCTV from reception. I could do with another pair of eyes, though. There's no way round having to check video footage manually, and there are the recordings from Clifton to go through as well.'

It's the first time he's ever asked for help, and it makes me realise that up to now, I might have been taking his ability to work technological miracles for granted. As usual, though, where my son-in-law is concerned, my mouth responds faster than whatever the bullet left of the sensible part of my brain.

'You mean you are actually admitting that a human being can do a better job than one of your fancy computers?' He doesn't take the bait, just responds with a raised eyebrow and an irritatingly tolerant smile. I give in and hold up a hand. 'I'll see what Grace manages to get out of the chief constable. If not, I'm sure George Saint won't say no to some overtime, especially if he's within sniffing distance of the canteen. Anything else to report?'

He shakes his head. 'Not yet. I've got a couple of local antique dealers to contact when their shops open, and I can get on with checking out the staff lists DI Sillitoe has just passed over.'

'I'll be going to interview Iris and Jacob Malden again later this morning, sir,' Robbie says. 'Mrs Malden is being discharged at ten, and Karen Wyatt is going to call me when they are settled at her son's place – a penthouse over on the harbour – one of those posh ones where the management fees cost more than the average mortgage.'

'Good.' I toy with the idea of mentioning last night's conversation with Joyce, but decide to keep it to myself for the moment. After all, there wasn't a great deal that would be relevant to recent events. Nevertheless, I say, 'Try to get the son's angle on his relationship with his father – without the mother present if you can. Karen might have picked something up, too. She's pretty perceptive when it comes to family dynamics. Also, find out where the money came from for the apartment – father, or son? You never know, it might have a bearing on something.'

I think for a moment, working out the priorities, and make a decision. 'Polly, I want you to go over to Portishead and see if we can't get more sense out of the Bridge Close victim's daughter, Mrs …'

'Turner,' Shaw says helpfully. 'Cathy Turner.'

I give her a nod. 'Thanks, Molly. We need to know if there's any reason, however unlikely, why her father might have been targeted.'

Sillitoe gives me a questioning look. 'Sure, boss, but why not send DC Shaw? She looked after Mrs Turner yesterday, so she's a familiar face …'

'But not an experienced interviewer,' I interrupt. 'At least, not yet. Besides, I want her to come over to Clifton with me and take over from Draper. He can come back here and make a start on the CCTV footage, at least until we get more bodies in to help. Plus, when you've finished in Portishead, get over to Weston and see what you can find out about the victim's brother. Hopefully he'll turn up sooner or later.'

She shrugs. 'Whatever you say, boss.'

Shaw is blushing furiously, and I try, probably with minimal success, to give her a reassuring smile. Her time will come, I'm sure of it, but with so much at stake, that time is definitely not now.

'What about me, boss?' Daz asks, clearly disappointed that I haven't put him in charge of the new recruit.

I have a feeling Molly Shaw is more than capable of taking care of herself when it comes to unwanted attentions. Nevertheless, I make a mental note to keep a close eye on my sergeant, who, if the station rumours are true, has developed a worrying tendency towards recreational bed-hopping. What he does on his own time is his business, but if it starts to affect his work, it will definitely become mine.

'Maggie is up to her eyes in post-mortems,' I say. 'I'd be happy if an experienced officer was attending just in case they come across anything vital.'

'Oh, sodding hell!' he mutters under his breath, then gives me a resigned grin. 'I suppose somebody has to do it. At least if she's doing PMs all day, she won't have brought that wretched Cyril into the office.' He turns to Shaw, who is looking suitably confused. 'Maggie's dog,' he explains. 'Well – not so much a dog as a fart machine. She takes it in with her sometimes when she's working late in the lab.'

'She does it on purpose,' I add, 'when she wants some peace and quiet. That animal can clear a room quicker than a bomb scare.' I glance across at Blue, dozing under my desk, who meets my eye, stretches, gives an ostentatious yawn and drops her head back onto her paws. 'Okay everyone,' I go on. 'Let's get moving – any promising leads, pass them on to our resident geek here –' I gesture towards Larson '– otherwise, we'll aim to regroup by the end of the afternoon.'

I leave Blue with Larson, along with a strict instruction not to let George Saint feed her more than half a sausage roll, and set off for Clifton with Shaw in the passenger seat. As I drive, I bring her up to speed on everything we know so far and she listens without interrupting. When I've finished, I glance across to find her staring at her knees, frowning with concentration.

'Any questions?' I ask.

'I don't think so, sir,' she replies, 'although you said there was no sign of a break-in, right?'

'That's right,' I say. 'So, what do you conclude from that?'

'That the victim knew his attacker, or attackers, and let them in, or …'

'Or what?' I prompt.

'Well,' she says, after a short pause for thought, 'A house like that usually has a lot of security – you know, alarms on the doors and windows, video doorbells, security cameras, stuff like that. I was thinking that people usually set any alarms at night, or if they go out during the day. What if someone got into the house in the daytime while the security systems were off, and waited until after dark? It would explain how they got in without raising an alarm, and if that's what happened, it might not have been someone known to the victim.'

I almost bring the car screeching to a halt. It's so bloody obvious I can't believe I didn't think of it. But then, it's not often I have three simultaneous and apparently motiveless murders on my plate. On the positive side, my instinct about what makes a good detective seems to be holding up. I have a feeling my passenger's days in uniform are well and truly numbered.

'Well done, acting DC Shaw,' I tell her. 'Bloody well done.'

Out of the corner of my eye, I see her smile and relax back into her seat.

We arrive at the Malden house to find DC Draper jiggling up and down on the front step, meaning he's either found something interesting, or he's desperate for a pee. At least, I notice, he's remembered to put on a pair of nitrile gloves before poking around inside the house. He runs across, barely giving us time to get out of the car.

'There's something inside I think you should see, sir,' he says, and then, catching sight of Shaw, stops in his tracks, doing a comical double-take. I go to make the introductions, but realise there's no need.

Shaw grins. 'Hi, Colin. Hard at work, I see. Chief Inspector Crow asked me to help out. I hope that's okay with you?'

Draper carries on gaping for another ten seconds, realises he's looking like an idiot, and pastes on a smile. 'Hi Molly,' he manages to stutter. 'Great to see you. You look …' He struggles for a word, and finally comes up with, '… different.'

I mentally roll my eyes. Of all the officers in West Hill, it appears I've managed to select the heartthrob of virtually every unattached policeman in the station under the age of thirty-five. Bloody marvellous! Shaw, however, isn't having any of it.

'You were saying you had something to show us, Colin?' she says, taking the words right out of my mouth.

'Oh.' He pulls himself up and turns to me. 'Yes. Sorry, sir. Yes – come and look at this.' He bounds back up the front steps and disappears inside. Shaw and I exchange a look, sigh in unison, pull on our gloves and follow him in.

We find him at the top of the stairs, pointing at the wall above the stairwell.

'There, sir,' he says.

I look up and see a glass-fronted wooden display case containing six daggers – daggers that as far as I can tell, look identical to the ones found in the three corpses currently lying in Maggie's morgue.

'Bloody hell!' Shaw blurts out, beating me to it. 'Isn't it one of those stuck in Mr Harcourt?'

I turn to her, surprised. 'You saw that?'

'Of course, sir. I managed to get a good look while we were waiting for the SOCOs to arrive. I thought it was really weird, leaving it there like that.'

Shaw shoots up another notch in my estimation. Unlike Draper, she clearly isn't afraid of the more unpleasant aspects of detective work. In fairness, though, Draper has made a good spot.

'Well done, son,' I say to him. 'But no, whatever was left in the chests of our victims, it wasn't one of these. There aren't any spaces in the case, and the collection looks like it hasn't been disturbed for a while. 'Colin, do you think you can shin up onto the baluster and take a look at the case?'

He eyes the distance, checks his weight on the wooden rail and hoists himself up.

'There's a keyhole on the side of the case,' he says, 'but no key.'

'Go carefully,' I tell him, 'and see if it's locked.'

He gingerly slips a finger under the lip of the case and tests it. 'It is, sir,' he reports, and then quickly takes his hand away. 'I think there might be some prints. There's dust on the top of the case, but it's been rubbed off in places – fairly recently by the look of it, and there are a couple of faint smudges on the glass.'

'Right.' I pull out my mobile. 'Take a few photos, as close-up as you can, and get down. We need to get a SOCO up there before we do anything else.'

He does as he's told, sends the pictures to my phone and waits while I make the call. 'Are there any other offensive weapons in the house?'

'A few,' he replies. 'It looks like Mr Malden was a bit of a collector. There are the swords in the hall, a brace of pistols over the fireplace in the lounge, and more in the study behind the desk. There's a suit of armour as well along the landing, and it's holding some sort of spear – you know, like in King Arthur's time. There aren't any more daggers, though, as far as I can see.'

'Okay. Thanks, Colin, good work. I want you to get back to the station, and ask Larson to run Malden's name past the dealers he's in touch with. If he's that much of a lover of ancient weaponry, they may know of him. Then, give him a hand with the CCTV footage; see if we can find out who's visited the house recently. DC Shaw can wait here for the SOCO, and check for any documentation relating to his collection. While you're at it, get in touch with the ambulance service, and find out which paramedics attended yesterday morning. We'll need to speak to them again.'

Draper looks disappointed, but thankfully doesn't argue. When he's gone, I lead Shaw back downstairs, and head for the reception hall.

'You want to know about the alarm, sir?' Shaw asks.

I nod. 'The paramedics would have been first on the scene. If the security system was armed, they would have needed to switch it off. It was off when we arrived, but that's no surprise – there have been God knows how many people tramping in and out since yesterday, and there's still a couple of uniforms out front.'

There are two doors at the front of the house – a main, heavy oak front door, leading into a vestibule, and an inner door, part-glazed with two stained glass panels. The alarm system is just inside the inner door, a fairly sophisticated system with a keypad. Whoever came in would have needed the code. I think back to Larson's comments during our last case, when we came across a similar system guarding an old Manse in Wales – a system he was able to get into in less than a minute. It was amazing, he told me, how many people buy an expensive security system, and then use a family birth date or the name of their pet as the password. More than once, he's demonstrated that with enough knowledge and determination, there is no system that can't be hacked. A quick examination of the rest of the house shows us that every door and window is alarmed, and presumably connected to the same circuit.

'Right,' I say, when we end up back in the main hall. 'Hang on here, and when forensics turns up, ask them to get those daggers over to Maggie as soon as possible, and dust the case for prints. I'm sure they will have done the entry alarm already, but check to make sure. While you're waiting, go through all the paperwork in his study. You're looking for any insurance policies, inventories of contents, plus other stuff you think might be important.' I think for a minute, and then add, 'Get copies of birth, marriage and death certificates too.'

'Sir?' she asks, looking puzzled.

I smile. 'When you start looking into a person's past, Constable, you never know what you are going to find. When you've finished here, DC Draper can come and pick you up.'

'Don't worry about that, sir,' she says, with a grin. 'It's only a couple of miles. I'll get an *Uber*. Where will you be, sir?'

'If anyone needs me,' I tell her, 'I'll be at the pathology lab.'

7

I find Maggie in her office, poring over her computer screen. She doesn't look up when I walk in, but flaps an arm towards a chair.

'Grab that, Al, and come round here,' she demands, and I do as I'm told.

'What am I looking at?'

She taps the right side of the screen with the tip of her pen. 'That's the weapon used on the first victim. The one on the left is one of the photos your young DC took earlier this morning. John Larson cleaned it up and sent it over a few minutes ago. What do you think?'

I lean forward and peer at the two images until they start to blur. 'They look identical,' I conclude, sitting back and rubbing my eyes.

'They are,' she says. 'Either they are a pair, or one is a perfect copy of the other. One of my assistants should be at the house now, and once the daggers have been bagged, I've asked her to bring them straight back here. We'll get any prints off the case, too, and fast track the analyses. Mr Larson has requested at least one of the daggers taken from the bodies, and one from the house to take for expert evaluation. If you are agreeable, I'll try to get one of each completed by the end of the day.'

'Do it,' I say, 'and let him know as soon as they are ready. He can come and pick them up. Anything else?'

She nods. 'Yes, but not helpful I'm afraid. In Malden's case, the weapon was clean as a whistle – no fingerprints, and so far, no DNA apart from Malden's own. I predict it will be the same with the other two. Whoever put them there must have cleaned them pretty comprehensively, and worn gloves. As for the cause of death, as I suspected, it wasn't the stab wound. That was post-mortem.'

'So, what did kill him?' I ask, trying not to let my imagination run riot.

'I can't be one hundred per cent,' she replies. 'But there was water in his lungs – not much, but enough.'

'You're telling me he drowned? Jesus Christ! How? Was he killed and then arranged in the chair after death?'

'Again, I can't say for sure at this stage, but it's very unlikely. You've heard of waterboarding, I take it?'

I open my mouth, but for several seconds nothing comes out. I've seen a lot of things during my too-long career, but the idea of torturing elderly people to death for no apparent reason is way beyond normal, even for West Hill.

'Dear God!' I say eventually. 'Is it the same for all of them?'

She shrugs. 'You'll have to wait until all three PMs are completed, but I'd say it was a pretty good bet, wouldn't you? Your sergeant's down there now with Maisie, watching the second one. They should be just finishing up. I'll take over for the third this afternoon. Will you be there?'

'No. I'll hang on and have a word with Daz, and send Draper over after lunch, if that's okay.'

She grins. 'You're a hard man, Al. Don't worry, we'll look after him. I know you can't see it, but that lad does have promise, you know. He's keen, and he's sensitive.'

'He's also a bull in a bloody china shop,' I say. 'He'd do better if he didn't act before engaging his brain.'

She gives me a sidelong look. 'Now why does that remind me of someone I know?'

I can't help but smile. 'Okay, Maggie,' I concede. 'Point taken.'

We're interrupted by a tap at the door, and a white-coated lab assistant comes in, holding an evidence bag.

'You wanted this?' he says. 'It's the weapon we took from Malden's body. The six daggers from the house have just come in. What would you like us to do with them?'

Maggie gestures to me.

'Get prints and DNA from at least one as soon as you can,' I say, 'preferably the one that matches this.' I point to the bag.

The assistant frowns. 'We do have a lot of …'

'You heard the man,' Maggie interrupts. 'Drop everything else until you have whatever you can find on at least one of them. After that, prioritise the prints taken from the case they were found in.'

The man nods. 'We'll be as quick as we can, Professor.'

'I'll keep an eye on it,' Maggie says when he's gone. 'With luck, we'll be able to get the other knife to you by the end of the day if everything goes smoothly.'

'Thanks, Maggie.'

There's another knock at the door, and Daz Jackson comes in, looking less bushy-tailed than usual.

'Well,' he says, 'That was fun. Dr Phillips says death was most likely by drowning. I mean, it makes no sense. If you're going to stab someone, why not just stab them and have done with it?'

Maggie and I exchange a look. 'I'll give you all the gory details when we get back to the squad room,' I tell him. 'I'm going to send Draper over for the afternoon session.'

'Christ, boss,' he comments. 'Are you sure? Knowing Colin, he'll probably pass out and land on the body.'

'Don't worry, 'Maggie puts in. 'I'll have someone there to catch him before he contaminates anything.' She gets up. 'I'd better go and see how they're getting on in the lab. As soon as there's any information, I'll send it through.'

I'm almost at the door when another thought strikes me. 'Can you get someone over to the harbour to take DNA samples from Mrs Malden and her son?' I ask Maggie. 'We'll need to eliminate them from any results you manage to get. DC Wyatt is with them, so assuming they give their consent it should be pretty straightforward.'

She nods. 'No problem. I'll send someone over now.'

I give her the address and head back to West Hill.

Jackson and I arrive at the station more or less at the same time. There's no news from George, and both Robbie and Sillitoe are still out. Larson and Draper are bent over their respective computers, silent except for the clacking of keyboards.

'Is the DSI in?' I ask.

Larson glances up and nods. 'Around an hour ago,' he says. 'Do you want an update?'

'Yes,' I reply, 'but we need to speak to Grace first. We'll be down in half an hour.'

I grab Jackson's arm and propel him out before he has a chance to say anything, Bluebell trotting at my heels. He gives me a quizzical look.

'What's this all about, boss?' he asks, as we step into the lift.

I'm about to tell him to wait until we're with the DSI when my mobile rings. It's Sillitoe. I put her on speaker.

'I'm on my way back from Weston now, boss, 'she says. 'But I thought I'd better let you know we've got a problem.'

'What kind of problem?'

'James Harcourt, the third victim's brother – apparently, he's gone missing. He has two daughters, and one of them rang Cathy Turner while I was interviewing her, asking if he was with her. He hasn't been seen since William Harcourt's body was found yesterday, and he was supposed to be at a hospital appointment this morning. I've just been speaking to the daughter, and she said it's something he would never miss. There's no sign of a break-in at his house, or any indication of where he might have gone. I've flagged him up as a vulnerable missing person, and the local uniforms are going through his stuff to see if it throws up any clues, but there's not much else I can do there. I'll tell you the rest when I get back – around twenty minutes if the traffic is okay.'

I tell her to come straight up to Grace's office when she arrives, and hang up.

'Bloody hell! That's all we need.'

'What do you think, boss? Is he a suspect?' Jackson asks.

'At this moment,' I reply, 'I've got no idea. It's unlikely, though. He's in his eighties and in poor health by the sound of it – I can't see him torturing his own brother to death and then sticking a knife in his chest, can you? But it's my bet he knows something. It sounds to me as if he thinks he might be the next victim and is running scared. If that's the case, let's hope we find him before the killers do.'

Grace's door is already open, and she waves us in with one hand, the other reaching for the filing cabinet drawer where she keeps a supply of dog biscuits. She hands one to Blue, who settles herself under the desk with a contented grunt.

'Gosford is giving us a couple more bodies from head office,' she announces. 'One of them is pretty good with IT, so that should help. They should be here later this afternoon. Are we any further forward?'

I give her a quick precis of events at the Malden house and cut to the chase. 'From what Maggie says, it looks like he was tied to a chair and had water poured down his throat until he drowned. The dagger was inserted after death.'

'Her assistant found the same cause of death in the second victim,' Jackson puts in, 'and it's a pretty safe bet the third will be the same.'

She stares at us in horrified silence for a moment, and finally mouths, 'Jesus!' under her breath. 'That's unbelievable. These people were old, and probably very frail. Who the hell would want to do something like that? And why, for God's sake? Is Maggie sure?'

'As sure as she can be at this stage,' I say. 'Plus, we've now got a potential fourth victim – James Harcourt has gone missing, according to Polly. She's on her way in now.'

Grace sits back and massages her temples between little finger and thumb, a clear signal that we have a problem.

'You realise we've had the press breathing down our necks since yesterday?' she says. 'Malden was a fairly well-known figure with fingers in a lot of pies, despite his age. Plus, the rumours about the three cases being connected are starting to run wild. By all accounts, the local rag is set for a Gothic horror headline in the morning. The price of your two extra officers was my attendance at a press conference this evening – you can thank me for that later. In the meantime, we all need to be on the same page, Al. What are your thoughts?'

I think about it for a minute. 'I don't see any harm in giving basic information,' I reply. 'It's pretty obvious the cases are connected. There are details we should hang onto for now, though, in particular, the disappearance of James Harcourt. You know what the press is like – they'll have him down as prime suspect and start a nationwide manhunt which could end up with us having another victim. The other thing is the connection between the murder weapons and Malden's collection of antique memorabilia. The less speculation about that, the better, and until we have more information, I don't want to spook the mother and son, at least not yet.'

'I don't think we should mention the drowning part either,' Jackson suggests. 'It could be the killers are hoping we haven't noticed that.'

'I doubt it' I reply, 'but I agree. We should play along with the knife in the heart theory for the moment. Anything we can do to make the killers complacent works in our favour.'

'Agreed,' Grace decides, 'although given their performance so far, I don't think complacency is a part of their mindset. I'll do my best to give the press just enough to damp down the feeding frenzy and get them out from under our feet. If it comes to it, I can call the chief editors in for a private meeting to emphasise the need for caution at this stage. They usually play ball if they believe extra publicity might be a threat to life. We should be able to get them to play down any risk to the general public. We don't want all the pensioners in Bristol barricading themselves in and arming themselves with kitchen knives.'

There's a tap on the door, and Sillitoe joins the party. Grace gets up, dispenses coffee to everyone to give my DI a minute to settle herself, and grabs another Bonio for Blue.

'I thought it was cold here,' Sillitoe says, rubbing some warmth back into her hands, 'but it's bloody freezing over in Weston – seventy-mile-an-hour winds expected by tonight, according to the forecast.'

'At least that should keep the burglars in front of their TVs and let us concentrate on more important things,' I comment. 'You said you had some information, Polly?'

She nods and takes a slug of coffee. 'God, I needed that. Yes – I had a long conversation with Cathy, William Harcourt's daughter. Her husband is with her now, so he was able to add some details, too. While I was there, one of James Harcourt's daughters rang, and it's clear the two families are pretty close. Cathy is just as worried about her Uncle Jim as his kids are, and can't think where he might have gone. He was due at Weston hospital for a set of important tests – a problem with his kidneys – and they are all adamant that he would never have missed it. He's been on a waiting list for over nine months according to his GP. He didn't tell anyone he was going anywhere, and when I had a quick look through his house, it was obvious he'd just done a massive supermarket shop – the fridge was full and there were still bags of dried goods on the kitchen table.'

'So, he left unexpectedly, and in a hell of a hurry,' Grace says. 'What else, Polly?'

'Cathy is William's only child, and James has two daughters, Rachel, living close by in Weston, and Sarah, married with two grown-up children, in Yorkshire, near Wakefield. That's where the whole family originally came from. William and James – known as Bill and Jim – grew up there, and there was a third brother, William Michael, known as Mick, a lot younger than the other two. Bill was the eldest, born in 1934, and Jim in 1938. Mick, though, didn't come along until 1964 – that's thirty years after Bill.'

'And where is he, now?' I ask.

'He died,' she replies, 'just over two years ago, leaving an ex-wife and two adult children, a girl, Susan, and a boy, Billy. The names William and James run through the generations, which makes things a bit confusing, and sometimes there is more than one William or James in the same generation, hence the use of second names. The thing is, Mick Harcourt had a criminal record. I haven't had time to run it through the system, but if you don't mind, Ma'am …'

'Be my guest,' Grace says, and vacates her chair to give Sillitoe room.

'We wait while she scrolls through the database, and finally says, 'Here we go. William Michael Harcourt – Christ! This record is as long as your arm! It starts in 1978 with possession of class A drugs, dealing, assaulting a police officer, burglary, car theft, and a four-year sentence for GBH – and all that was before 1982. There's nothing major in the next ten years, though – just a few possession charges. Then, in the early nineties, there was a spate of arrests for domestic violence resulting in release without charge, and finally one conviction, a twelve-month suspended sentence and a restraining order. I assume it was at that point the wife gave up and left him, presumably taking the kids with her.'

I quickly do the maths. 'So, he died in his late fifties – did Cathy Turner say how?'

'Self-neglect, she said. He didn't get on with brother Bill at all. They hadn't spoken for years, not since Mick was sixteen or so. The relationship with Jim was pretty rocky, too, from what I could gather. She said that Mick's body wasn't found for more than a fortnight after his death. I've asked Mr Larson to check it out and dig up the coroner's report and death certificate, but Cathy says the cause of death was drowning.'

8

By the time we get back downstairs, both Molly Shaw and Robbie Robbins are back, huddled round the coffee machine getting acquainted. I see Sillitoe and Robbie exchange a look – the kind I remember getting from Chrissie when we were still together and she was on the wrong side of pissed off with me. Robbie turns back to her conversation with what looks like exaggerated bonhomie. My DI simply scowls, and heads straight to her office to check her emails. I curse under my breath. The last thing I need from both of them right now is the distraction of a lover's tiff, especially as acting DC Shaw seems to have grabbed the attention of both Jackson and Draper. I want to remind them all that this is a serious crime unit, not a sodding lonely-hearts club. At least, I think with some satisfaction, the only extra-marital love affair my son-in-law is likely to have will be with something square, metal and equipped with a mains power supply. I go over to his workstation.

'Got anything yet?' I ask.

'Nothing from the CCTV footage so far,' he says, 'but I've just been looking at a bunch of papers that Robbie photographed over at the Malden house. She found a metal cabinet with files sorted into categories. She said she thought whoever did the paperwork was very methodical – everything very neat and in its place – almost obsessive in fact. The house is Georgian, and there are deeds and sale information right back to when it was built. There are records of every car they ever owned, and so on. She didn't bother sending all that, but you asked for information on the family. There are birth and marriage certificates for Charles Malden's side of the family going back God knows how long – at least a hundred years. He had some pretty impressive ancestors. There isn't so much for Iris's family, but her documents and those of her parents are there.'

'So, what's missing?' I ask, although I'm already pretty sure what he's going to say.

'Jacob Malden,' he says. 'There's no birth certificate. Plus, there may be something else. Robbie said that each document was filed individually in a plastic sleeve, all the sleeves placed in a ring binder and locked in the cabinet. There was a single binder for all the births, marriages and deaths, and there were two empty sleeves next to each other, presumably one of them was for Jacob's birth certificate. It seems to be the only gap in the record, so I can't think what might have been in the other one.'

I nod slowly, and close my eyes, recalling the scene when I first arrived there, and Iris Malden's statement from the hospital. She smelt burning and thought her husband had lit a fire. Someone thought something was so important – and so damning – they burned it in front of the victim, very likely before they killed him, perhaps to make some sort of a point?

'How did you know something was missing?' Larson is asking.

I open my eyes. 'Lucky guess, son. What about those daggers? Any luck there?'

He sighs and moves on. 'Scottish dirks,' he corrects me. 'I've spoken to a couple of dealers, and they both know Malden, one of them well. He was a collector, as you suggested. I've got an appointment in …' he looks at his watch, '… an hour. Did you manage to get hold of one of them? It would be better if he had more than just a photograph.'

I pull out the evidence bag and hand it over. 'Don't remove it from the bag, and don't let it out of your sight.' He gives me one of his meaningful looks. I think about an apology, dismiss the idea and add, 'By the way, is there any way of disabling a keypad alarm from the outside?'

He thinks about it. 'You mean the one at the Malden house? The keypad is inside, so I'd say probably not unless there is a power cut. Even then, there's bound to be a battery backup, so you would still need to know the code to disable it. Do you want me to go and take a look?'

'No – I don't think it would be worth it. I have a feeling whoever got in had an accomplice inside or was let in by the owner.'

'You mean Malden knew his killers?'

'Possibly – or he was forced to let them in. But I can't see him opening his front door to a total stranger after midnight, can you?'

I leave him with that thought, and pack Draper off to the pathology lab, looking as if he's likely to lose his lunch before he gets there. I head for my office, and beckon Robbie to join me.

'Anything interesting to report?' I ask her.

She frowns. 'To tell the truth, sir, I'm not quite sure. Jacob is very protective of his mother. He didn't want to leave me on my own with her. She still seems a bit confused, but her story hasn't changed. She can't think why anyone would want to hurt her husband, she didn't see anything, and why do we keep asking. They both protested about having DNA taken until Karen had a word and calmed them down.'

'That's not too unusual,' I say. 'It's an invasion of privacy whichever way you look at it. Plus, people immediately assume they are suspects.'

'Are they?' Robbie asks, raising an eyebrow.

'Right now,' I reply, 'everybody is. What did you think of Jacob?'

'Not much. He struck me as a bit of a bully.' She blushes, and I interpret the word 'bully' as a euphemism for 'total arsehole'. 'I'm afraid I had to threaten to arrest him for obstruction, sir, when he refused to leave Mrs Malden's room. Sorry if I did the wrong thing, but he poked his finger at me and called me a stupid, bloody-minded little cow.'

'Did he, indeed? In that case you were quite right, Robbie,' I say. 'I won't have anyone pushing my officers around, whoever they are and whatever the circumstances. I think it's time I paid Mr Malden a personal visit. But talking of circumstances …' I take a breath and bite the bullet. 'Tell me to mind my own business, but is everything all right otherwise? No problems I should know about?'

She stiffens. 'Not that I can think of, sir.'

In other words, I think, keep my nose out of her personal affairs. Fair enough, I suppose, as long as her spat with Polly Sillitoe doesn't become my business. There's a tap at the door and Larson sticks his head round.

'I'm going to see that antiques dealer,' he says, 'but I thought you'd want to see this first.' He hands me a printout. There are three grainy photographs, taken from the Downside CCTV footage – one male, two female. 'We've isolated these three individuals as part of a group that came in with the night shift on New Year's Eve. None of them signed in or had a pass. There were fifteen other agency staff members, all of whom did sign in, and their identities have been verified one way or another.'

'What agency?' I ask.

'An outfit called Daisychain. Their main office is over near Queen's Square.'

'Okay, thanks,' I say. Finally, we've got some leads to follow up.

Larson has already left when I call the rest of the team together. After a moment's thought, I decide maybe putting Sillitoe and Robbins together might not be the best idea, at least until they've sorted out their domestic problems. Besides, there's a lot Molly Shaw needs to learn, and she won't do that stuck in front of a screen in the squad room, especially if it means being in the same place as Daz Jackson. What is it, I think bitterly, about relationships and police work that just doesn't mix? Given what happened between me and Chrissie, I ought to know better than most. Back then, as a rookie trying to climb the greasy pole, I ignored the advice of the old hands. Now, as a cynical DCI in charge of a hormone-driven team, I see all the impending fuck-ups, and know that, just like my own superiors back then, I can do bugger all about it except wait for the inevitable crash.

In the end, I send Shaw and Sillitoe to see what they can get out of Daisychain. 'If they start making noises about confidentiality,' I say, 'tell them we'll be back with a warrant and go through every single worker on their books. That should put the wind up them, especially if they think Immigration might start sniffing around.' I turn to Jackson. 'Daz, get over to Weston and liaise with them – make sure they are pulling out all the stops looking for James Harcourt, and then go and see the daughter, Rachel. In particular, see what you can find out about exactly how Mick Harcourt died, when, where, and why. I know it's a long shot, but I've got a feeling there's a link with our victims somewhere, although what the bloody hell it is God only knows.'

He grins. 'Yes, boss. I'll see if Weston has a female officer to take along if you like, just in case.' He doesn't need to explain in case of what. Much as the idea of Daz Jackson in the company of any eligible policewoman isn't my favourite thought at the moment, he's right. These days, things need to be strictly by the book. 'I'll get the DSI to ring through and make sure you've got a suitable officer,' I tell him. 'If possible, we could do with an FLO with the daughter anyway, and Karen is tied up with the Maldens.'

I give Robbins an apologetic shrug. 'Sorry, Robbie. I'm afraid you'll be minding the shop. Someone needs to be here when the extra officers arrive from Portishead, and in the meantime, there's still the footage from that car enthusiast in Clifton to go through. The DSI will be here with Blue, so any issues, you can give her a shout.'

She nods, resigned. 'No problem, sir. Where will you be?'

'I think,' I say, 'it's about time I got better acquainted with Jacob Malden. If he tries it on with me, he may find he's bitten off more than he can chew.'

I'm halfway to the harbour when my phone rings. Thanks to my son-in-law, the hands-free function has become less of a mystery and I manage to pick up. It's Maggie. She sounds excited, which is always a sign that she's found something interesting.

'Where are you?' she asks.

'On my way to visit Jacob Malden,' I reply.

'In that case,' she says, 'you definitely need to come over here first.'

I don't argue, just turn around and head for the pathology lab. When I arrive, I spot Maggie coming out of the main lab, looking as if she's just gone six rounds with an all-in wrestler and won by a submission.

'Where's the fire, Maggie?' I ask, catching up with her as she yanks off her surgical gloves and readjusts a crumpled lab coat.

She heaves a huge sigh, and greets me with a rueful grin. 'You just can't get the staff these days,' she complains as we make our way up to her office. 'I was just having to give a couple of lab assistants a dictionary definition of the word "yesterday", which is when I need some of these results. It's a bit like telling Cyril he can't have any more treats until after his walk.'

'Tell me about it. So, what have you got?'

The grin widens. 'A nice little puzzle for you. I was just trying to get the final piece sorted, but I suppose it's a bit much to ask. Still, it's a good thing I caught you before you see the Maldens again.' She pours us both coffee and fires up her computer screen. 'Come round here,' she says. 'I'll show you.'

I drag a chair to her side of the desk and sit. There are three images, each containing a DNA profile. She points at the first one. 'This was taken from our first victim, Charles Malden. The second,' she points again, 'was taken from a hairbrush in the main bedroom, and there isn't much doubt it belongs to Mrs Malden. The DNA sample we're processing now should confirm that. The third sample is from a toothbrush in the bedroom frequently used by Jacob Malden. I asked your DC to find out whether anyone else has used that room in the last few months, and both Mrs Malden and her son said it was reserved solely for his use. The house has two guest rooms for when other people visit.'

She's interrupted by her desk phone. She listens, then says, 'Thanks Maisie,' hangs up and clicks away with her mouse. 'Maisie just got the result I was waiting for,' she says. 'Hang on.'

I manage to hold onto my patience, and a minute later a fourth sample appears on the screen alongside the other three. Maggie looks triumphant. 'Bingo! That does it!'

'Does what?' I ask, staring at the images with no clue what they are actually saying.

'It confirms, beyond doubt,' she replies, 'that Jacob Malden is completely unrelated to Charles Malden.'

That makes me sit up. 'That might explain it.' Maggie frowns at me, confused. 'Joyce has known them most of her life,' I explain. 'She told me that when Iris got pregnant, Charles booked her into a private clinic in Yorkshire, on account of her age and the risk to her, and to the baby's health. But it also makes sense if she had an affair, got pregnant and went away to give Charles time to deal with it. I imagine it would be a tough situation. It might also explain why Charles and Jacob didn't get on.'

'It would,' she agrees, 'if it were true. Unfortunately, it isn't.'

'Meaning?'

'Meaning,' she says, 'Charles Malden is definitely not Jacob's father – and Iris Malden is definitely not his mother.'

For a moment I'm struck dumb, and sip my coffee, mulling it over. 'So,' I say slowly, 'either something happened to Iris's baby, or …'

'Or Iris was never pregnant in the first place,' Maggie finishes for me. 'My money is on the latter. It would be easy enough to check, but you would have to get her to consent to a physical examination, and that might be the tricky part. There might be something in her medical record though, if you can get access to it.'

'I'll put it on the list,' I say. 'So, if Jacob isn't the Maldens' son, who the hell is he?'

'Ah,' she says, beaming with self-satisfaction. 'I think I can help you there.' A few more mouse clicks, and the three initial images disappear, replaced by another, which she places side by side with the one from Jacob. 'This is the profile of Jacob Malden's actual father.'

She looks at me expectantly, as if waiting for a round of applause. 'Come on, Maggie,' I say quietly, just about holding onto a fit of exasperation, 'I don't have time for twenty bloody questions – stop buggering about and tell me. Who is it?'

'Jacob's father,' she says, 'is none other than your third victim – William Harcourt.'

9

I sit in my car in the lab car park, trying to make sense out of it all. At least I now have a link between Charles Malden and William Harcourt, and Jacob and Iris Malden are right in the middle of it. I go through what we know so far. Fifty years ago, Iris Malden went to Yorkshire to have a baby – but not her baby – someone else's. She and Charles came back with William Harcourt's son, who they somehow successfully managed to pass off as their own. The first question is, did Jacob know he wasn't their natural child, and if he did, when did he find out? Secondly, did he know the identity of his real father? That leads neatly to the third question – if Iris wasn't Jacob's mother, who was? As for the elaborate nature of the murders, the only link I can see is the fact that William Harcourt's brother, Mick, died by drowning. I make a note to find out more details on that death. Meanwhile, there has to be a link between Malden, Harcourt and Alice Walker. If there was a genetic relationship between Alice and Jacob or any of the other victims, I'm sure Maggie would have found it. Finally, why is Harcourt's brother, James, on the run? He plainly knows something we don't, so finding him is even more of a priority. One thing is very clear. Maggie was right – confronting Iris and Jacob Malden right now might be a serious mistake.

'Bloody hell,' I mutter to myself, and set off back to West Hill, hoping Larson is back from his interview with the antique dealer, and prepared for some very late nights.

I find Robbie hunched over a computer screen, together with two DCs I don't recognise, presumably the officers sent over from

Portishead. They all look tired, and probably suffering the effects of too much caffeine.

She looks up and gives me an apologetic shrug. 'Nothing on the Clifton CCTV, boss,' she says, and indicates the two newcomers. 'This is DC Miller, and DC Blunt. We've managed to get through around seventy hours between us. How far back do you want us to go?'

I exchange greetings. 'You mean no one visited the Maldens in three days?'

'Only The next-door neighbour, Mrs Fontwell. She went round there several times, the last visit at lunchtime on New Year's Eve – it looked like she was taking a cake or something. She and Mrs Malden went out together once, the day before that, and came back with shopping – from the local corner shop by the look of the bags. Mr Malden went out three times, but not on the day before he was killed. The only other visitor was their son, Jacob. He came round two days earlier, on the 29th.'

'Not on New Year's Eve?'

'No – at least, not by the front door. There's a gate at the back, though, so he could have come in that way.'

'And so could anyone else,' I comment. 'Bugger it! Has Larson been back?'

'He rang in around five minutes ago,' Robbie tells me. 'He's on his way now.'

'Okay,' I decide after some thought. 'Go back another twenty-four hours, and then knock it on the head for now. I have a feeling things will take another direction before too long.'

I head for my office and call Karen Wyatt with an instruction to stick to the Maldens like glue and let me know if anything seems slightly off, however trivial, and then let Grace know I'm back. By the time I put the phone down, Larson is on his way through the squad room to my door, looking pleased with himself. I wave him in.

'I've got some interesting news,' he announces, sitting down and dumping a stack of paper on my desk.

'Congratulations, son,' I reply. 'Join the club. What's all this lot?'

'The antiques dealer was very helpful,' he says. 'A guy by the name of Joseph Cavill, owner of Cavill Antiques on Park Row –

very upmarket, and a specialist in militaria. He and Malden go way back. He says the dirk I showed him was one of six purchased by Malden over a period of ten years, in the 1980s and 90s. He dug up the original receipts, and back then the total cost was approximately fifty thousand pounds. These days, you could double that at least.'

'Bloody hell!' Clearly, killers who leave fifty grand's worth of antiques stuck in their victims definitely aren't interested in the money.

'I showed him the photo of the one you found at the Malden's house earlier,' Larson goes on, 'and he says there isn't much doubt it's a replica. No two dirks are identical. He'd have to examine them to make sure, though.'

'I'll get the rest from Maggie as soon as she's finished with them,' I say. 'We'll get Cavill in as soon as we have them to take a closer look, plus verify that the other two from the victims are also part of Malden's collection.'

I can't help thinking that the six replica dirks in the cabinet could have been placed there at any time, not just in the last few days, and given their position, high up above a stairwell, Malden would very likely not have noticed the switch for some time. If that is the case, going through all the CCTV footage could turn out to be a monumental waste of manpower. It also puts Jacob Malden firmly in the frame. As a frequent and trusted visitor, he would have had more than enough opportunity. I shuffle my priorities and make a decision.

'I need you to do some delving for me,' I tell Larson, and briefly explain Maggie's most recent discoveries.

'You're joking!' is his response, and he follows it up with, 'What are we going to tell Joyce and Chrissie?'

'Nothing,' I reply, 'at least, not right now. It's an ongoing investigation, and until it's over, neither of us is going to say a word, understood?'

He nods. 'And Rosie?'

That one's tougher. 'Officially, the same,' I say, remembering the times I used to regularly break the rules and discuss cases with Chrissie, more for my own sanity than anything else. I also remember the strain I put her under – serious crime isn't exactly a good topic for casual conversation. As a prison psychologist, Rosie is a different proposition, but even so …

He interprets my expression pretty accurately. 'Don't worry,' he says. 'I get it. So, what do you want me to focus on?'

'Several things,' I answer. 'We need to know exactly where in Yorkshire Iris Malden went in 1966 – it might have been a private hospital, hotel, sanatorium, or possibly they just rented a property for her to live in. Chrissie and Jacob were born around the same time, so you could be looking at a two or three-month window, say from the end of March to the end of June that year. Joyce said she thought it was somewhere in the Dales, so concentrating on that area might be a good place to start.'

'That's a hell of a big area,' he comments. 'Okay, what else?'

'Jacob Malden's birth certificate. It's missing from Charles Malden's records. I want to know where Jacob was born and registered, and any information on an official adoption if you can find it, in particular, details of the natural mother. There's also the question of whether or not William Harcourt had other children we don't know about. Cathy Turner told us she's an only child, and that clearly isn't true – she has at least one half-brother. Was she lying to us, and does she know of any others? That isn't your concern, though. Just see what you can dig up. Pick one of our two new boys to help. Grace said one of them knew his way around a computer.'

'Is that it?' he asks, and I catch a hint of sarcasm in his tone.

'No,' I say. 'If you can, try to dig up anything you can find on Alice Walker. Sillitoe has looked into her history and come up blank as far as relatives are concerned. The home has no record of next of kin, and her fees were paid by the council. We know she worked in health at some point, but not much else. Some record of where she's been and when might be useful.'

'Right.' He gets up, but pauses at the door and turns back. 'Do you mind if I grab some lunch first?'

I'm about to make a caustic comment when I realise the mention of food has made my stomach rumble. I look at my watch – it's getting on for mid-afternoon, and breakfast seems no more than a distant memory.

I nod, dig into my pocket for my wallet, and hand him a twenty-pound note. 'Good idea, son. If you're going down to the canteen, will you grab me a sandwich? I've got a feeling we'll be here quite a while yet.'

He thinks about complaining, but in the end just shrugs, takes the note and heads off towards the lift. I stick my head out the door and call Robbie in. 'Do you fancy a bit of overtime?' I ask.

She gives me a look I'm not expecting – almost one of relief. 'Sure, boss. What do you want me to do?'

'Give Cathy Turner a call and ask her to be available at home this evening, say, six o'clock or thereabouts. I need to ask her some questions, and I'd prefer to have a female officer present, just to be safe. She might be in for a bit of a shock.'

Robbie raises an eyebrow, but doesn't ask any questions. 'No problem,' she says, and goes off to make the call. She and Polly Sillitoe have been an item for a couple of years, and have managed quite successfully to keep work and home life firmly separate – until now. Unless they sort themselves out pretty quickly, I'm going to be lumbered with a big problem, one that usually results in one of those concerned asking for a transfer. In this case, I can't see Sillitoe going anywhere, and Robbie Robbins is a good officer, one I don't want to lose. I'm mulling over what to do about it when Larson comes back in carrying several packs of sandwiches.

'I wasn't sure which to get,' he says, so the canteen said I could take what we didn't want back down later.'

I pick out bacon, lettuce and tomato, while my son-in-law tucks into something green, and ominously luminous. I decide not to ask what it is. 'You might as well hand the rest around,' I suggest. 'I don't expect anyone else has eaten either. I forgot to ask earlier – did you manage to track down the details for the brother, Mick Harcourt?'

'Yes,' he replies. 'Give me a minute and I'll send them across to the whiteboard.' I follow him out, and after a few mouse clicks a set of documents appears on the display. 'His death certificate is dated 10th November 2021,' he tells me, 'although from what I've been able to gather, the actual date of death couldn't be determined with complete accuracy, as he had been dead several days before he was found.'

We both chew on our sandwiches for a minute or two, taking in the details.

'Okay,' I say eventually, 'walk me through the main points.'

'According to the police report,' Larson says, 'the body was found by his daughter, Susan, at his home. He was in the bath, semi-clothed – he'd managed to partially undress but was still wearing underwear and socks. There was a small quantity of alcohol in his blood, plus anti-depressant medication, but not enough of either to cause unconsciousness or death. There had been mental health problems for some years, but according to the daughter he was never suicidal. There was evidence of a blow to the back of the head, not of sufficient force to fracture the skull, but enough to either stun or knock him unconscious. The injury was consistent with the victim slipping and hitting his head on the bath tap. Cause of death was drowning, there was no direct evidence of foul play, and so the coroner returned a verdict of accidental death.'

The hairs on the back of my neck are prickling. Maybe Mick Harcourt's death was an accident, but in the light of recent events, maybe it wasn't. There's something else, too, that I can't quite put my finger on.

'Before you do anything else,' I say to Larson, 'can you root out a copy of Mick Harcourt's birth certificate? We might as well go for a full house.'

'You're the boss,' he replies, and heads back to his computer, still chewing on his radioactive sandwich.

It occurs to me as I reach my desk that given Mick's criminal history, it's possible he's on the DNA database. I call Maggie and ask her to check, and to compare it with the samples from the others she's collected so far. Then, I make my way upstairs to bring the DSI up to speed and, of course, make sure she hasn't fed Blue too many gravy bones.

It takes me around an hour to go through all the details, while Grace listens without interrupting, eyes closed, fingers steepled under her chin.

In the end, she just shakes her head. 'What the hell is going on, Al?'

I'm about to answer when her phone rings. She picks up, listens, replies, 'Yes, Maggie, he's here. Hang on, I'm putting you on speaker.'

'What is it, Maggie?' I ask.

'That profile you asked me to look at,' she says, and I catch a touch of incredulity in her voice. 'You were right about it being on the national database. You did say Michael Harcourt, younger brother of your third victim, yes?'

'Yes,' I reply. 'That's right.'

'Wrong,' she says. 'Michael Harcourt is not William Harcourt's brother. He is, however – or was –William Harcourt's son.'

There's a silence as Grace and I take this in. It makes sense, particularly in terms of the age gap between them. But why would William want to pass Mick off as his brother? I shovel that question to one side. Maggie is speaking again.

'There's more,' she says, 'if you are interested.'

'Go on, Maggie,' I reply.

'I hope you're both sitting down. I ran Michael Harcourt's profile against Jacob Malden's, and guess what? They are full siblings. In other words, William Harcourt was their father, and the same woman – whoever she is, or was, is their mother. And before you ask, there is no record of the mother's DNA on file that I can find, so who she is, exactly, is something you are going to have to find out. I did a comparison with your second victim, Alice Walker, and no match.'

'Okay, thanks Maggie,' I say, and Grace hangs up.

Grace and I stare at each other for a moment, until finally Grace asks, 'Do you think Jacob knew about Mick?'

'No bloody idea,' I answer, 'but if I had to bet on it, I'd say yes. The real questions are, did Cathy Turner and James Harcourt know, who is the mother, and how many more of them are there?'

Grace thinks for a minute, sighs, and then says simply, 'Shit!'

10

I'm on my way to Portishead with Robbie Robbins when a call comes through from Dick Fosbury.

'I thought you'd like to know,' he says, 'one of my constables took it on himself to check the local animal sanctuaries, looking for those dogs of yours, and came up trumps. Two Alsatians were dumped outside an RSPCA shelter near Weston in the early hours of this morning. They checked the ID chips and they are definitely Harcourt's dogs. They tried ringing the number on the tags but it was discontinued – Harcourt must have changed his number and not updated the information. They were about to send someone out to the house when my PC contacted them. He's gone over to the sanctuary now to take a look.'

'Thanks, Dick,' I say. 'I'll be seeing the daughter in a few minutes. She might want to take them on – if not, maybe you can recruit them for our dog unit.'

'As if I haven't got enough hassle already,' he replies, and hangs up.

'Doesn't that mean whoever took them must have known the victim?' Robbie asks.

'Not necessarily, Robbie,' I reply, 'but likely. Whoever they are, they must be animal lovers, to be bothered enough to make sure they would be well looked after. We'll have to wait and see what Cathy Turner has to say about it.'

We turn up at a small, modern terrace close to Portishead Marina. The door is answered by a giant of a man in jeans that can't quite accommodate the results of an expanded waistline, and a T-shirt allowing the display of well-muscled arms festooned with an assortment of tattoos – without doubt, the figure of a man who has spent half a lifetime sitting behind the wheel of a large truck. I take an involuntary step back, but when he speaks, the tone is friendly, and he holds out a hand, first to me, then to DC Robbins. We exchange introductions, and Mr Turner – Roy – ushers us through to the lounge.

'I'll put the kettle on,' he says, and shrugs. 'I've done nothing but make tea since I got back. Cathy won't eat, you see. I'm afraid she's in a bit of a state, what with everything.'

'I understand,' I reply. 'Tea would be good, thanks. I'm afraid we have some news that might come as a bit of a surprise, but if you like, we can wait until you're with her.'

He frowns, but gives us a nod. 'I won't be long – it had just boiled anyway.'

In the lounge, we find Cathy Turner curled on a sofa wrapped in a blanket, even though the heating is on 'sauna' setting and I'm sweating under my thick overcoat. Robbie has already unzipped her Parka and is glowing like a light bulb. Cathy hardly looks up as we walk in, just waves in the general direction of the armchairs. We take off our coats and sit.

'I know this must be a very difficult time,' I start, and her head shoots up, fixing me with a frosty glare.

'What would you know?' she spits. 'My father's been murdered, and the best you can do is come round and drink tea. You should be out there, looking for who did it – you won't even let me have his body to bury. They say I might have to wait for weeks – months even …'

She puts a hand to her mouth, stifling a sob. Robbie shifts in her seat and I give her a nod. 'We're very sorry about all this, Mrs Turner,' she says, 'and I assure you, we're determined to catch whoever killed your father. But to do that, we need as much information as possible, and anything you can tell us might help.'

Roy Turner chooses that moment to come in with a tray of tea and biscuits. He sets it down on the coffee table and joins his wife on the sofa, giving her a gentle hug.

'Come on, love,' he says, 'you know everyone is doing their best. If we can help, that's a good thing, isn't it?'

She nods, wipes her eyes on a tissue and blinks at us. 'Yes, of course. I'm sorry. Please, ask your questions. I'll help if I can.'

'Thank you, Mrs Turner,' I say. 'First, though, I have some news about your father's dogs. I thought you might like to know they are safe and well. They were taken to the animal sanctuary over in Weston.'

She perks up at once. 'Bonnie and Clyde are all right – oh, thank God! I thought they must have been – you know …' She trails off, but then turns to her husband. 'You have to go and get them, Roy. The poor things won't know what's going on – Dad would hate them to be locked up in a place like that.'

Roy doesn't look too keen, but does his best to attempt a reassuring smile. 'I'll go first thing, love. The centre will be closed now. The dogs will be fine just for one night. I'll get them back as soon as it opens, I promise.'

'Whoever took them obviously cared about them,' I say, 'and made sure they were somewhere safe. But we wondered whether perhaps they went with someone they knew, and trusted. Can you think of anyone?'

She manages a short laugh. 'Bonnie and Clyde? Those two are as soft as grease. They might look scary, but they're more likely to lick you to death than bite. But to answer your question, no – I can't think of anyone.'

'Ah, I see.' I do my best to hide the fact that another possible source of evidence has just gone down the pan. I take a deep breath. 'There is something else I need to ask, if you can put up with us a little longer.'

She glances at Roy, who squeezes her hand. 'Just say if you're feeling too tired, Cath. I'm sure the officers will understand.'

'I'm not too tired,' she replies. 'I just want it all over and done with.' She turns to me. 'What do you want to know?'

'Just a little about your family history,' I say. 'I assume your parents were married a long time?'

'I don't see what …' she starts, and then shrugs. 'They would have been married fifty-one years this year. Mum died three years ago. She was two years older than Dad – just old age, the doctors said. I don't think Dad got over it. He missed her so much after she'd gone.'

'And the rest of your family – uncles, aunts, grandparents and so on – did your mum and dad get on with them okay?'

She frowns. 'Why do you ask that? Actually, no, not all of them. He definitely didn't get on with Grandad. Old Bill, he called him. Dad thought that was funny, seeing as he was always getting arrested and his name was Bill.'

'Do you know why he kept getting arrested?' I ask.

'Violence, mostly,' she replies. 'He used to beat up his wife and children, and was always getting drunk and into fights. He was okay with me, though, as far as I can remember. We moved down here when I was four, and we never saw him again. Uncle Jim had already moved down with his family the year before, and he didn't think much of Old Bill either. We got the odd Christmas card from Grandma, but that was about it.'

'And what about your other uncle – Mick? Did you ever see him?'

She shakes her head. 'We all kept well away from him. Dad hated him and said he was just like Grandad, a nasty piece of work, and we shouldn't have anything to do with him. You know he died a couple of years ago? Dad was up in Wakefield at the time, visiting other family, but he didn't bother going to the funeral. Neither did Uncle Jim, although he did stay in touch with Mick – said he felt sorry for him – God knows why.'

God may well know, I think, but so do I. The question is, does she? From what I've seen so far, either she's completely ignorant, which I can't quite believe, she's in complete denial, which is possible, or she's a damned good actress. Robbie and I exchange a look. It's clear she doesn't want to pick it up, so the next step is down to me.

'I'm sorry I have to ask you this,' I say, 'but was your father's marriage to your mother his first? Did he ever speak of anyone else, before they met, perhaps?'

She looks genuinely shocked, although, in my experience, that doesn't necessarily mean much.

'Of course not! Mum was the love of his life – he always said so. There was nobody, before or after, if that's what you're thinking.' Again, she looks to her husband, 'Why is he asking these questions? What is he trying to say? I don't understand.'

There's just the faintest hint of something in her tone that makes my suspicion gel into a certainty. Cathy Turner understands only too well. As if in agreement, a tremor runs through my left hand –

a remaining legacy of the brain injury, and one normally triggered by a sudden jolt of adrenalin.

Roy Turner immediately leaps to her defence. 'This is ridiculous. Are you accusing my wife of something? Can't you see she's upset enough already – perhaps you'd better leave, come back another time.'

Whatever it is, he knows, too, I decide. 'I'm sorry,' I say. 'I'm afraid we can't do that. I can only ask you to believe me when I say that these questions are very important, and may have a bearing on your father's death.'

Robbie jumps in. 'We're not accusing you of anything, Mrs Turner. We just want to understand why your father might have been targeted, and we can't discount the possibility that it could be something to do with people he knew a long time ago. We really need you to help us if you can.'

Cathy slumps back in her seat with a sigh of defeat. 'There was a rumour,' she starts, and her husband gives her an encouraging nod. 'Around a year before Uncle Mick died, my cousin Rachel told me Mick's daughter, Susan, had been down to see Uncle Jim, and there had been a huge row. Susan said Mick had told her the truth; that he wasn't Dad's brother at all, but in fact his illegitimate son, and that Jim knew all along, but my dad had told him to keep it quiet, because he didn't want my mum and me to find out he had another child. Mick told her the family had forced him to lie about it all his life, and that Dad had threatened to kill him if he ever told anyone.'

'And did you believe this story?' I ask.

'Of course not! The whole thing was ridiculous. Mick was always trying to stir things up, make as much trouble for us as he could. He was a drug addict – did you know that? He was completely off his head most of the time, and it was no surprise when he finally managed to kill himself. I feel sorry for Susan and Billy, of course – I've nothing against them, and they grew up decent enough, thanks to their mother. But I think everyone else was relieved that we wouldn't have to put up with his lies and shit-stirring anymore.'

My mind goes back to the coroner's report Larson dug up – *a small quantity of alcohol in his blood, plus anti-depressant medication, but not enough of either to cause unconsciousness or death.* It just doesn't fit with Cathy Turner's image of a drug-addled accidental death.

'Mrs Turner,' I say, hunting for the right words, 'I'm afraid what I need to tell you might be a bit upsetting.' I pause, and see her stiffen, her grip tightening on her husband's hand. 'We looked at your late uncle's DNA profile, and it appears he wasn't lying. He was, in fact, your father's son – your half-brother.'

For a long moment, she stares at me as if I've grown an extra head, even though I'm sure that what I've just told her is simply confirming what she already knew but didn't want to admit.

Finally, she finds her voice. 'You looked at Mick's DNA? Why? What does it have to do with anything? We never saw him or had anything to do with him or his family – he lived two hundred miles away, for God's sake, and he's been dead over two years, so what the hell has it got to do with my father's death?'

There's no attempt at contradiction, I note, and her reaction is more shock at the fact that we've uncovered the family secret than at the information itself.

'At this moment, we aren't quite sure,' I say honestly, 'but we have to pursue every avenue of enquiry. You said your father was visiting family in Yorkshire around the time of Mick's death. Are you quite sure they didn't meet up? Perhaps he went to see your cousins?'

She shakes her head. 'I told you, he wanted nothing to do with any of them. They all hated us as much as we hated them, and Mum would have been very upset to think he'd been anywhere near them. He went with Uncle Jim to visit Sarah and her family. Rachel was already there, and they planned to give her a lift back.'

'Can you remember exactly when that visit took place, and how long he and your uncle stayed there?' I ask. 'Just for our records, you understand.'

She sniffs. 'As it happens, I can remember exactly. It was November 5th – bonfire night. Sarah's daughter went into labour – that's why Rachel was there, to help out. They went to be there for the birth, and stayed a month. They all came back at the beginning of December – the second or third – I'm not sure of the exact date, but I can look it up if you like.'

'Thank you, that won't be necessary.' I get up, and nod towards Robbie. 'I know all this is very difficult for you,' I say, 'and you have been very patient with us. I can assure you we are doing everything we can to find whoever is responsible. DC Robbins will stay in touch with you, and if you have any questions or worries, just call us and ask for her, or for me.' I take a step, and have another thought. 'You wouldn't happen to have an address and phone number for your cousin, Sarah? We might need to speak to her, and it will save us having to look it up.'

'I'll get it for you,' Roy Turner says, getting up to show us out. 'It's in the hall, by the phone.'

At the front door, he roots through an old-fashioned card index. 'It belonged to Margaret, Cathy's mother,' he explains. 'She couldn't bring herself to get rid of it, because all the addresses are in Margaret's writing. Ah – here it is.'

He stands clear while Robbie digs out her phone and photographs the card, and then stands in the open doorway, watching as we drive away – making sure we've actually gone, the suspicious part of me suggests.

'What did you make of it, Robbie?' I ask as we pull out onto the Bristol Road.

'I'm not sure,' she replies. 'They must know about the other murders, yet neither of them mentioned it, not even to ask if they were connected.'

'True – anything else?'

'I think they knew stuff they weren't saying, but I couldn't work out what. I mean, Mrs Turner acted like her dad was pure as driven snow, but she knew about Mick, so she must have known he'd had affairs with other women. Boss – why didn't you tell her about Jacob Malden? Do you think she knows about him, too?'

'I think, Robbie, that now is not the time. It's not clear yet whether or not Jacob himself knows, and we need to establish that first. I was tempted, though, and initially, it was part of the plan. For now, maybe we should keep our powder dry. The less Cathy Turner thinks we know the better. Plus, there's something else to consider.'

'What's that, boss?'

'Ah – you need to work on your powers of observation, Detective Constable. The Turners claimed they had never had anything to do with Mick Harcourt or his family, and that Cathy's mother would have been particularly upset at any contact between them. That's understandable if she knew that Mick was her husband's love child, yes?'

'I would say so,' Robbie replies. 'If I thought my partner had had an affair ...'

She trails to a halt, and coughs. I glance across to see her staring out of the window, biting her lip. Is that really what her spat with Polly Sillitoe is all about? As if I haven't got enough to contend with, damn it.

'Okay,' I say, moving on. 'If William Harcourt's wife was so set against Mick, how come his address was in her card index in her handwriting?'

11

Half way back to the station, my phone rings, and Sillitoe's voice comes through the car speaker.

'I think we're getting somewhere with our rogue care worker,' she tells me. 'The agency kicked up a bit of a fuss at first, but in the end, they identified two of the three individuals – the male, and one of the females. They are both regular kitchen and cleaning staff at several homes in the area, and according to Daisychain, have both been reported in the past for failing to adhere to security protocols. They say it isn't uncommon among some of their staff to either forget or, more likely, avoid signing in, particularly those with refugee status who have had bad experiences in their country of origin. The third, though, highlights a different problem. Some workers are registered with more than one agency, sign up for simultaneous shifts, and get someone else to do one of them in return for a cut of the wages. It's a racket they claim they are trying to stamp out, but they're probably not trying all that hard. In this case, the worker should have been a woman by the name of Kylie Berman, but her photo didn't match the image on the CCTV.'

'Did you get an address?' I ask.

'Better than that. We paid her a visit and she tried to make a run for it out the back door, so we arrested her on suspicion of fraud. We've just got back and dumped her in a cell. I thought you might want to have a word before the duty brief gets here.'

'You bloody well bet I do,' I reply. 'I'll be there in around fifteen minutes. In the meantime, you might like to let slip that we're thinking of adding "accessory to murder" to the list. It might help move things along a bit.'

'Or bring them to a grinding halt,' Sillitoe says. 'She's pretty scared, and if the brief is half decent, they'll realise it's not the time to go "no comment".'

'Let's hope so,' I say, and hang up.

It's gone 7.30 pm by the time we get back up to an almost deserted squad room. Sillitoe is in her office and, unusually, the door is closed. I see her glance up, catch Robbie's eye and quickly look away. Enough, I think, is enough.

'Get yourself home, Robbie,' I say, and add, 'Polly will want to be around when this care worker is interviewed, so she'll probably be here a while yet.'

Once she's gone, the only other person in the room is Grace, who is sitting where Larson should be, frowning over something on the computer screen.

I sent everyone home,' she says. 'They all looked shattered. John's taken Blue, and says to pick her up from his place when you're done here. He also said Rosie was sorting out food if you want it. You look pretty knackered, too. If you want to leave the interview to Polly, I don't mind sticking around as backup.'

'Thanks, but no,' I say. 'There are a couple of questions I want to ask, so I'd like to sit in – I'm happy for Polly to take the lead, though.' I also want to have a serious word with my DI, but keep that to myself for the moment.

'Fair enough, but there's something you should see first. John did some more digging while you were out, and look what he came up with.'

I grab a chair and go round to Grace's side of the desk. On the screen is a copy of a marriage certificate. William Harcourt married Margaret Chisholm at Wakefield registry office on 10th October 1973.

'This doesn't tell us anything we don't already know,' I say. 'Cathy Turner said it would have been her parents' fifty-first anniversary this year.'

Grace grins. 'Agreed, it doesn't tell us anything. But this does.' She clicks the mouse and the first document is replaced by a second. 'Take a look.'

It's a second marriage certificate. This one is dated 25th July 1965, and details the marriage of William Harcourt to Anne Marie Blake at the church of Saint Jude, Rubery, Birmingham.

'You're sure it's the same William Harcourt?' I ask.

'John is positive,' Grace replies. 'He looked into it a bit further, and the results are very interesting. Between 1966 and 1972, William and Anne had five children, two boys and three girls.'

'Christ!' I can't help saying. 'I know some people like big families, but five in six years – that's what I would call over the top.'

'Apparently,' Grace goes on, 'St Jude's is a Catholic church. If Anne's family was old-school, contraception wouldn't have been an option, even in the 1970s.' There's a long pause before she adds, 'Catholics don't go in for divorce either.'

It takes a minute for the penny to drop. So much for Cathy Turner's mother being the love of her father's life. I blink at the certificate, and then at Grace. 'He didn't get divorced? Are you sure?'

'Quite sure,' she replies. 'Whatever else our Mr Harcourt was, he was definitely a bigamist.'

At once, several questions spring to mind. In particular, were the Turners aware of this? If so, and they only found out recently, it might provide some kind of motive, especially as Cathy Turner seemed to have been very close to her mother. Equally, there are five abandoned children and an ex-wife, if she's still alive, with an axe to grind, somewhere in the Midlands. What I can't quite see is the link between this new information and our other two victims, Charles Malden and Alice Walker.

'We need to find out what happened to Anne Harcourt's children,' I say. 'If she had the first in 1966 and it was a boy…'

'You think he might have been adopted by the Maldens?' Grace finishes for me.

I shrug. 'We have to check, even if only to eliminate the possibility.'

'Agreed,' she says, 'but not tonight, Al. John can get onto it in the morning. You and Polly have a prisoner to deal with, and as you've declined my offer of assistance, I have a very good bottle of claret at home with my name on it.' She turns off the computer and gets to her feet. 'If you want my advice,' she says on the way out,

'I'd get over to your daughter's house as soon as possible. I'm reliably informed there's one of Joyce's steak pies in the oven.'

I tap lightly on Sillitoe's door and see her tense, then slump back in her chair and heave a sigh of relief as she realises it's me.

'Evening, boss,' she says as I go in. 'Are you ready for Ms Berman?'

'Not quite,' I reply. 'I think there's something else we need to discuss first?'

Her eyes narrow. 'Such as?'

'Oh, come on, Polly,' I say. 'We've known each other a long time. Tell me to mind my own business, but whatever's going on between you and Robbie is starting to spill over, and it won't be long before the rest of the team starts to notice – that's if they haven't already. We've got enough to contend with without having to walk on eggshells until the pair of you sort yourselves out.'

She thinks about making a protest, but decides against it, and holds up a hand. 'Sorry, boss. I suppose it's my fault – it always seems to be these days. Robbie blames it on this.' She raps a knuckle on her left leg, the one that was amputated just below the knee after being almost bitten off by a drug dealer's attack dog a couple of years ago. 'She was brilliant just after it happened – I don't think I would have come through it without her. Now, though …'

'You don't need a mother hen?' I suggest.

'I suppose that's it, partly,' she admits, 'but it's frustrating, you know? She says I haven't been the same since, and to be fair, she's got a point. I've been a bit difficult to live with the last few months. I can't help thinking that if it hadn't been for this,' she slaps again at her bionic leg, 'I'd have made DCI somewhere by now. It wouldn't work here, of course – you've got that corner all sewn up. It would most likely mean a transfer to God knows where. I told her I was thinking about it, and since then she's been accusing me of just about anything you can think of – the list is longer than a jumbo toilet roll, for fuck's sake. The latest idea is that I want to get away from her because I'm having an affair – it's ridiculous – for one thing, when would I find the bloody time?'

'Sounds to me like she's feeling a bit overpowered, Polly,' I say. 'You're not just her partner, you're also her senior officer. You're holding all the cards here. As for your career, don't be in too much of a hurry – nobody wants a DI whose eye is on the greasy pole when it should be on the job. Plus, don't forget, Robbie is a damned good detective. If you're not careful, she will be the one jumping ship to take up a promotion.'

She opens her mouth, but I cut her off. 'In the meantime, I'm the senior officer here, and right now, a bad atmosphere in the team is something I don't need. So, sort it out so we can all concentrate on whoever murdered three people before the body count gets to four – got it?'

She glowers for a moment, then breaks into a wry smile. 'Got it, boss.'

I give her a nod. 'Come on, then – let's go and get this interview out of the way so we can both go home.'

By the time we get down to the interview room, Kylie Berman's brief, a young duty solicitor lumbered with the night shift, has already arrived and had time to talk things over with his client. He greets us with a weary smile and leans across to whisper in her ear. Kylie herself is hunched in her chair dabbing her eyes with what looks like her solicitor's handkerchief, and at his prompting looks up and blinks at us, a rabbit caught in the headlights.

'I never did nothing,' she blurts out, between sniffs. 'I wasn't there, right? I don't know nothing about no dead woman, 'cos I was somewhere else and I can prove it, so you can't fit me up neither.'

'I've explained the situation to my client,' the solicitor puts in, 'and I have advised her that under the circumstances it would be in her best interest to cooperate fully with your investigation.'

'Thank you,' I reply. 'It's Mr Davison, isn't it? We've met a few times before.'

'Yes, Chief Inspector. Good evening – and to you, Inspector Sillitoe. Hopefully, we can clear all this up without too much difficulty.'

'Let's hope so,' Sillitoe says, and goes through the routine, beginning the recording and stating the names of those present. 'Before we start, Ms Berman,' she says, putting on her reassuring voice, 'would you like a cup of tea, perhaps, or coffee? And do you mind very much if we call you Kylie? It might make things a bit easier.'

My DI's tone has the desired effect, and the woman calms down a little and takes a deep breath. 'I don't want no bloody tea,' she says, still sniffing, 'and you can call me what you like. But I never murdered nobody. I told you, I was somewhere else, working, innit? I got witnesses, right?'

'We understand, Kylie,' Sillitoe says. 'You have been arrested on a charge of fraud – nothing else at this stage. We know you didn't murder anyone, but we think you may be able to help us find out who did kill one of the residents of Downside nursing home in the early hours of Monday morning. The more help you can give us, the easier your situation will be, do you understand?'

Kylie looks at us, then her brief, who nods his encouragement, and back to us again. 'I don't know nothing,' she says sullenly, but at least she's a lot calmer.

'The fact is,' I tell her, 'you might have been working, but you weren't where you were supposed to be, were you, Kylie?'

'That's not my fault,' she protests. 'I got three kids at home, and the money's shit. There's a bloody cost of living crisis on in case you hadn't noticed, but I suppose you lot wouldn't know about that. I had to buy new school uniforms for two of 'em last week, and I ain't got nothing left for food unless I double the shifts. I can't be in two places at once – I ain't fucking Derren Brown.'

'So, you sign up for more than one agency, and farm out some of your shifts for a cut of the wages – would that be fair to say?'

She lowers her eyes, wringing the handkerchief between her fingers. Reluctantly, she nods. 'Yeah, suppose so.'

'And the women who take your shifts – are they all people you know?' Sillitoe asks.

Kylie shrugs. 'Some, but not all. Word gets around – there are lots who do it. We wouldn't have enough to live on otherwise.'

'You say word gets round. How? From neighbours? Other care workers?'

'Other people doing the job, mostly.' She answers. 'Someone says they've got a mate wanting a shift, and if we get double booked, there's always somebody wants to take it on. They do the shift, and we get thirty quid a time. If it's a twelve-hour shift they do all right, and so do we. The agencies, they don't check, see?'

'And how do they get paid?' I ask.

She gives me a sly grin. 'That's easy. I got different bank accounts. Three agencies, three bank accounts. The money goes in there, and then I pay the other person cash, minus my commission.'

'And you don't have any issues with security?' She looks blank, so I elaborate. 'When someone takes a shift that you are supposed to be doing, how do they get in and out of the care home without anyone noticing it isn't you?'

She blinks at me as if I'm stupid. 'Are you fucking kidding me?' She sighs. 'Come to think of it, you look like the kind of bloke who's never mucked out a toilet in your life. The thing with most of these places is, they don't give a fuck who does the job as long as somebody does. We're just the ones in the blue overalls – or green, or pink, whatever – who turn up and do all the shit jobs that nobody else wants for shit money. They don't care who we are as long as it's done. Night shifts are best. Nobody's around, and if you keep your head down that's all you are – just a number in the headcount, yeah? I got some regulars, and give everybody a copy of my signature to sign in, but sometimes they forget, so I go through the book next time I'm there and make sure, so we all get paid.'

She's warming to the topic now, and sticks her chin out, proud of her misplaced ingenuity, and oblivious to the fact she will, without doubt, have no job at all to go back to, and may well end up with a custodial sentence. It likely won't make much difference, though, as there will be plenty of offers of work at thirty quid a shift when she gets out.

Sillitoe takes it up. 'Kylie, I'd like to talk about New Year's Eve. Were you working that night?'

She bites her lip, tightens her grip on the handkerchief, and glances at her brief again. He nods.

'No,' she admits. 'I was supposed to be, but I weren't. There was a party, right? Down at the Rifleman's. Everyone was going. I had two night shifts booked – it's double time, see – one at Downside, and one at Forest Gate over in Easton. There was another worker from Daisychain had tried to get the New Year shifts and hadn't been able to, so I said she could do my one at Forest Gate. There's a waiting list for the holiday shifts because of the extra cash, and she was a long way down it. If anyone asked, we'd just say we'd swapped. Nobody did, though.'

'And what about your shift at Downside?' Sillitoe asks. 'Did a colleague of yours ask to take that one?'

Kylie shakes her head. 'Nah – it was this woman I hadn't seen before. A friend told me about her, said she was desperate for cash and needed extra work. She'd done some shifts at other places, and was all right, my friend told me. I met her in the coffee shop down at the West Hill Price Cutter – you know the one?'

I nod. 'I know it. Go on.'

'She said she needed to do the New Year's Eve shift because of the extra money, and she was willing to pay forty-five quid. I said fifty, on account of it being the bank holiday, and she agreed.'

'And did she give you a name, this woman?'

Kylie shrugs. 'She said her name was Nina, but I know it wasn't because of the way she looked when she said it. I said I didn't care as long as she did the shift, and arranged to meet her and hand over the cash on Friday night. We get paid on Friday, see, so I can't take any money out till then.'

'So,' I say, 'You've arranged to see this Nina on Friday – where? What time?'

'Rifleman's, eight o'clock,' Kylie replies. 'That's what we said.'

Sillitoe leafs through the folder she's brought with her and pulls out a copy of the CCTV image from Downside's front desk.

'Is this the woman you met?' she asks.

'Yeah,' Kylie replies without any hesitation, 'that's her – well, it looks like her. It's a fucking awful picture though.'

Sillitoe takes the photo back. 'Thanks, Kylie. I think that will be all for now.'

'Just one more thing,' I say quickly. 'Did you know Alice Walker – the lady who was murdered?'

Kylie screws up her face. 'Everybody knew her. She was a right fucking bitch, always ordering us about, especially the night shift. Every five minutes it was "fetch me this, tidy up that, wipe my arse …" I told her one time, I said, we're not her bloody servants, and it's not our job to run around waiting on people like her hand and foot. If she wanted posh treatment, she should sod off somewhere else and pay for it. Can I go now?'

'Not quite,' Sillitoe says. 'You are going to be charged with some very serious offences under the Fraud Act. However, we are willing to allow bail if you agree to certain conditions.'

'What conditions?' Kylie asks, with more than a hint of suspicion.

'First, that you agree to stay in or around your home, and report to us daily. You will be given the details before you are allowed to leave. Second, a police officer will be with you when you keep your appointment with Nina on Friday.'

'I don't want to meet her, not if she done what you said, and killed that old woman. I know she was a right cow, but I don't want to see anybody who goes around murdering people – it's not safe.' She thinks for a second, then adds, 'And having you lot there won't be safe neither. Anyone turns up in a uniform, they're likely to get more than they bargained for in that place, and I don't want my mates thinking I'm a snitch.'

'Nobody will think that,' I assure her. 'We won't be in uniform, and you won't even see us. Someone will talk to you before Friday, and take you through what we need you to do. In the meantime, it would be in your best interest to keep it to yourself. You have been very cooperative so far, and if you help us, we'll do our best to put in a word for you. Okay?'

She nods. 'Yeah. You'd better make sure that woman don't come sniffing after her money before Friday, though. I know her face, and I don't want to get stabbed or nothing.'

With that thought, we leave her to the duty sergeant and make our way back upstairs.

'Christ almighty!' Sillitoe says as we head to our offices to grab our coats. 'How stupid can you be? She was bound to get rumbled sooner or later. I wonder how many more of them are at it – no wonder the care system is on its knees.'

'Not just stupid,' I say. 'I'd add desperate to the list. From what I could see, she wasn't doing it for drug money, or to keep herself in fags and booze. She's on her own, with three kids and a job that only pays a fraction of what it should. It's no wonder people like her break the rules to stay on top of things.'

Sillitoe stops mid-stride and gives me a concerned look. 'Are you sure you've completely recovered from that shot in the head, boss? Kylie Berman has been systematically ripping off the care system, probably for years, an elderly woman is dead as a result, and you're defending her?'

I smile. 'You're right, Polly. Maybe I'm getting old, or maybe I'm just very tired and very hungry. At least if it turns out I'm starting to go soft in my old age, I know I've got the human equivalent of a Rottweiler waiting in the wings. Now, bugger off home, and for God's sake be nice to Robbie. I don't think I could cope with another day of you two sniping at each other across the squad room.'

12

When I finally get to my daughter's house, there's no sign of my son-in-law. Rosie pulls me into the kitchen and insists I eat before I go up to join him in the spare bedroom he uses as his home office. To prevent any argument, Blue ducks under the table and distributes her not inconsiderable weight on my feet.

'You do realise you're over-compensating,' Rosie says, sliding a large slice of steak pie onto a plate and handing it over before I can launch into my usual complaint about Larson not paying enough attention to his family.

'For what?' I ask, through a mouthful of pastry.

She shakes her head. 'Just because Mum didn't like it when you used to get too involved in your work, it doesn't mean I feel the same – and it doesn't mean John ignores us either. It wouldn't hurt you to admit, once in a while, that the two of you have more in common than you think.'

That, I think to myself, is probably what I'm afraid of. 'How is Joyce,' I ask, changing the subject.

'Still a bit upset,' Rosie replies, 'but she's okay. Mum's just finished a commission for an advertising outfit in town, so she's free to look after her for a while.' She pauses, clearly wanting to say something, but not sure if she should.

'Go on,' I say. 'What's on your mind?'

'John told me,' she says, 'about Jacob Malden not being Iris's son.'

'He shouldn't have,' I comment before I can stop myself. 'That information is confidential.'

'Are you saying you never discussed any of your cases with Mum?' There's an accusing edge to her voice.

'You know I did,' I reply. 'That's one of the reasons we ended up getting a divorce.'

'And you don't want to see that happen to me and John. See, you do like him after all.'

I finish the pie and put down my fork. 'For God's sake, Rosie …'

She's smiling. 'The thing is, I spoke to Mum about Jacob – don't worry, I didn't tell her what John told me – and she said to tell you to be careful around him. She didn't like him much when they were children.'

'Why?' I ask. 'Did she elaborate?'

'A bit. She said he was a terrible bully at school, always pushing the other kids around and getting into trouble. She also said she thought it was partly to do with his father – the two of them didn't get on, and Charles was always accusing Jacob of being tied to his mother's apron strings. It's possible they were simply too alike, strong personalities butting horns. Anyway, Mum said the problems between them never really went away, although they tolerated each other for Iris's sake.' She shrugs. 'I thought you might find it useful to know that.'

I nod. 'It certainly fits with the reports I've had from the officer who interviewed him. But you're a psychologist – do you think his mother might have been a target as well?'

'It's possible,' she replies, 'but on the other hand, if he was scared of his father, he could have seen her as his protector – his safe place, and his behaviour outside the home would have been a reaction to his lack of control behind closed doors. I know Gran was very fond of Charles, but from what Mum says, and other hints I've picked up, he was pretty ruthless when it came to getting his own way. I suppose that's why he was such a successful businessman and politician.'

'In other words,' I say, 'Charles was a bit of an arse, and like father, like son? Do you think maybe Charles wasn't so keen on the idea of children, and had Jacob mainly to keep his wife happy?'

'It's one theory,' she answers after a moment's thought. 'But men like that tend to place a lot of value on the continuation of the line – having an heir to the throne if you like. Charles would probably have wanted that more than he disliked the idea of a child running around disrupting his life. It could explain why he and Iris kept Jacob's origins quiet – the importance of preserving the bloodline and all that.'

The more I hear about Jacob Malden's history, the more, I think, it puts him firmly in the frame. Abandoned by his natural father and barely tolerated by his adoptive one, I can understand his feeling more than a little pissed off, but whether that resentment was enough of a motive for murder … Then again, I've known people kill for much less on the streets of West Hill. Demonstrating motive isn't the only problem, though. However ingenious a criminal is, I've yet to come across one who can be in three places at once.

Rosie plonks two mugs of coffee on the table. 'Here. You'd better go and save John from himself. You're not the only one who has had a hard day, and I've got a date with a heated blanket and reality TV. I'll probably be asleep by the time you two have finished, so let yourself out.'

I find Larson juggling with two keyboards, completely absorbed in the array of images and documents laid out across three large screens. He barely looks up as I enter, find a small corner of the worktop away from the electronics to dump the mugs, grab a spare stool and sit beside him.

'Grace told me about Harcourt's first marriage,' I say, and it's possible …'

'It isn't,' he interrupts, sits back and finally gives me his attention. 'Pass me that mug, will you? I've got quite a bit to tell you.'

I swallow my annoyance and give him his coffee. He clicks at his mouse, sending a flurry of documents flying across the screens, snapping into place like the squares on a Rubik's Cube.

'One interesting thing,' he says, waving a finger at the screen, 'is that he committed to a Catholic marriage, yet still kept up his relationship with Mick and Jacob's mother. He was supporting another family when Jacob was born, which might explain the adoption.

He points at a photo of a couple with a girl of around ten or so. 'This is William Harcourt at around age forty, with Margaret, the woman he bigamously married later on, and their daughter, Cathy Turner. The resemblance between William and Jacob is quite striking.' He highlights another image and slides it across the screen to sit next to one of Jacob Malden. 'Mick Harcourt, he explains, 'taken around two years before his death. I did a trawl of Facebook.'

If I thought Jacob and his natural father looked alike, the familial link between the two brothers is even more obvious.

'I did some more rooting around, he says, 'and came across this.' He brings up a copy of a document.

I scan the details and sit back, scratching my head. 'Is this who I think it is?'

He nods. 'William Michael Cawley, known as Mick, born August 20th, 1964; father: William James Harcourt; mother: Patricia Joan Cawley. Look where the birth was registered.'

'Bridlington – that's East Yorkshire – not quite the Yorkshire Dales, but close.'

'Exactly. That's where Joyce told us Iris Malden went when she was supposedly pregnant. Also, as Mick and Jacob are full siblings, we now know the name of Jacob's natural mother.'

'Don't tell me – you looked her up?'

He smiles. 'I've made a start.' He pulls up more documents. 'I haven't had time to get more than the basics. Patricia Joan Cawley, born May 8th 1945 – VE day, would you believe? She was born in Balsall Heath, Birmingham, and died in August 1978; cause of death, myocardial infarction – a heart attack. She got married in 1969, again in Balsall Heath, to a man by the name of Jack Donlan. I haven't managed to get any further, so all we know so far is that she had at least two children with William Harcourt prior to her marriage.'

I let out a long breath. I'm about to tell Larson to knock it on the head for the night when it hits me. 'Jesus bloody Christ!' I mutter, and my son-in-law gives me a questioning look.

'What?' he asks.

'It might be nothing,' I admit, 'but we're looking for reasons why these three people should be targeted, and what kind of message the killers are trying to send by killing them in such a specific way, right?'

He nods. 'Right. So, what are you thinking?'

'Mick Harcourt drowned in his bath,' I say, 'and we now learn that his mother died in her thirties of a heart attack. Like I said, it might be just a coincidence that each victim was systematically drowned, and then had a knife stuck through their heart.'

'But why?' he asks. 'What's the motive? It sounds to me like William Harcourt was the kind of man most women would be pleased to see the back of, and Jacob landed on his feet, financially at least, when he was adopted by the Maldens, assuming there *was* a legal adoption. Patricia married a few years after Jacob was born, so she had clearly moved on. Suddenly turning up years later and going on a killing spree doesn't make sense.'

'That,' I reply, 'is because there is something we don't know that makes it all hang together – at least, we don't know it yet. But it's late, and you need to go and keep your wife company. I need to go home and get some sleep. Tomorrow, try to get all the information you can about Patricia, and what happened to her before and after she got married. In particular, I want to know how she ended up having a baby in Yorkshire, and where exactly she had it. Think you can manage that?

'I can have a good try,' he says, and turns back to his screens, but I grab his shoulder.

'Not now, for God's sake. Go and remind yourself what my daughter looks like.'

He sighs, but does as he's told and follows me downstairs.

I wake up to a day that even Blue doesn't want to venture into. I open the front door to a vicious downpour of freezing rain, whipped into icy daggers by a brisk northerly wind. My normally enthusiastic guard dog plonks her backside firmly on the mat and shoots me a look that plainly says, 'Don't even think about it.' In the end, I boot her into the back garden to take care of the essentials, after which we make a mad dash to the car and sit for five minutes with the heater on full, breathing in the scents of sodden overcoat and wet dog.

It's well past 8 a.m. by the time I manage to pull into the station car park and try to keep up with Blue as we sprint through the deluge to the main doors. George Saint greets us with a raised eyebrow.

'Bit nippy out there,' he says, with his usual flair for understatement. 'The canteen's had a run on full English breakfasts this morning – only had half a dozen sausages left when I got in.'

'I hope you did the right thing and left one for somebody else,' I reply. 'Anything interesting to report?'

'We're a few uniforms down for the next hour or so, on account of the weather. There have been half a dozen minor accidents clogging up the main roads. As far as your lot is concerned, Mr Larson came in half an hour ago, and the DSI's been in since seven. Polly and Robbie are on their way, and so are Draper and Shaw. They're all stuck over by Bristol Bridge – the main road has flooded. Daz Jackson rang in to say there was a five-mile tailback on the M5, so he won't be here for a while, yet.'

'What's he doing on the M5? He only lives a mile down the road.'

George shrugs. 'I didn't ask him. He was in Weston yesterday, though, so maybe he stayed over – there was a lot of thick fog down that way last night.'

'Right. I suppose I'd better go and see what my son-in-law is up to.' I make for the lift, but change my mind halfway and take the stairs down to the canteen in the vain hope of snatching one of the remaining sausages.

Five minutes later, I get to the squad room clutching the only offering left until the catering delivery truck gets through – a couple of fried egg sandwiches. I throw my coat into my office and take them over to join Larson.

'Here – if you don't want one, I'm sure I can manage both.'

He grabs one gratefully. 'Thanks. I didn't get the chance to have breakfast – the school's closed because the pipes have burst and three classrooms are flooded, and Ben was an absolute nightmare this morning.' Before I can say anything, he adds quickly, 'I offered to stay home and help Rosie, but she more or less chucked me out, said this was more important and she'd manage. It's a good thing she's not back at work until Monday.'

'Is he still going on about that smartphone?'

'Like a stuck record. He's got a real stubborn streak. This morning, he wanted to go to Marcus's house and threw a tantrum when we said the weather was too bad. I'm afraid he blames me for it all, so I'm hoping Rosie will be able to talk him down if I'm out of the way.'

'For what it's worth,' I tell him, 'I think you made the right decision. It's bad enough having one technology geek in the family.'

He throws me a look and takes a bite of his sandwich. 'So, do you want to know what I've dug up since last night?'

One thing I can say about my son-in-law – once he gets started on something, he simply doesn't quit. Neither, I reluctantly admit, do I. 'Go for it, son,' I say, which earns me another exasperated look.

He finishes his sandwich, drags at least half a dozen documents onto his screen and fires up the new giant whiteboard. 'It will be easier to follow on there,' he says, and we both walk over and stand in front of it. 'Patricia Joan Cawley,' he says, 'was admitted to Greendale Lodge Nursing Home – a euphemism back then for a mother-and-baby home – on the outskirts of Bridlington on August 10th 1964. As we know, she gave birth to Mick on August 20th. She discharged herself, with her baby, on August 31st.'

'What happened to her after that?' I ask.

'There's no way of knowing from these records,' he replies. 'There may be hard copy notes on file at the home itself, or it's possible someone who worked there is still alive who remembers. It's a long shot, though, as Patricia would only have been nineteen at the time, and most of the staff would have been older than that.'

'Okay. So, she had Mick, disappeared with him, and within a short time he popped up in the Harcourt family home in Wakefield, with no sign of Patricia. What else do we know?'

'That in 1966 Patricia was back at Greendale Lodge giving birth to Jacob Malden,' Larson says, 'except he wasn't Jacob Malden then.' He gives me a self-satisfied grin. 'You wanted to know what the two missing documents were from the Malden house. It's my bet they were these.'

He points to two images on the screen. 'We have a birth certificate for David Cawley, born to Patricia Cawley on October 2nd 1966. Approximately six weeks later, Iris Malden appeared in Bristol with her baby, and a couple of weeks after that, we have an official adoption certificate for Jacob Charles Malden. Interestingly, this time Patricia remained at Greendale for the intervening six weeks, and only left after Jacob had been handed over to the Maldens.'

'Do we know why? It seems a long time to be stuck there after a birth, unless there were complications. Perhaps she had nowhere else to go?'

'It's possible, but Rosie thinks it's unlikely. There was an idea back then that babies singled out for adoption should be left with the natural mother to allow breastfeeding – "breast is best" and all that. It was a cruel system – it meant that there would be time for the mother to bond with the child, at which point it would be snatched away and given to the adoptive parents. Rosie reckons it was often against the mother's will, but they would be made to sign the papers within minutes of the birth, often even beforehand, so when the moment came, she had no choice.'

I take a moment to think that information through. 'You're saying,' I say eventually, 'that Patricia Cawley had at least one child taken from her without her consent, and possibly two. What on earth were her parents thinking of?'

'Their reputations, most likely,' Larson says sourly. 'Having a child out of wedlock was virtually a mortal sin back then, and girls were regularly packed off to a mother-and-baby home when their pregnancy became obvious. The child was snapped up by a happily married, or at least a legally married couple who couldn't have children of their own, and the natural mother was sent back home as if nothing had happened – if she was lucky. At least she wasn't in Ireland – you must have seen all the programs about the laundries, and girls locked up in those places for years, sometimes their whole lives. It's unthinkable now.'

'Let's hope so,' I say. 'So, she had the second child, it was given to Charles and Iris Malden, and then what?'

'Then, quite a lot, but we haven't finished with the first part yet. Just hang onto your hat. In 1964, she gave birth to Mick, and in 1966 to David, a.k.a. Jacob. In July 1965, she was in Greendale again, giving birth to a daughter, Rita; father, William Harcourt. Rita was adopted by a couple from the East Midlands and renamed Helen Stone.'

I walk across to the coffee machine, more to contain my fury than anything else. William Harcourt might have been politely described, forty-odd years ago, as a 'love rat'. In modern language, the label that best fits is 'total fucking bastard who abandoned at least two women and several children, not including Cathy Turner, leaving a trail of misery in his wake'. And he didn't even, I remind myself, go to his eldest son's funeral, even though he was only a few miles away at the time. I pour two mugs of coffee, go back to the screen and hand one to my son-in-law.

'Is that it?' I ask.

'Not quite,' he replies. 'I said Patricia Cawley married in 1969. It turns out the marriage was annulled later in the year. I haven't been able to determine why just yet, but for an annulment, a reason has to be given, so I should be able to get that information, given time. However, it looks like she did finally find someone to settle down with, although they never married. She had three more children, all daughters, in 1970, '72 and '73. The middle daughter died in infancy, but the other two survived and took the name of the father – McAndrew. They lived in Birmingham until her death in 1978.'

I let out a long sigh. Far from narrowing down the list of suspects, Larson's researches have at least quadrupled it, and we still haven't found a connection between the two male victims and Alice Walker.

I pat him on the back. 'Great work, son,' I manage to say. 'Keep going – something's got to start making sense somewhere.'

'What are you going to do?' he asks.

'Right now,' I reply, 'I haven't got a bloody clue.'

At that moment, the desk phone in my office rings.

'Are you sitting down?' Grace asks.

I groan. 'Don't tell me there's been another one.'

'There has – but thankfully not on our patch. East Midlands has just rung through. They saw our cases come up, and say they've got an identical one, in a village just south of Burton-on-Trent. A woman by the name of Emily Stone was found dead in her living room yesterday morning. The thing is, Al, their pathologist has estimated the time of death as the early hours of New Year's Day – exactly the same time as our three. Their DSI is ringing back to my office in an hour. While we're waiting, perhaps you'd like to come up and give me an update.'

13

I grab Larson and we head up to the DSI's office, where I leave it to him to explain the tangle of paperwork he's managed to collect overnight. When he's finished, Grace sits back and runs a hand through her hair.

'Well,' she comments, 'at least we have a definite link between three of the victims – two of ours, and the one up near Burton-on-Trent.'

'Don't forget Mick Harcourt,' I remind her. 'If my hunch is right, his death might be what started all this off.'

'And it all goes back to Patricia Cawley and her three children with William,' Larson puts in. 'What we don't know yet is where Alice Walker fits in. I haven't managed to find any kind of record prior to late 1967, which is a bit strange – there should be a birth certificate at least, but so far, nothing. The only thing we do know for certain is that she's not genetically related to the other victims, nor to the Cawley children.'

Grace's computer pings, and she gestures for us to bring our chairs and squeeze in next to her on the other side of the desk. 'This will be DCI Moffat from East Midlands,' she says, and clicks to accept the video call.

DCI Bernard Moffat is around my age, a veteran officer with the determined expression of a man well used to chasing shadows in darkened rooms.

'It's all a bit of a puzzle,' he starts, when Grace has made the introductions. 'The body was discovered yesterday, and initially, we thought it was a stabbing, maybe a burglary gone wrong, but our pathologist gave the cause of death as drowning, and the stab wound post-mortem. The knife was left in the body – a weird-looking thing

– some sort of antique dagger. It was Rick – Rick Baines, our pathologist – who cottoned onto the similarities with your cases. He knows your woman, Maggie Ainsworth, and had a chat with her last night.'

'You say the body was found yesterday,' I say, 'yet you think the death occurred in the early hours of January 1st? How come it wasn't discovered sooner?'

'That's the thing,' he says, scratching his greying beard. 'The woman, a Mrs Emily Stone, was a widow, and her daughter, Helen, was away, and didn't get back until early yesterday. She walked in and found the body. That's fair enough, but I think you might find this interesting. When we asked the daughter to account for her movements over New Year, she said she'd been away visiting friends in the West Country – a place called Worle, if that means anything to you?'

I nod. 'It's a village – well, more a giant housing estate these days – bordering on Weston-super-Mare, which is a place of interest to us in connection with these deaths. You say you interviewed Helen Stone?'

'That's right, with one of my DCs,' he replies. 'She seemed a very pleasant woman – in shock, of course. She was able to provide an alibi from the hotel she stayed in. They confirmed she had booked in for three nights from December 29th to 31st, and checked out at around 5 a.m. on January 1st, so that puts her in the clear.'

'For your murder, maybe,' I tell him, 'but not for ours. Hang on.' I ask Larson to dig up the CCTV photo of the woman Kylie Berman identified as Nina and put it up on the conference screen. 'Do you recognise her?' I ask Moffat.

He stares at the image for a moment, open-mouthed, and then manages, 'Well, bugger me! That's Helen Stone, no doubt about it. Where was this taken?'

'At Downside Nursing Home in Bristol,' I answer, 'just before the murder of Alice Walker, one of the residents. I think it might be a good idea to put out a warrant for her arrest, and we'll do the same. According to the care worker she swapped places with, she's due to meet up with her on Friday to get paid, but I'd say the chances of her turning up here are less than zero.'

'I'll get on it right away,' he says, and breaks off briefly to give a string of instructions to his DI. When he's done, for the next half hour we go through the whole complicated story, while Moffat listens, mainly in silence and with growing incredulity. 'So,' he says when we've finished, 'You think this has something to do with the deaths of Patricia Cawley in 1978, and Mick Harcourt in 2021? Some kind of revenge campaign? But why now? Cawley died of natural causes forty-six years ago, and there was no reason to suspect foul play at the time. It's the same with the more recent death – accidental, according to the pathologist and the coroner. You've got to admit, it's a bit of a stretch.'

'I won't deny that,' I say, 'but what you've said convinces me we're on the right track. We are looking for at least four killers now, and I'd be very surprised if they weren't all related. The trouble is, there are so many possible suspects we don't know who else might be involved apart from Helen Stone, and Jim Harcourt is still missing. Whether that's because he's a suspect or a potential victim is anybody's guess. Let us know when you've picked up Stone, and we'll take it from there.'

He's about to sign off when his internal phone buzzes, and he gestures for us to wait. He listens, frowns, and then comes back to us.

'It looks like Helen Stone's been tipped off,' he says, clearly unhappy. 'There's nobody at the house, and a neighbour says she saw her leave with an overnight bag around an hour ago, looking like she was in a hurry. She took her car, so hopefully it won't take us long to track her down.'

'Jesus bloody Christ!' I mutter. 'How the hell did that happen?'

'Well, don't look at us,' he retorts, stiffening. 'Until a minute ago she was a witness, not a suspect!'

I can't disagree with him. 'Leave it with me,' I say, 'and keep looking. I'll update you as soon as we have anything to report. Meanwhile, I think it's time we pulled in Jacob Malden, and put the wind up one or two other people while we're at it.'

He gives a curt nod and signs off.

It seems Moffat isn't the only one feeling a little pissed off, as Grace sits back in her chair, folds her arms and raises a questioning eyebrow at me as Larson and I scuttle back to the right side of her desk.

'That's just marvellous,' she comments sourly. 'Somebody's fucked up somewhere. Any ideas?'

'Just one,' I say. 'Sillitoe should be here by now, and I think our next move is to haul Kylie Berman back in. I have a feeling there was something she conveniently forgot to tell us last night.'

When we get back downstairs, the rest of the team has finally arrived, and the room is a fug of damp coats, steam from the coffee machine and the smell of bacon rolls. Clearly, the supply truck has battled its way to the canteen. Blue, trotting at my heels, shoots me an accusing look, demanding to know what happened to her morning sausage. Sillitoe obliges, dumping her dripping Parka and following me into my office, tearing off a lump of her breakfast bun on the way. She hands it to Blue, straightens up and shrugs.

'Sorry we're late, boss – it's bloody awful out there.'

'Looks like I'm not going to be the most popular person in the room, then,' I say. 'I need you to go and haul Kylie Berman back in.'

The bun stops halfway to her mouth. 'What, now? Come on, boss – give me a break!'

'You're having it,' I reply, pointing to her breakfast. I give her a summary of what has just gone on upstairs, and her shoulders slump.

'Damn it! It's my fault – I should have checked for a contact number when I arrested her, or at least during the interview.'

'I was at the interview too,' I remind her, 'and I'm the senior officer. If it makes you feel any better, I'll bring Jacob Malden in, so we'll both get soaked again. You take Colin with you. Where Berman is concerned, subtlety isn't required. I'll take Molly Shaw. Jackson and Robbins can go and collect Cathy Turner. I want all three of them in one place, and if we need to, we'll bring Iris Malden and Jim Harcourt's daughter in as well. They all know something, and none of them are going anywhere until I know as well.'

I'm about to issue instructions to the rest of the team when my phone rings.

'Sorry about this, Al,' Grace says. 'You need to come back up to my office. There's someone here who wants to see you. I think it would be a good idea to bring John with you as well.'

There's something in Grace's tone that warns me not to ask questions. I have a quick rethink and decide to send Jackson over to pick up Jacob Malden, and Mollie and Robbie to Portishead. I figure that if things are already in motion, and Grace's visitor has other ideas, it will be too late to do anything about it. Leaving Sillitoe to sort it all out, I grab Larson and we make our way back out to the lift.

'What's it all about?' he asks as we head down the corridor.

'You know as much as I do, son,' I reply, 'but by the sound of it, whatever it is, it will be something we don't need.'

Grace's visitor is, at a guess, in his late forties, tall, kitted out in a bespoke three-piece suit that probably would have cost me at least a month's salary, and looks like he belongs to the same gym as my son-in-law. He gets up as we walk in and holds out a hand, first to me, then to Larson.

'Chief Inspector Crow,' he says, with just a hint of a Yorkshire accent, 'and Mr Larson. Pleased to meet you both. I'm Detective Chief Superintendent Horner, Humberside Police. My given name is Francis, but everyone calls me Jack.' He lowers a hand to Blue, who sniffs suspiciously, wags her tail and makes a beeline for Grace's filing cabinet.

'Humberside? That's a bit of a journey,' I comment, as Larson and I sit down, 'Is there something we can do for you – Jack?'

He grins. 'I caught the train down last night, at your chief constable's suggestion. I've got some information you might find interesting, and I have a feeling we can perhaps help each other out.'

I glance at Grace, who gestures for me to take the lead. 'Fire away,' I say. 'We're all ears.'

I don't suppose there's a pot of coffee going spare?' he says. 'This may take a while.'

14

He takes his time pouring a coffee and helps himself to a Bourbon cream from the tray a young constable has just thoughtfully delivered. 'I suppose I'd better start at the beginning' he says finally. 'It's my guess you haven't got very far with your background checks.'

'You guess right,' I tell him. 'Do you want to tell us why?'

'I intend to,' he replies, 'but you will have to be patient. It's a long story, and one that starts back in the 1960s, before any of us were born, when my former boss was just a young detective sergeant. He's in his nineties now, and it's one of those cases he's never been able to let go – you know how it is. Some things just stick.'

I grunt my agreement, thinking of Darius Kyriaku, the hired killer who shot my sergeant, nearly killed me, and whose dog left Polly Sillitoe with an artificial left leg. I know only too well how some experiences simply never go away.

'Of course,' Horner goes on, 'we all know what happened to a lot of unmarried mothers after World War II – packed off to a mother-and-baby home or a religious institution to give birth, only to have their babies forcibly taken and handed over to respectable married couples desperate for a child. It's hard to believe now that it was a fully legal practice in most cases, sanctioned by the state.'

'I don't think there are many who haven't heard the stories,' Grace puts in. 'It's recently become one of the great scandals of modern times.'

He nods. 'What a lot of people don't realise is that things changed in the early sixties. The "free love" era was just around the corner, and the pill was on the scene. It was supposed to be for married women only, but that was never going to work. Anyone eager enough could get hold of it. One of the consequences – apart from the rise in cases of sexually transmitted diseases – was a huge drop in the number of newborns available for adoption. Single women were either using contraception or going it alone with limited support from the welfare state. To the criminal gangs, it was a goldmine. Childless couples were desperate, and single mothers who could be coerced into giving up their babies were lucrative cash cows.'

'You mean women like Patricia Cawley,' I comment.

'Exactly so,' he agrees. 'She was one of the victims of a baby trafficking outfit on the Northeast coast.'

'And they owned the mother-and-baby home at Greendale Lodge?' Larson asks.

'Not directly,' Horner replies. 'The home itself was owned and run by a Catholic charity for women who suffered from various health problems and whose families couldn't afford expensive treatment. Naturally, falling pregnant out of wedlock was a definite health problem, and there was a wing of the Lodge specifically set aside to deal with unmarried mothers. They received young, pregnant Catholic girls from all over the country. I don't know how far you've managed to get with the Cawley case, but I can fill in a few details. Pat suffered from severe asthma and a weak heart. Her parents were Irish, originally from a village just outside Dublin, and moved to Birmingham in the late fifties. They were practising Catholics and active members of the Irish ex-pat community, so they had connections. Patricia was sent to Greendale at the age of six on account of the asthma. In those days, the preferred treatment was removing the child from an inner-city environment and into a rural setting with lots of fresh air. She remained at Greendale until she was eleven, then went back home. Reading between the lines, things probably didn't go well for her, being packed off to an ultra-religious, restrictive institution for five years, and then back to an equally stifling home life. What records we have show that she was reported as a runaway several times during the next six years, was picked up by the local police and carted back home. There's nothing on file for the next couple of years, but then …'

'Then, she met William Harcourt,' I finish for him.

'That's about the size of it,' he says. 'Bill Harcourt was already well known to West Yorkshire police. The whole family was on just about every watch list – police, social services, you name it. The father, Bill senior, had done several stretches for burglary, assaulting a police officer, and violence in general. His son was a bit savvier though, and we never managed to pin anything on him. It was always some other sucker in the firing line when it came to it. Word was, he had a protection racket going by the time he started primary school, taking a fee to stop the bullies nicking kids' dinner money. Anyway, he grew up to be a bit of a magnet for the girls, especially the young, innocent ones. I think Pat Cawley thought she was headed for the full works – roses round the door and all that. Then, she fell pregnant. Harcourt must have thought something of her, because he hovered in the background, and when her parents packed her back off to Greendale he followed her up there.'

'Don't tell me,' I say. 'When he got there, he realised there was some kind of racket going on, and thought he'd try to get in on the action.'

'Got it in one,' Horner says, with a grin. 'But it didn't quite work out the way he planned.'

'Hang on a minute,' Larson pipes up. 'All this happened, as you say, before any of us were born, so how come you know so much about it all? Surely a lot of what you're telling us is pure assumption?'

Horner shakes his head. 'Far from it, Mr Larson. Like I said, my old boss was very familiar with the Harcourts, and with the Greendale case. It was his obsession, if you like – we all have at least one, and this was his. He always said it would come back to haunt us one day, and given this latest spate of murders, looks like he was right. His information came straight from the horse's mouth, so to speak. Not the young horse – from Bill Harcourt senior. He was the true patriarch of the family. You have to understand – their mindset was entirely focused on family – much like your Charles Malden and his faux aristocratic roots, I suspect. Think *The Godfather* on benefits, if you like. Old Bill ruled his family with a rod of iron, and Bill junior was his eldest son and heir. It follows that selling off his first male offspring wasn't going to be an option. A girl would have been different. But it turned out Pat had a son, and Old Bill laid down the law. There was a massive row between father and son, and while they were arguing about it, Pat got wind of Harcourt's plan and absconded, taking the baby with her. She tried to go home, but didn't get any welcome there, and ended up on the street. Finally, in desperation, she took the child to Old Bill Harcourt, and he took it in.'

'That explains how Mick came to be passed off as William's brother,' Grace puts in. Up to now, she's been listening quietly. 'So how did the trafficking operation work, and how did Charles Malden come to be involved? You said the home was run by the church – were they part of the racket as well?'

'Again, not directly,' he replies. 'I suspect the church authorities were well aware of what was going on, but turned a blind eye as long as they got their regular charitable donations. Although they owned the building and land, it wasn't a closed system, and a lot of the professional medical staff were from secular backgrounds. The mother-and-baby home was in an annexe, cut off from the rest of the buildings, and although it was administered by an order of nuns, most of the professional staff – midwives, doctors and so on – were brought in from outside. The board of directors consisted of the head of the order, a local priest and a bishop, politicians and business people – you know the sort of thing. In this particular case, the business interest consisted of two local gang bosses masquerading as property developers, but in reality, adding baby trafficking to their portfolio of high-value criminal activities. They targeted prospective parents who were desperate and willing to pay – up to a hundred grand in some cases. They even offered a payment plan for those without ready cash, and of course, that fed into their loan shark operations. For them it was win-win.'

'Christ almighty,' I mutter to myself, and then, 'So how did Charles Malden get involved? Presumably, he was one of the beneficiaries?'

'Indeed, he was,' Horner replies. 'But unfortunately, nothing could be proved. He was on the board of directors of a neighbouring private health clinic, one that shared resources with Greendale Lodge from time to time. There is no direct connection between Malden and the traffickers, and all the adoption documentation was bona-fide, but it's possible he paid them a handsome sum. It would never have made it to court though, and now, of course, it's too late.'

'So how come Old Bill Harcourt didn't object to that arrangement?' Larson asks. 'Surely Jacob was in the same category as Mick – another heir?'

Horner smiles. 'You've heard of the "heir and a spare"? The second son was the spare, and I think by then Old Bill had decided he couldn't cope with more babies in the house. As for the middle child, Rita, a.k.a. Helen Stone, she was a girl, and so worthless as far as the Harcourts were concerned. Unknown to Patricia, she was kept at Greendale for more than a year before she was sold off to the Stones at a cheaper price. Female children weren't treated much better than their mothers – just commodities to be used and farmed out for as much profit as the gangs could get.'

I glance at Grace, whose lips have stretched into a thin line of disgust. Larson simply shakes his head in incomprehension. Horner and I both know such things still happen, but thankfully not as frequently, thanks to changes in attitudes and, not least, advances in medical science. Criminal gangs these days have more lucrative and less risky markets to exploit.

'So where does Alice Walker come into all this?' I ask. 'So far, we've dug nothing up on her at all.'

'Ah.' Horner leans forward and pours himself another coffee. 'I was getting to that – it's the reason I've made the trip down in person. It's better not to put certain things in writing – you understand, Chief Inspector?'

Suddenly, the truth of the matter hits me like a splash of cold water. 'Oh, for fuck's sake …'

Grace conducts a minute examination of the woodgrain in her desktop – clearly, she has already been told the lie of the land.

'I wonder if it might be prudent to, er …' Horner coughs, and nods towards Larson.

'Mr Larson stays,' I tell him. 'I can vouch for the fact that anything he hears will remain completely confidential.'

'Of course,' Larson says, looking confused.

'What DCS Horner is about to say,' I go on, for my son-in-law's benefit, 'is that Alice Walker is not our victim's given name, and that's why we can't find any history.' I meet Horner's eye. 'My guess is we're talking about witness protection – am I right?'

Horner smiles. 'Quite right, DCI Crow. The woman you know as Alice Walker was a former nurse who worked as a newly qualified midwife at Greendale Lodge in the sixties. I'm afraid I still can't tell you her real name, even though it won't make any difference to her now. It might, however, affect others who are still alive and at risk. Alice realised what was going on there, and came to the police hoping we would do something about it. She was bright enough to understand that if she made a fuss the criminals wouldn't have any qualms about silencing her. She agreed to continue to work there, and at the same time try to find out all she could about the chain of command, who was pulling the strings and what was happening to the money. She was an extremely brave woman. She almost single-handedly supplied us with all the evidence needed to wind up the whole operation. My old boss was able to trace a huge payment straight into the bank accounts of two of the ringleaders. Both were arrested and convicted.'

'So,' I say, 'it's possible Alice Walker was working there when Patricia Cawley had her children, and she may have been one of the midwives involved?'

'She *was* the midwife,' Horner replies, 'and it was seeing Cawley lose her three babies that alerted her to what was going on, although the arrests didn't take place until 1967, and she didn't start working for us until around a year before that.'

'Okay. In that case, as far as Patricia was concerned, Walker was the woman who snatched her children. She would have had no idea that her midwife was, in fact, a whistle-blower.'

Horner nods. 'Nobody knew except the police and the protection service, and if we did our job properly, that remains the case.'

'I think,' Grace says, 'it might be useful to speak directly to your former boss if possible. I notice you haven't told us who he is.'

'My apologies,' he answers. 'I was advised by his medical team not to unless you asked directly. He is over ninety years old now, you see, and in very poor health. However, since you do ask, He is former Detective Chief Superintendent Donald Harris. He is currently in a nursing home near York, receiving constant medical care, hence my presence here, as he couldn't make the journey himself, and even if he could, he has, let's say, communication difficulties following a stroke a few months back. I will, however, be reporting back to him, and he is happy to answer any questions you may have. I can relay his responses back to you.'

'Don Harris?' Grace's eyes widen. 'There's a name I haven't heard in a while.' She turns to me. 'I did a short stint with the drugs squad up in Yorkshire when I was a DC – he was a bit of a legend up there back then, even though he was on the verge of retirement by that time.'

'Still is,' Horner says, with a smile. 'This is the one case he was never able to wrap up completely, and like I said, it's still very much on his mind.'

'What do you mean?' I ask. 'You said the ringleaders were caught and convicted.'

'I said two of them were,' he replies. 'There were three, and he never managed to identify the third man, the one who was really in charge. As soon as the other two were arrested, he vanished into thin air, and despite all Don's efforts, he wasn't able to trace him. A year later, the top brass decided the third man theory was pure imagination, and the case was closed.'

'But you don't think so?'

Horner shakes his head. 'Don wasn't one for flights of fancy. He maintains there was someone else, and that's good enough for me. Mind you, whoever it is must be either very old or dead by now, and it's highly unlikely he's connected with your case, or with the one in East Midlands. Still, it's something you needed to know, as it's one reason why the decision was taken not to reveal Alice Walker's true identity. She wasn't the only one, you see. Just like three people were running the trafficking outfit, three insiders were working for us. Alice was a midwife, the second was a secretary, and the third was a woman who, by some stroke of fortune, was seeking to adopt. Don managed to get her and her husband to agree to help set up a honey trap. They let it be known they didn't have much money, and would be willing to accept a child of any age and gender. The trap worked, and in April 1967 Don got all the evidence he needed to achieve the convictions, without making it look as if the couple had been involved with the police at any stage. They never needed to give evidence, so no need for protection in their case. It took some doing, but once all the fuss died down, he liaised with social services, and the couple were able to go through the proper procedures and adopt the child legally. And that is where, from your point of view, things get interesting.'

'Interesting how?'

'The administrator's name was Emily Stone, and the child they adopted was Rita Cawley, now known as Helen Stone.'

15

By the time Larson and I get back to the squad room, a definite headache is beginning to crystallise near the spot where Kyriaku's bullet left a neat hole. Sillitoe and Draper are still out, but Jackson is hovering by his desk, communing with Robbie and Molly Shaw.

'We're getting complaints from uniform,' Jackson says as I go over to join them. 'They've just made four arrests over at Cabot Rise and when Polly and Colin get back, we'll be taking up three interview rooms. They are asking if we can't put at least one of ours in a cell to free up some space.'

'What are the arrests for?' I ask.

'Three dealing class A drugs and one offensive weapon,' he replies. 'The usual thing, and all with previous. I told them that as neither Turner nor Malden are actually under arrest it wouldn't be appropriate, but DI Fosbury isn't too happy.'

'I'll have a word,' I say. 'We can put Kylie Berman on hold when she gets here, though. She might be a bit more forthcoming after an hour or so in a cell. Tell Polly to take her straight down, and I'll deal with Jacob Malden first. You can sit in if you like – I'll be around half an hour, so grab yourself a coffee. It won't do any harm to give them a bit of time to think about things.'

'Will do, boss.' He grins. 'Looking forward to it – he made a hell of a fuss when I brought him in. His mother was a bit upset, too, but Karen Wyatt's looking after her, so she should be okay.'

'Good.' I make for my office and beckon my son-in-law to follow.

'What do you want me to do?' he asks after I've closed the door.

'It may come as a surprise, son,' I tell him, 'but at this moment I haven't got a bloody clue.'

He sits, frowning, while I ring down to Dick Fosbury. Three of his four prisoners, he tells me, can quite happily stew in the cells while awaiting their briefs, but the fourth, being only thirteen, needs a suitable room where he can be interviewed with his social worker present and bailed as quickly as possible. It means Kylie Berman will have to wait a little longer, but that's fine with me.

I'm about to turn back to Larson when my phone rings, and DCI Moffat is on the line from East Midlands.

'We've found Helen Stone's car,' he says, 'in the railway station car park at Burton-on-Trent. One of my lads went through the platform CCTV, and we got her boarding the 09:31 headed for Bristol Temple Meads. Looks like she's coming your way.'

'Why the hell would she do that?' I ask, half to myself. 'For someone trying to evade arrest, it seems like a pretty stupid move. She must know we'll be watching for her. Do you know what time it's due at Bristol?'

'12:02,' he answers. 'I've already informed the authorities at all the stops south of Birmingham – we were too late to monitor the others, but if she tries to get off anywhere from New Street onwards, she'll be intercepted.'

I look at my watch – it's just coming up to eleven.

'Thanks,' I say. 'I'll get someone over there, and let you know if and when we pick her up.'

I hang up and get back onto Dick Fosbury. His response is predictable.

'For fuck's sake, Al!' He heaves an irritated sigh down the phone. 'I've got my hands full downstairs, you've commandeered the interview rooms, and it will take at least four bodies to cover the railway station exits. What's the matter with sending a couple of your DCs?'

'It will only take two uniforms outside the entrance if I add Shaw and Robbins on the concourse,' I say. 'Plus, I'll rope in the transport police to monitor the CCTV and give us a heads up when she gets off the train. We know what time it's due, so it shouldn't take more than half an hour. She is a murder suspect, after all.'

I hear a grunt and another sigh. 'I suppose that does trump a kilo of cocaine and a machete. Okay, Al. Send Molly and Robbie down and they can liaise with my two. Mind you, if today carries on like this, I'll leave you to explain to George Saint why he's having to dust off his stab vest and go out on the beat.'

Thankfully, I only get minor grumbles from Molly and Robbie when I explain they are going to have to head back out into what is still a barrage of hail and sleet. The lure of what could be a major arrest on their records is enough to offset any objections. I realise, as I try to decide just how much pressure to put on Jacob Malden, that with the exception of Colin Draper, I've given my two most inexperienced DCs a pretty big ask, and one which, if they balls it up, might have far-reaching consequences. I watch them leave, noting the grim determination on each face, and somehow know that the pair of them are going to be just fine. As they reach the door, they bump into Sillitoe and Draper, fresh in from their mission to apprehend Kylie Berman. Sillitoe flashes Robbie a smile, and there's a brief touch of hands in the doorway. At least that's one problem solved, for now.

I try to clear my mind of concerns about Helen Stone, and call Jackson in. 'You ready?'

'You bet, boss,' he says, rolling his shoulders. 'How do you want to play it?'

'Slowly,' I say. 'Right now, what we need most is information. A confession – whatever there is to confess – is secondary. Run down to the evidence room and grab those two dirks we got from Maggie – the original and the replica. We'll see what he has to say about those.'

I'm about to walk out of my office when I realise Larson is still waiting patiently on the other side of my desk. Trying to prioritise the avenues of enquiry in this case has become like trying to untangle a plate of overcooked spaghetti. Maybe, I think, it's time to at least eliminate some of the less likely angles.

'I want you to see what you can dig up on Harcourt's children from the first marriage,' I tell Larson. 'And look into Pat Cawley's daughters as well – the ones she had later. We might as well see what the full picture looks like, even if it's only to discount some of the blind alleys. Plus, Mick Harcourt had a son and a daughter, so we should look them over as well, just to be thorough.'

He raises an eyebrow. 'Anything in particular I'm looking for?'

'Good question, son,' I say, realising I'm clutching at an awful lot of straws. 'Maybe I'll know more when I've spoken to Malden and Turner, and hopefully Helen Stone as well. I suppose the main thing I want to know is whether there was any communication between them – right now there's no evidence they even knew of each other's existence, but if they did and were talking to each other, that's a whole different scenario.'

He nods, understanding where my admittedly vague train of thought is going. 'I'll do my best,' he says. 'At least I've got the two temps from Portishead to help out. That should make it a bit easier.'

He's already making his way to his computers, so I join Jackson, who is out in the corridor clutching bags containing the two knives, and head down to the interview suite.

When we get there, I find Grace waiting for us in the observation room. 'I thought I'd come and take a look,' she says. 'Something tells me this is going to be a hell of a lot more interesting than staring at a screen in my office.'

'Be my guest.'

I glance at Jackson, who shrugs. 'Do you want to sit in?' he asks.

She shakes her head and gives him a smile. 'I wouldn't want to deprive you, Daz. I'll watch from here and give you the benefit of my wisdom. Have you got a plan?'

'Short and to the point, for now,' I say. 'I'd like to get an idea of what all three of them have to say before going into too much detail – that's assuming things go smoothly and we get our hands on Helen Stone in half an hour's time. We'll see how their answers stack up before committing to anything – Jim Harcourt is still missing, and if he is a potential fifth victim we can't afford to bugger about following false leads.'

'You've got that right,' she says. 'Good luck!' She takes charge of Blue and settles herself in front of the observation screen.

Jacob Malden is clearly not in the best of tempers, despite having been served proper filter coffee in a china mug, complete with a small plate of assorted biscuits – a ploy designed to evoke a touch of complacency in anyone 'helping with enquiries.' This particular suspect, however, is anything but complacent.

We get off to a predictable start.

'What the hell do you think you're doing?' He shoots to his feet, a perfect combination of self-righteousness and bluster. 'I demand to see my solicitor immediately – you have no right to keep me here …'

Jackson's hands curl into fists, although thankfully he keeps them firmly by his sides, takes a couple of deep breaths and reaches for his chair. I do the same and we both sit, allowing Malden to pace the floor and continue his rant for another thirty seconds. He finally runs out of steam, stops pacing and stares at us.

'Please,' I say, trying to sound calm and reasonable, 'sit down, Mr Malden.'

He grinds his teeth, eyes flitting from one to the other of us, realises he's getting nowhere fast, and flops heavily into his chair on the other side of the table.

'First of all,' I explain, 'I need to remind you that you are not under arrest, and as you see, at this point nothing is being recorded. We simply wish to clarify a few points with you, so surely a solicitor is unnecessary? If you insist, though, just give us the details and we can contact him or her on your behalf.' He opens his mouth, but I cut him off. 'I assume you want to do all you can to help us find your father's killer. If that is not the case, you are, naturally, free to leave at any time. Of course, that wouldn't create a very good impression, so I would urge you to cooperate with us, however irksome it may seem. I'm sure your mother would want that, too – yes?'

I see him tense, the cogs starting to whirr, but after a minute's silence he nods, and slumps back in his chair.

'I'm sorry,' he mumbles finally. 'It's just that … I'm concerned about Mother, you know? She isn't in good health, and I don't like to leave her just now, what with everything. Of course I want to help, although I have no idea what use I can be – I've already told you everything I know.'

'We understand,' I say. 'It's a difficult time for everyone. You may think you've told us everything, but it's surprising how small, insignificant details can often be very important. For example, I'm sure you are aware that whoever attacked your father burned something in the room where he was found?'

'Yes. Mother said she smelled something burning, and that's why she went downstairs. Nothing was missing, though – I thought she must have been mistaken.'

'She wasn't,' I tell him. 'Two documents were missing from your father's study. We believe someone searched them out – just those two – and deliberately burned them in front of him before he died.'

His eyes narrow in genuine puzzlement. 'That's unbelievable – what documents?'

I take a deep breath. 'Your birth certificates – both of them.'

He blinks, and gapes at me. After a long silence, he whispers, 'Both of them? He kept both of them?' He clears his throat, and says, louder, 'Why? Why would somebody do that?'

'We were hoping you would be able to tell us,' Jackson puts in. 'You knew you were adopted?'

He stiffens, but nods. 'Yes. Dad told me when I was eight or nine. He made me swear not to tell anyone, though. He said it might make life difficult for me, and best to keep it quiet. I didn't see why, but …' He shrugs. 'It's been a bit of a sore point over the years. I told him it was more for his benefit than mine – like everything else in his life, I suppose. He had a reputation to keep up, and having a cuckoo in the nest wouldn't have done anything to help that along.'

A note of bitterness has crept into his tone. 'So, you and your father didn't get on?' I ask.

Another shrug. 'We had our ups and downs – more downs, to be honest, as I got older. I often think he took me on just to keep Mother happy. I was always much closer to her. But he changed his tune a bit when I left home and made a success of things in my own right.' He falls silent for a moment, staring at his hands, and when he speaks again, there's a slight catch in his voice. 'You know, on Christmas Eve, he actually told me he was proud of me? I can't remember him ever saying it before, not in so many words. And a week later, he was …'

He tails off and rubs a hand across his face. I search for any signs that he's faking it, but can't find any.

'You can't think of any reason why someone would want to destroy your birth certificates? I ask.

He shakes his head. 'No. I mean, nobody knew, except for me and my parents – and I suppose the people involved at the time, but that's more than fifty years ago, and they are probably all dead by now. I don't understand.' He stiffens again, defensive. 'What are you trying to suggest?'

'We're not trying to suggest anything,' I say. 'As I said, we are simply trying to gather as much information as possible. I'd like you to look at something and tell us if you recognise it.'

Jackson reaches down, produces the plastic bag containing the replica dirk, and pushes it across the table. Malden picks it up, looks at it briefly, and then pushes it back.

'It's my father's,' he says. 'There's a set of them in the house, in a display cabinet.' The reason for the question dawns on him. 'You're saying whoever did it used this? He was stabbed with one of his own knives? Jesus – I …'

'Actually,' Jackson interrupts, 'he wasn't stabbed with this knife.' He places the second bag on the table. 'It was this one.'

Malden snatches it up, turns it over in his hands, grabs the other and does the same, giving each a minute examination. Eventually, he sets them down and taps the first bag with a finger.

'This is a fake. How the hell …?'

'You sound pretty sure,' Jackson says. 'Bit of an expert, are you?'

Malden bridles. 'Of course I'm sure. Dad was the real expert, not me, but I used to go to the auctions with him when I was a kid, and he showed me how to spot a replica. It's pretty obvious when you know what to look for, and even clearer when you've got the genuine one for comparison.'

'So,' Jackson goes on, injecting a hint of sarcasm, 'you know enough to spot a fake, yet you didn't notice that all six – what do you call them? Dirks, is it? You didn't realise that all six dirks in the cabinet above your father's staircase had, at some point, been replaced with replicas?'

His mouth flaps, but I put my oar in before he has a chance to respond. 'The thing is, Jacob, we're looking for someone who had access to your father's house for long enough to replace every knife in that cabinet with a fake, who was very familiar with the collection, and who was enough of an expert to have these replicas made and substituted for the real ones without your father being any the wiser. I don't suppose you have any idea who that might be?'

We're interrupted by a knock at the door, and Robbie Robbins pokes her head round.

'Sir, do you think I might have a quick word?'

I glance at Malden, who has gone white as a sheet, nod to Jackson, who sits back and folds his arms, and join Robbie outside in the corridor.

'We've just brought Helen Stone in, boss,' she says.

'Well done, Robbie,' I tell her. 'Was she any trouble?'

'That's the thing,' she says. 'We didn't pick her up – she picked us up. She got off the train and we followed her to the exit, but when she got through the barrier she went straight up to one of the uniforms at the main door and told him she wanted to speak to a detective straightaway, and please could he take her to a police station. He called us over, and she just said "Thank God for that", and that she would only speak to the person in charge of Alice Walker's case. We've put her in the soft room for now with Molly, but she's looking pretty shaken up.'

'Christ almighty!' I mutter, seeing another of my theories heading at breakneck speed for a brick wall. What sane murderer walks up to a policeman and demands to be arrested, for God's sake? 'Okay. Go down and make sure she's got a cup of tea, and tell her I'll be along in a few minutes. I just need to wrap up here. What about Cathy Turner?'

'She's in a state, too, according to the DI, but it's hard to know how much she's putting it on. Colin's keeping an eye on her.'

'In that case, she'll keep,' I say, 'and so will Kylie Berman.'

I rejoin Jackson, and with some inner relish apologetically inform Jacob Malden that something has come up, and our interview has been temporarily suspended, but despite the inconvenience, we would be very grateful if he could bear with us for a little while. He opens his mouth to object but thinks better of it. Jackson throws Malden a satisfied smile and follows me into the observation room to join Grace, who is staring through the mirror and stroking her chin thoughtfully.

'What do you think?' I ask her.

'I'm not sure,' she replies. 'He's not the most pleasant of characters, but that doesn't mean he's a liar or a murderer. It's a good time to take a break, though, let him think things through for a bit.'

'Agreed,' I say, and quickly tell her the state of play with Helen Stone.

She gives me a puzzled frown. 'That's interesting. Well, as she's demanded to see a senior officer, she might as well see both of us. Daz, maybe you'd like to go and sort out Kylie Berman, see if we can charge her with wasting police time and withholding evidence along with everything else.'

'My pleasure, Ma'am,' he replies, and heads off to the cells.

'Okay, Al,' she says, gesturing towards the corridor. 'Let's go and see what Helen Stone has to say.'

16

Robbie meets us outside and hands me a folder. 'DCI Moffat rang through while you were with Jacob Malden,' she tells me. 'I've brought him up to speed, and he's sent through some more details and forensic photographs on the Emily Stone murder. They're all in there, together with the CCTV footage from Downside care home.'

'Thanks, Robbie. Great work. Has Helen actually been charged?'

'We arrested her on a charge of fraud when we picked her up,' she says. 'She didn't make any objection, and we thought murder would be a bit premature. I hope that was okay?'

'Perfect.' I decide to test the water. 'How about you and Polly get started with Cathy Turner, see what you can get out of her? I'm pretty sure there's a fair bit she's not telling us about her relationship with her "uncle" Mick – and with Jim Harcourt as well. She may not know the full story, but I've got a feeling she might be protecting someone.'

Robbie flashes a smile. 'No problem, boss – we're on it.'

'Looks like your little pep talk with those two had the desired effect,' Grace says when Robbie has gone. 'Maybe you should consider a new career in counselling.'

'Tell my therapist that and he'll probably take legal action,' I reply. 'Mind you, when it comes to dealing with real policemen, he hasn't got a bloody clue.'

'Do any of us?' she says, with a mischievous grin. 'Let's go and see how Ms Stone deals with a couple of real police detectives.'

We find Helen Stone hunched in the corner of the sofa in the 'soft' interview room, usually reserved for child witnesses or victims of violent crime. She has my new DC's hand in a death-like grip and is trembling uncontrollably. Despite my naturally suspicious nature, I can't quite picture her brutally drowning and stabbing a defenceless old lady, or anyone else, for that matter. I glance at Grace and see from her expression that she's thinking the same thing.

'It's all right, Helen,' Molly says, gently extricating her hand as Grace and I sit in armchairs opposite. 'This is my boss, Detective Inspector Crow, and his boss, DSI Helston. They'll listen to everything you have to say, and I promise you, they will take it all very seriously. All you need to do is tell the truth, and it will be okay. I have to go now, but I'll come back later. Don't worry – it will be fine.'

Molly shoots me a questioning look and I give her a nod as she makes her way out. Helen Stone glances from one to the other of us, blinking with terror like a child that's just been dumped by its parent in a crowded classroom on the first day of school.

'I didn't do it,' she blurts out before we can say anything. 'You've got to believe me – I didn't do anything to Alice. I wouldn't have – she was my mum's best friend, and now they're both …'

She stumbles to a halt, unable to actually say the word – 'dead', and starts to sob. Grace does the honours and hands her the box of tissues from the coffee table between us. Thankfully the outburst doesn't last long, and Helen blows her nose, dabs her eyes and sits back, her face a mess of blotches.

'Sorry,' she mumbles, wringing a tissue between her hands as if it's an enemy she wants to strangle. 'It's just, you have to believe me. I know I shouldn't have – you know – pretended to be that other woman – but I couldn't think of another way to get in without anyone seeing me.' She bites her lip and adds, 'But it was too late anyway – I got there too late.' She shakes her head and tries to wipe her eyes, realises the tissue is in shreds and casts around for a waste bin. Grace obliges again, and Helen gives her a weak smile. 'Thank you.'

'Perhaps,' I say, with a growing sense that the ground is shifting again, and not in a direction that is going to make my life any simpler, 'you'd better start at the beginning. You admit impersonating a care home worker to gain access to Downside with the specific aim of getting to Alice Walker, yes?'

She nods.

'Okay. You understand that your actions were against the law, and you have been arrested for that offence?'

She nods again. 'It was the only way …'

I hold up a hand. 'What we want to know is, why? And because you have been arrested on suspicion of fraud, we need to conduct a formal interview – that means everything you tell us will be recorded. If you would like a solicitor present, we can delay the interview until one arrives and you've had a chance to talk to them. Do you understand?'

She has suddenly gone very pale. 'You want to record what I say? No – you can't! I mean, it's too dangerous. I came here because I thought I could explain everything, and then you'd help, but you won't, will you? You think I killed Alice, just like the other policeman thinks I killed Mum, and as long as you can put someone in prison you don't care who it is, or that they might get murdered as well.' She shudders, but thankfully doesn't start crying again. 'I shouldn't have come. It's just going to make everything worse, isn't it? Mum said not to trust anybody, not even the police, but I thought if I came back down here it would be different. But it's not. There's no way out, is there?'

Once again, she stutters to a halt. Grace takes over. 'Listen, Helen, I don't know what you are afraid of, but I give you my word, you are safe here. Believe me when I say that the last thing we want is for an innocent person to go to prison. If you are being threatened, or intimidated in any way, we can help, but only if you tell us exactly what's going on. Chief Inspector Crow is right. We do have to conduct a formal interview, but before we do that, how about you just explain everything – no recording, just the three of us, and then, if we decide you need some sort of protection, we can make sure that happens. After all, if you didn't want to talk to us, you wouldn't have risked the journey to come here – right?'

There's a long silence, and then she finally nods. 'It looks like I have no choice,' she says. 'I have to trust you. I didn't go to the care home to hurt Alice. My mother sent me to warn her. When I got there, the home told me that Alice had expressly told them no visitors were to be allowed in to see her, no matter who they were, or what they wanted. I didn't know what to do, so I waited outside and spoke to one of the care workers coming off shift. She said Alice wouldn't have a cleaner in her room, even to change the bedding. Everything had to be left outside the door. But the worker said if I really wanted to get in, she knew somebody who would swap places with me on condition I let her take thirty per cent of the wages. I didn't see any other way, so I agreed.'

'And the care worker you swapped with was Kylie Berman,' I say.

Helen nods. 'Yes. She explained what to do, and said if I wanted to meet her later in the week, she'd give me the money, minus her cut. Of course, I didn't want any money. I managed to get in with the late shift and went straight up to Alice's room. I knocked on the door and she didn't answer at first. But when I told her who I was and that Mum had sent me, she let me in.'

'What time was this?' Grace asks.

'It must have been just after midnight,' she replies. 'She told me she already knew why I was there, and she was more worried for Mum than for herself. She was in a home, with plenty of security, but Mum was on her own. I realised, then, that maybe it was all a trick to get me away, and that Mum was in danger, so I left, and took the first train I could back home. When I got there …'

'It was too late and your mother was dead,' I finish for her. 'And as soon as you left Alice, someone killed her, too. Is that what you're saying, Helen?'

'Yes. But you won't believe me, will you? I was in both places, at both times, and Mum and Alice are both dead. Therefore, I murdered them. It's a no-brainer, at least, as far as you're concerned.'

'I suppose that's how it looks,' I agree, 'but looks can be deceptive, and it can be dangerous to jump to conclusions, so every good policeman tries to examine every angle. As it happens, I am a very good policeman – at least that's what people tell me, and DSI Helston is probably even better. But why come back here? You have to admit, it looks more than a bit suspicious, running away like that. You haven't done yourself any favours.'

'That woman – Kylie – rang me,' she replies. 'She asked me to give her a phone number in case anything went wrong with the shift, or we had to change the meeting date, so we swapped numbers. I suppose that was a bit stupid of me. Anyway, she rang me and it was awful – she said I'd got her into trouble with the police, and that I was a murdering … well, I won't say everything she said, but she was screaming at me, and told me the police had my photograph and I was going to be arrested. I panicked, but when I got to the train station I thought if I could get to you first and explain everything it might be all right.' She gives a helpless shrug. 'I didn't know what else to do.'

'You did the right thing,' Grace says gently. 'It took a lot of courage to hand yourself in like that. As for Ms Berman – the woman whose shift you took – she is safely under arrest and not likely to bother you anymore. But, if you want our help, you have to tell us the whole story, right from the beginning.' She gets up, pokes her head outside, tasks the duty constable with providing more refreshments, and then resumes her seat. 'First of all, perhaps you can tell us the relationship between your mother and Alice Walker? We already know that both were instrumental in helping to convict members of a child trafficking gang around fifty years ago, and that Alice had to take on a new identity as a result.'

'You know that?' Helen looks shocked. 'But it was supposed to be secret – the courts said nobody would ever be able to find out who Alice really was, or that Mum and Dad were part of it.'

'You're right,' I say, 'and we still don't know her original identity. But we have been told what your parents did – they must have been good people, and very brave.'

'They were,' Helen agrees. 'And so was Alice, and Lizzie …'

'Lizzie?' I ask. 'Who was Lizzie?'

Helen claps a hand to her mouth. 'Oh! I shouldn't have said – Lizzie was a secretary who worked at Greendale Lodge. There were three of them, you see – Alice, Lizzie and Mum. They went to the police together, because they wanted to see it all stopped. I only ever knew them as Alice and Lizzie, their new identities after the trial. Mum never told me what their names were before. She said it was safer not to ask. But she did tell me the whole story when I was in my mid-twenties. I knew I'd been adopted, but it was around that age I started to get curious about who my real parents had been, and whether I had brothers and sisters – you know the sort of thing.'

'So, Grace says, 'you knew you had two brothers?'

She nods. 'Yes. Mum knew who they were, and who had adopted them, because she did a lot of the paperwork at Greendale. She gave me the information but warned me to be very careful with it, and not to make any rash decisions, especially as far as my father and older brother were concerned, as both of them were involved in crime, one way or another. I knew about David, too, and that his name had been changed to Jacob, but in the end, I decided to follow my parents' advice, and not rake things up. As for my natural mother, nobody knew what happened to her after David was born. I tried to trace her, and got as far as a marriage certificate, but then it was a dead end, so I suppose I convinced myself she'd found some happiness, and left it at that.'

'So, you never met with either of your brothers, at any time?'

'No. As I said, I thought it was best to let things lie. I've often wondered if that was the right decision, but I suppose it's too late now. The thing is, I know Mum kept in touch with my brother Mick – I think she felt responsible somehow for where he ended up. Then, around two years ago, just after New Year, she got a phone call, and everything changed. I was with her at the time, and I remember asking her several times who it was because I could see she was getting more and more upset. She must have been on the phone for more than half an hour. When she finally hung up, I asked her again, but she wouldn't tell me, and said not to worry, everything was fine. I knew it wasn't, though. From that time on she started to suffer with her nerves. She'd been a really confident, active sort of person before, but after that call, she became anxious about everything – she stopped going out, had new locks and a security alarm fitted, and wouldn't answer the door to anyone she didn't know. In the end, I moved in with her – Dad had died, you see, and I never married, so it was easy enough to rent out my house for a while. I was planning to move back as soon as she got better, but she never did.'

'And you have no idea who that phone call was from?' I ask.

She shakes her head. 'I tried to get her to talk about it, but she always refused. I caught her several times on the phone to Alice and Lizzie, and I'm sure that's what they were talking about, but as soon as she realised I was there she just clammed up and told me to go away and mind my own business.'

'So, what changed?' Grace asks. 'You say your mum asked you to come to Bristol to warn Alice about something. Something must have happened to make her change her mind.'

In response, Helen reaches for her overcoat, pulls an envelope out of an inside pocket and pushes it across the coffee table. 'This came for her in the post last Friday. I don't know who sent it. I'm sure Mum did, though. I found it in her bag after – you know, after …' He falters, takes a deep breath, and goes on, 'She wouldn't let me see it, but it explains why she was in such a state on Friday night. I thought she'd finally lost her mind – I almost rang for an ambulance, because she was going on about the phone being tapped, and Alice being in danger, and I had to go and warn her, and on and on like that until I agreed to go.'

I dig into my jacket and pull out the pair of disposable gloves I've learned to always carry around just in case. I pull them on, pick up the envelope and examine it. The postmark is Hull, posted first class on Christmas Eve. I wonder, briefly, if the letter had been meant to arrive earlier, although given the usual festive season delays, the sender might have anticipated that it probably wouldn't arrive until several days later than normal. I carefully pull out the contents, a single sheet, with a short, typed message. I hold it up so that Grace can see as well.

They know about A. Phone not safe. No police. Send H. Urgent. E.

'So, you did as your mother asked,' I say, 'and came down to Bristol to see Alice. But what were you supposed to do when you got there? Did she give you any other instructions?'

Helen nods. 'She said to try to get her away from the home if I could. I had no idea how, but I'd promised I'd try. I went to Weston-Super-Mare, because it was some way from Bristol, and it's a holiday place, where lots of people are coming and going all the time, so I thought we might be safe there, and then I could bring her up to our house the next day. But when I got there, I realised leaving Mum had been a mistake. I got my things and went back home, and found – well, you know the rest. I tried – I really tried, even though I didn't believe Mum then. I do now, but …'

She dissolves into tears again, and I'm suddenly struck by the fact that if this woman is telling the truth, she's witnessed two horrendous murders in the space of a few hours, and one of them was her mother's. Her version of events is wild and unbelievable, but in my experience, no guilty person would expect us to give such an incredible tale an ounce of credibility. And that's what makes me believe every word. I glance at Grace, and as usual, we're on the same page. Helen Stone's story is just too stupid to be false.

'Just two more things,' I say. 'When you came down to see Alice, were you aware that your father, William Harcourt, also lived in Bristol, and that his brother, James, lived in Weston, quite close to where you stayed?'

She stares at me blankly. 'No. I – no, I had no idea. Mum never mentioned them – only Alice.'

'So,' I go on, 'you also didn't know that the night Alice and your mother were killed, William Harcourt was also murdered, and so was your brother Jacob's father, Charles Malden?'

She has gone completely white, and for a moment I think she is either going to faint, or vomit all over the sofa. Luckily, she does neither, and manages to recover herself, although when she speaks, it's in an unsteady whisper. 'No – I mean – Oh, God!'

'Thank you, Helen,' Grace says. 'We'll leave you alone for a while now, and send in DC Shaw to look after you while we investigate further. Is there anything else you'd like to tell us before we go?'

She frowns, shaking her head. 'Mum was right,' she mumbles. 'I thought she was starting to lose her mind – dementia or something – but she was right, wasn't she?' She looks up suddenly, meeting my eye. 'What if she was right about everything? I mean about the phone not being safe, and not to talk to the police? And what about Lizzie? Will whoever it is kill her, too? I don't understand.'

'Neither do we,' I tell her. 'But we will, I promise you. Whatever is going on, we'll get to the bottom of it, and in the meantime, try not to worry. You'll be safe here. Do you know where we can find Lizzie? We can check, and make sure she's okay.'

'Not exactly,' she answers. 'She lives in Lancashire, somewhere near the coast, I think, but Mum never gave me an address. She never wrote them down either – it was her rule, she said, just in case – in case of something like this, I suppose. She only told me where to find Alice as I was leaving to come down here. I'm sorry, I know that's not much help.'

'It's all right,' I say. 'At least we know where to start. We'll try not to be too long. If there is anything you need, just ask DC Shaw.'

'You think she's telling the truth?' Grace asks as we make our way up to the squad room.

'I've got a horrible feeling she might be,' I reply. 'And if she is, where the hell does that leave us? There is one thing, though – that letter – it was signed *E*. If we assume "E" stands for Elizabeth, then it was most likely sent by this Lizzie, that is if Lizzie exists, and Helen said Lizzie lives somewhere on the Lancashire coast.'

'But the postmark on the envelope,' Grace finishes for me, 'tells us it was sent from Hull – the other side of the country.'

'Bloody hell!' we both say in unison.

17

Daz Jackson is waiting for us in the squad room, wearing what can only be described as a triumphant grin.

'I really enjoyed that, boss,' he says, rubbing his hands gleefully. 'Berman admitted calling Stone and warning her not to come back to Bristol, so I charged her with wasting police time and withholding evidence. It's a pity I couldn't add breaking bail conditions, but unfortunately she wasn't due to report until after we re-arrested her. Still, I suppose that means we don't have to keep her in and involve Social Services to see to the three kids. What do you want done with her?'

'I doubt she'll try to make a run for it now,' I reply, 'and she can't do much more damage, so you might as well let her go pending an appearance at the magistrates' court. At least that will give Dick Fosbury an extra cell to make use of.'

'It bears out part of Helen's story as well,' Grace points out, 'which means we must seriously consider everything else she's told us. I suppose there is one quick way to check out whether or not she was telling the truth when she said she'd never met her brother.'

'Are you joking?' I ask, feeling an uncomfortable twitch somewhere near where my lunch is supposed to be. 'Bloody hell, Grace – that's a bit of a risk, isn't it? Aren't Social Services supposed to be involved in situations like this?'

'Come on, Al – they're not teenagers. From what I've seen so far, they're both perfectly able to cope with surprises. And being surprised at the sudden appearance of a sibling you've never met is pretty hard to fake, wouldn't you say? We can take Jacob across to the soft room, leave them alone, and see what happens. You and I can observe, and of course, the security camera is a requirement in any case. If they do already know each other, it will stick out a mile.'

'And if it goes tits up,' I say, 'it was your suggestion, not mine. But right now, that isn't my main concern. If what Helen says is true, her mother was pretty adamant that the police shouldn't be involved, and the message she supposedly received said *No police*. Yet both Emily Stone and Alice Walker were part of a police operation to bring the traffickers down, so logically, contacting the police at any hint of trouble should have been their first move.'

'Don't worry, Al,' Grace replies. 'That wasn't lost on me, either. In fact, I thought it a little odd that a DCS from Humberside should feel it necessary to make a long and expensive trip just to tell us something he could easily have explained on the phone. It's not as if the force has never heard of secure lines.'

'So,' I say, 'we have an unexpected visit from a senior officer, sent by his former boss to check us out, and Helen Stone's mother gets an anonymous – well, almost anonymous warning letter from the same area. You said you knew Don Harris? What was he like?'

Grace grimaces. 'He was what you would have called a typical tough, old-school copper, the type who always got his man, and not averse to beating the odd confession out of his suspects.' She pauses, and grins. 'Thinking about it, that's a bit like someone else I know. Even you would have drawn the line at some of the stuff he used to get up to, though. That kind of behaviour was fairly normal back in the sixties, and he didn't mellow much over the years. He didn't take to female detectives much either, unless it was between the sheets or making the tea.'

'In other words, you didn't like him much,' I suggest.

She sniffs. 'The man was a complete arsehole. But he got results, and the top brass thought the sun shone out of every orifice. He was on the edge of retirement when I was a wet-behind-the-ears DC, and he wasn't too happy about a woman being on his team. I ended up mostly stuck behind a desk typing up reports and twiddling my thumbs. I won't say it wasn't a useful experience, though. When you have to do battle with your colleagues as well as the criminals, it definitely toughens you up a bit.' She pauses, thinking, and then adds, 'He was, without doubt, a bit of a loose cannon, and bent the rules to get results, but then, most of his generation did. It doesn't mean he was corrupt, necessarily.'

'But we can't rule it out,' I say. 'Meanwhile, we still have Cathy Turner's story to get straight.' I turn to Jackson. 'Anything from Polly yet?'

He shakes his head. 'They're still at it, boss. Last I heard Cathy was refusing to say anything unless her husband was there, and when they said no, she asked for a brief. Do you want me to go and check?'

'Oh, for fuck's sake! It looks like "wasting police time" is going to win the charge of the day competition. Send Colin down to tell them they have my permission to formally charge her with whatever they think fit and to tell her if she wants a solicitor, it's the only way she'll get one. Where is Colin, by the way?'

'In with Jacob Malden,' Jackson replies. 'I thought it best not to leave him alone, and Colin's got strict instructions not to open his mouth for any reason short of a bomb scare.'

'Very wise,' I comment, 'although once that lad gets going, most suspects would sign a confession just to shut him up.'

'For goodness' sake, you two,' Grace says, with just a hint of irritation. 'That boy's got enough to contend with without the pair of you sniping at him all the time. He's a sensitive soul – something neither of you would know anything about. At least he follows instructions, which I have to say makes a pleasant change. It wouldn't hurt to take him down the pub with you once in a while, make him think you value his contribution – and believe me, he'll make one sooner or later, you wait and see.'

'Down the pub?' Jackson heaves a sigh. 'Oh, well, at least it would be a cheap night – he only drinks orange juice.'

We make our way back down to the interview rooms, and I send Jackson off to fill DC Shaw in on the plan, then finish processing Kylie Berman. We find Jacob Malden seething with indignation and frustration, and DC Draper standing diligently in a corner, lips firmly sealed, reminding me of one of the fake Roman statues in Charles Malden's front garden. Grace gives me a pointed look, and in response I smile as sweetly as I can manage, tell him to take a break and grab a coffee, then go to see if he can help Larson with the Internet searches.

As he disappears, Jacob rounds on us, practically foaming at the mouth. 'What the bloody hell are you lot playing at? I've been stuck here for hours.' He jabs a finger at Grace. 'And who the hell are you?'

'I'm Detective Superintendent Helston,' she replies smoothly. 'I do apologise for the delay, Mr Malden, but I'm afraid we had a rather important issue to deal with. Thank you for your patience. However, I'm sure we can sort everything out quite quickly now. If you will follow us, there is someone we would like you to meet.'

He stares at us, eyes narrowing in confusion. 'Who? What do you mean? Look – will you please just tell me what's going on?'

'If you will just come with us, sir,' she repeats, gesturing towards the open door.

He hesitates, realises he's on a hiding to nothing, flaps his arms in a half-hearted shrug and heads for the door. When we get to the soft room, I leave Malden with Grace at the end of the corridor and call Molly Shaw to join me.

'I've told Helen there is someone here to see her,' she says, 'but nothing else. Is that okay?'

'Perfect,' I answer. 'Give us a minute to get to the observation room, show Jacob in, but no introductions, and then go and take a break.'

I nod to Grace, who leads a frowning Malden up to the door. He opens his mouth, but thinks better of making any objection and just shakes his head.

'This officer will show you in,' she tells him, 'and we'll catch up with you in a few minutes.'

In the observation room, we see Helen tense as the door opens, and then, as she catches sight of Jacob, a hand flies to her mouth and we hear her sharp intake of breath. She gets unsteadily to her feet, blinking as if to dismiss a hallucination. Likewise, Jacob takes two steps into the room and freezes, staring at his sister in disbelief. Now that the two of them are together, the resemblance is undeniable, not just physically, but in the expressions, the subtle gestures – there's just under a year's difference in their ages, but they might as well be twins.

'There's no way those reactions can be faked,' Grace comments, as we both watch the encounter, fascinated.

'I agree,' I murmur. 'But is it because they really have never met before, or are they just surprised to see each other here?'

Helen has recovered herself a little, and takes a tentative step forward.

'David?' she whispers. 'You're David, aren't you? Oh, my God!'

For once, Jacob Malden is lost for words. He carries on staring stupidly for a few seconds and then rubs a hand across his face, makes an attempt to pull himself together, and says, 'Jacob – my name is Jacob, now. I – I mean – who *are* you?'

His tone makes it more of a plea than a question.

'Helen,' she answers. 'I'm Helen, but I used to be Rita – Rita Cawley. I …'

Her legs start to give under her, and Jacob finally comes to life and jerks forward to catch her. They both land on the sofa, and I suddenly see another side to him as he takes her hand, strokes it gently, and then reaches for the water jug on the coffee table, pours a glass and hands it to her.

'Sorry,' she says. 'I didn't mean to …'

'I didn't know,' he says, with genuine confusion. 'They never told me. Why? Why didn't they say something, for God's sake? All this time, and …'

Suddenly, beneath all the bluster and aggression, I catch a glimpse of the small boy, abandoned by one father, bullied by the other, spending years building his defences against yet more rejection and relying on the only person who gave him unconditional acceptance – his adoptive mother, Iris Malden. And now, in the blink of an eye, he is beginning to realise that she, along with everyone else, kept him in the dark.

I turn to Grace. 'I don't know about you, but I'd stake my pension on this being the first time they've set eyes on each other.'

She nods. 'At least that answers one question. I think it's probably a good time to give them as much privacy as we can under the circumstances.' She flicks off the audio. 'What's your next move?'

I think for a minute, not wanting to admit that in truth, I've got as much of a clue as a seasick sailor in a rowing boat in a force nine gale. Then, something occurs to me. 'Up until now, we've assumed that Jacob was responsible for the substitution of those dirks, or at least complicit. He almost condemned himself by stating that no one else could have entered the house. But if he didn't do it, someone must have – maybe someone he wouldn't consider – like a cleaner, or a care worker? I think it's time for me to have a word with my son-in-law.'

'And while you're doing that,' she says, 'there are a few things I want to check out with Humberside – in particular, the state of Don Harris's health. DCS Horner struck me as being a little over-protective, and I'm not comfortable about having to rely on him being Harris's only mouthpiece. If I get anywhere, I'll let you know. In the meantime, send one of the Portishead temps down here to keep an eye on the reunion, but tell him not to intervene unless they suddenly try to kill each other.'

Back in the squad room, my first move is to send Draper down to the canteen for sandwiches, after which I call Larson into my office.

'How far have you got with finding information on the relatives?' I ask.

'Some way,' he replies. 'What do you need?'

'Photographs,' I say. 'In particular, pictures of James Harcourt's two daughters, and Mick's children, plus anything else you've managed to dig up on Cathy Turner.'

He shrugs. 'That should be easy enough. They are bound to have images somewhere, either official or on social media. Nearly everybody has these days. I've been trawling through Cathy's background, and come up with nothing so far. Just as she said, the family moved to Bristol when she was a small child, she's been here since, never been in any kind of trouble – a couple of speeding fines and that's it. Give me ten minutes and I'll see if I can pull out some decent pictures of the others. Why?'

'Let's just say I want to eliminate them from our enquiries – or not, as the case may be.'

He nods and heads back to his computer. Draper gets back with a pack of chicken sandwiches, and I've just taken the first bite when Sillitoe taps on the door.

'I've sent Robbie off to get some lunch,' she says, flopping into a seat on the other side of my desk. 'I don't mind admitting, I'm knackered – Cathy Turner was bloody hard work. She's hiding something, boss, but I'm buggered if I know what it is. It's as if something's scaring her more than we are. She's got a great line in turning on the waterworks as well – perfect timing, and once she starts, you can't get a thing out of her.'

'Okay,' I say. 'Leave it for now, and with a bit of luck, we'll be further forward later this afternoon. Go and have lunch with Robbie, and I'll catch up with both of you in an hour or so.'

Larson comes back in with a printed sheet of head-and-shoulders photos. 'Best I could do at short notice,' he says. 'Luckily, both of James Harcourt's daughters are on Facebook and haven't triggered any of the privacy settings. They probably don't realise that anyone can access their pages. They're both there, plus Cathy Turner and Mick Harcourt's children, Susan and Billy. I'm still working on the rest, but at least you've got five to be going on with, if that's any use. I've put the names on the back.'

'I've got a feeling we may not need the others,' I say, 'but it's worth having them, just in case.' I catch sight of Molly Shaw, take the sheet and grab the rest of my sandwich. 'I'll fill you in when I get back.'

'You're welcome,' he mutters as I head for the corridor, gesturing for Molly to follow me.

I'm about to breeze into the soft room when Molly grabs my arm.

'I'm sorry, sir,' she stutters, jerking her hand away, cheeks turning pink. 'Do you think – maybe – we should give them a bit of warning – just in case …?'

'In case of what?' I ask, my mind starting to boggle, but realise she probably has a point. After all, a reunion between long-lost brother and sister could, I suppose, be defined as 'delicate'. I give her a smile. 'You're right, Molly. Want to do the honours?'

She nods, blushing even more, this time with relief, taps lightly on the door, and waits a couple of seconds before pushing it open. Helen and Jacob are huddled together on the sofa, hands clutched tightly, and Jacob's ashen face tells me that in the last half hour or so, he's learned a great deal about his family history that he'd very likely rather not know. They both eye me with a fair dose of apprehension as I make my way to one of the armchairs and sit down, Molly Shaw taking another.

'Helen says,' Jacob starts, making a supreme effort to keep his emotions under control, 'that my parents – my father – that he paid for me. She says that some gang stole me from my real mother, and he knew about it, and he bought me off them – like he would buy a sack of potatoes from a supermarket, or order a takeaway. Is that true? Did Mother know? Was she part of it as well?' He rubs a hand across his face and shakes his head as if trying to dismiss the idea. 'And did you know about it, too? Am I the only person who didn't?' He attempts an accusing tone, but doesn't quite manage it.

'I know this is a lot to take in,' I start, and he bridles at that, but I don't give him a chance to interrupt. 'We only became aware of the possibility earlier today – and at this time, it is still only a possibility. We can't say anything for certain without more information, and believe me, Mr Malden, we intend to get to the truth. What I can tell you is that some adoptions were perfectly legal, and at this stage, we can't jump to conclusions. Meanwhile, I'm hoping both of you can help us out. Jacob, you said you couldn't think of anyone who might have had access to your parents' house recently?'

'No,' he replies. 'I told you, they rarely had visitors, and over Christmas, just me and Edith – Edith Fontwell from next door. Mum had another friend, Joyce something-or-other – Barrett, is it? She was at the hospital with her daughter, but I don't think she'd been to the house for quite a while.'

'Okay,' I say. 'I think we can discount Mrs Fontwell and Mrs Barrett. I want you to think back, say, over the last year or so, and tell me if you remember anyone else being in the house – builders, perhaps, or care workers – someone your parents wouldn't have known well. Think very carefully.'

There's a silence as he sits, brow furrowed, eyes screwed shut, scouring his memory. Finally, he opens his eyes and shakes his head.

'I can't think of anyone. They had a problem with the boiler last spring and had to get a plumber in, but he couldn't have been there more than a couple of hours and I was with him the whole time. I wanted to make sure he wasn't ripping them off – it happens with old people – tradesmen come, do nothing and charge a fortune. He was fine, though. The only other time is when Mum and Dad went away for a week last summer, to the Lake District. They asked me to look after the place, so I stayed there with my girlfriend.'

'Your girlfriend?'

He colours slightly, and shrugs. 'Well, not really a girlfriend – someone I met, a woman down for a conference at the Grand Hotel in the centre. I met her in the bar while I was waiting for a client.

We hit it off, she didn't like the hotel, so she stayed with me for the week. It was fun, but we didn't swap numbers or anything like that.' He shrugs again. 'We had a good time, she went home, and that was that.'

'And what was her name, this woman?'

'Tricia, she said – I don't even know her last name, and didn't ask. It was just one of those things.'

With an effort, I keep the frustration out of my voice. 'So, you and this "Tricia" stayed for a week in your parents' house while they were away. I assume you didn't take the week off, so what did she do while you were working?'

'She was at her conference, I suppose,' he replies. 'She left in the morning, around the same time as me, and we met up again in the evening.'

'At the house, or in town?'

'Mostly in town, but a couple of times at the house, when her sessions finished early and she wanted to shower and change.'

'Okay,' I say. 'So, if she finished early and wanted to take a shower, and you didn't get back till later, how did she get in?'

It finally dawns on him what I'm driving at, and he turns a worrying shade of grey. 'Oh, Christ!' he mutters. 'I gave her a key – and the code for the alarm.'

'Jacob,' I say quietly, 'I'm going to show you some photographs. Let me know if there is anyone you recognise. Helen, I'd like Jacob to see them on his own, and then I'll show them to you, okay?'

She nods and turns away. I hand the sheet Larson provided me with across to Jacob. He runs his eye over it, takes in a breath, and points to the first image, top left.

'That's her!' he says, blinking in confusion. 'That's Tricia. How the hell …?'

'Thank you,' I say, and hand the sheet to Helen, who shakes her head.

'I'm sorry,' she says. 'I don't know any of these people – at least, I don't think I do.' She looks closer and then hands the sheet back to me. 'No – I thought for a minute two of them looked familiar, but no, I don't recognise any of them. Who are they?'

For a moment, I'm tempted to tell them, but now, I think, is not the time. Instead, I make a decision, and hope it's the right one.

'Jacob, I know this has been a very difficult few hours for you. If it's any consolation, you have been a great help. DC Shaw will take you home, and I would urge you to stay there with your mother for the time being. Given the situation, I need to know that both of you are safe. DC Wyatt will remain with you at your flat, so if you need anything, just ask her.'

I turn to Helen. 'There is still the matter of impersonating a care worker and gaining unauthorised access to the nursing home,' I tell her. 'Despite that, I would, in normal circumstances, release you without charge, although you would still be under investigation. However, I am concerned for your safety, and to be frank, I haven't the manpower to give you adequate protection, so the best option would be for you to stay here until we can sort something out.'

'Why can't she come with me?' Jacob asks. 'You said your policewoman would be staying at my apartment, so why can't she keep an eye on all three of us?'

I heave an inward sigh of relief that the gamble, for the moment, has paid off.

'Are you happy with that?' I ask Helen, and she smiles for the first time since she entered the station.

'Yes,' she answers. 'Yes, of course. But you haven't answered the question. Who are those people in the photographs?'

'I'm afraid I can't tell you that just yet,' I reply. 'I hope we will be able to explain everything, but it may take a little time.'

I wait until Molly Shaw has taken the two of them off to commandeer a patrol car, and then make my way back up to the squad room, wondering how the hell I'm going to break the news to Jacob Malden that the woman he picked up in a hotel bar was, in fact, his cousin, Rachel, daughter of the missing James Harcourt.

18

Back upstairs, Grace is waiting for me, her expression telling me things haven't quite gone smoothly with Humberside police.

'Get your coat,' she snaps. 'We've been summoned. As if we haven't anything else to bloody well do!'

'I take it we've upset one of Gosford's golfing buddies?' I say, as we make our way down to the car park.

'Apparently,' she replies, through gritted teeth, 'I have impugned the reputation of one of the most revered detectives in Yorkshire. I was put through to their ACC, and given an earful of bullshit about DCS Harris's illustrious career, and how dare I try to besmirch his good name, plus the good name of one of their best current serving officers, and a complaint would be made immediately to my commanding officer. He wasn't kidding either. I had the chief constable on the phone within five minutes, and he's demanding to see us both in less time than it takes to drive to Portishead.'

'I don't suppose you mentioned to him that we're short-handed, and a bit busy trying to solve three murders, for fuck's sake – four, if you count the one in East Midlands, plus a manhunt for a missing potential victim?'

Her answer is a grunt as she slams her car door and we set off for head office at a speed that, if it wasn't for the look on the DSI's face, would have me politely suggesting that she switch on the Blues and Twos.

We arrive to find Chief Constable Gosford pacing impatiently in front of his floor-to-ceiling picture window, hands clasped behind his back, looking as if he's just accidentally sat on a six-inch nail. His secretary starts to formally announce us, but he shoos her away with a flap of the hand.

'You two bloody well took your time,' he growls, directing us, with another curt flap, to the chairs normally reserved for visiting dignitaries.

Grace and I exchange a quick glance. Whoever has brought on his fit of pique, it doesn't seem to be us.

'I've just had words with Humberside's chief constable,' he explains, as we warily take our seats. 'With a bit of luck, her ACC will be out of a job by teatime. Of all the bloody cheek …'

He stalks across to his desk, jabs the intercom button and snaps an order for coffee, then plonks himself into a leather armchair opposite us. After a couple of deep breaths and a derisive snort, presumably aimed at his northern counterpart, he treats us to the hint of a grin.

'Looks like we've poked a bit of a hornet's nest up there,' he says. 'It seems this retired chief superintendent you're looking into has a bit of a boy's club going among the serving officers. He clicks a finger, they run to do his bidding – you know the sort. I thought that kind of crap was reserved for the Met.' He snorts again. 'God forbid it would ever happen down here – at least, not on my watch, I can promise you that.'

The flustered secretary comes in with coffee, and there's a short hiatus as she pours, sets down a plate of biscuits, and scuttles out again. Gosford picks up his cup and stares out of the window, frowning.

'Sir?' Grace ventures, when the silence becomes awkward. 'Is there something we need to be aware of?'

He blinks, as if just remembering we are there. 'My apologies, Superintendent, Chief Inspector,' he says, 'but this sort of thing really makes my blood boil! Apparently, your visitor, DCS Horner, was not acting officially, at least, not according to their chief constable. We can't touch him, because he got the go-ahead from the ACC, so his arse is more or less covered. However, it turns out that both Horner and the ACC are in the retired DCS Harris's boy's club – with the emphasis on "boys". Their chief constable is definitely not eligible for membership, and she's been trying to stamp it out ever since she took up the post, but of course, she's got nowhere fast.'

'You think Harris was bent?' I ask.

'Nothing was ever proved,' Gosford replies, 'but I'd be surprised if he wasn't, one way or another. Nobody gets results like his without bending the rules at some point. And that's the problem – he got results. As far as half the local force is concerned, he's the big hero – he says jump, and you can hear the thump of police issue riot boots hitting the ground ten miles away.'

'Horner told us Harris is in a nursing home, and couldn't talk to us because he's recently had a stroke,' Grace says. 'You think that's a ploy to keep us at arm's length?'

'Perhaps, Gosford replies, 'but perhaps not. There's only one way to find out.' He turns to me. 'Crow, I want you to go up there first thing tomorrow. I've arranged for you to meet directly with the chief constable – the fewer people in the loop, the better. I want you in that nursing home, and I don't care if you have to use sign language, you find out what he knows, and what's going on – clear?'

For a minute I just stare at him blankly. When I do think of something to say that won't land me on a disciplinary charge, I say, 'Sir – you do realise I'm heading up a triple murder investigation here? Plus, we're short-handed …'

'For God's sake, Chief Inspector,' he snaps, 'you think I don't bloody well know that? But tell me this – who is Harris more likely to talk to – a ranking officer, or some wet-behind-the-ears constable? And he's sure as hell not going to respond to your DI, for obvious reasons – my apologies, Grace. The man's a complete misogynist along with whatever else. I'm sorry, but that's my decision, whether you like it or not.' He softens a little, and adds, 'Believe me, I don't like it either, but I'm sure DI Sillitoe will do a sterling job in your absence, and with luck, it won't be for more than twenty-four hours. We're having the wool pulled, and that makes me angry. It also makes me think there's something going on that is going to make a huge difference to our case – and DI Moffat's.'

I can see I'm presented with a fait accompli, and can't disagree with him, although, given the attitude of the top ranks towards women golfers, his comment on misogyny in the force almost makes me choke on my coffee. Grace has to feign a cough.

'I see what you mean, sir,' I manage to say. 'I'll book a train up there first thing.'

'Good,' he says, 'and take someone with you – not a female officer – we don't want to give him any ammunition in that department – not that I'm implying anything, you understand. It's just that I get the feeling we need to tread with care, if you take my meaning. What about that young DC of yours? Draper, is it? He's fairly innocuous from what I hear. He might as well be useless up there as a spare part down here – be a good experience for him.'

I struggle for words, and finally come up with, 'Sir – you can't be serious!'

'Deadly,' he replies. 'Get it sorted, and report to me personally as soon as you get back. I have every faith in you, Chief Inspector. Don't let me down.'

And that's it.

'Don't be so hard on him,' Grace comments as we get back into her car.

'Who?' I ask. 'Draper, or the chief constable?'

She laughs. 'Both, I suppose. But Gosford, unlike some, didn't get where he is by being stupid. Yes, he's a political crawler, but you can't say he hasn't got his finger on the pulse, and he's honest. To be frank, I wouldn't have his job for any money.'

'Me neither,' I agree. 'But Draper? Christ all-fucking-mighty!'

'I told you,' she says. 'That boy has qualities. You just haven't seen them yet. And when you do, you'll appreciate them, mark my words.'

'You're the boss,' I say, and spend the rest of the drive back to West Hill in miserable silence.

As Colin Draper stands in front of my desk, giving me a fair impression of a grounded fish, I get the awful feeling I look much the same. I make a conscious effort to keep my mouth closed, and my expression mildly encouraging – or at least, not actively hostile.

'You want me to go with you – to Yorkshire?' He pauses, trying to think it through, and then adds, in a sudden stroke of genius, 'It's a long way up there, sir.'

‘Which is why,’ I say, stifling a sigh, ‘I need you to be here at 5.30 a.m. It’s a four-hour journey each way, and their chief constable is meeting us outside York station at 10.30, so we need to catch the 6.30 a.m. train. In the meantime …’ I push a very thick folder across my desk. ‘I want you to go through this. It’s a record of all Harris’s activities while he was on the force – career moves, operations he was involved in, arrests and so on. The more we know before we meet him, the better. You can take me through the main points while we’re on the train.’

He visibly perks up at the thought of having something useful to do, reminding me once again of a dog that’s been thrown a tasty bone. Blue, curled under the desk, seems to agree, and lets out a quiet bark that might be the canine equivalent of amusement.

‘Yes, sir – I’ll make a start right away.’

He grabs the folder and heads for the door. ‘Colin?’ I say, before he makes his escape.

‘Sir?’

‘Bring your big coat. If you think it’s cold down here, believe me, it will be bloody freezing up there.’

On his way out, he bumps into Sillitoe and Robbins on their way in, looking exhausted, but jubilant.

‘We finally got something, boss,’ Sillitoe says, as I gesture for them both to sit.

‘It took all afternoon,’ Robbie adds, ‘but she crumbled in the end. She’s scared to death, boss. The day after her father’s murder, she got a threatening call telling her to keep her mouth shut, and if she told us anything, she’d be next on the list.’

‘Whose list’ I ask.

‘That’s just it,’ Sillitoe says. ‘She said she didn’t know, and we believe her. I said we needed to have access to her phone and she almost fainted – said if whoever it was found out she’d talked to the police, they’d come after her. The thing is, she doesn’t have any idea what it is she’s been threatened not to talk about. I’m pretty sure she’s completely out of the loop, but whoever it is assumed her father had filled her in. We’ve got to treat her as a potential victim, not a suspect.’

‘Shit!’ is all I can say to that. ‘So, we have three of William Harcourt’s children, all of whom were possible suspects, and are now in need of protection as potential victims, for goodness’ sake!’

Sillitoe shrugs. 'It looks like it, boss. Sorry – we did our best.'

'And you got a result,' I acknowledge. 'Well done, both of you. The problem now is, someone has to stay with Cathy Turner while the threat remains.'

'How about Molly?' Robbie asks. 'I know she hasn't got FLO training, but Cathy seems to trust her.'

'Good call,' I say. 'Robbie, can you see to that? And then, both of you go and take some time. This day's been long enough, and Polly, you will be in charge for twenty-four hours as of tomorrow morning, so you should get some rest.'

Robbie goes off to finish up, and I fill Sillitoe in on the afternoon's events. 'I want Rachel Harcourt picked up first thing in the morning. Somebody from the Weston station should be keeping track of her movements, so hopefully they've been keeping their eyes open and she hasn't gone anywhere. Her explanation of what she was doing at the Malden house with Jacob should be interesting. Draper and I should be back from York by mid-evening, but if you hit any problems, I'll be on the end of my mobile.'

'You're taking Colin?' is her first comment. 'Bloody hell!'

'Gosford's idea,' I explain. 'But he's the least indispensable officer here, so I suppose it makes sense. Plus, he seems to enjoy paperwork, so I've left him to go through Harris's file. If we dredge anything up tomorrow, I'll let you know, but I have serious doubts.'

'By the way,' she says, with a hesitant smile, 'you were right. It's all sorted, with me and Robbie. You don't have to worry about it, okay?'

'If it means I'm not going to lose two of my best officers anytime soon,' I reply, 'that's good news.'

She grins. 'The truth is, boss, I'm just waiting for you to jump ship and take up a new career in marriage guidance so I can grab your job.' Thankfully, she doesn't hang around for my reply.

My next task is to sort out Blue for the next day or so.

'You're going where?' my son-in-law comments, eyebrows shooting up in surprise. My next statement almost makes them disappear altogether and gives me a distinct feeling of Deja vu. 'You're taking who? Bloody hell!'

'Don't you start! Can you manage Blue until I get back?'

'Of course. She'll be a good distraction for Ben. I'm going to stay on for an hour or so – I've got a search running and I need to wait until it's finished before I power down. I'll pick her up on my way home.' He checks his watch. 'It's just after five now – say, 7 o'clock at the latest?'

Canine lodgings arranged, I grab my coat and make my way downstairs before I get collared by anyone with an issue requiring a senior officer – Dick Fosbury in particular, who by all accounts is still grumbling about the lack of cell space. I don't quite make it to the car park, as George Saint intercepts me at the front desk.

'I hear you're off to Yorkshire,' he says, leaning on the counter and chewing on a chocolate muffin.

'You hear right, George – a place called Howden – somewhere near Hull.'

He straightens up, showing more than his usual expression of casual interest. 'I went up there with the wife last year – stopped off on our way to the Dales. They do bloody good fish and chips – cook the chips in beef fat – makes all the difference to the taste. Ours down here just use oil. That's why they're always soggy.' He pauses, warming to his favourite subject. 'There's this café in Goole we went to – it was pissing with rain, and they had a notice in the window. It said, *Don't stand outside feeling miserable. Come in and get really fed up*.' He chortles, and then puts on his serious face. 'Listen, Al, if you get the chance, there's this place, in Howden high street, called "The Kitchen". They do pastries to die for! Do me a favour and nip in there if you get the chance. One of their cream cakes would keep me going for a week!'

'They must be the size of Vista House, then,' I say, marvelling at our desk sergeant's global knowledge of food emporiums, although I shouldn't be surprised. 'I'll do my best, George. In the meantime, if I get any emergency calls, don't put them through. I've got a feeling I'm going to have my work cut out on this one.'

He gives me a grave nod. 'You've got that right, Al,' he agrees. 'I hear you're taking young DC Draper with you. Bloody hell!'

19

As soon as I get through my front door I know something is wrong. Blue stops in the doorway, rigid, ears pricked, and lets out a menacing growl. A second later she's launching herself towards the back of the house, barking frantically. I take the hint, grab the first thing that comes to hand – a giant golfing umbrella – and cautiously follow her to the back door. When I get there, she's scrabbling at the woodwork, but the bark has turned into an anxious whine, her tail wagging more with excitement than aggression. She gives me a pleading look, which in human terms conveys the thought, *for fuck's sake open the bloody door!* Much as I trust her judgement, I'm not going to take her word for it, though.

'Who's there?' I demand, tightening my grip on the umbrella.

A familiar voice answers. 'Jesus, Bird Man – hurry the fuck up and let us in – we're getting bloody pneumonia out here!'

I slide back the bolts and open the door to reveal a very bedraggled Clive Gingell, plus two other kids behind him, both kitted out in hoodies several sizes too big, pulled down over regular Parkas. One of them dashes out and straight into my arms as Clive and his other companion squeeze past into my kitchen.

'What the … Ben? Ben, is that you?'

He's sobbing so hard he can't get his breath, clinging onto me as though his life depends on it. I realise that now isn't the time for an interrogation, so just hold him tight, stroking his hair and making appropriate shushing noises. The other boy with Clive is in a similar state, tearful and shooting me terrified looks. Clive drags out a chair and flops into it, shaking his head as if, for once, he doesn't quite know what to do. My mobile chooses this moment to start ringing, and I root it out of my jacket with one hand, still holding onto Ben with the other. It's Rosie.

'Dad?' She's in a panic, hardly able to get the words out. 'It's Ben – he's not here, and I don't know where he is …'

'He's with me, Rosie,' I say quickly. 'He's fine – he's all right. He was waiting for me when I got in, just a couple of minutes ago.' For a long moment, all I can hear is her wild attempts to slow her breathing. 'Do you hear me, sweetheart?' I say. 'He's okay and he's here. There's another lad with him – do you know who it might be?'

There's another pause, and she manages to get herself under control. 'Thank God!' she says, and then, 'Marcus, his friend. I thought Ben must have gone there, but when I rang his mum, they couldn't find him either, and …'

'Okay,' I interrupt. 'Just calm down, call your mother and get her to come and look after Alex. Let Marcus's parents know they are both safe. But, listen to me. Give me half an hour with them and I'll meet you at the station, yes? We can talk it over then, when I know more. Right now, they are both scared to death – I'd say partly because of the trouble they think they're in. They came here for a reason, so maybe I can find out what this is all about before we jump to any conclusions. Have Marcus's parents notified the police?'

'Yes,' she replies. 'As soon as we realised they were both missing, we rang 999. It will have gone through to West Hill, and I'm expecting a patrol car any minute.'

'When they arrive,' I say, 'tell them the boys are with me. I'll phone through and let them know, too. In the meantime, try not to worry. We'll sort this out, I promise. Have you told John yet?'

'I was about to,' she replies. 'I thought it was best to call you first – I don't know why …'

'You did the right thing,' I reassure her. 'Call him now, although it's probably gone round the station already, and tell him to stay put and wait for us. Tell Marcus's parents to meet us at West Hill station as well. I'll bring the boys in as soon as I've had a chance to calm them down and have a chat with them both.'

What I don't tell her is that the person I most want to talk to right now is Clive, who is still, uncharacteristically, slumped in one of my kitchen chairs. Normally, when Shark Johnson, West Hill's local gangster kingpin, sends him on an errand to my back garden, he can't wait to make a swift exit over the back fence. Clearly, Shark has a message for me. But first things first.

'It's all right, Ben,' I say, giving him a squeeze. 'Why don't you and your friend get out of those wet things and take Blue into the lounge? I'll turn the fire on and bring some hot cocoa in. I just want to have a quick chat with Clive first, okay?'

Ben, thankfully, has recovered a little, and nods miserably. 'It's all right,' I repeat. 'We'll sort this out, okay?'

He nods. 'Okay, Grandad.' He pauses, and then says, 'Please don't tell Mum and Dad.'

'I can't promise that,' I say, honestly. 'They've been very concerned about you. But you don't have to worry about that now.'

I shoo the boys into the lounge with a couple of bath towels, turn the heater on and return to the kitchen, where Clive is staring at his trainers, hands stuffed into the front of his hoodie.

'I'm making cocoa for the boys,' I say, rooting in a cupboard for a saucepan. 'You want some?'

It's a question I'm guessing, from his confused expression, he doesn't get asked very often. He thinks it through and then shrugs.

'Yeah – why not?'

There's a silence while I get on with the task, hand him a mug and take the others through to Ben and Marcus before joining him at the table.

'So,' I ask him, 'what's the story?'

'Your kid shouldn't come down our way,' he says. 'He's bait, know what I mean – him, and his friend. Shark said to warn you. Kids like that, they ain't safe down by Vista House.'

'Is that where they were? Christ almighty! What were they doing there? And how come you were with them?'

'Jesus, man!' He thumps the table in frustration. 'You bloody lot never give up with all the fucking questions – anybody would think I'd kidnapped them or something.'

'I don't think that, Clive – I'm very grateful you brought them here – and I'm sorry if I'm asking questions, but their parents are going to ask me, and I've got to tell them something. Help me out, here – yes?'

He thinks, takes a gulp of his cocoa, and nods. 'Fair enough. There's this nonce, right? Just got out and come back home, thinks he can set up shop again around here, carry on like he did before.

Shark won't let that happen – been trying to get him out, yeah? He says the police can't do nothing 'cos they can't catch him at it, but he's at it all right – fucking paedo.'

I feel a sudden chill. 'You mean Carl Barton, released from prison four weeks ago? Christ – it didn't take him long! And you're saying he was with Ben and Marcus?' My left hand has started to tremble, and I've come out in a cold sweat.

Clive shakes his head. 'He never got to them – one of us keeps an eye, especially at night.'

By 'keep an eye', he means Shark Johnson sends his stooges out after dark to practice a little persuasive intimidation – messages painted on the doors, smashed windows, dog shit and fireworks through the letterbox – the usual treatment for sex offenders trying to disappear into the murky depths of West Hill.

Clive is talking again. 'I was out on an errand and saw him lurking around by the underpass. Then I saw the two kids. When they got close, I recognised your daughter's boy, and I knew he shouldn't have been out – it's fucking dangerous – I wouldn't let my little brother walk around down there on his own, and we live there! Anyway, I saw them walking in the nonce's direction, and when he saw them, his ears pricked up, like he was waiting for them, and he started walking towards them, so I went over and they looked really scared, so I said I'd bring them here. When the queer fucker saw me he legged it. I reckon he was expecting them, so I rang Shark, and he said to make sure they got here, and to tell you, get the bastard off our patch, or he'd do it for you.'

I nod. 'And would you say all this in court?' I ask.

Clive's lip curls into a cynical grin. 'Fuck off! You got your kid and his friend – you don't need me.'

'But they never saw his face,' I point out, 'and he never actually did anything – you got there first, thank God. We can't haul somebody in just for walking down the street.'

'Why not?' He juts his chin out defiantly. 'You stop us all the fucking time!'

'That's because …' I start, but then sigh. I'm banging my head on a brick wall. 'Fair point,' I concede. I consider for a second, then thrust out a hand. 'I'm very grateful to you, Clive. I owe you one, okay? If you ever need anything – anything legal, that is – you know where I am.'

He hesitates, and then takes my hand. 'You got it, Bird Man.'

He gets up, and stops at the door. 'Check your kid's phone,' he says, 'or his computer. That's how the fucker gets 'em. And if the kid says he's had his phone nicked, you should search his place. Shark heard he might be storing up crack in there, know what I mean?'

And then, he's gone. Despite the circumstances, I have to smile. I quickly ring through to West Hill, fill George in on events and ask him to put me through to Dick Fosbury. I tell Dick I've had a reliable tipoff concerning a stash of crack cocaine in a flat currently tenanted by one Carl Barton, convicted and recently released paedophile, and while his boys are turning the place over, it might be worth grabbing any phones or computers on the premises.

'Do me a favour and let the DSI know I'll be in with Ben and Marcus in around half an hour,' I add, and then turn my attention to the problem waiting in my lounge.

The boys have taken off their wet coats and the oversized hoodies, presumably provided by Shark Johnson to stop them catching their deaths, and are huddled by the fire wrapped in the towels, Blue resting her head on Ben's lap. They look up as I walk in, both pale and still trembling, partly with cold, partly because they are still terrified. I sit on the sofa, and at once Ben scrambles up next to me. Marcus hesitates for a second, then comes across to sit on my other side, both desperate for comfort. I put an arm around each of them, wondering if, for one second, they realise what might have happened if it hadn't been for West Hill's main gang boss and his teenage chief errand boy. The thought makes me shudder.

'You want to tell me about it?' I ask, when they're both settled.

'It was my fault,' Ben blurts out, trying to hold back tears. 'I told Marcus about my phone, and he said he'd ask his friends if anyone had a spare one. I've got fifty pounds on my Kidcard that Great-grandma gave me for Christmas, so I said I'd give them that.'

'I got this mate I talk to on the gaming site,' Marcus says. 'We play football on it – he's Bristol Rovers and I'm City. I asked everyone, and he came back and said he could get an iPhone for a tenner.'

'That's a pretty good deal,' I say. 'So, what's his name, this mate of yours?'

'He said his name was Charlie, and he goes to the learning centre on the other side of West Hill. He said if we could meet up with him halfway, at the betting shop by Vista House, and bring the ten quid, he'd hand it over. He said if Ben came along he'd make sure it was all set up right and let him test it out.'

'So, you both sneaked out, met up and made your way over to Vista House. How did you manage that, Ben? Climb down the drainpipe?'

Ben reddens. 'Mum went in the garden because a plant pot fell over. I went out the front while she was putting it up again. Sorry, Grandad.'

'Okay – so what happened when you got to Vista House? Did you meet Charlie?'

They both shake their heads, and Marcus bursts into tears. 'Charlie put a pin on my phone so we'd know where to go,' he says, between sniffs. 'But we'd just got there when someone came up on a moped and took my phone and pushed me over. Then we didn't know where to go anymore, and this other boy came up and said to go with him and he'd take us to your house. He wouldn't say what his name was, but he said you were his mate.'

'So we went with him and he brought us here,' Ben finishes.

'And you're sure you never saw Charlie? You don't know what he looks like?'

They both shake their heads. 'But he might be still waiting for us,' Marcus says. 'I haven't got my phone anymore, so I can't tell him we're not coming, and it might be dangerous if he's on his own. Can you send somebody to look, Mr Crow? If he gets hurt, it'll be our fault.'

If I get hold of Carl Barton, I think, getting hurt will be the least of his worries.

'It's okay,' I tell them. 'We've got some policemen out looking for him right now. I think it's about time I took you two over to the station.'

'Are we being arrested?' Ben asks, starting to panic again.

'No,' I assure him. 'You haven't broken any laws, but we'll need to take statements from both of you and get a description of the person who snatched Marcus's phone. Plus, your parents are waiting for you there, to make sure you both get safely home.'

By the time I pull into the car park, all thought of the potential dire consequences of their outing has flown from the boys' minds, and they are both excitedly bouncing up and down on the back seat. Ben, I realise, has never been inside a police station, or seen where I work.

'Can I see your office, Grandad?' he's asking, 'and can we see where you put the prisoners, and where …'

'Enough!' I snap, getting out, releasing Blue from the hatch and opening the rear door to usher them out. 'Any more of that and I'll ask Sergeant Saint to lock the pair of you in a cell until your parents are ready to take you home.'

It's a wrong move, as the suggestion is greeted with 'Wow – cool!' in unison from both boys. I swear under my breath.

It seems the whole station has stayed on to witness the return of the prodigals. George, I know, should have been off shift two hours ago, and there's a gaggle of uniforms around the front desk. Our entrance is greeted with a round of applause, which only serves to cement my grandson's temporary celebrity status.

'DSI Helston's taken Rosie and Marcus's parents up to your squad room,' George says. 'Inspector Fosbury says can you drop the boys off up there and then go down to his office? Mr Larson's in there with him, and there's something you need to see.'

In Fosbury's office? He ought to be with Rosie, for God's sake. I manage not to swear out loud in front of the children, and shepherd my charges to the lift.

I find Grace, Rosie and Marcus's parents in a huddle around the coffee machine. Rosie rushes across as soon as she sees us, ragged with worry, and grabs Ben so tightly that he struggles to take a breath. Marcus runs over to his equally haggard-looking parents, and there's a brief scrum. Grace and I exchange a look and she joins me as I head back to the door.

'Thank God they're both safe,' she says. 'From what I hear, it's no small thanks to Shark Johnson and the Gingell boy. Uniform picked up Barton within minutes of your call, and John's been going through his phone and computer – looks like we've got enough to prove he's breached his licence, and charge him with God knows what. He's only been out a month, for God's sake. John's down in Dick's office.'

'I know,' I reply. 'I'm on my way there. Thanks for staying on, Grace.'

'I'll be here until it's all sorted,' she says. 'Don't worry.'

I glance at Rosie, who is still holding onto Ben for dear life. She gives me a nod and a weak smile, and mouths, 'See you later.'

In the time I've known my son-in-law, I've seen him frightened, sad, happy, tired, mildly irritated – but never before have I seen him incandescent with rage. He's pacing up and down, hands balled into tight fists, breathing hard. The look in his eye as I walk through into Dick Fosbury's office almost makes me take a step back. He stops pacing when he sees me, and jabs an accusing finger under my nose.

'Before you say anything,' he spits, 'do not tell me to calm down. I will not fucking calm down. The only way I will calm down is if you give me the key to that sodding bastard's cell and leave me with him for five minutes – no – make that two. It will be long enough – more than long enough, you can bet on that.'

'You want me to join you?' I ask. He stares at me for a long moment, and then turns away with a snort, running a trembling hand through his hair, which has become a tangled mess. 'Actually,' I go on, 'I came to tell you that Ben's upstairs with Rosie. He's still a bit shaken up, but he's fine.'

He freezes, every muscle rigid, but then lets out a long sigh, and with it, some of the tension. At last, he turns back to me and nods.

'He's fine,' I repeat, 'and will probably feel even better when he sees you. Why don't you go up, and let Dick and me see to this?'

He blinks and takes another deep breath, sanity trickling back.

'Yes. I should …' He shakes his head. 'Sorry. I'll just – sorry.' He heads for the door, and I pat his shoulder as he squeezes past.

'Thank Christ for that,' Fosbury comments when he's gone. 'I thought I was going to have to lock him in an interview room – not that I wouldn't feel the same if it was one of mine.' He narrows his eyes at me. 'Are you okay, Al? What with the lad being your grandson and all …'

'I'm fine, Dick,' I reply, 'although I wouldn't trust myself in the same room with Barton for thirty seconds, never mind two minutes. I take it you've got enough to send him back inside for the duration?'

'Plenty.' Fosbury smiles. 'Looks like Shark Johnson did us a big favour. Barton started up within days of his parole coming through, the bastard. John Larson went over his laptop and found three aliases on different gaming sites, all claiming to be eleven-year-old boys. Charlie was one of the names – the one your grandson's friend, Marcus, was talking to. It was a real stroke of luck he had his phone nicked and they got lost before they reached the rendezvous point. Between you and me, it's likely young Gingell was there keeping an eye on the phone thief – Shark doesn't like that kind of independent activity on his patch – disturbs the smooth running of his business. Still, I suppose we can't complain – the boy did a good job keeping the lads safe, and Shark's helped us get Barton back off the street, even if his motives aren't exactly public-spirited.'

'What about Ben and Marcus, now?' I ask. 'I assume you will need statements from them?'

'Yes, but not tonight. I've had a call from Vice, and they are going to send one of their DCs round to each of them in the morning. They didn't see anything or meet up with Barton, thank goodness, so there's probably not much Ben can say, and with luck, there might be a record of communications on Marcus's computer, and in his phone records, even though we don't actually have the phone. I'd say send them home for a good night's sleep. At least Barton isn't going anywhere except back to prison.' He smiles. 'I hear you're going up to Yorkshire first thing. Maybe you ought to get your head down for a few hours as well?'

'I'll do that,' I say. 'Thanks, Dick.'

Back up in the squad room, I pass on the news that the boys can go home, and Marcus's parents gratefully usher him out in the company of one of Fosbury's PCs. Ben, clinging now to his father, holds out an arm as I enter, and I find myself in an awkward three-way hug. Larson gives me a tentative smile, and for a brief moment, we're united in a state of mutual relief.

'Will you come back with us?' Rosie asks. 'There's plenty of food at home, and you've got to be off early in the morning.'

I think about it and reluctantly shake my head. 'Thanks, but I'm fine,' I tell her. 'Just take Blue – it will do Ben good to have her around. I'll check in when I get back, okay?'

My son-in-law raises an eyebrow, but says nothing. Neither of us has eaten since a sparse lunch. This isn't the right moment to be a spare part, though. I give Ben another bear hug and make my exit, at the same time rooting out my mobile to order a takeaway from the local curry house. I'm about to leave the building when I hear a shout, and turn to see Larson jogging towards me.

'Everything all right?' I ask as he catches me up.

'It is now,' he says, 'although Ben's a bit upset you're not going to join us for dinner.' He hesitates. 'Thanks – for looking after him. When I think of what might have happened …'

'It didn't,' I say, 'and it's not me you should be thanking, it's a teenage thug from Vista House. Tell Ben I can't stay because I'm on the trail of three murderers – that should cheer him up. And it's not all bad – the experience should put a stop to his moaning about a smartphone for a while.'

'Not just that,' Larson says, with the hint of a grin. 'He and Marcus have vowed not to go near a computer ever again – just as well, as I was going to lock him out of all his devices for a week anyway – he'll have to make do with old school entertainment, like jigsaws and board games – and homework of course. But I just wanted to say, good luck for tomorrow. Grace says this Harris character is a bit of a hard nut, and you need to be careful.'

'Don't worry, son,' I tell him. 'I always am.'

20

The journey up to York is, as it turns out, unexpectedly peaceful. Within ten minutes of leaving Bristol, and having managed to upgrade our tickets to first class for the paltry sum of a tenner each, Colin Draper is curled in his seat, snoring quietly. I grab a coffee and a Danish pastry, and settle back to scan the background material on Harris I gave him to read through the night before. It's clear from the highlighting and scribbled notes in the margins that my young DC must have been working on it most of the night. I have to admit that he's done a pretty good job, and despite having had just as little sleep after the previous night's drama with my grandson, I can't begrudge him the chance of a little downtime.

After flipping through just a couple of pages, it's clear why Harris was something of a celebrity in his day. His resume includes a raft of medals – long service, exemplary service, a Queen's Gallantry medal – even a photo taken after the presentation at Buckingham Palace in the mid-1970s. I vaguely remember being invited to be presented with my own medal after the shooting that left me with a hole in my frontal lobe, and responding with a barrage of the best invectives my damaged brain could manage. Despite my protests, I got the bloody thing in a brown padded bag through the letter box. I remember ignoring it for a fortnight, thinking it was a tax return.

Don Harris, though, seems to have revelled in the glory of his many achievements, from rescuing a toddler from a frozen lake to bringing down three of Yorkshire's major crime syndicates within the space of ten years. It's an impressive portfolio. The file includes letters of commendation from two chief constables, both now most likely deceased, and several glowing testimonials from officers of all ranks, junior and senior, spanning a period of more than twenty years. The current chief constable has definitely done her homework, and Draper's judicious highlighting has made it easy to conclude that the former DCS Harris has been firmly placed in the 'untouchable' category. Any attempt to so much as wag a finger in his direction is going to be met with serious resistance. I stow the file, sit back and, following Draper's example, close my eyes and take a much-needed nap.

Draper shakes me awake as the train pulls into York, and I notice a cold cup of coffee on the table in front of me.

'Sorry, sir,' he says, as I haul myself reluctantly out of my seat. 'I thought you might be wanting one, but I didn't want to wake you.'

'That was thoughtful of you, Colin,' I reply, shrugging on my coat, and down it in one, slowly gathering my wits. 'Thanks. What was the CC's name again?'

'Manly, sir,' he says. 'Chief Constable Michaela Manly.'

'Christ,' I comment, as we shuffle to the doors and disembark onto a platform that's coated in frost and a good five degrees colder than where we've come from. On the other side of the barrier, I search the crowd for a uniform but draw a blank. I'm hunting for my phone when a stout figure swathed in a massive overcoat, scarf and woolly hat bowls up to us and sticks out a hand.

'Chief Inspector Crow? And DC Draper I presume,' she says, shaking my hand and giving him a nod and a smile. 'Chief Constable Manly – and before you say anything, I've heard them all.' She grins. 'Come on, I've got a car waiting, and it's too bloody cold to hang about outside.'

She sets off at a trot, and we follow her out to where a car is hovering on double yellow lines, engine running. 'You sit in the front,' she says to Draper, and gestures for me to join her in the back seat. 'This is my trusty assistant, DI Lola Campbell.' She points at the driver. 'As far as the rest of the station is concerned, we're taking the day off to have lunch and hit the market in town. I thought it best not to give Harris's cronies the heads up on your arrival. I've arranged for you to see him at 1 p.m., which gives us time to grab a late breakfast – or early lunch. I can help fill in a few more details at the same time.'

I'm rapidly warming to Humberside's chief constable. She's about as far from Gosford as anyone could get, and in many ways reminds me of Grace, and her ability to get to the heart of any situation quickly and with unsettling accuracy. I'm well aware, though, from my long friendship with my DSI, that even in these enlightened times, a woman battling to prove her worth in a world dominated by testosterone needs to be twice as smart as most of her colleagues.

The car drops us near the Shambles, and Manly guides us through a maze of stalls and narrow streets to a small café tucked away behind the market. We settle ourselves with generous plates of fish and chips (the best in town, she tells us), and pots of tea. Draper, I notice, has abandoned his usual impression of an excited kangaroo, and seems transfixed by his portion of chips. I conclude that he is probably overawed by being in the presence of both his chief inspector and a chief constable – which is probably just as well.

'You've had time to read through his file?' She asks. I nod, and she goes on, 'Then you can see why it's tricky. A small, but very vocal number of our serving officers have connections to Harris one way or another – relatives or friends of men who were on his teams – that sort of thing, and they include some very senior policemen, not to mention local government officials and so on. It's pretty clear he didn't get his reputation by doing things by the book, but up until now, he's managed to keep any dodgy dealings well under the radar. DCS Horner, who came to see you …' She sighs and shakes her head. 'He's the nephew of one of Harris's DIs from back in the day. My ACC, Jim Cracknell, was a DS just before Harris retired. It's a similar story throughout the force. When he finally pegs it, his send-off will probably be one carriage short of a state funeral. You can see what I'm up against.'

'But…' Draper blurts out, and we both turn to stare at him. 'Sorry,' he says, 'but surely, if DCS Harris had been involved with the trafficking gang, wouldn't he have gone out of his way to protect them? I don't see what the advantage to him would have been to expose them and have them all arrested. It doesn't make sense.'

Manly spears a chip and grins. 'That, young man,' she says, jabbing her fork in his direction, 'is the question, or at least, one of them. We know from the records that there were three individuals involved, and two were arrested and convicted. The third was never caught, and Harris claims he never managed to uncover his identity. He's made a great show over the years of continuing to pursue the third gang member and bring him to justice – his swan song, so to speak.'

'Yes,' Draper persists, 'I see that, but if he was involved with the gang, why make such a big thing of it? Why not just keep quiet? And what's he got to do with all these murders, and why now? And …'

'DC Draper!' I snap, trying hard not to roll my eyes, and failing.

Manly, however, is stifling a laugh. 'He likes asking the sixty-four-thousand-dollar questions, your lad, doesn't he?' She turns to him with a tolerant smile. 'You keep asking, Detective Constable. They're all the right questions. The trouble is, we don't know the answers – not yet. That's why you and your boss are here. If we can sneak under the wire and put the former DCS Harris on the spot, maybe he'll answer some of them. Talking of which, eat up – we should get going. The home he's in is just outside Goole, and that's a half-hour drive, plus, Lola will have to drop you a ten-minute walk away. At this stage, I don't want my interest to become too widely known – if there are members of my force protecting him, any hint I'm sniffing around will only lead to a closing of ranks.' The chip on the end of her fork finally finds its way to her mouth. 'You, Chief Inspector, are my Trojan horse. I'll be staying here, and Lola will pick you up and bring you back when you've finished.' She grins, and gets to her feet. 'In the meantime, I intend to hit the shops. Good luck, Chief Inspector.'

Exactly forty minutes later, I announce us over the entry intercom of what looks like a very expensive private nursing home – a former mansion house set in at least a couple of acres of well-manicured grounds. Draper echoes my first thought.

'I don't know about you, sir, but I can't see a police pension covering the cost of a place like this.'

'You're not wrong, son,' I agree. 'Still, we need to keep an open mind. One of the best policemen I know is the son of a hereditary peer and went to Eton.' I can't help but smile when I think of Inspector Jerry Forbes, and the cross-border investigation into a serial killer of teenage girls that brought us together back in the autumn.

I notice Draper is also grinning. 'You mean Inspector Forbes? I suppose you're right, sir. He was amazing!'

There's a definite note of hero-worship in his voice, so I can't help saying, 'Are you suggesting that I'm not amazing, Detective Constable?'

He starts to blush violently. 'Of course not, sir – I mean …'

'Relax, Colin,' I say. 'If you're going to get ahead in the force, you'll have to learn to recognise when you're having your leg pulled.'

He's saved from having to reply, as the main door opens, and a man a good six inches taller than me with biceps thicker than my thighs appears in the gap. He looks us over, wipes a hand down the front of a white nurse's uniform that has been so liberally starched it resembles a bullet-proof vest, and holds it out for me to shake. I oblige, and find his grip firm, but surprisingly gentle. He ignores Draper completely.

'If you'd like to follow me, sir,' he says, and sets off back inside without a backward look.

We follow him down a hallway, through an opulent lounge and into a much smaller sitting room, where a very elderly man cocooned in a blanket is almost swallowed by a huge leather armchair close to the window. Two similar chairs have been arranged so that the three form a semicircle looking out onto the tastefully manicured grounds. Before I can introduce myself, the nurse butts in.

'Will you be needing anything else, Mr Harris?'

'Thank you, Dennis – perhaps our guests would like some coffee?' He turns to me. 'Columbian – I have it shipped in direct from the growers once a month.' He throws me a look that is almost a challenge.

'I'm sure we'd love some,' I say. 'I'm …'

'Chief Inspector Crow – the famous hero of West Hill. I expect you've been mugging up on my background, as every good policeman should, so you'll forgive me if I have done likewise. Please,' he gestures to the two waiting armchairs, 'take a seat – and your young lad, too – can't have your bodyguard standing around like a spare part, can we?'

Draper opens his mouth, and quickly closes it again when I give him a look. 'This is Detective Constable Draper,' I tell Harris, who gives him a slight nod, and we both sit. Dennis pads silently in with a tray, places it on the wide window sill, and pads out again.

'I'm afraid you'll have to be mother,' Harris says, addressing Draper. 'You might as well make yourself useful, since you're here. Mine's black, three sugars, and if I've done my homework, your boss takes his the same.'

'Don't you mean, your friends in the force have done your homework?' I comment as Draper sets himself to the task.

Harris answers with a shrug and a sly smile. 'You want to ask me about one of my old cases, I gather,' he says, taking the cup my DC is holding out to him. 'Apparently, people are being murdered left, right and centre and you think the killings might be connected to the Greendale Lodge business, back in the 1960s.'

'More than just think,' I say. 'It's pretty clear there's quite a big connection – so big, in fact, that you saw fit to ask DCS Horner to travel all the way to Bristol to explain how. He also took great pains to advise us that you were extremely unwell and unable to speak to us. Did you ask him to say that, too?'

Another shrug. 'Young Jack is a good man, but occasionally he does take too much on himself. I did have a minor stroke a few months back, but as you see, I have recovered quite well. I think he was worried that excessive stress might lead to another – I've put him right on that. I'm sorry if he gave you the wrong impression, but I'm sure he only had the best of motives.' He pauses, brows coming together in the impression of a puzzled frown. 'When Chief Constable Manly rang this morning to tell me you were coming, I admit I was a little surprised. All this cloak-and-dagger stuff really wasn't necessary, you know – all you had to do was ring through to me directly and I would have answered any questions you have without you wasting your time travelling up here. But then, it's just typical of Manly. Women like her spend half their lives trying to get to the top, and when they manage it, they waste their time having paranoid fantasies that their male colleagues are out to get them instead of actually doing the job. I'm sure you take my point.'

'I'm sure I don't,' I reply, as calmly as I can manage. 'But as we *are* here, perhaps you could give us your take on current events. I've been told the original case is of some importance to you, so you must have some thoughts on who might be responsible for these murders, and why the killers have chosen to act now, decades after the original events?'

He grunts, and takes a sip of his coffee. 'You have obviously read up on the original case, so you know two of the main suspects were caught and convicted. The thing is, they weren't much more than hired heavies – neither of them had two brain cells to rub together. They were just the monkeys – the organ grinder vanished into thin air, and we never found out who he was.'

'But you carried on looking.'

'I don't like unfinished business.' His mouth twists into a snarl, momentarily revealing what lies beneath the veneer of civility. It's quickly hidden, and he goes on, 'The bastard made a fool out of me – and one of my DCs was crippled for life in the raid. He had to leave the force and killed himself two years later – couldn't live with it. From what I hear, you know how it feels to lose a man in the line of duty.'

I nod. 'I think anyone who has been in the force more than twenty years knows what it feels like. But you're still looking, yes?'

There's the definite hint of a smirk. 'I'm retired, Chief Inspector Crow. I'm sitting in a nursing home, waiting, as they say, for God. The only thing I'm looking for is peace and quiet – and decent coffee.' He lifts his cup. 'Cheers.'

'Of course,' I say. 'And being retired, you no longer have access to police files – unless you're being slipped the odd titbit by the members of your little club. I know that if it were me, I'd be tempted.'

He holds up his hands in mock horror. 'That,' he pronounces pointedly, 'would be illegal. I wouldn't want to get a serving officer into any trouble.'

'I'm pleased to hear it. I wonder if we can clarify some points on the original case, then. We know that two of the victims were whistle-blowers working undercover with your team – the woman we know as Alice Walker, and Emily Stone. We also have evidence of a third, a former secretary, and we believe her life may be in danger, so if you can give us any information that can lead us to her, it would be very helpful.'

Draper opens his mouth, but I silence him with a look. Harris shakes his head. 'That is only partly true. Yes, we were approached by a third individual, a clerk working in a different department of Greendale Lodge. I interviewed her, but ultimately decided against involving her – I found her much too flighty, and prone to gossip. She would have been a liability, and we were already taking a huge risk with the other two. It would only have taken one careless word and the whole operation would have come crashing down.'

'Yet you offered her protection, a change of name and so on. Why?'

He lets out a derisive chuckle. 'I'm afraid your information is inaccurate, Chief Inspector. We did nothing of the kind. If she moved away and changed her name, it was not due to any intervention by us.'

I try not to sigh in frustration. 'All right – but if she wasn't part of the operation, at least you can tell us her name – the name she went by in the 1960s?'

This time, he does laugh. 'Look at me, Chief Inspector – I'm an old man, and you're asking me to remember the name of one girl out of hundreds I've interviewed over the last fifty-odd years? If you're so desperate to go on some wild goose chase after an over-dramatic child with a vivid imagination, be my guest. You'll probably find her in the records, somewhere down in the basement of Hull police station. If you're going to do that, though, I'd recommend wearing a face mask – there must be a foot of dust on everything down there by now.'

'I might just do that,' I tell him. 'Over-dramatic, with a vivid imagination, you said? It sounds like you have a pretty good picture of her in your mind – shame you can't remember her name.'

The mask finally slips, and he presses a buzzer, conveniently placed on the arm of his chair. Dennis the minder is at his side in less than ten seconds.

'I'm afraid this interview is over, Chief Inspector Crow. I'm feeling rather tired, and it's time for my medication. I'm sure you can find your own way out.'

He makes a great show of struggling to his feet and shuffling through the door, aided by the obscenely muscular Dennis.

'Sir …' Draper starts, as we get up and head for the exit.

'Not now, Colin,' I say, navigating through the lounge and back to the main door. CC Manly and my DSI are right, I think to myself. Don Harris is a complete arse, and worse, he's a very clever one.

But he made one error. Whoever, and wherever the woman now known simply as 'Lizzie' is, she's important – not least, because Harris doesn't want us to find her.

It's a ten-minute walk through a pleasant stretch of wooded parkland to where Lola, our chauffeur, is waiting to take us back to York. We're around halfway there, passing under a stand of leafless and frosted oak and birch trees, when two men appear on the path in front of us, done up in regular West Hill style – jeans, black hoodies and balaclavas that I'm pretty sure aren't meant as protection against the cold. Draper comes to a halt, and I glance behind to see two more similarly dressed thugs sauntering casually towards us. There's no escape through the trees, and it's clear none of them are out for a mid-afternoon jog. When all four are within two feet of us, one of the pair in front, the one closest to Draper, reaches into his hoodie. It all kicks off so quickly I don't even have time to swear. I feel a dull thump in my back, and the last thing I remember is falling, my head hitting the gravel hard, and a great deal of yelling and shouting, slowly fading until all that is left is grey silence.

21

I have a vague memory of flashing blue lights, a lot of shouting, and several faces looming over mine – green and blue uniforms – and Colin Draper, his expression one of complete panic. At least, I remember thinking, he's alive, and looks unhurt. I try to tell him to calm down, that I'm fine, but nothing comes out. There's a sharp prick in my arm and I feel myself starting to drift. When I surface again, I'm in a hospital bed in a dimly lit room, hooked up to some machine or other. Someone is gripping my hand, and I try to turn my head, realise that's probably not a good idea, let out an involuntary grunt and give up.

The grip tightens, and a voice from somewhere to my left says, 'Al? Oh, thank God! For a while I thought …' Chrissie's tear-streaked face appears above me. 'It's okay, Al,' she goes on. 'You're going to be fine; do you hear me? Everything's going to be fine. You just need to rest for a bit, that's all.'

She doesn't have the chance to say anything else, as there's a flurry of activity around me, and before I can reply, she's gone.

The next time I open my eyes everything is brighter, and the pain in my head has receded to a manageable level. Chrissie is back, sitting by the bed, a plastic cup of coffee in one hand, a paperback in the other. I try to shuffle myself a little more upright, and she jumps at the noise, abandons the book and reaches across to plump the pillow and help me into a sitting position. The tears have been replaced by a radiant smile.

'Welcome back,' she says, and leans across to kiss my cheek. I try to reply, but my mouth feels full of sandpaper. At once, she pours a glass of water from the carafe on the bedside table and holds it to my lips. 'You had us worried for a while,' she says, as I drink. 'The doctors say it was a heavy knock on the head. They were concerned about a bleed on the brain, so they've been monitoring overnight. You were concussed, but that's all, thank God. Plus, the knife missed all the vital organs – it was a glancing blow, thanks to your DC Draper. He probably saved your life …'

'Chrissie?' I finally manage to get a word out and grab her hand. 'Slow down, love. I hardly remember anything. You need to take your time, okay? But first, I could do with some coffee – and maybe a slice of toast? My stomach thinks my throat's been cut!'

'Al!' She gives me her disapproving look. 'Don't say such things – it very nearly was!' She pulls out her mobile and dials. 'John? He's awake, and he's going to be fine … Yes, I know – it's great news. He wants coffee and toast. Okay – bye.'

'Breakfast coming up,' she says. 'Anything else?'

'Larson's here? Chris – what the hell's going on? How long have I been here, and where is "here" exactly?'

She smiles tolerantly. 'You are in Hull, and you've been here since the ambulance brought you in yesterday afternoon. You had a severe concussion and a stab wound in your left side, which turned out not to be serious, but you lost a lot of blood. Chief Constable Manly phoned through to West Hill, John came to pick me up, and we came straight here.'

'You've been here all night? Jesus, Chrissie – you must be exhausted.'

'I'm fine, Al. John and I have been taking turns, and we managed to get a hotel room nearby so we could get our heads down for a few hours. As for what happened …' She shakes her head and lets out a long breath. 'You were attacked – you, and DC Draper. According to him, there were four men, and at least one of them had a knife – the one who stabbed you. Colin went for him and put him off his stroke, otherwise, we probably wouldn't be having this conversation. He put him on the floor and was laying into a second one when a group of cyclists turned up. The other thugs ran off when they saw they were outnumbered, but the one who stabbed you was arrested – Colin broke the bastard's leg – and he broke another one's nose! The cyclists called an ambulance and the police, and helped with some first aid until the paramedics arrived. And here you are, thanks largely to your DC and a band of middle-aged men in Lycra.'

I take a moment to piece the information together. 'Where is Colin?' I ask finally.

'In our hotel room,' she replies. 'He was here until three hours ago, but John made him go and get some rest. He was pacing up and down outside your room all night.'

'Was he hurt?'

She grins. 'A bruised rib and skinned knuckles, but otherwise fine. You owe him, Al – big time.'

'I suppose I do.' I try to laugh, which results in a sharp pain in my side.

'Careful!' Chrissie says. 'You've got ten stitches where the knife went in.'

'Thanks for letting me know,' I comment, and squeeze her hand. 'You know, Grace told me that Draper had hidden depths. I didn't believe her. I bloody well do now!'

There's a light tap on the door and Larson sticks his head round. 'Okay if I come in?'

'If you've got coffee with you,' I say, 'be my guest. I hope you remembered the toast.'

He grins. 'Glad to see you're back to your old self,' he says, and sets down a tray with a bacon sandwich and three coffees, one black with three sugars.

In a moment of weakness, I raise my coffee in a mock toast. 'Cheers – and thanks, John – for coming all this way, and bringing Chrissie.'

'You're more than welcome,' he replies, 'and before you ask, Rosie is fine – worried, of course, but fine. Ollie White got back this morning and he's taken over my job until I get back, so you don't need to worry. I'll update you later. The doctors say you should be fit enough to move this afternoon, so we can drive you and Colin back home. There will be plenty of time to swap notes.'

Another knock announces DC Draper, who nervously pokes his head round the door.

'Come on in, Colin,' Chrissie says, before I have a chance to object, and gets to her feet. 'We'll leave you two alone for a while – I could do with some breakfast and a few hours' sleep before we drive back, and Chief Constable Manly says she'll be over to see you in about half an hour if you're up to it.'

'Do I have a choice?' I ask.

She rolls her eyes. 'As if you want one! Come on, John, let's take our coffee elsewhere.'

I'm left with Draper, shuffling uncomfortably from foot to foot at the end of the bed.

'Sit down, Colin, for God's sake,' I tell him, 'or at least stop swaying about like a tree in the wind.'

'Yes, sir – sorry, sir.' He does as he's told. 'They said you were feeling a lot better, so I thought I'd check in.'

'And you've been outside all night, from what I hear,' I say. 'I also hear you are responsible for my still being alive, and for causing grievous bodily harm to two of our assailants. Is that true?'

He blushes, and studies his fingernails. 'Some of it, I suppose, sir.' He hesitates. 'I mean, I had to do something. One of them pulled a knife and was heading straight for you. I didn't mean to hurt him that much, honestly – it was just instinct I think.'

'Christ almighty! Where on earth did you learn instincts like that? You do realise you could have been killed?'

He gives me a reticent smile. 'I don't think so, sir. Whoever they were, they weren't experts – they were way too slow.'

'Not experts? And you are? Jesus, Colin!'

'Well …' He coughs, and turns even redder. 'Sort of, sir – in kickboxing. I've been doing it since I was a toddler. My Dad is a kickboxing trainer down in Southampton, and he taught me. I was a trainer myself before I joined the force, and I've kept it up, as a hobby, ever since. It's a really good way to relieve stress, sir.'

I stare at him, desperately trying to imagine my ineffectual, over-eager DC beating the shit out of people twice his size over ten rounds in a kickboxing ring. On reflection, I decide, the term 'ineffectual' doesn't really fit any more.

'How come I didn't know any of this?' I ask. 'There's nothing about it on your record.'

He shrugs. 'It's not the sort of thing you want spread around – you know what the squad room's like. I'd rather you didn't say anything, sir, if that's all right.'

I want to laugh, but remember the stitches in my side and decide against it. 'I give you my word, Colin, your secret is safe with me – but one thing I can tell you – next time I walk into a situation that might turn sour, there's nobody I'd rather have watching my back. You earned your keep yesterday, son, and I won't forget it.' There's a short, awkward pause, until I change tack. 'I'm told the one who knifed me is in custody. Has he said anything?'

'Not much, sir,' Draper replies. 'He only got out of surgery a few hours ago – he's in a ward upstairs with his leg in traction, so he won't be going anywhere. All the local hospitals are looking out for any admissions with a broken nose as well, but no luck so far. I can't see a thug who's had his nose bashed by a policeman strolling into A&E. We've got the knife, though, and it's gone off for fingerprint and DNA analysis. There is one funny thing …'

He frowns, and I let the cogs whirr for a moment before losing patience. 'What? Come on, Colin – spit it out!'

'Sorry, sir. It's just, they weren't kids – at least, the one we arrested isn't. He's in his mid-fifties, I'd say. I don't know about the others – it was hard to tell with the masks, and they all seemed pretty fit, but it's odd, don't you think?'

'Very odd,' I agree, 'and interesting. So, tell me, what did you think of ex-DCS Harris?'

'I didn't like him very much,' Draper answers, without hesitation. 'I don't think he liked us much either.'

'I'm pretty sure he didn't. But what do you conclude about the information he gave us?'

He bites his lip, working himself up to it, and finally says, 'If you don't mind me saying, sir, I think he was pissing us about.'

This time I can't help but laugh, which ends in a splutter as my stitches make themselves known. 'I don't mind at all, son,' I say, once I can speak. 'I couldn't have put it better myself. So, give me your thoughts. How, exactly?'

'For one thing,' Draper replies, 'all that stuff about DCI Horner telling us he couldn't talk because of a stroke. That was, well, bullshit. He told Horner to say that, but pretended it wasn't his idea when we got there and saw for ourselves.'

'Agreed.' I can see my young DC growing in confidence as he thinks it all through. 'Go on.'

'I reckon he's definitely got men inside the force working for him, and I bet he's got somebody going down into those archives right now to make sure we can't find anything. I told CC Manly about that, sir, and she said she'd make sure nobody had access until her officers have brought up any files that are there. I hope that's okay.'

'Too bloody right it is,' I say. 'Well done, Colin.'

'And then there's this third woman – Lizzie, or whatever her name is,' he goes on. 'He was lying about not being able to remember her, and it's my guess he did involve her in some way. What I don't understand is, why? You'd think that if he's still trying to solve the case and find the third man, he'd be more concerned about her safety, and about the other victims as well. He didn't seem to care about any of them.'

I nod. 'You know, Colin, if you carry on like this, you might make a pretty good detective. But I'll tell you what's bugging me most of all. Nobody knew we were going to see Harris except Chief Constable Manly and, presumably, her assistant, and the receptionist at the home who was told to expect us. According to Manly, she was given instructions not to tell Harris, or anyone else, precisely who we were or the nature of our business. Yet he knew, and had all his ducks in a row by the time we got there. For what it's worth, my money's on the charming Dennis. Not only that, he had his heavies ready and waiting for us when we left.'

Draper looks genuinely startled. 'You think he hired those people to beat us up?'

'I think he wanted to do more than that, son. If I read it right, he wants us out of the way permanently, and what better method than a random knife attack in a public park? The whole force would have been out hunting for a gang of cop killers with no connection either to him and his cronies, or to our murder investigations. You said the one that got caught was in his fifties?'

'That's right. He certainly doesn't look like your average opportunist phone thief.'

I smile. 'Well, we're still here, and with luck, Manly's team will be able to identify our assailant and connect him to Harris. He must be really worried we're going to uncover something pretty damning if he's willing to take that kind of a risk.'

'Like what, sir?'

'I don't know,' I reply, 'but I'm damned sure I'm going to find out.'

22

Several hours, and a good deal of poking and prodding later, I'm pronounced fit to travel, on condition I take it easy and don't move around for a few days. In the intervening time I've had calls from a concerned Grace, who refuses to tell me anything apart from that everything is under control and she'll give me a full report when I get home, and Rosie, who takes a good twenty minutes to convince that I'm not at death's door. Finally satisfied, she puts Ben on the line, who wants to know when he can go to the police station again, because it was 'well cool', and then Alex, who very seriously informs me that there is a big chocolate factory in York, and am I going to bring her some back? As I end the call, there's a tap at the door, and without waiting for a response CC Manly strolls in carrying two large boxes, looking both relieved and a little self-satisfied.

'Glad to see you're still with us,' she says, dumping the boxes at the end of the bed. 'You'll be pleased to know we've identified the attacker and charged him with attempted murder. With a bit of luck, the only way he'll ever get back on the street is when his body is taken to the crematorium. He's denying he knew you were a policeman, of course – says he was hard up and he and his mates decided to replenish the coffers with a bit of random mugging. DC Draper has given his statement, and if it's okay with you I'll record yours before you leave.'

'No problem,' I say, 'although I was flat on my back and semi-conscious through most of it. Who is he, then? Colin said he was a bit old for a mugger.'

'That's where it gets interesting,' she replies. 'His name is Geoffrey Wicks, aged fifty-eight, a list of convictions as long as your arm, mainly for drug and gang-related offences – nothing in the last ten years, though. He used to be a minder for one of the big dealers in Hull, but around a decade ago there was a gang war and another outfit took over. Wicks wanted payback, so he started feeding us snippets of information on the new boys. Guess who his handler was?'

'Not Harris – he would have been well out of it by then.'

'Not Harris,' she confirms, 'but close – your recent acquaintance, DCS Jack Horner – a leading light in Harris's boys club. Plus, I take it you met Harris's pet manservant over at the home?'

I nod. 'You mean Dennis? I've never seen anyone look more out of place in a nurse's uniform.'

She grins. 'His only connection with nursing is providing the profession with more patients when the whim takes him. He's kept his nose clean recently, though, and Harris pays handsomely for his services. Those services include protection, of course, and keeping an ear to the ground. It's pretty certain he was the one who tipped Harris off about your visit. He is also – you'll love this – Geoff Wicks's nephew.'

'Jesus! So, Harris really did want us out of the way. He wasn't very subtle about it, though – does he think he's that untouchable?'

'Probably,' she replies, 'but I don't think he's that stupid. It's my guess Dennis was acting off his own bat. He's never been the sharpest tool in the box, and I expect he thought he was doing his boss a favour. I wouldn't like to be in his shoes when Harris learns about it, though.'

'What about Harris's claim that he never took on a third whistle-blower? Did Draper tell you about that?'

The air of self-satisfaction returns. 'He did – he's got a near photographic memory, that boy. I'd keep a close eye on his progress if I were you.'

'I'm starting to get the message on that one,' I agree. 'If he's going to get anywhere, he's going to have to get a bit more confidence in himself, though.'

'That's your department,' Manly says pointedly. 'It sounds to me as though you haven't given him much of a chance so far. If he were mine, I'd find a bit more time for him. We can't all be go-get-'em tough guys, and sometimes the quiet, subservient types are the ones who come up trumps.'

'Yes, Ma'am,' I say. 'You can be sure I'll pay more attention to him when I get home. Let's just say I'm starting to appreciate his qualities.'

'Good,' she says, and smiles. 'Anyway, he got us looking for the old records before the boy's club got to them, and hence,' she gestures to one of the boxes, 'here's what we've got. I'm afraid I don't have the manpower to go through every page at high speed, but if you've got someone who can trawl through it all, you might find something useful. A job for DC Draper, do you think? I'd bet you any money that he's your man when it comes to paper archives.'

I smile. 'I've got a guy on the team who's a genius with computer records,' I say, 'and I think if there's anything to find, between the pair of them, they'll find it. Leave it with me – it shouldn't take too long once they get going. One thing you could focus on, though – the mysterious Lizzie, who is supposed to have sent a message to Emily Stone. Stone told her daughter that Lizzie lived in Lancashire somewhere, but the note she allegedly sent to Emily came from Hull.'

'It's a puzzle,' she agrees. 'I'll do as much delving as I can, and send through updates, plus anything else I manage to get. In the meantime, you were muttering quite a lot in your sleep – about someone called George – a friend of yours?'

'You could say that,' I reply. 'We joined the force together. He's our desk sergeant now.'

'That figures.' She points to the other box. 'Apparently, you'd promised to go to The Kitchen in Howden to get him some cake. He's clearly a connoisseur – the place is famous in these parts. I rang the local station and asked if someone could nip round there. There should be enough to keep your friend – and the rest of your team – going for a day or two. Just call it a "get well soon" gift. Now, let's get this statement over with, and I can leave you in peace – for the moment.'

Five hours later, we arrive back in Bristol to a barrage of yet more rain and hail. Larson drives straight past my street and, ignoring my objections, pulls up outside Chrissie's and Joyce's place in Clifton.

'Sorry,' he says, with a shrug, and aims a thumb over his shoulder at Chrissie, sitting beside me in the back seat. 'Not my idea – and it's more than my life's worth to argue.'

I glance across at Chrissie, whose expression tells me not to even think about it, and let out a resigned sigh. 'Just for tonight,' I tell her, and she treats me to a derisive snort, gets out and stamps round to my side to help me onto the pavement.

As soon as I try to stand up I realise she's got a point, and meekly let her take my arm, guide me up the path and through the front door. The entire family is in attendance, and it's clear that the children, both in their pyjamas, have been given strict instructions not to run up for their usual hug, as they both hang back beside Rosie, and Ben has one hand firmly on Blue's collar in case of accidents.

'They wanted to stay up until you got here,' Rosie says, coming up and pecking my cheek. 'They were worried about you.'

Alex trots up and takes my hand. 'Are you going to die, Gandi?' she asks, her little brow furrowing.

'Not tonight, sweetheart,' I say, ruffling her hair, 'and now you know I'm still alive, isn't it time you were in bed? I'll see you in the morning, I promise.'

'You too, Ben,' Rosie says. 'Take Blue up with you, and your dad will be up in a minute, okay?'

Ben thinks about objecting, but gives up at a look from his mother and trudges off upstairs, Blue in tow. Rosie follows with Alex, leaving me alone, for the moment, with Chrissie.

'Come through and get yourself settled,' she says. 'I've let Mum know we've arrived, and she's on her way back. She's been over to visit Iris Malden, more out of curiosity about Jacob's new sister than anything else, I think.'

'News travels fast,' I comment, sinking into the sofa. Chrissie sits beside me, takes my hand, and I realise, with a small shock, that she's crying again. 'It's all right, love,' I say, putting an arm around her. 'Everything will be all right.'

She sniffs and pushes herself away so that she can look me in the eye. 'It's not, though, is it?' she says. 'And it never will be. I thought …' She hesitates, and lets out a long sigh. 'I thought,' she goes on, 'that after the divorce things might be different. I met Terry

– look what a disaster that turned out to be – and then you were shot and nearly died, and …'

Again, she pauses, and gives my hand a tight squeeze. 'I was there – at the hospital, every day – I told Mum and Rosie not to tell you. I was trying to move on …' She gives a humourless laugh. 'I'm not sure where to – maybe to a place where I wouldn't have to sit, watching you die, or wait at home for that knock on the door – you know what I'm saying? I knew you wouldn't change, and I thought if I stayed away, then maybe the constant worry would stay away too – out of sight, out of mind. I suppose that sounds childish.'

'No,' I say. 'No, it doesn't. It sounds like you did the only sensible thing you could do under the circumstances.' I give her a squeeze. 'It doesn't look like your plan worked very well though. From where I'm sitting, it seems you're still worrying.'

I hear a rueful laugh, and she relaxes against me. 'Listen, Al, I …'

The sound of my mobile shatters the fragile moment. Chrissie sighs again, and gets to her feet.

'I'd better go and help Rosie,' she says. 'Mum will be back any minute, and those cakes you brought back need to be in a fridge.'

With that, she disappears, and I dig my phone out of my pocket.

'Welcome back,' Grace says. 'I've just picked up your mother-in-law, and she's invited me back for dinner if that's all right with you?'

'Sounds like an offer you can't refuse,' I reply, 'as long as you bring me up to speed on what's been happening down here.'

'Quid pro quo,' she says, with a laugh. 'I'll see you in around fifteen minutes.'

I hear Larson coming down the stairs and try to get up off the sofa. I'm still struggling when he sticks his head round the door five minutes later.

'How are you doing?' he asks.

I think about telling him that I'm not an invalid, can manage perfectly well and to mind his own bloody business, but decide that under the circumstances, behaving like an arse is probably not the way to go.

'As well as can be expected, I suppose,' I manage to reply. 'I could do with some of those painkillers they gave me at the hospital – and a glass of whisky to wash them down.'

'Are you sure you should …' he starts, and then grins, delves in my holdall, pulls out a bottle of pills, pours me a generous tot of Scotch from Joyce's drinks cabinet, and hands them both over. 'If you keel over,' he warns, 'don't expect me to call the ambulance.'

He's about to leave when I have another thought. 'How's Draper?' I ask.

'I dropped him off at the station,' he replies. 'I offered to take him home, but he said he wanted to get his report done while everything was fresh in his memory. Polly Sillitoe is still there, and from what I hear her brief is to manhandle him to an Indian restaurant in town for a surprise party, meticulously arranged by Daz. He's the hero of the hour, whether he wants to be or not.'

I smile. 'Nice thought – he's earned it. Mind you, I'm not sure curry and beer is his thing.'

'You never know,' Larson comments drily. 'After all, until yesterday nobody thought kicking the shit out of armed assassins was his thing either.'

A commotion at the front door is followed by the appearance of Joyce and Grace. After a strict order not to move from the sofa and a promise that food won't be long, Joyce goes off to the kitchen, and my son-in-law disappears upstairs to tuck in the children.

'You had us worried for a while,' Grace comments.

'I had me worried,' I answer. 'It's just a flesh wound, though – a bloody painful one, but not serious. Colin put the bastard off his stroke.'

'I told you he'd come in handy,' she says, grinning, but then becomes serious. 'You believe Harris was behind the attack? It's what CC Manly thinks.'

'Not directly. It was far too obvious. I think his minder realised we might be a threat and decided to do his boss a favour. I suspect Dennis isn't Harris's favourite person at the moment.'

Grace nods. 'The question is, though, what is he afraid we're going to find out?'

'If I had to take a guess,' I reply, 'I'd say he knows who is responsible for the murders, or at least has a pretty good idea. The fact he doesn't want to tell us means there's history between him and whoever is pulling the strings.'

'The third man?' Grace suggests.

'Possible,' I agree. 'If so, he's been lying about not knowing who he is for decades. For my money, the key is the woman – Lizzie, or whatever her name really is. It's when I tried to question him on what he knew about her that he clammed up. According to Helen Stone, she was a third whistle-blower, and like Alice Walker, she got police protection after the case. Harris denies her involvement and says she was rejected as an informant. Then there's the letter Helen's mother received before her death, warning her she might be in danger, which resulted in Helen's trip to try to warn Alice. It feels to me like a ploy to get Helen out of the way, and maybe frame her for Alice's murder at the same time – two birds with one stone.'

'And if we were really blinkered,' Grace puts in, 'we would do exactly what we were expected to do – put all our energy into pursuing the supposedly wronged children of William Harcourt, all out for revenge on the father who abandoned both them and their mother.'

'Except whoever it is miscalculated,' I say. 'Firstly, we're not that stupid – yes, we've lost some time going after Jacob and Helen, but we could have gotten ourselves completely bogged down with all the other children, grandchildren, and on ad infinitum. In fact, we did, for a while. Second, sending Jack Horner down to Bristol was a mistake – maybe the first Harris has made in a long time, but given his low opinion of women in general, and female senior officers in particular, he probably thought it would work. In his mind, he expected that Manly would see it as cooperation, and you would be intimidated by a visit from the shadowy world of police protection. The plan backfired on both counts. Finally, the clumsy attempt on my life – and Draper's, don't forget – has a touch of desperation about it. All efforts at diversion failed, someone got out of line and made a dumb move.'

'So, who benefits?' Grace asks. 'Not Harris – that little stunt just makes him look guilty as hell. And if you're right, and he does know who's behind these murders, why is he protecting them? There can't be any mileage in laying himself open to a charge of assisting an offender, or worse.'

'Maybe the alternative *is* worse,' I suggest. 'I can only see two possibilities. Either Harris is in willing partnership with whoever is orchestrating the killings, or he's being forced to keep his mouth shut. Neither option looks particularly pretty.'

Grace hesitates, and takes a deep breath. 'It looks like Harris isn't our only problem, Al. Weston police went to pick up Rachel Harcourt this morning, and she wasn't at home. There was supposed to be someone watching the house and keeping a tail on her in case she made contact with her father, but they were called away to an incident on the Locking Road. By the time they resumed surveillance she'd left – and it looks like she won't be coming back. We've applied for a warrant to enter and do a search, but we won't get it until tomorrow.'

'Oh, for fuck's sake, Grace!' is all I can think of to comment, and then, as an afterthought, point to the bottle of Scotch Larson has left on the coffee table. 'At least we can toast one success – Daz Jackson finally managed to get DC Draper into a curry house.'

23

I'm rudely awakened by a blinding shaft of sunlight that hits me right between the eyes through a gap in the curtains. I groan, swear, and gingerly push myself into a sitting position. So far, so good – the stitches in my side protest the movement, but the pain is far more tolerable than the night before. My head is much clearer, too, although I can't quite remember how I got from the lounge to Chrissie's spare room, thanks to last night's combination of whisky and pain killers. The house is eerily quiet, and I'm trying to decide whether to risk the trip down to the kitchen when there's a light tap at the door, and Chrissie comes in carrying a tray loaded with coffee and croissants.

'How are you feeling?' she asks, setting the tray down and sitting on the edge of the bed.

'Much better, thanks,' I reply. 'Where is everyone? And what time is it?'

'Eleven o'clock,' she replies. 'Rosie and John went home last night. They'll both be at work by now. It snowed in the night – not enough to bring everything to a halt, but the schools are still closed. Ben and Alex are in the back garden with Mum, building a snowman. Blue's out there, too – I don't think she's seen snow before, and she's finding it a bit of an adventure.'

'Eleven? Jesus, Chrissie! I need to …'

'You need to stay right where you are,' she snaps, but follows up with a grin. 'Those are your boss's orders, not mine. Grace said to tell you the warrant came through and they are going through Rachel Harcourt's house now, plus, Polly is picking up Cathy Turner again, and John is helping DC Draper with that box of files you brought back from Hull. There's nothing you can do until they get back from Weston, and she will come and pick you up if you insist on ignoring medical advice – which I assume you do?'

'You assume right,' I say, as she pours us both coffee. I point to her mug. 'Looks like you're planning on staying a while.'

She nods. 'We didn't quite manage to finish our conversation last night.'

She avoids my eye, staring into her coffee mug, and suddenly there's a knot in my stomach. As usual, my first thought is that she's met someone else, or if she hasn't, she wants to back away, and tell me that this latest near disaster is just one too many.

I reach out and squeeze her arm. 'It's okay, Chrissie. Whatever it is, just say it – I'm already sitting down, and it's not as if I'm going anywhere right now.'

That draws a faint smile. 'I hope it's not that bad,' she says, 'but I've been thinking – the money I gave you before Christmas – do you still have it?'

'Of course,' I reply, trying to hide my surprise at the question, and also my suspicions of all manner of dire scenarios that might have prompted it. 'I haven't had time to even think about it, never mind spend it. But listen, Chrissie …' I take her hand. 'I don't need it, and if you're in any kind of financial trouble …'

'Oh, for God's sake, Al!' She bristles, but then lets out a bitter laugh and sighs. 'I suppose I can't blame you for thinking the worst – after all, it was me who lost our savings in the first place.'

'Then what? If there's anything you need, you know I'll help if I can.'

'I know. It's just that – well, I've been thinking, and I wondered if …' She bites her lip, takes a breath and starts again. 'I've been thinking about the divorce, and everything that's happened since, especially to you, and to Rosie – she would be in prison if you hadn't been there to clear up the mess I made of it all.' I open my mouth to protest, but she silences me with a look. 'I divorced you because I thought I couldn't live with you anymore. I know it's a bit late, but over the last few years I've realised I can't live without you either.'

She pauses again, and this time I realise she's waiting for me to say something. 'It sounds like you have a suggestion,' I say finally. 'What did you have in mind?'

This time, her laugh is a mixture of relief and incredulity. 'After everything that's happened – Terry, Rosie, me getting scammed out of all our savings – after all that, you can't think of anything else to say?'

'I suppose,' I reply, 'I could have asked you to re-marry me, but I didn't think that would go down too well.'

A flush of colour rises to her cheeks and she looks away. 'Perhaps not right now,' she admits. 'But I thought maybe … maybe we could put our money together and buy a place between us – somewhere on the coast – a little cottage or something that we could both use as a bolt hole. We could choose it together, and use it separately – or together sometimes if you wanted to – just for us, away from everything, and …' She falters, and gives me a nervous glance.

I squeeze her hand. 'It's a great idea, Chrissie. When this case is over, we can start looking – together. I'd like that.'

She nods, and leans across to kiss my cheek. 'When this case is over,' she says, 'there will be another one, and then another, and …'

'Not this time,' I interrupt. 'I promise, Chrissie. Not this time.'

By the time Grace arrives, I've managed to get up and make myself reasonably presentable. In stark contrast to yesterday, the front garden is bathed in brilliant sunshine, reflecting off a sprinkling of snow – enough to keep the children amused, but no problem to the smooth running of the city. I watch from the lounge as she makes her way up the path to the front door. Sillitoe and Larson are with her, which means something important in the case has shifted. Chrissie ushers them in and goes off to make more coffee, firmly closing the lounge door behind her.

'It looks like things are finally beginning to move,' Grace starts, making herself comfortable in an armchair. 'That trip of yours to Humberside has really stirred things up. John and Polly have been working on it since around five this morning, and we've got quite a bit to tell you. First things first, though. A thorough search of Rachel Harcourt's house in Weston has come up with bugger all so far, unless you count the fact that it looks like her disappearance was rushed, but nevertheless planned. She was going to do a runner at some point, and made sure nothing incriminating would be left behind.'

'That's probably as good an admission of guilt as we're going to get,' I say. 'But why leave it until now? And where to?'

'It looks like she was tipped off, probably by the Turners,' she replies, 'and as for where, it's my guess it's to wherever her father is. I was hoping there would be some clue in the house somewhere, but nothing yet. We haven't given up, though, so there's still a chance we'll find something.'

'So, she's known where James Harcourt is all along?'

'We think so,' she says. 'Unfortunately, we can't prove it – yet. I've been in touch with DCI Moffat in East Midlands, and he's setting things in motion to get hold of the other daughter, Sarah, as it's more than likely she's a part of it as well.'

'How do you know?' I ask.

She gestures to Sillitoe, who takes over. 'It was partly Molly Shaw's idea,' she says. 'We knew Cathy Turner was hiding something, and it was pretty clear she was scared. We checked her mobile and the house phone and found more than a dozen calls from the number registered to Rachel, and also several from Sarah.'

'Surely, that's to be expected,' I comment. 'They are cousins, and with one parent dead and the other missing, it would be odd if they weren't talking to each other, or even collaborating.'

'That's true,' Sillitoe replies. 'But then, Molly suggested we checked the husband's phone as well, and bingo!' She roots in her rucksack, digs out an evidence bag and a pair of nitrile gloves. 'Roy Turner was a bit reluctant to hand it over,' she says, pulling on the gloves and carefully taking the phone out of the bag, 'but when we explained we could get a record of just about everything on it, and charge him with wasting police time at the very least, he dropped his objection. There are two calls from a particular number, one lasting just over a minute, and the other is a voicemail.'

She dials and puts the phone on speaker. It's a man's voice, with a Northern accent – not quite the same as Harris's, though, and I guess it's perhaps a different part of Yorkshire, or maybe Lancashire. The message is short, and chilling.

Tell your wife to remember, the Mother Superior sees all and hears all. You know what will happen if she forgets.

There's a short silence while I ponder this, until I finally say, 'Who the bloody hell is the "Mother Superior"?'

'That was our first question,' Larson says, 'and we have a theory about that. The second question was, "Who is the man leaving the message?" We think we can answer that one, too.'

'Surely, that's easy enough,' I say. 'Just find out who the caller's number is registered to.'

He gives me his familiar long-suffering look – the one that tells me I'm teaching Granny to suck eggs. 'He used a burner,' he says simply. 'However, the one thing DSI Helston did find in Rachel's house was a collection of old home videos, filmed around forty or so years ago on VHS tape. Most of them feature James Harcourt with Rachel and Sarah as young children. Some also include William and Mick. One strange thing is that James's wife isn't present in any of the ones we've viewed so far. You'd think she'd feature in at least one or two. I've got Colin and Ollie White trawling through them all as we speak.'

'And the relevance of all this is …?' I ask, aware that I'm being both impatient and unreasonable.

He smiles. 'Quite a few of the videos have sound,' he answers. 'I ran a comparison between the voicemail from Roy Turner's phone and the soundtrack of a couple of the tapes and got a match. I still need to run through more samples to confirm, but I'm ninety-nine per cent sure the message on Turner's phone was from James Harcourt.'

'Good God!' I mutter. 'You think he might be Harris's third man?'

Sillitoe nods. 'And all the time we've been treating him as a potential victim, when he should have been our prime suspect. If we'd known earlier, we could have thrown a lot more resources into finding him, but he's had time to go to ground anywhere. We're checking to see if he might have left the country, and we've alerted all airports and ferry terminals, but we're definitely on the back foot.'

'When was the last call?' I ask.

'Six days ago,' she replies. 'It was made from somewhere near Leeds, but he could be anywhere by now.'

'Thanks to Cathy and Roy Turner,' I grumble. 'You interviewed them, Polly, so how come you didn't check their phones earlier? I hope you've bloody well charged the pair of them now!'

Sillitoe bridles, but Grace gets in first. 'What purpose would that serve?' she snaps. 'There were no grounds to treat them as serious suspects, so don't blame Polly. The likelihood is, we'll need them as witnesses down the line, and they've already been threatened by Harcourt. We need them to cooperate with us, and they won't do that if they feel even more intimidated.' She puts on her head prefect's expression. 'I know you've got a pain in your side, Al, but that doesn't mean you can get away with being a pain in everybody else's arse.'

'Why not?' I retort. 'I wouldn't want to change the habit of a lifetime.' She sighs, but the corners of her mouth twitch upwards in a slight grin. I hold up my hands and nod an apology to Sillitoe. 'Point taken, Ma'am.'

Chrissie chooses this moment to come in with coffee. 'Mum wants to know if you'd like sandwiches,' she says. 'It's almost lunchtime, and it will save you all having to sort out food when you get back to the station. We're making some for the children anyway, so it's no bother.'

The suggestion is met with universal enthusiasm. 'So,' I say, when she's gone, 'is James Harcourt the organ grinder, or just one of the monkeys?'

'That's the big question,' Larson replies, 'which brings us to the "Mother Superior" thing. I've been delving into James's history, and Colin's gone through that pile of documents you brought back – he must have been at it most of the night. He was mainly looking for any references to the woman we know as Lizzie. Harris says she was considered as an informant but rejected as unreliable. If that's the case, there should be some record of the interview, even if the subject isn't mentioned by name. Colin found meticulous records of the activities of Emily Stone, and also Alice Walker. Pseudonyms were used throughout, but comparing the content with what we already know, their identities are pretty clear. There are also reports on two other potential candidates, both male, but nothing on any other females. Either Lizzie is a fiction, or someone got to the files before we did.'

'Bugger it!' I comment. 'It was a long shot, though. Harris was too quick to point us to the archive – he knew damned well it had been sanitised – probably years ago. So, what about James Harcourt? Did you manage to dig up anything interesting on him?'

'That depends on what you call "interesting",' he replies. 'We know he grew up in West Yorkshire, second son of Old Bill Harcourt, and just a couple of years younger than his brother, William. He got married in 1967, to one Lisa May Buckley, and they had twin daughters, Rachel and Sarah, a few months later. They separated early in 1969, but it looks like they stayed on good terms. He stayed close by until the children left school, and moved down to Weston when Rachel got a place at what was then Bristol Polytechnic – University of the West of England now. Until he retired, he worked as a self-employed Jack-of-all-trades builder, and by all accounts was fairly highly regarded by his clientele. Before that, though, it's all a bit murky. I managed to find a record for him as the director of a limited company dealing in mainly imported timber in the 1960s and 70s.'

'Couple that with several convictions in his teens for possession, threatening behaviour and aggravated burglary, and it's a good bet he wasn't just importing planks of wood,' Grace puts in. 'He did a couple of six-month stints in a young offender's institution, but nothing more serious than that. Then he seemed to fall off the radar. However, some of the company he kept definitely didn't.'

'Between 1963 and 1966, the company had a co-director, a man called Matthew Brennan, well known to the police as a fraudster and local mob kingpin,' Larson says, taking up the tale. 'In 1966 Brennan shot and killed a rival gang boss, and was sentenced to life. He died in prison. He and Harcourt had been friends since childhood, and there's no doubt their company was a cover for a range of illegal activities.'

'Including child trafficking?' I ask.

'It's highly likely,' Grace says, 'but nothing was ever proven. Back then, the force didn't have the technical resources we use nowadays, so hard evidence was more difficult to find. In fact, I doubt it was ever considered. There would have been much more emphasis on drug smuggling.' She nods for Larson to go on.

'Now we get to the interesting bit,' he says. 'James Harcourt continued as sole director of the company until the late 1970s, when it appears to have been liquidated. It's impossible to say what happened to the assets – we're looking at a good forty years ago, but there are no records of Harcourt ever claiming benefits, and his handyman business in Weston was very casual, so wouldn't have earned him a fortune. Yet he owned a fairly substantial property, and both his daughters' houses were paid for in cash, the source of which is unclear. I don't have access to the bank records, but I'd put any money on those funds coming from offshore accounts.'

There's a tap at the door, and Joyce comes in with a huge pile of assorted sandwiches, closely followed by Bluebell, who does a round of enthusiastic greetings before settling herself at my feet. Joyce diplomatically bows out and leaves us to chew on both sandwiches and new information in silence.

I'm halfway through my second helping of ham and mustard when the tumblers start to click into place.

'It's all of them,' I declare, wondering why it's taken this long for me to see it.

'All of who?' Grace asks.

James, Rachel, Sarah and Lisa – the whole family,' I say. 'They could have done it, if they were all working together. The three murders down here were committed at roughly the same time. We can place Rachel in the Malden house, alone, sometime before the killings, with the opportunity to replace those knives with fakes – and to lift Jacob's birth certificates. She knew how to disable the alarm, so it's my bet she's the one who killed Charles Malden, while James was in West Hill murdering his brother William. Allowing for a small time difference – say around a thirty-minute window for time of death, either of them could have gotten to Downside Nursing Home and Alice Walker. We need to go through all the CCTV footage of the reception area again, plus footage from the rear of the building if there are cameras there – has anyone checked?'

'We didn't see the need once we'd identified Helen Stone,' Sillitoe says. 'I'll get onto it right away.'

I give her a nod. 'Meanwhile,' I go on, 'Sarah was in Burton-on-Trent making her perfectly timed attack on Emily Stone.'

'And what about Lisa?' Larson asks. 'Where does she fit in?'

'That's where I need you to make a leap of faith,' I reply. 'All I know is that in my admittedly damaged mind, it makes sense. You say James and Lisa separated in 1969, yes?'

Larson nods. 'James started divorce proceedings, but never went through with it.'

'I'll bet he didn't,' I say. 'I haven't quite worked out why, yet, but I have a feeling it was more a business decision than an emotional one. It suited them to look as if they were apart – it's a known strategy in criminal circles – when one member of a couple is threatened, feigning divorce helps protect the other. The question is, in this case, who was protecting whom? Maybe it worked both ways. In any case, I'm pretty sure it was a sham. The point is, we have the historical Greendale forced adoptions, the fact that one of the main criminals was never caught, four current murder cases all connected to Greendale Lodge, and an attempt to frame the adopted children for at least two of the killings. One of those attempts – sending Helen Stone down to try to warn Alice Walker, was instigated by a woman about whom we have a conspicuous lack of information, and who goes by the name of Lizzie – am I the only one who sees a link – a tenuous one, granted – between James Harcourt and the mysterious Lizzie?'

Grace blinks at me, and then catches up with my thought.

'Christ almighty, Al,' she says. 'Lizzie – Lisa? It's a long shot, but if it's true, it's no wonder Don Harris tried to hide the fact that he tried to recruit her.'

'What if he didn't try?' I say. 'What if he succeeded? He recruited an informant who was feeding him misinformation while passing valid information on the police operation back to the criminals, and that's how come he never caught whoever was masterminding the whole thing.'

'And you think that might have been James Harcourt?'

'Actually,' I reply, 'I'm not too sure. If – and it's a big if – the Mother Superior is, in fact, Lisa Harcourt, a.k.a. Lizzie, we might have fallen into the same trap Don Harris did – assuming the head of the operation was a man. Just think of it – Humberside's greatest misogynist fucked over by a woman. No wonder he's kept it quiet all these years. I think we'd better bloody well get hold of James Harcourt. Then, we'll find out.'

24

I walk into the squad room to a round of applause from the assembled team, plus a couple of whistles from Daz Jackson and the newly returned Ollie White, fresh from a week in the Med, sporting world class panda eyes and a white stripe at his hairline that no amount of combing has managed to conceal. Draper, I notice, is hunched over his desk, looking distinctly sheepish. I announce a briefing in fifteen minutes, and beckon him to follow me into my office.

'Are you sure you're all right?' I ask. Close up he looks even more as if he's just got back from an all-night rave.

'Sorry, sir,' he says, flushing. 'It's just – well, I don't really drink much you see, and I'm not sure, but I think someone might have put a couple of vodkas into my orange juice last night. I've just got a bit of a headache, that's all.'

I just about manage not to grin, and at the same time decide to have a stiff word with the prime suspect for that sort of prank, Daz Jackson. 'I'm sure they didn't mean any harm, Colin,' I reassure him. 'It's just their way of saying thank you for saving my arse – but even so, it's not on. If you want to go home and sleep it off, that's fine with me.'

He straightens up. 'No, sir – of course not. I've had some painkillers, and I'll be fine once they kick in, honestly.'

'Good,' I say. 'In that case, if you're up to it, I'd like you to go over to Weston, hunt down someone from their forensic team and get them to find you samples of Rachel Harcourt's hair, or a toothbrush – anything that might give us decent DNA, plus the same from her father's house. Then, rush them over to Maggie Ainsworth at the lab. Tell her we want an urgent comparison and need the results yesterday. If she complains, she can give me a call. Think you can manage that?'

'Yes, sir, of course.' He makes his way out, relieved to be out of the limelight.

Back in the squad room, I put forward my theory concerning Lisa Harcourt, and ex-DCS Harris's possible involvement with her, together with the possibility of all the murders being committed by James, Rachel, Sarah and possibly Lisa. There's a long silence while everyone thinks it over, until Jackson finally voices the word that's on everybody's mind.

'Why?'

I nod for him to go on.

'I mean,' he says, 'yes, they could have done it, and there's some circumstantial evidence, especially as far as Rachel Harcourt is concerned, with her pretending to be someone else to gain access to Malden's house, switch the daggers and so on, and there's James's voicemail to Roy Turner, but why? What's the motive? And why would James want to murder his own brother? Sorry, boss, but it just doesn't make sense.'

'I know, Daz,' I say. 'We don't have a motive and we don't have any hard evidence – we don't even know if Lisa Harcourt and the woman who sent the note signing herself "E" are the same person. The one individual I'm pretty damned sure does know is Don Harris, and when I questioned him on Lizzie's identity, I had a gang of thugs trying to permanently warn me off minutes later. I think that tells us Harris knows exactly what's going on – he knows who and why, and either he's not cooperating because he's in it up to his neck, or because he's been running scared for the last forty years, or both. I'm not convinced that his reputation is the only thing he's protecting, and one way or another, I'm going to find out exactly what his involvement is. The other avenue to the truth is the Turners. It's time they realised how much trouble they're in with us, so we need to lean on them until they get the message. Polly and Daz – that's your job. Cut the "good cop, bad cop" routine, and go for "mad, bad and dangerous to know", okay?'

'You got it, boss,' Sillitoe says, with an enthusiastic grin in Daz's direction.

I consider for a minute, and then add, 'Molly, the Turners – Cathy in particular – seem to trust you. Let Daz and Polly play the tough guys, and whenever there's a break, go in with tea and sympathy – you know the sort of thing. Tell them we'll protect them, make sure nobody gets to them, whatever they want to hear. People often say things when they are off-guard, especially if they're nervous. Do you think you can manage that?'

She looks dubious, and glances nervously around the rest of the team. She's built up a relationship with Cathy Turner, and it's a hard step to take – one of the big differences between the mindset of an average uniform on the street and the work of a halfway decent detective. She's at a crossroads, and everyone else knows it.

She blinks once, stiffens, and says, 'Yes, sir. I'll do my best.'

'Do more than your best,' I tell her. 'Lives may depend on it.'

I turn to my son-in-law. 'I want you and Ollie to keep looking for any more records that might give a clue as to where Lisa Harcourt might be. If we work on the assumption that she's still somewhere in the north of England, that might help focus the search – not much I know, but it's something. I'm fairly sure that wherever she is, the rest of the family will be close by. Robbie – get over to Jacob Malden's flat and see if you can get Iris talking about her visit to Yorkshire when Jacob was adopted. Ask her what and who she remembers – you never know, she may have seen something significant without realising it. Take some photos with you, of James and William Harcourt, and Don Harris, preferably as they were in the 1960s if we can dig any up. There's a slim chance she might recognise one of them. Also, Helen Stone might have more to tell us if we ask the right questions – for example, did her parents ever get any odd visits, letters or phone calls that created an uncomfortable atmosphere – just follow your instincts and see where it goes.' I take a breath. 'Does anyone have any other suggestions?'

Larson waves his hand in the air. 'There's still the case of Mick Harcourt's death,' he says. 'Given the hints that it may not have been an accident, even though that was the coroner's verdict, there may have been some accusations or statements made around the time of the inquest that haven't been gone through.'

It's a reasonable point. 'Good idea,' I tell him. 'Add it to the list.'

'What about you, boss?' Sillitoe asks.

'First,' I say, 'I'm going to the lab. There are a few things I need to discuss with Maggie. Then, I'm going to try to think of a way to get to Don Harris that doesn't end up in another visit to A&E.'

'Do you have any idea,' Maggie complains, yanking open one of her desk drawers with unnecessary force, 'just how many requests I've got in my pending file? Damn it – where the bloody hell did I put that bag of humbugs?'

'Try the other drawer,' I suggest. 'And yes, I know you've probably got dozens of jobs outstanding, but I'll bet there aren't any other quadruple murder cases on your books.'

'Aha!' She pulls out a crumpled paper bag and throws it triumphantly on top of a sheaf of papers. 'I knew they were somewhere. Help yourself.'

I take one and examine it dubiously. 'Christ, Maggie – how long have they been in there? This one's gone completely soft.'

She shrugs. 'No idea – six months, maybe? Don't be so picky – the texture might be sub-optimal, but they taste the same.' She peels off an unpleasantly gelatinous wrapper and pops one into her mouth. 'That's better. Now I can think. You say you want a DNA analysis on three samples?'

I nod. 'DC Draper is on his way with two of them – from a hairbrush belonging to Rachel Harcourt, and a couple of used razor blades he picked out of James Harcourt's bin. The other is the letter I sent through that was received by Emily Stone.'

'Ah – that was an interesting one.'

'You mean you've looked at it already? For God's sake, why didn't you say?'

She grins. 'As you've pointed out, Al, it is relevant to four murders, and I've been working on it with Rick Baines over in East Midlands. I didn't want to say anything until I got a result from him, and he only got back to me around an hour ago. I would have called you, but as I knew you'd be coming over I thought I'd wait.'

I can tell from the smug look on her face that she's working up to a big reveal, and realise I'm holding my breath.

'Well?' I ask, after a suitable pause for effect, 'Are you going to spit it out, or do I have to guess?'

She relents and gives me a nod. 'In my experience, and probably in yours as well,' she says, 'it doesn't matter how careful a criminal is, they can never cover their tracks completely. There's always at least one little forensic mistake. In this case, there are two. There are several sets of fingerprints on the envelope – to be expected, as it was sent by post, and handled by goodness knows who. The letter itself, however, has only three. Thank goodness your people had the good sense not to handle it without gloves. We've identified one set as belonging to the fourth victim, Emily Stone. I'd take a guess that one of the other two belongs to her daughter, Helen. The third, by process of elimination, will be the writer of the letter.'

'That's useful to know,' I say. 'We can take prints from Helen easily enough, to tell us which is which. It doesn't get us any closer to identifying whoever wrote it, though.'

'Not by itself, no,' she agrees. 'And that brings me to the second mistake. Whoever wrote it licked the envelope to seal it. There was enough saliva to get a profile.'

For a moment I'm lost for words. 'You're bloody joking!' I say finally.

'I think the phrase you are looking for is "Thank you, Maggie",' she says, grinning. 'And once your DC arrives with the samples from the Harcourts, we should be able to get those profiles and compare them – assuming that's what you were about to ask for?'

I have to laugh, which sends a painful jolt through the stitches in my side. 'Why do all pathologists have to be wind-up merchants?' I comment, when the pain has subsided.

'We all watched *Star Trek* in the sixties,' she replies, without taking a beat. 'You remember Scotty – tell the boss a thing will take days – do it in hours and your reputation hits the ceiling. There's a lot to be learned from TV.'

'Pity you never watched any consumer programmes.' I point at her bag of rancid humbugs. 'You might have learned something about sell-by dates and the risk of salmonella.'

'Chief Inspector,' she says, putting on an air of mock condescension, 'in all my years of establishing causes of death, I have never yet come across a case of salmonella caused by out-of-date confectionery. That's not to say it's impossible, but I'd put the odds at several billion to one. Take Cyril, for example – I had a friend who worked for the Department of Agriculture, and he found a chicken that had been frozen since 1944. Nobody wanted it, so I took it home, and finally defrosted it a few years ago. I thought it best to try Cyril with it first, and no ill effects at all – I had a roast chicken dinner the next day and I'm still here. Mind you, Cyril had terrible wind …'

'I thought you said there were no ill effects,' I comment, imagining the inevitable results of Cyril's post-prandial flatulence.

I'm saved from further discussion on the state of Cyril's digestive system by a tap at the door, and Draper makes an appearance with two plastic evidence bags. He still looks a bit pasty, and after looking him up and down, Maggie takes matters into her own hands.

'Grab a seat, young man,' she says, and fires up the coffee machine, relieves him of the bags and slips out to deliver them to her assistant.

'Whatever you do,' I have time to warn him, 'if Maggie offers you a humbug, don't take one. I think they've been in her drawer since the abdication.'

'Thanks for the warning, sir,' he replies, 'but I can never eat anything when I come over here – it's the thought of what they might be doing downstairs, if you know what I mean.'

'I don't think any of us likes that part of the job, Colin,' I say, 'any more than we like discovering the victims. You'll have to get used to it, though, if you're going to be part of a unit that deals with serious crime. What I've never understood is why anyone would want to become a pathologist and stare at people's innards all day.'

'And I've never understood,' Maggie says, hovering in the open doorway, 'why anyone would want to be a police officer and spend their days getting stabbed or shot at. Each to their own, I suppose.' She pours three coffees and settles herself back behind her desk. 'I've put Maisie straight onto those samples. We'll get them done as soon as possible and compare the results with the ones from the envelope. As soon as you get prints from Helen Stone, send them across and we'll eliminate them. With a bit of luck, that will just leave the ones from your suspect.'

'Thanks, Maggie,' I say. 'All we need now is some way of getting the information we need from ex-DCS Harris, and I can't see him cooperating anytime soon.'

'I'm afraid I can't help you with that one,' she says. 'Although …' She pauses, and sips her coffee thoughtfully. 'From what I've heard, he had a bit of an attitude when it came to gender politics. Do you know if he was ever married?'

'He still does have an attitude,' I reply, 'and if he *was* married, he certainly isn't now.'

'Well,' she goes on, 'he's getting on a bit, so he might have been widowed, but what if he was divorced at some point? Men like that tend to be control freaks at home, and when the wife finally gets fed up with it and leaves, it's usually with a pretty big axe to grind. It might be worth hunting around to see if there's an ex – maybe even more than one – still alive and longing for the chance to get her own back.'

Draper and I exchange a glance. 'Maggie,' I say finally, 'you're wasted as a pathologist – you should have been a policewoman.'

25

Two hours, and a hefty dose of pain killers later, I'm in my office, wondering whether it might be wise to take at least some notice of the hospital's advice not to overdo it, when there's a sharp rap at the door and Larson bursts in, looking excited.

'I think we're onto something,' he says, and then stops, looking concerned. 'You know, you look bloody awful.' He checks his watch. 'It's almost five, and it's started snowing again. Maybe I should give you a lift home? I can transfer the files to my laptop and take you through it all there?'

For once, I don't have the strength to argue, and manage to swallow my usual knee-jerk resentment at any positive suggestion my son-in-law makes.

'I've had better days,' I admit, 'but …'

I'm interrupted by the grating tones of *Also Sprach Zarathustra* – Larson's ringtone. He picks up, listens, says, 'Hang on, I'm putting you on speaker,' and sets the phone on my desk. It's Rosie.

'Hi Dad,' she says. 'I'm on my way to Clifton. We're all going to stay there tonight – Mum and Gran are concerned about the snow. Mum says, will you come over here, too? Otherwise, they'll spend the whole night worrying about you as well.'

Larson raises an eyebrow, and I let out a sigh of defeat. 'Tell your mother we'll be there in around an hour,' I say, and end the call. 'I need to catch up with Polly and Daz before we go,' I tell Larson.

I don't add that getting out of my chair might turn out to be a bit of a struggle until the painkillers kick in. Larson has already figured that out, though. 'I'll send Colin down to the interview rooms if you like,' he says, and I nod.

A few minutes later, Jackson and Sillitoe appear, looking tired and frustrated.

'We're getting nowhere fast,' Sillitoe says, flopping into a chair. 'The husband is still refusing to say a word – he's trying to protect his wife, however misguided that may be. As for Cathy, I'd say we need to call in the duty psychiatrist. The state she's in, I'm not sure she's fit to be charged. If we're going to hang onto her much longer, we could be laying ourselves open to all kinds of trouble if it turns out she isn't faking it.

'And if we let her go,' Jackson puts in, 'and she decides to do something stupid, that could rebound on us, too.'

'Do it,' I say. 'Either she's fit to be charged, or fit to be sectioned. Either way, she will be in a secure environment and out of harm's way. You can charge the husband though – he's clearly been withholding information. We've got enough to do that, at least, and it means we can hang onto him for the time being. Once the duty medic has sorted out the wife, you can both go home. The same goes for Molly. Do you know what's happening with Robbie?'

'She's still over with the Maldens,' Sillitoe answers. 'Karen needed a break, so Robbie's taken over until tomorrow. With luck, she'll be able to get more out of Iris this evening – I've arranged to meet up with her first thing in the morning.'

'Thanks, Polly – and you too, Daz. Fingers crossed we get a bit more movement overnight, one way or another.'

Fifteen minutes later, I'm satisfied I can leave things to tick over at the station until morning, and only have one more important task to see to. I retrieve a large paper carrier from the squad room fridge containing half the cakes and pastries kindly donated by Humberside's chief constable, and then head downstairs with my son-in-law to where George Saint is ensconced, as usual, behind the counter at the front desk.

'Courtesy of Chief Constable Manly,' I tell him, dumping the bag on the counter.

He takes a peek, blinks, and for once is lost for words. Eventually, he manages to tear his gaze away from the assorted cakes, pastries and sausage rolls from Howden's Kitchen, and manages to comment, 'Bloody hell!' He quickly follows it up with, 'Thanks, Al – this lot will keep me going for a few days.'

'It would keep a normal person going a few weeks,' I reply, 'and you owe me, George.'

'The thing about bribery, Al,' he says, deadpan, 'is that usually works.'

My mind goes back to ex-DCS Harris. 'You know,' I say, 'I've been thinking the same thing myself.'

Despite my impatience, I know that whatever Larson has uncovered, I'll need to revive my mental faculties in order to take it in, so stick to less taxing subjects on the way home.

'How's Ben?' I ask.

He frowns. 'I'm not sure. I sat him down last night and we had a long talk, but he still doesn't quite understand how much danger he and Marcus were in, and what could have happened if Clive Gingell hadn't been around. I suppose it's all a bit beyond kids of that age. All he can talk about is how exciting it was to see where his dad and grandad worked. I'm hoping Rosie can get through to him – she can be much more terrifying than me!'

'She takes after her mother,' I comment. 'Believe me, son, once she gets going, Ben will be on a hiding to nothing.'

He doesn't answer, but I see the corner of his mouth quirk into a smile. After a short silence, he says, 'That boy – Clive – I keep thinking maybe there's something Rosie and I can do for him. After all, he may well have saved Ben's life. What do you think?'

I consider, and then reply, 'It's a good thought, but not a very practical one. After the business with Kyriaku, I made an agreement with Shark Johnson and got the kid into school. He's a bright lad, and so far, Shark has kept to his side of the bargain. It's a very fine line, though. If it gets known he's receiving gifts from the police, or people working for the police, he could easily be taken for an informant, and his life would be on the line. If you give him something valuable, he'll either sell it, someone will steal it, or Shark will get his hands on it and Clive will never see it again. If you want to leave it with me for a few days, though, I'll try to think of something.'

He nods. 'I suppose you know these people better than I do. I'm just the resident nerd after all.'

There's no answer to that. When I glance across at him, though, I catch the tail end of a grin as he pulls up outside the Clifton house. The snow is settling in earnest as we make our way up the path. Ben and Alex are glued to the front window, mesmerised by the sight of flakes as big as thumbnails swirling in the light from the street lamps. Their heads disappear as they rush out to greet us at the front door. For the next five minutes, we're subjected to a barrage of barking from Blue, and two over-excited children competing over who can shout the loudest. Eventually, Larson takes charge and puts on his rarely displayed stern face, accompanied by an equally intimidating – at least to young children – 'shut-up-or-there'll-be-trouble' voice, and the cacophony subsides.

'Sorry, Grandad,' Ben says, when he's got his breath back. 'I forgot you'd been stitched up.'

'Don't worry, it happens all the time,' I mutter, and seeing his confused expression add, 'It's fine, Ben. It's not every day it snows like this. Your Dad and I have to talk now – why don't you take Alex into the kitchen to help with dinner, and we'll get together later.'

They both reluctantly troop off, and my son-in-law and I breathe a joint sigh of relief.

'I'll go and grab a couple of beers, and let everyone know we'll be working for another half-hour or so,' he says and leaves me to sink gratefully onto the sofa in the lounge.

A couple of minutes later, Larson reappears with his laptop and two bottles – a craft beer for me, and his usual lager.

'You're going to find this very interesting,' he says, powering up the machine and setting it on the coffee table so that we can both see. 'It looks like Maggie Ainsworth's suggestion was on the nose.' He brings up four photographs, all of young women – a couple of them very young, I'd guess in their mid-teens. 'I've arranged them in chronological order.' He points to the first image. 'This is Harris's first wife, Elsie. They married in 1954. He was twenty, she was nineteen. They divorced in 1963. She cited unreasonable behaviour and adultery. She was successful on the unreasonable behaviour, but the adultery accusation was dropped. I think I know why.'

He indicates the second photograph. 'Lorna, the second wife – aged fifteen in 1963. If the charge of adultery had stuck, he would have been convicted of having sex with a minor.'

'Jesus!' I mutter. 'He must have pressured her into making that one disappear – or got someone to do it for him.'

Larson nods. 'He married Lorna two weeks after she turned sixteen in 1964. There was an age gap of fifteen years. She filed for divorce in 1968, again citing unreasonable behaviour and adultery. This time both counts succeeded.' He moves on. 'The third wife, Miriam, lasted five years – married in 1970, died of cancer in 1975. Finally,' he points to the fourth image, 'Jean, married Harris in 1983, aged twenty. He was fifty. They separated six years later, but it was another seven years before the divorce. She left the marital home and was taken in by a refuge. Reading between the lines, it's possible she tried to get a divorce on the grounds of domestic violence, but was coerced into dropping it. Once they had been apart for the statutory length of time, she didn't need his consent so was able to get the divorce without his input.'

'So, where are they now?' I ask. 'One died, but what about the others? And were there any offspring from any of these marriages?'

Larson shakes his head. 'There were no children. Elsie and Jean are both now deceased, but luckily for us, Lorna is still alive, in her mid-seventies, and – you won't believe this – living in South Gloucestershire, less than twenty miles away.'

'Bloody hell! And thanks – that's great work,' I say, which draws a raised eyebrow from my son-in-law. 'But what is she doing in the West Country? It's a long way from Hull.'

'I thought you might ask that,' he replies. 'Lorna turns out to be quite an interesting character. After the divorce, she reverted to her maiden name – Villiers. Does "Lorna Villiers" mean anything to you?'

I shake my head. 'Should it?'

He laughs. 'I suppose it's not really your thing. She was an athlete and a bit of a trailblazer for women's sport back in the day. She managed to get sponsorship from a Gloucestershire conglomerate to compete in the 1972 Olympics and was one of the first women to run in the 1500 metres. 1972 was the first year of the event. She came sixth. Four years later, though, she won the bronze medal. Later on, she became a campaigner for women's rights and set up an organisation pushing for equality in sport. In the 1980s she was awarded an MBE for services to sporting charities. Apparently, she's still in good health and goes for a morning run every day. She never remarried, although I imagine she had plenty of offers – maybe those years with Harris put her off the idea.'

'Which means,' I say, 'if she's willing to talk to us, she could be a goldmine of information on Harris?'

'Grace has already contacted her,' he says, 'and Lorna's agreed to meet her, plus another officer, tomorrow morning at her home. I told Grace I'd pass the information on, and she said to tell you to be in her office by eight a.m. if you want to go along and you are recovered enough. If not, she'll take Polly.'

'Don't worry,' I tell him. 'I wouldn't miss it for the world.'

There's a tap at the door and Joyce pokes her head round to tell us Dinner's ready.

'How are you feeling?' she asks me.

I smile. 'Better,' I reply, 'than I have for quite a while.'

26

There's a definite glint of excitement in Grace's eye as we drive up the M5 towards Thornbury in South Gloucestershire.

'I'm afraid I've annoyed Polly Sillitoe,' she says, grinning. 'Apparently Lorna Villiers has been a heroine of hers since she was a kid. The thing is, she was one of mine, too. I heard her speak at a couple of London demos on women's rights when I was a constable. She was impressive. I couldn't pass up the chance to meet her face to face.'

'Let's hope it's worth it,' I comment. 'There's a lot of water passed under the bridge since you were a constable, and when Polly gets in a sulk it's a bit like trying to push a car with a flat battery up a steep hill.'

She laughs. 'Don't worry. I'm sure we'll need to talk to Ms Villiers more than once, and I promised Polly she could have second bite. After all, there's no point being DSI if I can't pull rank now and then.' She pauses to negotiate our way off the motorway and check the satnav for the next turning. 'It is strange, though,' she goes on, heading for the town centre, 'that all the time I was working under Don Harris, I never guessed there was any connection between him and Villiers. He never mentioned any of his wives, or talked about his home life – his only social activity seemed to be taking his male colleagues to the pub after work.'

'There was no reason to think they were connected,' I say. 'From what you and others have said, she seems to have been a bit of a firebrand in her day – not at all the sort of woman who would attract a man like Harris. Perhaps that's why the marriage failed. I just hope that whatever she has to say helps us get to the bottom of what's going on now. It all happened a long time ago, and we could be wasting our time.'

'It might have been a long time ago,' Grace replies, 'but she's the only witness we have who was on the scene when Harris was investigating Greendale Lodge, so we'll just have to cross our fingers she remembers something useful.'

We pull up at a modest detached house, part of a small housing development that I guess was built sometime in the 1970s, the kind that had its streets named after British wildlife – flowers, birds and so on. This particular estate opted for animals, and Lorna Villiers resides at number twenty-three, Otter Crescent. Her front door opens as we step out of the car, and we are greeted by a tall, lithe figure who looks closer to someone in their late fifties than mid-seventies. She strides down the path, opens her front gate and holds out a hand.

'You must be Detective Superintendent Helston,' she says to Grace, and then, to me, 'and Chief Inspector Crow.' Her handshake is dry, and firm, and there's a spark in her eye that tells me this is a woman who doesn't miss much. 'Come on in,' she says, with an infectious smile. 'I've got the kettle on.'

We're shown into a neat, tasteful lounge, one wall of which is filled with framed certificates charting our hostess's illustrious and varied career. There are awards for athletics, charity work, a degree in social policy, and an honorary doctorate from the University of Exeter. The most recent I can pick out is a photograph taken just a couple of years ago, of Villiers, surrounded by a group of teenage girls wearing tracksuits bearing the logo *Thornbury WAC.* She joins us, carrying a tray of tea and biscuits, and gestures for us to sit on the sofa, placing the tray on a coffee table and taking an armchair opposite.

'You said on the phone you wanted to talk to me about my former husband?' she begins, and can't prevent a ripple of distaste from flitting across her face.

'Ms Villiers,' I start, but at once she interrupts.

'Lorna, please.'

I nod. 'Lorna – I know this may be uncomfortable for you, but …'

She snorts. 'Not at all, Chief Inspector. Perhaps it might have been, a long time ago, but believe me, I haven't given Donald Harris a thought in more than fifty years. We weren't married that long, and a lot has happened in my life since then. I could even say I was grateful to him in a way. He made me a stronger person – showed me what I was capable of. What do you want to know?'

'What kind of person was he?' Grace asks. 'I mean, as a husband, rather than as a police officer. I know you probably can't tell us much about his work, but we'd like any insights you can give us about his behaviour during the time you were with him.'

She fiddles with the teapot, pours us each a cup, and then gives us a wry grin. 'You mean,' she says pointedly, 'was he really as much of a bastard as you think he was. The answer is, you don't know the half of it. I was fourteen when I met him. He was twenty-nine. I was still at school and training in athletics. I suppose I was already used to being controlled; up at 5 a.m. every day, including weekends, being bullied by male coaches into running faster, keeping my weight down, constantly doing exercises and watching my diet. You must know what life is like for young athletes with promise. I was a great hope for the future, and back then, one of the big pressures was to compete with the Eastern Block. That meant taking performance-enhancing drugs. I always refused, and the pressure increased. Don was chasing illegal drug runners at the time, and he interviewed me as part of one of his investigations.'

She pauses, and takes a sip of her tea. 'I didn't know then,' she goes on, 'that he had a thing about young girls. He was charming and good-looking – the kind of man you thought you could trust to look after you – and he was a policeman. In those days, everyone respected the police, thought they had integrity and would protect the innocent. He told me my coach was part of a drug dealing ring, and I could be implicated, my career ruined, but if I agreed to go out for dinner with him, he'd make sure it was all swept under the carpet. It would be easy for me to tell you I was coerced into it, but the truth is, I was mesmerised by him. I thought he was my guardian angel. Christ – I was only a kid, and I hung on his every word.'

'Was it true? About your coach and the drugs, I mean?' Grace asks. 'Did you ever find out?'

'It was a complete lie.' She shakes her head, presses her lips together in a thin line, and then sits back with a sigh. 'It was part of his – what do you call it? *Modus operandi* – I think that's the phrase. Pick your target, isolate them, make them think you are the only person they can rely on, that you are protecting them from some terrible fate … In a way it's true. The threat is real, but it's something the abuser creates to manipulate the victim. Don was in a position to construct whatever criminal charges he liked against just about anybody – girlfriends, colleagues, anyone who got in his way, and everyone knew he could make them stick. I didn't realise it at the time, of course. I was just madly in love, or thought I was.'

'Did you know he was married?' I ask.

She nods. 'He told me, but not until he knew I was in too deep to object. He spun me a line about his wife being an unhinged harridan who hated him and would do anything to make his life miserable. He was filing for divorce, he said – another lie – she was divorcing him. We'd been going out for around a year when his wife came to see me one night. She warned me to stay away from him, told me what he was really like, but of course, I didn't listen. I was besotted.' She sighs again. 'The divorce came through, and just after my sixteenth birthday, we got married. That's when the trouble started.'

'Trouble? What kind of trouble?'

She gives me an almost pitying look. 'I take it you've met the man. What kind of trouble do you think? He doesn't have real relationships – he controls people – women particularly, but not exclusively. He can't bear the thought of anything happening that he's not in charge of, whether that's at work or home. For me, that meant I had to give up athletics and become a housewife. Daily life was meticulously planned – what I wore, who came to the house, when I cooked, cleaned, did the shopping, and so on and so on. I had no friends, my parents were barely tolerated, and only when he was present and able to monitor our conversations. Within months it became a living hell. I was trapped. If I tried to leave, he made all kinds of threats. He was a policeman, beyond reproach, capable of ruining not just my life, but my family's as well, plus all my former friends. I have no doubt he would have carried out any threat he made.'

'But you did manage to find a way out,' Grace points out. 'How? Something must have happened to give you back some control.'

'Oh, it did,' Lorna replies. 'He was put in charge of the Greendale Lodge investigation. It was a long, drawn-out case. He never spoke to me about it, of course, but officers were coming and going at all hours, and I spent my time making coffee and food for them all. They behaved as if I wasn't there, so I pretty much learned everything that was going on. The other thing I learned was that he was having an affair with one of the women working at the lodge. A couple of his constables were in the kitchen one day, joking about it, wondering what the girl's fiancé would do when he found out she was "up the duff" as they put it. That's when I finally snapped. He'd always told me he never wanted children, you see, and that I should make sure I never got pregnant. I confronted him, and he became violent – he'd always been very careful not to abuse me physically, so I must have touched a nerve. I ended up in hospital with a broken arm. A policewoman came to take a statement, and although I was too scared to press charges against him, she got me a place in a women's refuge. I never went back.'

Grace and I exchange a look. 'Do you know who the other woman was?'

She shakes her head. 'Not by name, no. I tried to find out because I wanted her named in the divorce proceedings, but of course, everyone on his team closed ranks. All I managed to learn was that she was an employee at the Lodge – some kind of secretary. In truth, I was glad I didn't find out. Knowing Don as I did, I realised he probably used the same technique he did with all his women – a combination of charm and coercion.'

'You don't know, then, if the rumour about her being pregnant was true?' I ask. 'If she was, it would help us to know what happened to the child.'

'Oh, I'm sure it was true,' she replies, 'from the way his cronies were talking about it. But it wasn't just that. Don was going to contest the divorce until my solicitor threatened to identify the other woman and investigate a possible pregnancy, which would eventually have led to a paternity test. He folded immediately, and offered to admit to unreasonable behaviour and adultery on condition the identity of the other party wasn't revealed. I admit, I was a little surprised at the time, but I suppose he was protecting his reputation – and his bank balance if he ended up supporting a child.' She grimaces. 'One thing I do know for certain is that it wouldn't have been to protect the woman's honour. I'm sorry I can't tell you more.'

'Actually, Lorna,' I tell her, 'I think you've told us exactly what we needed to know. Thank you – you've been a great help.'

She cocks her head on one side. 'Is that right, Chief Inspector? In that case, I'm very glad to have been of assistance.'

Grace gets up and holds out a hand. 'I'm very pleased to have met you, Lorna,' she says. 'Will you be willing to speak to us again, if we find we need more information?'

'Of course,' Villiers replies, shaking our hands. 'I suppose you can't tell me what it's all about. A shame – I do have rather a curious streak, and if you are investigating Don Harris, that definitely piques my interest.'

Grace laughs. 'I promise you, as soon as the case is concluded, I will make sure someone comes and tells you all about it. We have a detective inspector on the team who has been following your career, and she would very much like to meet you.'

'Is that so?' Villiers says, with a twinkle in her eye, 'I will look forward to her visit, then, and wish you all the very best of luck with your investigation.'

'If I look like that when I'm seventy-five, I'll be happy,' Grace comments, as we head back to Bristol.

'Never mind looks,' I say. 'I'll settle for being able to remember my name!'

She glances across at me. 'You've got that expression on your face,' she says. 'The one that tells me you've got a handle on all this.'

'I think so,' I reply. 'I need to speak to Maggie again first, and if what I suspect is true, it means another trip to interview Harris.'

'Christ, Al! Are you sure you want to put yourself through that again? I can ask Manly if we need anything else from him.'

'No chance, Grace.' I smile. 'If my hunch is correct, I want to see the look on his face when he realises his past has caught up with him.'

We're interrupted by my mobile. 'Can you get over to the lab?' Maggie asks, and there is a definite note of self-satisfaction in her tone.

Grace answers for me. 'We're about twenty minutes away, Maggie,' she says. 'Get the kettle on.'

Thanks to last night's light snowfall, the traffic is lighter than usual even though the roads are well-gritted, and Grace makes it in fifteen.

'Well,' Maggie says, handing round coffee and sinking into her chair, 'this is a rare honour. It's not often we see you down here these days, Detective Superintendent.'

'Privilege of rank, Maggie,' Grace says, smiling. 'Delegation comes with the territory. I don't mind admitting, attending post-mortems was never my favourite part of the job.'

Maggie shrugs. 'You really ought to keep your hand in, Grace,' she comments. 'You can't let your DCI have all the fun – or all my Scotch.' She gives me a wink.

'There's no need to impugn my reputation, Maggie,' I tell her. 'But I take it the DNA results have come through? Why not put us out of our misery?'

'Indeed, they have,' she replies, rubbing her hands and leaning forward, elbows on the desk. 'I have to hand it to you, Al. I thought your hunch was a bit of a long shot, but it seems to have paid off.'

I feel a small stab of excitement. 'Go on, Maggie. I'm all ears.'

She nods. 'One step at a time, then. The first test was a comparison of the samples belonging to Rachel Harcourt and James Harcourt. No match.'

I can't help but let out a bark of triumph. 'Sarah and Rachel are not James Harcourt's children! So far, so good, Maggie.'

Grace stares at me, and I can see she's catching up fast. 'Bloody hell!' She mutters. 'Is this going where I think it is?'

'Next,' Maggie says, tapping the desk to regain our full attention, 'we compared Rachel's profile with the unknown sample of saliva from the envelope containing the letter sent to Emily Stone. There's a ninety-nine per cent probability that whoever licked that envelope is Rachel Harcourt's mother.'

'Lisa Harcourt is the mysterious Lizzie – oh, Maggie, you are a genius!'

'We still can't say for certain,' Grace warns, 'but it's a damned good bet.'

'You've done something else?' I ask, noting the gleeful twinkle in Maggie's eye.

'Chief Inspector,' she says, frowning in mock disapproval, 'as you well know, I hate to leave things unfinished. I've been in touch with CC Manly in Hull. As luck would have it, she already had a DNA profile from former DCS Harris. We ran comparisons, and guess what? Rachel and, by implication, Sarah Harcourt are Harris's children.'

It's Grace who gets in first. 'Jesus Christ, Maggie – that's bloody brilliant!' She turns to me. 'We've got him, Al. We've fucking well got him!'

27

For what seems like a long time, we sit in Grace's office, mulling over the implications of Maggie's findings. Eventually, she shifts in her chair, stretches and yawns.

'What time is it?' she asks.

'Just after 1.30 p.m.' I reply.

'In that case,' she says, reaching back and pulling out the bottom drawer of her filing cabinet, 'I'd say we're officially at lunch.' She pulls out her bag of croissants. 'So,' she goes on, taking one and handing me the bag, which doesn't quite fit my definition of lunch, 'what's your next move?'

'I'm just waiting on Polly,' I reply, 'and she's waiting on the duty psychiatrist. Last I heard he was on his way half an hour ago, so he should be with Cathy Turner now. Daz finally got her husband to crumble, after threatening to charge him with a handful of offences we probably wouldn't have been able to make stick. He's offered to stay here voluntarily to help with our enquiries. In truth, I feel a bit sorry for the poor sod. He loves his wife and just wanted to protect her, no matter how misguided that might have been.'

'And he was up against someone who thinks nothing of getting rid of anyone in her way – if you're right, and it is Lisa Harcourt who's behind it all.'

I let out a sigh, and bite a chunk out of something full of custard and apricots. 'That's the big question. I could be completely wrong, but as far as I can see the only person who knows for sure is Harris. I have to go up there again, Grace – as soon as possible. I need to see how Harris responds, and if Lisa is in Hull, I want to be there when she's found. I can't leave it to Humberside. It's not that I don't trust CC Manly …'

'But it's not Manly we need to worry about,' Grace finishes for me. 'Don't worry, Al. I'm with you on this one – literally. You're still recovering from a knife attack, remember? I'm coming with you, and we'll be taking a car. I think DC Draper deserves to be invited to the party as well, don't you? You never know – we might need a bodyguard!'

I'm about to reply when her desk phone rings. She listens, eyebrows coming together in a deepening frown. After around thirty seconds, she looks at her watch, says, 'We'll be with you by six,' and puts the phone down. 'Harris has just been rushed into hospital,' she tells me. 'Manly says it's a suspected overdose, and the doctors reckon it's touch and go.' She gets up and dusts the pastry crumbs off her sweater. 'Grab Draper, make sure he's eaten something, and I'll meet you in the car park in half an hour. Oh – and we'll be using a marked car, in case we need to blue-light past any obstructions.'

Back in the squad room, I send a delighted Draper bouncing down to the canteen to stock up on sandwiches for the journey.

Sillitoe rolls her eyes. 'Are you sure he didn't just trip over and break that guy's leg by accident, boss?' she asks.

'It did cross my mind,' I reply, 'but he did go on to break another bloke's nose – not even Draper can have that many accidents in the space of thirty seconds.'

She laughs. 'I suppose not. I wish he'd calm down a bit, though. All that enthusiasm wears me out.'

'Just face it, Polly,' I say. 'We're getting old. We were both probably just like Colin when we were his age.'

'Jesus Christ, I hope not!' she replies, and then grins ruefully. 'I expect you're right, though.'

'So, what's the news on Cathy Turner?'

She blows out a long breath. 'Not fit to be charged. The psych reckons she's at risk of self-harm, and he's arranging an ambulance to take her over to a secure mental health unit.'

'Good – at least she'll be safe and we don't have to use our resources to look after her. You might as well tell Daz to let the husband go with her. I don't think he'll want to be anywhere else, and while she's there he won't do a runner. Just to be sure, though, send Molly along with him in case he decides to say anything useful.'

'That'll make Dick Fosbury happy at least,' she comments. 'He hasn't stopped complaining about cell space since you went up to York. I've spoken to Robbie – nothing from Iris Malden so far. She remembers taking some photos while she was at Greendale though, so once Karen Wyatt gets back to take over the babysitting, Robbie says she'll go over to the Malden house and hunt around for old albums.'

'Good idea. If she does come up with a photo of the Lodge staff, tell her to liaise with Larson. It's a long shot, but any clue as to what Lisa looks like, then or now, will be a real help.' I look around for my son-in-law, but there's no sign of him. 'Where is Larson, by the way?'

She shrugs. 'He went out around fifteen minutes ago, said he had to go to head office in Portishead, and would be back in a couple of hours. He didn't say what for.'

'For God's sake,' I mutter. 'He's supposed to be part of a team – what the hell is he playing at?'

Sillitoe looks pointedly at her shoes. 'I'm sure that whatever it is, boss, there will be a good reason.'

I try to turn off my unreasonable switch. 'I'm sure you're right, Polly,' I manage to say. Her reaction tells me something I should have known already – that Larson is both popular and valued among the team. They also know there's friction between us, all coming from my side, and it's up to me to sort it. I remember that only a day or two ago, I was lecturing Sillitoe on her personal relationships, which are, on reflection, far less fucked up than mine. 'No problem,' I say. 'Just bring him up to speed when he gets back, okay? If we do get a photo, ask him if he can do a bit of wizardry on it and get an idea of what she might look like now.'

She smiles, mainly with relief. 'Sure, boss – and good luck with Harris. Fingers crossed he survives and we can get something out of him.'

'Amen to that, Polly,' I reply, and go off in search of Draper and my sandwiches.

Four hours, a bacon sandwich and a hefty dose of painkillers later, we meet CC Manly at the entrance to Hull Royal Infirmary. She and Grace greet each other warmly, and then she turns to me.

'Just can't keep away from the place, eh, Chief Inspector?' she says. 'At least this time you're walking in under your own steam. Let's hope it's worth the trip.' She winks at Draper, who is hanging back, shuffling his feet. I see him blush and give her a nervous smile.

'I hope so, too,' I reply. 'I take it Harris is still breathing?'

Manly nods. 'It's a miracle, given his age, but I'm told he'll make a good recovery. One of the nurses at the home got to him within seconds and managed to get him to vomit before half of it got into his bloodstream. They pumped him out as soon as he got here, and he's stable now – out for the count, but should be able to answer a few questions when he comes round. That won't be for a while, though, so I took the liberty of arranging rooms for you all at a decent hotel down the road if you want to freshen up. There's a very good Chinese restaurant down by the river, and I suggest we all go and eat – we might as well swap notes in comfort.'

There are no objections, and half an hour later we emerge from reasonably comfortable rooms at the Excelsior Hotel, a couple of streets away from the hospital. Manly, in a car driven by her sidekick, Lola, picks us up at the entrance, and we're whisked across town to a very impressive-looking Chinese restaurant on the waterfront. We're shown to a table looking out over the murky waters and mudflats of the Humber estuary, a landscape that reminds me of CC Gosford's view of the Bristol Channel. Unlike Gosford's office, though, these window seats are accompanied by what looks like a very impressive oriental menu. Draper, as usual, is doing his best to look as if he's on the menu rather than choosing something from it. I try to dredge up a remnant of my inadequate social skills, but Manly gets in first.

She reaches across and pats his hand like a maternal aunt. 'Listen, young man,' she says, with a disarming smile, 'you probably won't believe this, but when I was a humble detective constable, I remember sitting in on an informal meeting with my then DSI and the chief constable – at a restaurant very much like this. I was so nervous I took one look at the menu and had to make a dash for the loo – puked my guts up! Afterwards, the CC took me aside and told me he did exactly the same thing back in the day. He said that one thing he learned was never to pass up a good meal if your boss is paying. We're all on the same side, Colin, and we've left ranks at the door. If you want a tip, the Hong Kong sweet and sour is particularly good here – and so is the orange juice – freshly squeezed and nicely chilled. Fill your boots, kid – it's all on expenses!'

I see him visibly relax. 'Actually,' he says, with a shy smile, 'I think I'll go for the Chow Mein and a beer – if that's okay, Ma'am.'

She rewards him with a wide grin and another wink. A waiter comes across, and we put in our orders, then get down to business.

'You think it was a suicide attempt?' I ask.

Manly shrugs. 'It's possible, I suppose, but I wouldn't have said it was Harris's style. If I were to put money on it, my theory would be attempted murder dressed up as a suicide. It was a pretty clumsy attempt too, by all accounts – a load of sleeping pills crushed up in a glass of liver salts. Half of them didn't dissolve. If they had, Harris would have died before he got to the hospital. Who put them there is a question only he can answer.'

There's a pause as the waiter brings a bottle of red wine and two beers. When he's out of earshot, she goes on, 'So, given what we now know, do you have any theories?'

'At this point, it's hard to say,' I reply. 'We've established that Harris was lying about his relationship with Lisa, a.k.a. Lizzie. What isn't clear is his motive. It could simply be an attempt to cover up a monumental mistake that would have destroyed both his career and reputation – and still could, if it became known that Lisa infiltrated his operation because, not to put a finer point on it, he couldn't keep it in his trousers.'

'On the other hand,' Grace puts in, 'perhaps the affair was genuine, and Harris was on the take. If that's true, my question would be, was Lisa protecting her husband, James Harcourt? It seems the two of them were working together – still are by the look of it – and luring Harris into that relationship would be one way of getting him to keep his mouth shut about the identity of the so-called "third man". If he got himself in deep enough, he would have a lot to gain, but even more to lose. From what I remember, he never did have much of a moral compass.'

Manly nods and turns to Draper. 'And what about you, Detective Constable? What do you think?'

He glances round the table, sees three pairs of eyes on him, shuffles and clears his throat. 'Well,' he starts, fiddling with his beer glass, 'I don't think he'd try to kill himself. I mean, he isn't the type – whatever his problem is, he'd try to wriggle out of it.'

'A good assessment,' Manly agrees. 'So, you believe someone tried to bump him off? Who? And why – or, to be more accurate, why now? There have been four murders, and if you're right, three attempted murders – I'm counting the attacks on you and your boss – stemming from events that took place nigh on sixty years ago. So, what's changed? Someone must have kicked the hornet's nest, and kicked it pretty hard.'

Draper frowns, studying the gas bubbles in his beer for so long I almost crack and kick him under the table.

'I don't know, Ma'am,' he comes out with eventually, 'but I'm pretty sure Harris does. He knows what's happening and why, and I reckon whoever it was, they were worried he might spill everything to us. That's why they tried to get rid of us, to stop us talking to him again, and when that didn't work, they had a go at him instead.'

'And luckily for us,' I add, 'by the look of it that hasn't worked either. A good analysis, Colin – I think you might be right.'

Grace snatches the wine bottle and refills her glass, and then Manly's. 'Well,' she declares, with a definite note of frustration, 'the bastard had better not flake out on us now. He's probably our only chance of a breakthrough before somebody else gets killed.'

The arrival of food puts our deliberations on hold, and we plough through an array of dishes in silence, until the arrival of coffee and fortune cookies.

CC Manly cracks hers open with the enthusiasm of a child at a party and reads out the message. 'It says, *You are cleverly disguised as an adult*. One day, I'll get one of these things that tells me something I don't know. How about you, Detective Superintendent?'

Grace sighs. '*Two days from now, tomorrow will be yesterday*. Christ – any more like that and I'll need to go and lie down! Your turn, Colin.'

Draper fidgets, and practically crumbles his cookie to dust. '*Flattery will go far tonight*,' he says.

Manly chuckles. 'Now that *is* good advice.'

I realise everyone is staring at me, and I've got no chance of getting out of the game. When I see what's written on my slip of paper though, I have to smile. '*When working towards the solution to a problem, it always helps if you know the answer*,' I read out.

'Which brings us neatly back to the reason we're all here,' Grace comments, and takes a sip of her coffee.

My mobile chooses that convenient moment to ping. It's a message from Larson, with two photographs attached. When I see what he's sent, I can hardly believe my eyes.

Grace catches my expression. 'What is it?' she asks.

I hand her my phone. 'It looks like Iris Malden has come up trumps,' I reply.

She examines the photos and passes the phone to Manly, who whistles softly and hands it, in turn, to Draper.

The first image is a black and white group photo, all women. Some are unidentified, but Larson has thoughtfully added a message beneath, naming three of the figures. In the centre, holding a very small baby, is a woman of around thirty who, he tells us, is Iris Malden with six-week-old David, soon to become Jacob. On her right, in a nurse's uniform, a young, smiling Alice Walker is waving at someone on the other side of the camera. Iris, he adds, knew her as Jean, but couldn't, frustratingly, recall her last name. The woman on Iris's left, however, is a girl of maybe sixteen or seventeen, dressed in a conservative blouse and pencil skirt, and Larson's label identifies her as Lisa Harcourt, née Kelly.

The second image is of a much older woman, I guess mid to late seventies. Beneath it, Larson has written, *computer-generated estimate of Lisa Harcourt's current appearance.*

'Send me a copy,' Manly says. 'I'll get it circulated. If she is in the area, and it's a good likeness, we might have some luck. At least we've got something to shove in front of Harris's nose that he won't be expecting.'

She excuses herself to go and make some calls while we finish our coffee, and a few minutes later, returns to announce that Harris will be fit to receive visitors first thing in the morning. 'It's inconvenient, I know,' she says, with a shrug, 'but there's nothing to be done about it. Your rooms are booked overnight, so I suggest we all get some sleep and I'll send Lola to pick you up at 8 a.m. There's one of my constables outside Harris's door overnight, so nobody can get in or out without my say-so.'

'I don't mean to be rude,' Grace says, 'but can you trust your constable?'

Manly grins. 'Oh yes, I think so. She's my daughter.'

28

Lola drops us back at the hospital entrance at 8.30 a.m. The hotel is only a ten-minute walk away, but I get the feeling Manly isn't taking any chances, given the last time Draper and I took a short walk to the car. She meets us at reception, where a harassed doctor is informing her, in no uncertain terms, that visiting is restricted to two officers, for a maximum of twenty minutes, and that the patient can terminate the interview at any time.

'Well,' Manly says, disgruntled, 'I suppose we should have expected that. Given the restrictions, I suggest that as DCI Crow and DC Draper conducted the original interview at the home, they should be the ones to finish the job. What do you say, Grace?'

'Sounds fair to me,' Grace answers with a smile. 'It will give the two of us time to catch up over coffee, and if the first crack at him goes nowhere, we can always take the second turn.'

They head down the corridor towards the hospital café, and the doctor, still looking none too pleased, utters a curt, 'This way, please,' leads us to the lift, and up to Harris's private room on the third floor. 'I must remind you, gentlemen,' she says, before stalking back down the corridor, 'that Mr Harris is a very elderly man, and has just been through a traumatic procedure, especially for someone of his age. Excessive stress could severely impact his health, and any deterioration in his condition will be entirely your responsibility. Do I make myself clear?'

'As an unmuddied pool,' I reply, forcing a smile.

The young detective constable sitting outside is unmistakeably related to CC Manly, both in appearance and personality. She stands to greet us, with the same mischievous grin that is never far away from her mother's face.

'DC Manly, sir,' she says. 'I managed to get a quick look when the nurse came earlier, and the old sod looks in pretty good shape, so if he tries it on, don't let him take you in.' She turns to Draper. 'You must be the local hero – Mum told me all about it. Colin, isn't it?'

He nods, turning a delicate shade of beetroot. 'DC Draper,' he manages to say. 'Pleased to meet you.'

I note that she is blushing, too. 'Georgie,' she says, taking his hand and holding it slightly longer than necessary, 'short for Georgina.'

Oh, for God's sake, I think to myself. A distracted Draper isn't what I need right now.

'Come on, son,' I say, managing not to let my irritation show, 'let's go and show Don Harris our holiday snaps.'

The former chief superintendent is propped in bed, tethered to a drip on one side and a machine monitoring his vital signs on the other. He looks a touch less cocky than last time we met, but the glint in his eye tells me his mind is still just as sharp. He manages a cynical grin.

'I thought you'd be front of the queue,' he says, 'and brought your little sidekick with you again, I see. From what I hear, it turns out he's a pretty good minder after all – saved your arse last time you crossed the border into the savage north.'

I move across and sit in a chair that has been conveniently placed by the bed, while Draper hovers by the door. 'Looks like we've both had a bit of trouble,' I comment. 'I hope you don't mind if I sit down? The doc says I need to be careful until the stitches come out. Where's Dennis, by the way? Isn't he supposed to be looking after you?'

His face crunches into an expression of distaste. 'I had to let him go – didn't do his job properly, as you can see.'

'Obviously not. After all, he didn't manage to finish you off, did he?'

There's a quick flash of anger, but then he chuckles. 'Not one of Yorkshire's greatest intellects, I agree.' All hint of amusement vanishes. 'I knew nothing about the attack on you and your DC. You probably won't believe that, but you have my word. I've cut a few corners in my time, but I have never been responsible for a physical attack on a fellow officer, serving or not. I only discovered afterwards that Dennis was having ideas above his station.'

'I believe it,' I reply. 'As you say, he's not very bright, and he sent his uncle to do the dirty work.'

Harris barks out a laugh. 'You mean Geoff Wicks? Jesus bloody Christ! The man's almost as decrepit as me! He was a local mob heavy when I was a constable in short trousers. No wonder your lad was able to knock the shit out of him.'

The comment makes Draper shuffle his feet, but thankfully he keeps his mouth shut.

'So,' I say, 'if you weren't pulling Dennis's strings, who was?' The question is met with silence, and a meaningfully blank expression. 'Okay.' I shrug, and pull my mobile out of my jacket, 'maybe I can answer that one.'

I hold up the phone and show him the computer-generated image of an aged Lisa Harcourt. Again, there's no response, but I see a momentary widening of the eyes. It must, I think, be a fairly good likeness. I fiddle with my phone again, and bring up the file I asked Larson to send over as soon as I woke up this morning. I say nothing, just press 'play' on the video, and hold it up for him to see – a family scene of James Harcourt playing in a garden with Rachel and Sarah, both aged around five. This time the reaction is unmistakable. His mouth twists into a snarl, and he slumps back onto the pillow, breathing hard. The machine monitoring his heart rate beeps, and a second later the door bursts open and a flustered nurse bowls in, almost knocking Draper over.

I can see her squaring up to forcibly remove us if necessary, but Harris takes the initiative, grabbing her arm and hissing, 'Get the fuck out of my room,' not to us, but to the nurse. She comes to a standstill, confused, and Harris releases her, saying, more calmly, 'I want you to leave if you wouldn't mind. My friends and I were just sharing a joke, that's all. I got a bit excited. Everything's fine, now – just fine.'

'Are you sure, Mr Harris?' She looks dubious.

'I'm quite sure, my dear,' he says, with a patronising pat of her hand. 'Please, just go away.'

She sighs, glares at me, then Draper, and leaves.

'Where did you get that?' he asks, pointing at the video.

'From James Harcourt's house,' I reply. 'I expect you know he's disappeared, and that we are looking for him in connection with four murders.'

There's a silence, during which we stare each other down like a couple of ageing and bedraggled cockerels. Finally, he nods towards Draper.

'Tell Bruce Lee over there to bugger off. What I have to say isn't suitable for the ears of children.'

'Sir?' Draper takes a step forward, concerned and, I'm pleased to see, annoyed.

'It's all right, Colin,' I say. 'I'm sure you and the DC outside can find something to talk about for a few minutes.'

'But …'

'Just do as the man says,' I tell him. 'It will be fine. If I need you, I'll shout.'

He gives me a reluctant nod and disappears.

'Before you ask,' I say, 'We do have DNA evidence.'

'Of course you do,' he mutters. 'You're a clever bastard, DCI Crow. I would have liked you on my team back in the day.'

'Somehow,' I reply, 'I don't think we'd have gotten on too well. Perverting the course of justice has never really been my thing.'

He barks out a laugh. 'No, I don't suppose you're the type. But how did you work it out – about Rachel and Sarah, I mean? You must have had a tip-off from somewhere.'

'You know I can't answer that,' I reply. 'I already had my suspicions, though, and my source just confirmed it. I knew that whatever hold the boss of the Greendale Lodge trafficking gang had over you, it had to be watertight. Two illegitimate children are pretty hard to sweep under the carpet, and for whoever was running the show, they were – and still are, by the look of it, a pretty cast-iron insurance policy.'

'They were,' he admits. 'At least, they were part of it. But it looks like that particular ship has sailed. Christ! I nearly made it. Just a few more years, and I'd have gone to my grave with a bit of dignity. As it is …'

'As it is, your reputation is likely to be shot to pieces when it all comes out. Add to that domestic violence, sex with underage girls, corrupting other officers – that's quite a juggling act, keeping all those balls in the air for sixty years. You do know that both your daughters are now wanted murderers?'

'My daughters?' He lets out a derisive snort. 'Biologically, maybe, but they were never mine. It wasn't supposed to happen – the bitch lied to me. She knew exactly what she was doing, damn her, and so did her husband. They threatened to ruin me unless I kept quiet about their involvement in the Greendale business. I couldn't let them do that – I was damned good at my job – the best the force had. There are hundreds of dangerous bastards who would still be walking the streets if I hadn't been there to bang them up. For Christ's sake, Crow, I shut down their operation and got most of them convicted – what more could I have done? You would have done the same.'

'I doubt it,' I say, 'but I would like to know a few details about the operation at Greendale Lodge that will help to clarify our current investigation and, I don't mind admitting, satisfy my curiosity.'

He thinks about it, and then nods. 'Fair enough. I'd want the same – but off the record. It was all a long time ago, and there's nothing any of us can do about it now.'

'Except,' I say, 'maybe getting our hands on Lisa Harcourt and making sure she and her family spend the rest of their lives in prison. It's my guess that's what you want, too. I can't promise to keep you out of it altogether, but if you help us catch these killers, I'll do what I can – and don't forget, they are clearly targeting you, now, and you've just sacked your bodyguard – not a good situation to be in, if you ask me.'

'Dennis?' He grunts in disgust. 'Dennis was never my bodyguard. He was my keeper, sent to make sure I never put words in the wrong people's ears. When you turned up asking all the right questions, they got spooked – hence the attack on you and your boy. The problem for them is, Dennis decided to make a name for himself and fly solo, thinking that knifing a couple of policemen in broad daylight would earn him some brownie points. When that failed, he realised you'd probably come back, even more suspicious, so he had a go at me. Trouble is, he fucking well cocked that up as well, and I can imagine Lisa wasn't too pleased once she found out. He knew his card was marked, so he legged it. I wouldn't bother looking for him. He's probably somewhere at the bottom of the Humber by now, complete with lead boots.'

'Christ!' When I think of what Harris, despite his many faults, must have endured over almost sixty years of being under Lisa Harcourt's thumb, I almost feel sorry for him. The poor sod, by the sound of it, has been in a prison of his own making since the 1960s. 'Before we go on,' I say, 'just tell me they didn't get you to do other things, down the line. Tell me you haven't been working for them all these years. If you were ...'

'What do you take me for?' he snaps. 'I swear, Crow, I never did, not once. That was the agreement. They had something on me – I had even more on them. We made a deal. I kept my mouth shut about Greendale Lodge on condition they let me get on with my career. They knew that if push came to shove, I had enough to put the whole lot of them away, and to make it look kosher they gave me a couple of the major players. That kept my bosses satisfied, but you were right – the monkeys got convicted, while the organ grinders got away with it. I've always tried, over the years, to find a chink in the armour that would bring them down, but that woman is too clever. She was then, and she is now.'

'I'm surprised you're still alive, in that case,' I comment.

He laughs. 'Oh, they tried – several times. There were attempted car accidents, muggings, drownings – you name it. But after their third try, I gathered a small group of other officers around me, and I always made sure at least a couple of them knew the whole story and would spill if anything happened to me.'

'Like DCS Horner?' I suggest.

He nods. 'He's one of the current lot, yes. For the last fifty years, there's always been someone who can finger her and her wretched family if I die in suspicious circumstances, and she knows it. It's why I'm pretty sure Dennis will be dead by now. He's single-handedly brought her house of cards down. Well, we might as well finish the job. I'm too bloody old to play hide and seek with the mob anymore.'

'It's not just Dennis, though, is it? Something's happened recently that's kicked it all off again, and you know what it is, so for goodness' sake, Harris, tell me, so I can put an end to it, once and for all.'

The door opens again, and the doctor who escorted us to his room marches in, looking even less amenable than she did down in reception.

‘I thought I said twenty minutes,’ she says, pointedly examining her watch. ‘You’ve been here half an hour.’

I’m forced to push back my chair as she bustles around the bed, checking the monitor and drip, taking Harris’s pulse and brandishing a thermometer in the general direction of his face.

Before she can shove it in his mouth, he says, ‘And he’s staying another half an hour – longer, if need be, so you can bloody well sod off and wait till we’ve finished our conversation. If I die in the meantime, my solicitor can sue you later.’

She arches an eyebrow. ‘If you die in the meantime,’ she retorts, ‘it will cost this hospital a fortune storing your body and conducting an autopsy, and much as I hate to admit it, I’d rather save the NHS the cash.’

The thermometer finally reaches its destination, and there’s a short silence until she takes it back and checks the result. ‘You seem to be recovering nicely,’ she concludes, ‘so I suppose there’s no harm in your visitor staying a little longer. But if you feel tired or unwell, just press the button and someone will escort him out. Another half hour, and that’s all – understood?’ She glares at both of us and stalks out.

‘Bloody woman!’ Harris mutters, and then, ‘Why don’t you get your constable to nip down to the café and get us some coffee? If you want the whole story, it might take a while – and before you ask, no, I’m not supposed to be drinking caffeine. I’m not supposed to be alive, either, so I might as well break another rule while I’ve still got the chance. Tell him triple espresso, black, three sugars.’

I stick my head round the door and see that Draper has found himself a chair, although I’m not altogether sure he needs one, as DC Georgie Manly is practically sitting in his lap. When they see me, they jerk apart as if I’ve poked them with a cattle prod. I send him on his errand and go back inside.

‘Okay,’ I say, regaining my seat, ‘I’m listening.’

He heaves a sigh and closes his eyes, remembering. ‘I expect you already know the bare bones of it,’ he starts. ‘Horner told me you had some pretty sharp people on your team, including some civilian computer wizard. He’ll have gone through all the records, no doubt.’

'We've got a pretty good picture,' I agree. 'It's just a matter of fine details, particularly Lisa's role, and how that affected your investigation.'

He nods. 'We'd been trying to gather evidence on the main players in the trafficking operation for over a year and were getting nowhere. We knew it was happening, but they were clever and careful. Taking babies from unmarried mothers was a difficult area to police back then – some gave up their children willingly, others didn't. Either way, it wasn't illegal as long as the mother signed the right papers, so there was nothing we could do about it. The process only became criminal when the mob got involved and money changed hands – huge amounts in many cases. We knew women were being coerced into signing their babies away, but none of them would make a statement to that effect. There was too much pressure on them from their families, the church and, of course, the traffickers. Add to that the fact that not every child was trafficked. They had the perfect cover – a completely above-board adoption agency run by catholic nuns and sanctioned by the state, which by and large left them to it. The traffickers chose their targets carefully. They honed in on couples who wouldn't have met the criteria set out by Social Services, or who wanted to jump the very long queue and had the ready cash to make a deal.'

'What about Charles Malden?' I ask. 'Was he one of the ones who paid to adopt?'

Harris shakes his head. 'No. We thought at first he might be, and tagged him as a suspect – him, and his wife. We knew he was wealthy, and he was the kind of man the gang might go for. The other thing that alerted us was the appearance of James Harcourt's brother, William. We were pretty sure James was involved, and initially assumed William must be, too.'

'You're saying William Harcourt had nothing to do with his brother's activities?'

'Other stuff, probably – none of the Harcourts were particularly law-abiding, but as far as baby trafficking was concerned, he almost certainly knew, but wasn't a party to it. He was there because he'd gotten his then-girlfriend pregnant – three times in as many years, can you believe? I don't know who was more stupid, him or her. Anyway, I got the impression he'd been sent by Old Bill, the family patriarch, to make sure his kids weren't sold off like some of the others. There were arguments between him and James – they didn't exactly get on.'

I realise that what Harris is saying shows Cathy Turner in a somewhat different light. William might have been a petty criminal and a philanderer, but it now looks entirely credible that in later life he'd put his past behind him, and done his best for Cathy and her mother. It's quite possible that until the murder, her only image of him was as a normal, loving father. Cathy knew nothing, therefore the threats she and her husband received would have been terrifying, but meaningless to them. Harris is speaking again.

'It was William's girlfriend who gave us our breakthrough,' he goes on. 'Not directly, but one of the midwives had been present at the birth of her first child, and kicked up a huge fuss about the way the girl was treated. When she turned up again less than a year later, and the second child was taken, the midwife came to us, saying she knew what was going on and wanted to help, and a friend of hers felt the same. The operation was going nowhere, and I jumped at the chance.'

'That would have been Alice Walker?' I ask. 'And the friend was Lisa Harcourt?'

He nods. 'Lisa Kelly, although I didn't know that then. She called herself Lisa Connor. I had my doubts about her – she was only seventeen, working in the admin department, but she was sharp, and very pretty, which meant she had the eye of several men we suspected of being part of the trafficking ring. We recruited Walker first, and soon realised we'd hit a goldmine. As a midwife, she was pretty much under the radar – a woman in a nurse's uniform with access to all areas, just doing her job – as invisible as a waiter hovering at a table with a wine bottle. Within a couple of months, she'd managed to identify some of the staff on the gang's payroll, including a couple of senior nuns and a bishop, for fuck's sake. We were never able to make charges stick in those cases though. The law might have a long arm, but the church is like a bloody octopus.'

'So where did Lisa come in? We know you recruited her at some point. Was it before you started sleeping with her, or after?'

His brows come together in an indignant scowl, but then he shrugs an acknowledgement. 'After. Like I said, she was a very pretty little thing, and she had her eye on me from the moment I arrived on the scene. She was the one doing the chasing, and I wasn't going to pass up the chance of a good time. That was my first mistake. The second was suggesting she chat up a couple of the male orderlies Walker had put us onto as taking backhanders from the traffickers. I ended up telling her how far we'd got with the case, who was under suspicion, what our next move was going to be – just about everything. I told her she had a vital role to play, winkling information from her targets any way she could and feeding it back to me. What I didn't know at the time was that she was engaged to James Harcourt – the two of them were working together, and if anything, she was the driving force, not him. Ironic, isn't it? The one person I never suspected was a skinny little slapper in a mini-skirt and thigh-length boots, and yet she was the most dangerous criminal of them all. Jesus fucking Christ!'

'I suppose that's what comes of a lifetime of underestimating women,' I remark.

I'm saved his response by a commotion out in the corridor, following which the door bursts open and the doctor reappears, annoyance dial turned up to maximum. I get a quick view of Draper, a paper coffee cup in each hand, looking distinctly uncomfortable.

'Times up,' she says, fixing me with a look that makes it clear resistance is useless. 'Mr Harris needs medication, and we need to run some tests.' She turns to her patient. 'Caffeine and sugar, Mr Harris, definitely do not qualify as medication, unless you insist on taking up a bed for much longer than necessary.'

'We haven't finished,' Harris protests. 'For God's sake, woman, how long is this going to take? There are things the chief inspector needs to know – police business – it's important.'

'More important than your health?' she counters, and then sighs, and turns back to me. 'About an hour,' she says, 'assuming the tests are satisfactory. I'll let the police officer outside know when you can come back in.'

I nod and make my exit. In the corridor, Draper and Manly's daughter are still deep in conversation. I decide I might as well leave them to it, tell them to drink the coffee and set off downstairs to update Grace and the chief constable on what I've learned so far.

29

I find Grace alone, at a corner table right at the back of the hospital's coffee shop, elbows resting on the table and, a tell-tale sign, massaging her temples between little finger and thumb. I quickly scan the rest of the café – there's no sign of CC Manly. I realise that the coffee I was about to drink is still on the third floor with DC Draper, order two more, and take them across. She jerks upright as I pull out a chair and sit.

'Thanks,' she says, grabbing the mug and taking a healthy swallow. 'God, I'm tired. The CC had a meeting with some politician or other – said she'd be back in an hour. How did it go?' I give her a run-down of Harris's statement so far, and she shakes her head in disgust. 'That man is bloody unbelievable. Does he actually realise what he's done? If he'd come clean about all this decades ago, at least four innocent people would still be alive. Well, it's time the bastard pulled his head out of his arse and took responsibility. He won't wriggle out of it this time, and neither will the cronies who have been covering for him. Does he know where the Harcourts are hiding out?'

'I'm not certain,' I reply, 'but I'm pretty sure he knows what triggered the killing spree. With a bit of luck, I'll find out in half an hour or so. Whatever sparked it off, it was a serious enough threat to make them take drastic action. It's the complexity of it all that I can't understand – why go to such lengths to try to frame the children? It's just adding to the risk.'

'It's a good way of distracting us, though,' Grace says. 'They've had us running in all directions, and while we've been chasing dead ends, it's given them time to go to ground. Damn it – they could be anywhere by now.'

'No,' I say. 'They're close by. I can feel it. I just hope Harris has some ideas as to where they might be. In the meantime, maybe we could get Manly to pick up Horner. Now that Harris is talking, she can at least arrest him on suspicion of perverting the course of justice. We know there are others still in the force, but I doubt Harris will name them. He's thrown Horner to the wolves, though, and once he realises it, he might decide that continuing to protect Harris isn't worth it and give her the list.'

'It's worth a shot,' she agrees. 'I'll suggest it as soon as she gets back.'

My phone rings, and Draper comes on the line. 'The doctor said to tell you she's finished, and could you come straight up? Harris is creating a fuss, and threatening to discharge himself unless she lets you back in.'

'I'm on my way,' I tell him, and get to my feet. 'Wish me luck, Grace,' I say, and head back to the lift.

Harris is sitting up in the bed, looking distinctly rattled. 'Bloody doctors!' he mutters, reaching for the water jug. He struggles to lift it until I decide to help him out and fill his glass.

'Something you're not telling me?' I ask.

He grunts, empties the glass and holds it out. I refill it. 'Cancer,' he says, 'prostate. It was diagnosed a couple of years ago, and they said old age would probably get me before the tumour did. Looks like they might have been wrong.'

'I'm sorry,' I say, which draws a humourless chuckle.

'No, you're not – and neither am I if you want the truth. At my age, the alternative is spending my final years dribbling all over the bedsheets and having my nappies changed by a teenager who doesn't know which end to stick the safety pin. They've given me around six months.' He laughs, which results in a coughing fit. 'Just think,' he says when he recovers, 'if Dennis hadn't decided to spike my coffee with sleeping pills, I would have quietly made my final exit, and pretty little Lisa and her brood would have one less problem to worry about.'

'Not if it was up to me,' I comment. 'But you were about to tell me what's brought them out of the woodwork now. It must be something pretty big for them to resort to multiple murders – and why those particular targets? Alice Walker and Emily Stone, I can understand, but from what you've said, Charles Malden had nothing to do with the trafficking operation, and neither did William Harcourt. William knew about it, but families like the Harcourts generally don't go round shopping each other to the police.'

'Except that's exactly what he meant to do if I read things right,' Harris replies. 'You ask me what happened? Mick Harcourt happened. You know he drowned in his bath, a couple of years ago?'

I nod. 'We went through the records. The body wasn't found until sometime after death, and it was recorded as accidental.'

Wrong on both counts,' Harris says. 'Mick was always the cuckoo in the nest, thanks to Old Bill's insistence that he was raised within the family, and he grew up pretty bitter about the hand he'd been dealt. It was made worse when his father let slip that he had a brother and sister, and both had been adopted. He set out to find them, and although he never managed to locate his brother, he did somehow find out about Helen Stone. He contacted Emily, who told him that Helen already knew about him and had made the decision not to meet him or have anything to do with him. That was early in 2021. It resulted in several nuisance calls made to Emily – mostly a combination of alcohol and self-pity. By that time, his health was shot with drink and drugs, and he was seething with resentment at not having the chances his siblings had been given. What happened next is partly guesswork, but it's my belief he worked out what had gone on at Greendale, and threatened to expose James's and Lisa's involvement with not only that, but other things, too. It wasn't just child trafficking, you see. Guns, drugs, you name it – they were neck deep in organised crime all over Humberside.'

'So, they killed Mick to keep him quiet – it wasn't an accident?'

He nods. 'You need to understand, Lisa was, and still is, the star of the show – known as the "Mother Superior" within the organisation. She's the daughter of one Brian Francis Kelly – heard of him?'

I shake my head.

'Not many people have, even within the force. Kelly was one of the biggest OCG bosses in the north of England – operations in Manchester, Leeds and Hull. He had a knack for being invisible, and we never got him anywhere near a courtroom. He died in the late eighties. What I didn't know during the Greendale investigation was that his only child, Lisa, was being groomed as his successor even back then. She took over after his death, and for the last thirty-odd years she's been in charge of one of the most powerful crime syndicates in the country. She and James Harcourt have been joined at the hip since they were teenagers. They married soon after she got pregnant with the twins, went through a sham divorce at one stage, when a gang war blew up and James went into hiding with the kids for a couple of years, but they've never really been apart. You know what people call the pair of them? The iron fist in the granite glove. It's a pretty good analogy.'

'And presumably her daughters – *your* daughters – are set to inherit the whole setup,' I comment. 'It's no wonder you wanted to keep that quiet.'

'If it got out, it would destroy the reputation of the whole force – innocent or guilty, it wouldn't matter – and bring into question hundreds of convictions. Believe it or not, Crow, it isn't *all* about me. Yes, I fucked up at Greendale Lodge, but I wasn't going to let Humberside police get dragged through the shit because of it. It was three years of work, and we got good results. It was a trade-off – it's how the real world works.'

'Except your trade-off meant you got the minnows, and let the sharks go free to kill God knows how many others,' I point out. 'But you were telling me about Mick Harcourt's death. You have evidence it was murder?'

'Not personally, but I know someone who does. As I said, Mick was shooting his mouth off, threatening to go to a rival set-up and take the family secrets with him. The Harcourts were all involved with the Kelly empire in one way or another, and Mick, when he was sober, was one of Lisa's office boys, with access to a lot of sensitive material. Lisa wasn't going to tolerate that, nephew or not. She sent James to get rid of him, knowing Mick wouldn't be suspicious of a visit from his uncle. So off James went like an obedient lapdog, but he didn't realise that when he arrived, someone else was in the house.'

'Who?' I ask.

'Mick's granddaughter,' Harris replies. 'Mick was divorced, but he kept in touch with his kids. The elder, Susan, had a five-year-old girl, and that night Mick was babysitting while Susan and her partner went to some all-night party. The kid was in bed when James arrived, and Mick had had a couple of drinks to go with his anti-depressants – not enough to knock him out, but he was probably pretty relaxed. He'd just run a bath, and told his uncle to make himself at home while he got cleaned up. James must have thought luck was truly on his side. He waited until Mick was in the tub, bashed him on the head and held him under. The thing is, the kid woke up, heard voices and went to see who the visitor was. She was just in time to witness the whole thing. She got scared and ran back to bed, and James made a quick exit. He never knew she was there.'

'But surely,' I say, 'her mother or father would have found the body when they came to collect her the next day? The post-mortem says the body had been in the bathtub for anything up to two weeks.'

He nods. 'It was – and you're right. Susan came to collect the little girl around lunchtime the next day and found her cowering in the bedroom, unable to speak. She put two and two together and realised that if she reported the death, Lisa would find out the child was a witness and be next on the hit list. She waited a week or two, then went round to her dad's house with the kids, just like a normal visit, and claimed that's when she found the body. Nobody questioned it – accidental death, head injury from the bath tap, case closed.'

'So how come you know all this?' I ask. 'And what's it got to do with the other four murders?'

'Ah – that's where it gets interesting. For several months after Mick's death, nothing happened. The granddaughter was pretty traumatised, as you can imagine, and ended up in therapy. It took a while, but one evening she finally told her mother that she'd seen Uncle Jim in the bathroom that night, and it sounded like they were fighting. Susan knew Lisa had been behind the death, but had never for a minute suspected James. She told her grandfather, William Harcourt. William, naturally, didn't take it well, even though there was no love lost between him and Mick. When push comes to shove, family is family, and knocking off your brother's son is a definite no-no. He confronted James and said he'd find a way to bring him down. The thing is, William had been at Greendale, observed the whole operation – not just theirs, but ours, too, and he was no fool. He knew Malden had adopted Jacob and, more importantly, that Emily Stone had been working for us, and had adopted Helen. He also knew that Mick had been in touch with Emily, and if he knew, so did Lisa. He rang Emily to warn her, probably hoping she'd come to us with the information, and guess what? Emily contacted her two fellow undercover whistle-blowers, Alice Walker, and …'

'And Lizzie, a.k.a. Lisa Harcourt,' I finish. 'Dear God!'

He nods. 'My words exactly. So, put yourself in Lisa's shoes. There was no way she could know whether or not Malden had also been told about James's involvement in Mick's death, so she simply added him to the list. I think Emily and Alice would have come straight to us with the allegation if it hadn't been for Lisa. She probably spun them a line about it being too dangerous, and to wait until she'd spoken to me, that as long as their roles in breaking up the trafficking gang weren't exposed, they would be safe – God knows. Whatever she said, she persuaded them to say nothing for the time being. It took more than a year, but she managed to formulate a plan that would get rid of all four of them – Malden, Alice, Emily and William, while diverting suspicion away from James and onto William's children.'

'And that plan included turning Sarah and Rachel into murderers,' I say. 'Do you know who was responsible for each death?'

He shakes his head. 'My guess is as good as yours, but if I were pushed, I'd say James killed Charles Malden.'

'James? Not Rachel?'

'No – Rachel's job was to get hold of the knives from Malden's house, but they wouldn't have sent her to do the killing. She was one of the few people William Harcourt wouldn't have been suspicious of, on account of her relationship with his daughter, Cathy. She probably had a key to his house and visited regularly. She killed him, and then went over to Downside and murdered Alice Walker – that, or the other way around. Killing Alice would have taken less time, so she was probably first on the list. I'm pretty sure Emily Stone was down to Sarah.'

He pauses, and then says, 'If you want my opinion, I think Lisa's lost it. A family betrayal is a sign of weakness, and when she lost control of Mick, she panicked and sent James to sort it out. She wanted to keep it all quiet – immediate family only. If she'd sent one of her many anonymous assassins to do the job, she could have blamed it on a rival gangland killing, and William would have accepted that – hazard of the trade, so to speak. The fact that it was his brother was something he couldn't take. What followed has made her position even more precarious, and not just with the police. You know yourself that being at the top of the tree in organised crime makes you a target for every wannabe gangster in the country. Everyone is watching, waiting for that wrong step. She's fucked up and she's in trouble. And if I know little Lisa, she'll be looking for a way out, even if that means leaving James and the kids to take the rap.'

'So, where is she? Come on, Don, you must have some ideas. Even if you don't know for sure, you can take an intelligent guess. We both want to take her down, so help me out here, for Christ's sake. After all, it sounds to me like you've got nothing left to lose. For once in your life, do the right thing, even if it means handing in your daughters – the ones you supposedly don't care about? You never know, if the rest of the mob is after them, you might be saving their lives.'

He thinks about objecting, but then lets out a sigh and slumps back onto his pillow.

'Fuck you, Crow,' he mutters. 'If you want a guess, I'd say Lisa's far away by now. She may have taken Rachel and Sarah with her, but it's unlikely. It's not so easy to disappear if you've got the family in tow. There's a place here in Hull that she uses from time to time, one in Hornsea and one over in Wakefield. Hull is closer to the ferry terminals, and it's easier to catch a ferry than a plane, so that would be my bet. I'll give you the addresses. As for saving their lives, you might be too late, and if it's a choice between a quick death and a life sentence, I know which I'd choose. I've been living with that option for decades. As for James, they are most likely not travelling together. The escape route will have been planned years ago, and they will arrange to meet somewhere you can't get to them – South America would be favourite. Face it – you've missed the boat – literally.'

For a long, agonising moment, I wrestle with the urge to drag Harris out of bed and commit an act of grievous bodily harm.

He reads my thought and chuckles. 'Don't kid yourself, Chief Inspector. You're not the type – much too fond of playing it by the book.'

'Don't push your luck,' I hiss. 'Just give me those addresses, and I'll leave you to your own devices – or is that just "vices"?'

'Either way, it sounds like a reasonable deal. I wish you every success in your future endeavours, Chief Inspector Crow, and sincerely hope we never meet again.'

30

I grab a startled Draper and head down to the café, phone welded to one ear. By the time we get there, Manly, back from her meeting, is busy barking orders into her mobile, and both she and Grace are on their feet heading towards us.

'We're getting teams over to all three properties,' she tells us, 'with orders to surround each one, but not approach. Manly is liaising with the West Yorkshire serious crime squad to cover the house in Wakefield. If Harris is spinning us a line, I'll personally go in there and …'

She stops herself and clamps her mouth shut, hands bunched into fists. I can almost hear her teeth grinding.

'We'll soon find out,' I say. 'What about Horner? Has he been picked up?'

She nods. 'It was the first thing on Manly's list. With a bit of luck, he'll give us the names of any other officers who have been withholding information.'

Humberside's chief constable gets off the phone and comes across to us. 'All sorted,' she says. 'We might as well go and join the party. The Hull address is closest, so we can start there. We've got firearms units heading for each location, with orders to cover all entrances and exits, but not make a move until they get the order. If the Harcourts *are* in one of them, God knows what weapons they might have to hand.'

'And if they're not?' Grace asks.

Manly grins. 'Then I'll probably be writing my resignation letter in the morning, given how much it's going to cost. Come on – let's go and find out if I've still got a job.'

It takes us around twenty minutes to get through the city centre traffic, not wanting to draw attention by using the blue lights. Eventually, we make it across to one of Hull's leafy outer suburbs, where a plain-clothes officer flags us down a couple of streets short of our destination.

'We've been watching for the last fifteen minutes,' he tells us. 'There's been no one coming or going, and no movement inside. The curtains are all closed, so it's hard to say, but the place looks as if nobody's been there for quite a while, Ma'am.'

'Thanks, Eddie,' she says. 'Patch me through to whoever's in charge of the firearms unit, will you?'

He nods, pulls out his radio and makes the call. 'Sergeant Watkins, Ma'am,' he says, and hands it over.

'I can't say for certain that the place is empty until we get inside, Ma'am,' Watkins tells her, 'but so far we have no reason to think anyone's been there recently.'

'No reason to think,' Manly retorts, 'is not the same as knowing. Until we know, I don't want anyone going in there. What about a thermal imaging camera? Have you got one handy? And will that pick up anything alive that's inside?'

'It wouldn't do any good, Ma'am,' he replies. 'It won't pick anything up through the walls, and window glass will just reflect the radiation back to us. In any case, the curtains are all drawn, so it's impossible to either see in or get any kind of thermal image.'

'Shit!' she mutters. 'Okay, Sergeant. Stand by – and keep watching.'

She thrusts the handset back at the detective and rummages for her phone. 'We might as well see if there's a visual of the inside of the other two houses, but I've got a pretty good idea they are locked up just as tight. Sod it!'

We wait impatiently while she makes several more phone calls, jams her phone back in her pocket and swears. 'West Yorks decided they weren't going to wait any longer and sent their team in. They found the remains of a cannabis growing operation in the loft, but the drugs are long gone. Forensics is in there now, but I doubt they'll find any evidence of note.'

A small, nagging feeling starts up at the back of my neck, but for the moment, the meaning of it escapes me. 'What about the place in Hornsea?' I ask.

'Same as here,' she replies. 'No sign of any movement, inside or out.'

'You think Harris lied to you – sent us on a wild goose chase?' Grace asks me.

'It's possible,' I admit. 'It's also possible they have other bolt holes he doesn't know about, or they've been and gone – like he said, we could be too late.'

The detective constable's radio crackles into life, and Watkins comes back on the line. 'How long do you want to give it, ma'am?' he asks. 'It's a bit like *The Night Before Christmas* over here – not even seen a mouse move.'

She sighs and runs a frustrated hand over her brow. 'Five minutes,' she says at last, and checks her watch. 'That makes it 2.05 p.m. precisely. I want you and the Hornsea team to go in at exactly the same time. Are you in contact with them?'

'Yes, ma'am,' he replies. 'We'll let you know when the area's been made safe and you can come through.'

'Thank you, Sergeant – good luck, and keep your heads down.'

The wait seems to go on forever – in reality, it can't be more than ten minutes, but in those ten minutes, my mind has gone back to the night I sent my sergeant to the door of a nondescript terraced house in West Hill armed with a battering ram and a bullet-proof vest – a vest that did nothing to protect him from a perfectly aimed shot to the head, fired by a Greek assassin, and left that bullet lodged neatly in the frontal lobe of my brain. I realise my hand is shaking, and when the radio finally crackles again, it jerks so violently that Grace grabs hold of my wrist, a shadow of concern on her face. I swallow hard and give her a nod, cursing the weakness that never seems to go away entirely.

When Watkins speaks, he sounds dazed, reticent. 'Ma'am?' he says, and there's a long pause. 'It's all clear, but I think you'd better come and see this.'

Even before I get to the threshold, I find myself offering up a prayer of thanks to whichever deity decided to keep the temperature close to freezing. Despite the cold, a couple of well-fed blow flies chart a ponderous course past my nose and out into the front garden. The smell wafting from somewhere inside is thankfully faint, but unmistakable. Grace and I exchange a look, and Draper, coming up alongside me, takes a sharp breath and immediately turns pale.

'Don't worry, son,' I say, patting his shoulder. 'We can't go in until the SOCOs turn up with the appropriate clothing, and I doubt they'll want more than a couple of us tramping around, even when we're in our paper suits. It's probably going to be a while, so why don't you go and find out where the nearest cup of coffee is – with or without currant buns?'

'Yes, sir,' he says, and makes his relieved way to the end of the street, where a couple of uniformed officers are busy setting up a cordon.

A minute or so later, CC Manly joins us by the front door, Sergeant Watkins in tow. She gestures for him to speak.

'There are three bodies in there,' he says. 'We found the first one downstairs in the front room – elderly male, victim of a stabbing by the look of it. The other two are female, found together in one of the bedrooms, no obvious signs of injury, but we'll have to wait for the pathologist to determine cause of death.'

'The two females – could they be sisters?' I ask.

'I'm sorry, sir,' he replies. 'It was one of my AFOs who found them, and as all three individuals were clearly dead, we checked the other rooms and vacated immediately to prevent too much contamination. I can find the officer if you'd like to speak to them?'

'If it wouldn't be too much trouble, sergeant.'

He goes off, and returns a minute later with a woman in combats struggling to unstrap her bulletproof vest.

'You wanted to see me, sir?'

I nod. 'The two women you found upstairs – did you get a good look at them?'

'It depends on what you mean by "a good look", sir,' she replies. 'I didn't examine them closely – just enough to establish they were dead, which didn't take long. They were lying together on the bed as if they were asleep, but their eyes were open. It looked like they might have been put there – you know – laid out, arms crossed, the sort of thing an undertaker would do.'

'So, you saw their faces. Did they look similar, do you think? I mean, could they be related?'

She takes a moment, and then says, 'It's hard to say. Sisters, maybe? One was blonde, the other had darker hair and looked older. Sorry – that's probably not very helpful.'

'Thanks. Don't worry, I'll get a look myself once the SOCOs have finished. I was just being impatient.'

'One blonde, one dark, and different ages,' Grace murmurs. 'It doesn't sound like Rachel and Sarah Harcourt. You thought it might be them?'

I shrug. 'It was just an idea. Harris hinted at trouble brewing between different outfits, so a gang hit isn't out of the question.'

A white van comes to a halt at the front gate and disgorges a little band of ready-suited SOCOs. One of them comes over to us and gives Manly a friendly nod.

'Not often we see you at the business end,' he comments. 'This one must be important.'

'You don't know the half of it, Frank,' she replies. 'This is Detective Superintendent Helston and DCI Crow, from Bristol. They've got a professional interest in identifying the bodies as quickly as possible.'

He turns to us with a smile. 'Definitely important, then,' he says. 'Frank Baker, chief pathologist. I'd shake hands, but …' He waggles his gloved hands. 'If it's that urgent, I can take a couple of you in with me, as long as you suit up and don't go near anything. I'll get started, and tell one of my people to escort you in when you're ready.'

Five minutes later, Grace and I are conducted through to the lounge, where Baker is busy examining the corpse. I take one look, and there's no need for him to say anything.

'James Harcourt,' I murmur to Grace. 'Christ – how long has he been there?'

'I'd say getting on for a week,' Baker says, 'or thereabouts. It's strange, though …'

'That whoever did it stabbed him through the heart even though he was already dead, and left the knife in the body?' I finish for him.

He raises an eyebrow. 'Exactly so. I suppose you're going to tell me the cause of death, too?'

'How about drowning?' Grace puts in.

He nods. 'It looks like it. I don't think he would have known much about it, though. There are no signs of a struggle, so I'd guess he was unconscious when he was tied to the chair – drugs, perhaps, or alcohol, possibly both. There's a definite smell of whisky, so that could be what they used to drown him, or at least render him unconscious.'

Baker calls one of his assistants across to take over and leads us back out into the hall. 'Let's go and have a look at the other two,' he says. 'Maybe you can tell me what they died of as well.'

'At least,' Grace says as we follow him upstairs, 'we know what happened to five of Charles Malden's antique daggers. I have a feeling we're about to find the sixth.'

The scene in the master bedroom is rather different, however. The two women are lying on the bed, side by side, arms neatly folded across their chests, just as the AFO who found them had described. There are no signs of restraint, nor any injury, and each is dressed in a long, white towelling bathrobe. The hair has been combed, and whoever placed them there has even applied a little makeup to each face – blusher, powder, a touch of lipstick. This finishing touch makes the scene somehow more gruesome than the more violent death that occurred downstairs. The AFO was right about something else, too – one woman is older than the other – at least fifteen years older, maybe a little more. Between them, the killer has carefully placed the sixth and final dagger.

'Dear God!' Grace murmurs. 'What the hell is going on here?'

Before I can speak, Baker answers. 'Drugged is my guess,' he says, and points towards the dressing table. There are two wine glasses, one still containing a centimetre of what looks like white wine. 'Rohypnol, perhaps, or something similar – not enough to cause immediate loss of consciousness, but they wouldn't have been aware of what was happening, hence the lack of signs of a struggle. Whoever did it laid them out, blocked the nose and poured water down the throat, perhaps using a pipe or some such. I'll be able to say more when I've done the post-mortems.'

'How do you know?' I ask. 'They could have dragged the victims into the bathroom, and drowned them in the bath or the shower.'

He shakes his head. 'I don't think so. Barely conscious or dead bodies are pretty heavy, and there are no signs I can see of dragging or manhandling. Plus, they haven't been dead long, and the carpet is still wet between the bed and the dressing table. Do you know who they are?'

I nod. 'I know for sure who one of them is. The older one is Lisa Harcourt. The younger is either Rachel or Sarah, her daughter, but as Rachel and Sarah are – or were – identical twins, it's hard to say which one.'

'The question is,' Grace says, 'who killed them?'

'Not anyone from outside,' I reply. 'In the case of James, it could have been any one of the three, but my money's on Lisa. Then, for some reason, one twin decided it was the end of the line for both her mother and sister. She planned to make it look part of the pattern – drowning followed by stabbing – but maybe she couldn't bring herself to stick the knife in when it came to it. She laid them out as best she could, and left the dagger, perhaps as some kind of symbolic gesture.'

'But why, for God's sake?' Grace has resorted to massaging her temples between finger and thumb. 'And more to the point, where the bloody hell is she now?'

There's nothing more to do in the house, so we leave Baker to it, make our way out into the fresh air, and bring Manly and Draper up to speed. Draper has managed to ferret out a corner shop a couple of streets away with a coffee machine, and for a few minutes, we stand in silence, hugging paper cups and trying to work out our next step. The decision is made for us when Manly's mobile rings.

'He's done what?' She chokes, spraying coffee all over the pavement. She listens, her expression becoming more furious by the second. 'Right,' she says. 'We're on our way,' and jabs the *end call* button with enough force to break the phone in half. 'Hospital,' she spits, already jogging towards the car. 'Don Harris has discharged himself. Someone was supposed to be watching him, for fuck's sake!'

As we head back to the infirmary, this time with full-blown blue lights and sirens, the nagging feeling at the back of my neck starts to crystallise into a very unpleasant certainty.

31

For several minutes we hover at the end of the corridor while Humberside's chief constable vents her fury on the hapless PC who was supposed to have been stationed outside Don Harris's room, the tirade aided and abetted by her daughter, DC Georgie Manly, whom the uniformed constable had relieved just over two hours before. Eventually, Georgie leaves her mother to it and comes over to join us, flashing a quick smile at Draper along the way before reverting to a furious scowl.

'Bloody idiot,' she mutters, shaking her head, and then, 'Sorry, sir – ma'am, but it makes me so angry. The fool reckons he got called to a disturbance on the next floor – an assault on a nurse in ICU. When he got there, it was all over, and the bloke had run off. He went to help security do a search, but didn't find whoever it was, and he thinks he was away from his post no more than ten minutes.'

'That's more than long enough,' Grace comments. 'Was the nurse hurt?'

'Thankfully not,' Georgie replies. 'If you ask me, the whole thing was staged to get him away from Harris's room, give the old sod time to sneak out.'

'Agreed,' I say. 'The question is, where did he sneak to?'

The lift door opens, and the sour-faced doctor I encountered earlier emerges, looking almost as furious as CC Manly, who has by now just about run out of steam. The PC sees his chance and heads for the lift, doing his best to keep dignity intact and not run. It doesn't quite work – he looks like a competitor in a 5k walking race. Both Manly and the medic reach us at the same time.

The doctor gets in first, glaring at Manly. 'May I remind you that this is a hospital, not a football stadium? There are some very sick patients on this floor, and I will not have them subjected to a bunch of idiots screaming in the corridors. You are police officers, not drunken hooligans!'

Manly takes a deep breath. 'I do apologise, Doctor. I'm afraid my temper got the better of me. We are all very concerned for the welfare of Mr Harris. I don't suppose you have any idea where he might have gone?'

'He has been discharged,' she answers stiffly. 'His latest tests indicated a good recovery, and his niece undertook to keep an eye on him for the next twenty-four hours, so there was no reason to keep him in – we do have a chronic shortage of beds, you know, so if a family member is available, it makes life easier for us.'

'And you didn't think to inform the police?' Manly says, between gritted teeth. 'We also have a shortage – of manpower – and we don't station an officer outside a hospital room unless there is a very good reason.'

The doctor shrugs. 'I attempted to inform your officer, but he wasn't there, so I assumed you no longer had a reason – good, or otherwise.'

'Oh, for God's sake!' Manly mutters, taking the words out of my mouth.

I bring out my phone and scroll through the images provided by Larson. 'Did you see Mr Harris's niece yourself, or speak to her?' I ask.

She nods. 'We had a chat before they left,' she replies, 'about care, medication and so forth – a very nice woman, and very concerned about her uncle.'

I hold up the photo on my phone. 'Is the woman in this photograph?'

Again, she nods, examines it closely, and points. 'Yes, that's her. As I said, a very pleasant woman.'

'You're sure? The one on the right?'

'Positive. The bridge of her nose has clearly been broken at some point. It's been reset – a nice bit of correction, but just a fraction out of true. Only a surgeon would notice it. Oh …' She digs into her white coat and pulls out an envelope. 'On the way out, Mr Harris asked me to pass this to a Chief Inspector Crow.'

'That would be me,' I say, holding out a hand. She eyes me suspiciously, but after a pause, hands it over. 'One more thing,

Doctor – I assume Mr Harris will be returning at some point for more tests, considering his condition?'

Her eyes narrow. 'Tests? I don't understand what you might be referring to. He was checked before he was discharged, and there were no complications.'

'I mean for his cancer,' I explain. 'When we were talking earlier, he mentioned that his prostate cancer had become virulent, and there was a possibility he would have to be readmitted, or even remain in hospital for further treatment.'

She looks genuinely confused. 'I'm sorry, Chief Inspector. I have no idea what you're talking about. As far as I know, Mr Harris, as I said, is in good general health. We gave him a thorough examination, and if he had any kind of cancer, it would have been detected.'

I force a smile. 'Thank you, Doctor. I must have misheard. I apologise for any disruption. If Mr Harris has left and won't be returning, we no longer have any reason to remain here. If he does come back for any reason, I'd be very grateful if you could let us know.'

She responds with a nod and a derisive snort, and pads her way back down the corridor.

'The evil bastard!' Grace bursts out as we make our way back to the car. 'He lied to us about everything. He and Sarah – or Rachel – whichever one it is, must have been in it together, probably for years.'

'Rachel,' I say. 'I showed that doctor a photo of James and the twins, one on either side of him, taken not that long ago. She identified Rachel. She may not win a personality of the year contest, but I'd trust her to know exactly what she's talking about when it comes to surgery on a broken nose.'

'So, what was the point of all that about prostate cancer?' Manly asks. 'It sounds a bit over the top, even for an inveterate liar like Harris.'

'The point,' I say, 'was to make me and, by association, us, believe he was too ill to be a threat and wouldn't be going anywhere – bloody clever sod. It worked, didn't it? We went chasing off to the addresses he gave us, and I'd bet my pension he knew exactly what we were going to find.' I remember his sarcastic remark about me being too fond of doing things by the book. 'He also knew we wouldn't go straight in if we believed there might be armed criminals in there,' I go on. 'So, while we were all hanging around in the freezing cold, he and Rachel were busy making a neat getaway, the whole thing probably planned God knows how long ago.'

We walk the rest of the way to the car in silence and are about to get in when Draper pipes up.

'Sir – I was wondering if … I mean, would it be okay if …'

'For God's sake, Colin,' I snap. 'Just spit it out. It's too cold to stand around until your brain gets to where it's trying to go.'

He coughs. 'Well, it's Georgie – I mean, DC Manly, sir. She's just come off shift, and I sort of said I'd buy her a coffee before she went home if I had the time and it was all right with you – and with the chief constable of course,' he adds, risking a glance at CC Manly.

Manly grins. 'My daughter, Detective Constable, is her own woman. She does what she wants to, whether I like it or not. In this case, though, I think you both deserve a quick break – it's been a long day, and it's not over yet. What do you say, Chief Inspector?'

I let out a sigh. 'I suppose there's not a lot you can do for the moment. Meet us back at the hotel in, say, a couple of hours, okay? Mind you, the price is you driving us back down to Bristol later, so no alcohol.'

His face lights up like the Christmas tree still on show in the hotel foyer. 'Thank you, sir,' he says, and sets off back to the hospital reception at a run.

Ten minutes later, the three of us are in the hotel lounge, Grace and Manly attacking a bottle of claret between them, while I sip at a pint of very good local real ale.

'So, where the hell have they gone?' Manly mutters, downing half her glass in one and refilling it with more than a note of aggression.

'North Cyprus?' I suggest. 'Maybe Honduras, Morocco, Tunisia – anywhere they can count on being able to access their offshore accounts and not be extradited. From there, they can skip to just about anywhere. You can bet they've had false passports, plus complete identities set up for some time, and blocking the ports and airports won't get us anywhere. They had a two-hour start, and they're long gone. Harris has probably been in on it from the beginning. The only change is that he originally did his deals with Lisa. At some point, he decided Rachel was a better bet for his long-term future.'

Grace looks dubious. 'Surely, he wouldn't have had enough time – unless he knew that Rachel had already planned to get rid of James and Lisa – but to kill her twin sister? That's one hell of a thing. Whatever happened to family loyalty?'

'It depends on who you consider to be family,' I reply, 'and whether it rates above loyalty to the organisation. What's bad for the business is bad for the family, and now and then, there's a conflict between the two. We've seen it happen before. James and Lisa were a formidable team in their day, and still dangerous, but the fact is, they were starting to lose their grip. It was time to pass things on to the next generation, and from what I've learned about Lisa, she wasn't the type to let go. She and James had already gone as far as getting rid of Mick and William, and I don't think they would have been beyond setting up their own daughters if they became a threat. In fact, the easiest explanation is that Rachel found out they were planning to cut her loose – it doesn't explain why she killed Sarah, though – we may never know.'

'It doesn't explain why she chose to jump ship with Harris either,' Manly puts in. 'The man's on his last legs, for goodness' sake – a complete liability. Why risk taking him along if she wanted to make a quick getaway? It doesn't make any sense.'

'It makes perfect sense,' I say. 'Think about it. Harris has a happy band of less-than-upright coppers in the force who would go to a lot of trouble to protect him because by doing so, they are protecting themselves, and they include some fairly high-ranking officers. I'd guess he also has friends in other organisations as well – Customs and Excise, for example. He would have access to all the necessary documentation, and he'd know exactly who to go to if he wanted to get out of the country in a hurry. Harris is Rachel's passport, and she's also his daughter, so you're right, Grace. Family loyalty does count. Mind you, I'm not sure how long it will last once Rachel gets to where she wants to go. He may find his usefulness is limited after a while.'

'What about the message he left you?' Grace asks. 'What did it say?'

I realise the envelope the doctor passed to me is still stuffed in my jacket pocket. I pull it out and open it.

Please accept my apologies for the slight deception, it reads, *but as I'm sure you understand, it was necessary. I know it will be a disappointment to you and your colleagues, but the fact is, your investigation of my affairs was never more than a minor irritation. There were many more pressing matters to consider. By the time you read this, my daughter and I will be beyond your reach, so I advise you not to waste energy attempting to pursue two individuals who are, in the grand scheme of things, relatively unimportant. Instead, I urge you to focus on the information I have provided below. I give you my word, for whatever that is worth to you, that everything contained in the enclosed document is, to the best of my knowledge, entirely accurate and verifiable.*

I wish you good health and good luck

D. A. Harris, Detective Chief Superintendent (retired)

Along with this note, a sheaf of around a dozen sheets of paper, stapled together, is enclosed. I pass it to CC Manly, who leafs through it and whistles.

'Good God!' she mutters. 'If all this is genuine, it's dynamite. He's given us information on just about every big criminal operation in the area, past and present – names, dates, locations – everything we need. Plus, there's a list of those police officers who are compromised – who are on the take from whom, and for what. This can't be real.'

'Oh, I think it is,' I say. 'If you read through carefully, I think you'll find he's grassed up everyone who might have an interest in hunting him and Rachel down. The one thing that won't be there is any information on the operation of the Kelly outfit. His letter says that the police are just a minor consideration. He isn't just running from us – he's hiding from the rival mobs. If we can shut them down, we'll be giving him and, by implication, the Kellys, a free pass.'

'Not if I can bloody well help it!' Manly snaps, at which point her mobile rings. 'It's Frank Baker,' she tells us, and jams the phone to her ear. 'What have you got?'

For the next few minutes, Grace and I focus on our drinks, at the same time trying to read the various expressions crossing the face of Humberside's chief constable. She finally ends the call, takes a stiff swallow of her wine, and turns her attention back to us.

'Forensics found a third wine glass in the kitchen,' she says. 'Frank got his team to prioritise analysing the contents and identifying the prints. All of them contained wine – a Chardonnay, all from the same bottle. Two had traces of Flunitrazepam – that's Rohypnol to you and me. The third glass was clean. One of the adulterated glasses contained two sets of prints – Sarah's and Lisa's. The two others – one spiked and one clean – had Lisa's prints, and also Rachel's.'

She pauses, giving us time to work it out. When the truth dawns, I can't help but let out a grim chuckle. Grace raises an eyebrow.

'It looks like Lisa Harcourt finally met her match,' I say. 'It makes sense, once you piece it all together. We may never know why she decided her family had become too much of a risk. Perhaps Harris was wrong – we were becoming too much of a threat, and she was afraid that one of them would say too much if they were arrested. Maybe one or both of the girls got tired of waiting to take over, and she was being pressured into stepping down. Who knows? Whatever the reason, Lisa set out to get rid of all of them, and was probably still clinging to the idea that she could pin all the deaths on William Harcourt's kids. James was first. She got him blind drunk, drowned him in whisky, and used one of the two remaining daggers from Malden's collection. The daughters were more difficult. When they got to the house days later, she could have spun them a yarn – they'd had a row, maybe he got violent and it was self-defence, or he was drunk, fell and hit his head – anything plausible. But not to worry, she'd arranged the body to throw off whoever found it, and why didn't they all have a stiff drink before heading off into the sunset?'

'But,' Grace says, 'Rachel smelled a rat. Lisa poured the wine and handed out the glasses – that's why her prints were on all three. Sarah took hers, but Rachel managed to somehow swap hers for her mother's, hence her prints were on two of the glasses, but not on Sarah's. Christ!'

Manly has been sitting quietly, thoughtfully sipping her wine. She shifts in her chair and nods. 'Supposing,' she says, 'James was already drunk when Lisa got there. He was drunk and ready for a fight. All the information we have tells us that Lisa and James were devoted to each other and their kids. So, what happened? What could have made James turn on the wife he was so devoted to? Come to that, why would Lisa then try to murder her daughters? There is one reason I can think of, and it has nothing to do with the police, or with rival gangs.'

Grace provides the answer. 'Good God! James didn't know the twins weren't his. Somehow, after all those decades, he discovered his beloved daughters weren't his at all. And to rub salt in the wound, he found out that their real father was Don Harris.'

Manly nods. 'Rachel knew, though, and was probably the one who told him. It's clear that, unknown to Lisa, she had already formed a relationship with Harris, and they had put plans in place to make a quick exit. All Rachel had to do was light the blue touch paper and retire, as they say. If Lisa hadn't killed James, I'm pretty sure Rachel would have, and then gone after her mother. I don't think she counted on Lisa having the same idea, though, and when she realised what was happening, she had to improvise. I don't think she ever planned to harm Sarah – that was just collateral damage.'

'Hence the laying out of the bodies – a final sign of affection for her sister – perhaps even for her mother, in a strange way,' I add.

Manly checks her watch and pushes back her chair. 'Well, it looks like I'm going to be extremely busy for the next few days. I've got several policemen to arrest and a few organised crime groups to wrap up. There's nothing more you can do here, and if you set off now, you should be home before midnight.' She gets up and holds out a hand. 'It's been a pleasure working with you both. I'll keep you posted, and if we get a sniff of the whereabouts of Harris and Rachel Harcourt, I'll let you know, but don't hold your breath.'

There's a movement at the other end of the bar, and Draper makes a timely entrance, accompanied by Georgie Manly. He leans in close, whispers something in her ear, and she giggles, blushing. When they see us watching them, they jerk to a respectable distance, try, and fail to put on serious expressions before coming over to join us.

'Any chance of a lift?' Georgie asks her mother. 'I'm supposed to be cooking for the house tonight and I haven't even picked up the shopping yet.'

Manly tuts, treating her daughter to a mock frown. 'I am not a taxi service for the lower ranks,' she complains, 'but if you stay out of sight in the back seat, I suppose I can drop you at the supermarket. I'm not waiting, though. Believe it or not, I am a very busy woman.'

'Thanks, Mum.' She gives Draper a final wave, and they breeze out, leaving him shuffling his feet, but still grinning.

'And you can take that look off your face, Constable,' I say, feeling a distinct touch of envy. 'You've got a four-hour drive ahead, and I want to be in one piece at the end of it.'

He straightens up and just about manages to modify his expression. 'Yes, sir – sorry. Shall I get the car now?'

I nod, and glance across just in time to see the wink Grace gives him as he scuttles out in the direction of the hotel car park.

32

After what seems like a year, but is in fact little more than a week, I wake up to the blissfully familiar surroundings of my own bedroom, complete with the gently snoring bulk of a Doberman sprawled across my feet at the end of the bed. As I try to extricate myself, Blue opens one eye, utters an annoyed huff, closes it again, and goes back to sleep. It takes me another half hour to fully regain consciousness and make it out onto the landing, which still carries the faint scent of Rogan Josh, hastily grabbed from the just-about-to-close takeaway at eleven p.m. last night. I'm getting too old, I decide, blinking into the mirror and feeling a sudden, unjustified resentment towards young Colin Draper, flushed with the bloom of doomed infatuation, looking forward to an impossibly distant love affair that's likely to peter out within a couple of months. Still, I think, he can enjoy it while it lasts. Eventually, if he makes it and fulfils his dream of a career in the force, he will most likely end up jaded, divorced and with precious little social life. Then again, if he's sensible, he'll settle for a quiet life in the back office like George Saint, married thirty years, two kids, holidays in a caravan in Cornwall and a lifetime supply of sausage rolls. I shake myself out of it, shave, bundle Blue into the car and head for the station, accompanied by a steadily growing, uncomfortable sense of failure.

The mood in the squad room is equally subdued.

'The DSI's just been down,' Sillitoe tells me. 'She's filled us in on what happened. At least now we know the whole story – well, most of it. I've arranged to have Karen Wyatt pulled out of Jacob Malden's flat later this morning. If you like, I can go over there with Robbie and give them the good news that they are no longer under suspicion or in need of protection – unless you would rather do it yourself?'

'No, Polly,' I say, 'it's fine – you go ahead. I just wish we'd managed to nail Harris and Rachel Harcourt. I don't like unfinished business, and I can't help thinking it's not the last we'll hear from them. What about the Turners?'

'Cathy is still being treated, but they say she'll be fine and should be able to leave later today with appropriate anti-depressant medication. Roy's with her. Molly has already let them know that it's safe for them to go home, and that the Harcourts are out of the picture. I think Roy was pretty relieved we're not going to proceed with any charges.'

I nod. 'Tell Molly to stay with them until they're settled, and then come back in for the debriefing this afternoon. Is the DSI in her office?'

Sillitoe shakes her head. 'She's gone off to Portishead to report to CC Gosford. She said to tell you she thought you wouldn't mind if she went on her own as you probably had better things to do here.' She grins. 'I said you might be put out, but you'd get over it.'

'I'll certainly do my best,' I reply, mentally tossing up the relative merits of spending an hour in Gosford's office versus a day at my desk, which is metaphorically piled with a month's worth of paperwork. The paperwork wins, by a narrow margin.

By five o'clock, I've managed to make a very small dent in the folder labelled 'Expenses', catch up with the rest of the team, and drink several times the recommended daily dose of caffeine. Grace rings down to remind me that I'm meant to be recovering from an injury, and doesn't want to see me at work for at least a couple of days.

'And, by the way,' she adds, 'that's not a suggestion.'

I finally make it out of my office and down to my car. The one person I haven't caught sight of all day is Larson, and as I get Blue settled in the hatch, I notice that his car isn't in its usual spot in the station car park. Perhaps, I think, he's finally taken my advice and is spending a bit more time with Rosie and the children. I swing by the supermarket to pick up essentials and head home to a quiet and, hopefully, solitary night communing with my much-neglected TV. Anything, I think, apart from one of the police procedural reruns currently swamping just about every channel.

The next morning, I wake to a cold, crisp and sun-drenched winter's day, and spend the morning with Blue up on Clifton Downs. I suddenly feel very old, and very tired. I'm not sure whether it's the still painful gash in my side, the legacy of yet another near miss on the part of the grim reaper, or the failure to slap handcuffs on the wrists of the odious Don Harris that's getting to me. Maybe Chrissie is right after all, and the game just isn't worth the candle any more. By mid-afternoon, I'm back home putting the kettle on when the doorbell rings, and I find Larson on my front doorstep.

'I know you're supposed to be taking a couple of days off,' he says, only half apologetically, pushing his way into my lounge and hauling his laptop out of a rucksack, 'but I knew you'd want to see this.'

'Good afternoon, do come in, and would you like a cup of tea?' I reply, with more than a hint of sarcasm – unjustified, naturally, as I'm as eager to hear what he has to say as he is to tell me.

He throws me one of his irritating, knowing smiles. 'Sorry. Tea would be nice – thank you.'

I make the drinks and join him on the sofa. 'Okay. What's so important it couldn't wait a couple of days?'

'This,' he replies, swivelling his screen so I can see.

I squint at it for a minute and decide my next formal appointment will be with an optician. 'Just give me the highlights,' I say.

He nods. 'Okay, here goes. Chief Constable Manly has had the authorities checking arrivals and departures and going through CCTV footage at every local port and airport, figuring it would take too long for Harris and Harcourt to get much further without being caught. There was no luck, but then, she started looking at private airfields, initially within a fifty-mile radius of Hull. A flight took off shortly after the time you say you left Harris's room at the hospital from a small airfield just west of Hull, and landed at another close to Charles de Gaulle in Paris around two hours later. There was a pilot and two passengers, one male, one female. Once there, they refuelled and took off again as soon as they could, flight plan logged to a destination in southern Turkey. They used Irish passports in the names of Catherine Kelly and – you won't believe this – Harrison

O'Donal. They must have been pretty confident they'd get away with it.'

'Harrison O'Donal? The bloody cheeky bastard!' I let out a long breath. 'They must have planned it all a long time ago – they were out of the country before we'd even found the bodies, and there's bugger all we can realistically do about it now.'

'I don't know if it helps,' Larson says, 'but when I was a kid and one of the school bullies got the better of me, my Dad would always say, "If you sit by the river long enough, you'll see the body of your enemy floating by." It took me quite a while to work out what he meant – people like Harris overreach themselves eventually, and all you have to do is wait for them to make that fatal mistake.'

'You're right,' I say. 'It doesn't help. But I'll get him one day – if he lives long enough. And I'll get Rachel Harcourt, too. I have a feeling she'll be back. She's in charge of the family firm, now, and she's got too much to lose to stay away. By the way – what happened to you yesterday? Weren't you supposed to be in the office?'

He shifts his gaze to the frost-coated weeds in my back garden, clearly reluctant to answer. I'm starting to get seriously worried when he finally comes back to life, sighs, and pushes closed the lid of his laptop.

'I was over at Portishead,' he says uncertainly, 'for a meeting. It took rather longer than expected.'

'What kind of meeting?' I ask. 'Who with? That's the second time you've been over there. Is there something I should know?'

He nods. 'I suppose you'll find out about it sooner or later, as it will affect the amount of work I do at West Hill for a while. You can't mention it to anyone, though – I shouldn't be talking to you about it at all.'

Now I'm getting nervous. 'Believe it or not, son,' I say, 'I've been playing the game long enough to know the rules. If you're ...' Then it hits me, and I feel a cold, twisting knot in my stomach. 'You've been talking to the cloak and dagger mob – Jesus Christ! Why? What do they want? Whatever it is, it's something you don't want to get mixed up in. Do you have any idea how dangerous undercover work is? I can tell you for a fact that whatever you can imagine might happen, the reality is a hundred times worse. You must be out of your bloody mind to even consider it.'

He looks me in the eye, determined, but I catch a glimpse of the apprehension behind the outward calm. 'I haven't just considered it,' he replies, his tone even, 'I've agreed to it. You know police work isn't the only thing I do. I'm a software developer and a legal hacker. I know all the tricks and loopholes criminals use on the dark web, and I know how to get into their code, hopefully without being detected. After what happened with Ben, I – well, I want to help bring down the bastards that prey on young kids like him and Marcus. Vice is setting up an operation to infiltrate websites – the kind that have private members to share photos and videos of what they've been doing – you know what I mean. They need someone with my skills to infiltrate these so-called clubs, trace the ringleaders and shut their operations down. I'm going to do everything I can to make it happen. Discussion over, okay?'

There's going to be no reasoning with him. In the end, I just say, 'Have you told Rosie?'

'No,' he answers. 'I'm not going to tell her – and neither are you. This stays strictly between us. As I said, I shouldn't even be talking to you about it. It all kicks off in a couple of weeks, and they think they'll need me for around six months or so, maybe a year.'

'Six months? Well, we'd better hope serious crime takes a holiday until July, then.'

He gives me a sidelong look. 'Are you trying to say, Chief Inspector Crow, that I'm indispensable?'

I stomp out into the kitchen to wash up the cups.

Over the next couple of weeks, West Hill's most noteworthy event is the arrest of a previously law-abiding elderly married couple trying to make off from the local homeware store with a top-of-the-range electric heater. In their haste to get away, the husband accidentally drove his mobility scooter over his wife's foot, bringing an abrupt end to a low-speed chase through the car park. Luckily, no bones were broken, the couple were charged and released on bail, and returned home to find the owner of the store on their doorstep to present them with the stolen item as a gift. Given all the fuss about the cost of living crisis, it was the best publicity, he said, that his business had had for years.

'Do you think he's really thought it through?' Chrissie asks, between giggles, when I tell the tale. 'I mean, the poor man is going to have every pensioner in West Hill descending on his shop with a bag marked "Swag"!'

We're sitting in a cosy tea room in a picturesque Pembrokeshire fishing village overlooking the harbour. Between us, most of the table is taken up with a stack of property particulars – everything from quaint country cottages in need of renovation that will devour cash more quickly than George Saint can polish off a crate of sausage rolls, to state-of-the-art penthouse apartments with what the brochures describe as 'stunning sea views'.

It takes me a while to identify the mood that's been creeping up on me for the last couple of days – days spent checking out the beauty spots, visiting estate agents and, last night, walking along Whitesands beach with Chrissie, arm in arm, defying the blisteringly cold wind blowing in across the Irish Sea. It's contentment, I finally decide, and at the same time realise it's something I haven't felt since the last time I had a holiday – and that was thirty years ago, when Rosie was a baby, and Joyce had her for a week while Chrissie and I toured Anglesey in a beat-up old Ford Fiesta that broke down every fifty miles or so. I glance across the brochures and teacups at my ex-wife, and her smile tells me she's remembering, too.

'I think maybe it's time I thought about retirement,' I say.

Her eyes widen. 'Seriously?'

I nod. 'Seriously. I'm old enough to take a pension if I want it. I could spend more time with the grandchildren, take Blue for long walks, and wake up knowing I wasn't going to be stabbed or shot at. I could …'

'You could take up sky diving, or high wire walking – maybe explore the South American rain forest…'

'Yes! Why not?'

'Because, Al,' she says, laughing and shaking her head in exasperation, 'you'd be bored stiff within a week and impossible to live with. You're a policeman. You'll always be a policeman. You'll never be happy doing anything else. If you went to the rain forest, you'd be arresting the first parrot that squawked too loud and charging it with anti-social behaviour!'

'Being a policeman is what I do,' I counter. 'That doesn't mean it has to be what I am – at least, not *all* the time. I'm here, with you, and the last couple of days have been – well, different. I feel different …'

My mobile rings. I ignore it. Chrissie fixes me with a look, sits back and folds her arms. The phone keeps on ringing. I give her an apologetic shrug, defeated, press the button, and listen. When I hang up, she raises a questioning eyebrow.

'Two burglaries,' I tell her. 'One homeowner dead, two seriously injured. I …'

She reaches out and squeezes my hand. 'Go,' she says. 'I'll stay on another couple of days. If I find something I think we'll both like, I'll email you the details.'

'I don't have to …' I start.

'Yes,' she says, 'you do. You're a policeman, remember?'

I lean across the table and kiss her cheek. The thing about Chrissie, I think, as I key the ignition and set off on the long, solitary drive back to West Hill, is that she always has the last word.

ABOUT THE AUTHOR

H J Reed lives and writes in Bristol, where she graduated with a PhD in psychology and began a long career lecturing in psychology and criminology, both in mainstream universities and in the prison education system. Her evenings were spent writing novels and short stories in various genres and styles, and pondering on the strange workings of the criminal mind. After a number of publication successes, she gained an MA in creative writing and went on to teach literature and the arts. Now, she is able to follow her lifelong passion and write crime fiction full time. When she is not writing, she can be found being taken for long muddy walks by a middle-aged, temperamental toy poodle, or exploring the city that has been her home for more than five decades.

Did you enjoy *Thicker Than Water*? Please consider leaving a review on Amazon to help other readers discover the book.

www.hjreed.com

Also by HJ Reed

The DI Crow Series

Her Last Chance

The Killing Ground

A Fatal Pact

Printed in Great Britain
by Amazon

62900367R00153